Wonderland
Creek

Wonderland Creek

LYNN AUSTIN

BETHANY HOUSE PUBLISHERS

a division of Baker Publishing Group
Minneapolis, Minnesota

Published by Bethany House Publishers
11400 Hampshire Avenue South
Bloomington, Minnesota 55438
www.bethanyhouse.com

Bethany House Publishers is a division of
Baker Publishing Group, Grand Rapids, Michigan

Printed in the United States of America

Library of Congress Cataloging-in-Publication Data
Austin, Lynn N.
    Wonderland Creek / Lynn Austin
        p.   cm.
    ISBN 978-0-7642-0919-2 (hardcover : alk. paper)
    ISBN 978-0-7642-0498-2 (pbk.)
    1. Single women—Fiction. 2. Librarians—Fiction. 3. Kentucky—Fiction.
4. Depressions—1929—Fiction. I. Title
PS3551.U839W67 2011
813'.54—dc22   2011025214

Scripture quotations are taken from the King James Version of the Bible.

Cover design by Lookout Design, Inc.
Cover photography by Mike Habermann, Minneapolis

For Poppy
Never forgotten
Forever loved

CHAPTER 1

BLUE ISLAND, ILLINOIS
1936

If my life were a book, no one would read it. People would say it was too boring, too predictable. A story told a million times. But I was perfectly content with my life—that is, until the pages of my story were ripped out before I had a chance to live happily ever after.

The end came, appropriately enough, at a funeral. Not my own funeral—I'm only twenty-two years old—but Elmer Watson's funeral. He was a kindly old gentleman who patronized the public library here in Blue Island, Illinois, where I have worked as a librarian for the past year and a half. I knew Mr. Watson—or I suppose it would be more accurate to say that I knew his taste in books and magazines—and I thought very highly of him because of his reading preferences.

When I heard that his funeral would be held that day, I walked to the funeral parlor after work and took a seat in the back row by myself. My father, Reverend Horace Ripley, conducted the service. But first an entire host of Mr. Watson's boring relatives—long-lost cousins, sons, nephews, and in-laws—decided to get up and tell long-winded stories about how Elmer had once walked to the store with them, or bought a horse from them, or some such inane piece of history. None of these people could tell a decent story to save his life. I wasn't the only one in the audience who was yawning.

As the dreary eulogies dragged on and on, I pulled a book from my bag and began to read. I thought I was being quite subtle about it, glancing up every now and then, and nodding in sympathy as another one of Mr. Watson's fine character traits was eulogized. I could have added that he always returned his books to the library on time, but why prolong the service?

That's when my boyfriend, Gordon T. Walters, son and grandson of the funeral directors, tiptoed up behind me and slipped into the chair beside mine. I quickly finished reading the paragraph and stuck a bookmark in place before closing the book.

I expected Gordon to reach for my hand, but he didn't. He sat so stiffly beside me, all buttoned up in his dour black suit, that he might have been a corpse like poor Mr. Watson. I looked up at Gordon and smiled, but he gave me a funereal frown and shook his head. I hadn't realized that he knew Elmer Watson, but why else would he act so somber? When the service finally ended and we stepped outside through a side door, away from the other mourners, I discovered the reason.

"You were reading a *book* during a *funeral*?" he asked as if horrified. "Alice, how could you?"

"Well . . . it was a very good book," I said with a little shrug. "I couldn't help myself. I needed to find out what happened to the heroine."

"What difference does it make what happens in a stupid book? It isn't real. It's a made-up story. But a funeral, Alice—a funeral is real life!" He was gesturing wildly, as if unable to convey his outrage with mere words. I reached for his hand, but he wouldn't let me take it. We stood in a beam of weak February sunlight outside the funeral parlor where Gordon lived and worked, and we were an oddly mismatched couple—Gordon tall and dark-haired, myself, short and blond. Patches of snow dotted the grass and lay in dirty mounds around the parking lot as black-clothed mourners climbed into their cars for the trip to the cemetery. Mr. Walters sometimes needed Gordon to drive the hearse, but not today. Most of the time Gordon worked in the office, ordering coffins and collecting receipts and paying bills.

"I'm sorry," I told him, "but when a book is as well-written as this one is, it *seems* just like real life to me and I—"

"But reading at a *funeral*? This was a once-in-a-lifetime event. Elmer Watson will never be buried again."

"I certainly hope not," I muttered beneath my breath. "Anyway, I'm sure he wouldn't have minded. He used to come into the library all the time to check out books. He was a very nice man."

"You could have shown more respect for his family."

"They couldn't even see me. I was sitting in the last row." I didn't understand Gordon's outrage or why he was making such a big issue of this. "Come on," I said, taking his arm. "Walk me home."

"No." He peeled my hand away. "Why did you come to the funeral in the first place if you weren't going to pay your respects? And you weren't very respectful, Alice. If you wanted to read your stupid book, you should have stayed home."

I had been trying to make light of the incident until now because I honestly couldn't see why it bothered him so much. His unreasonable behavior made me defensive. "I didn't *plan* on reading—you make me sound like such a horrible person. But I started the chapter during my lunch break at work, and then I had to stop right in the middle of it when my hour was up. All afternoon I've been dying—pardon the expression—to find out what happened. So when the eulogies went on and on and I couldn't stop thinking about the characters, I decided to take just a tiny peek and . . . and how was I supposed to know that I would get pulled back into the story again? It's a wonderful book, Gordon."

He didn't seem to hear a word I said. He continued to glare at me with the solemn gaze perfected by his forefathers and immortalized in their portraits, now hanging in the mortuary's entrance hall. "I've been to hundreds of funerals," he said, which was no exaggeration since he'd been born in the apartment above the funeral parlor. "But I've never seen anyone reading a book during a memorial service." He was upset. I had to take this more seriously.

"Again, I'm sorry, Gordon. From now on I will eschew reading novels during funerals."

9

"You'll . . . what? You'll chew . . . what?"

"I said, I will eschew reading. It means to abstain from or avoid something." I had been waiting for an opportunity to use the word *eschew* after discovering it in my favorite literary journal and looking up the meaning. It had such a refined, tasteful sound to it—a wrinkle-your-nose, tut-tut quality. I thought this would be the perfect opportunity to try it out. How could I have known that the word would further infuriate Gordon?

"Confound it, Alice! Sometimes you act like you think you're better than everyone else."

"Wait. Are you calling me pretentious?"

"Maybe . . . if I knew what it meant. Does it mean snooty?"

"Listen, I can't help it if I have a broad vocabulary. I acquired it from reading."

"Did you ever stop to think that maybe you read too much?"

"That's absurd," I said with a little laugh. "Nobody can read too much. That's like saying someone breathes too much."

He sighed. His shoulders sagged. He shook his head. I thought he was going to say, *You're right. Let's forget it.* But he didn't.

"I can't do this anymore, Alice."

"Do what?"

"Fight about stupid things like books and big words. You live in a different world than I do. Everything you talk about comes from a book, not real life. I want a girl who has both feet on the ground. And more important, one whose nose isn't stuck in a book all day."

"I work in a library," I told him. "Books are my livelihood, just like funerals are your livelihood. Do I complain because you're surrounded by caskets and corpses all day?"

Gordon tipped his hat to a group of mourners as they walked past us on the way to their cars. When they were gone, he turned to me and said, "I don't think we should see each other anymore."

"What?" I felt a twinge of panic. We'd had arguments before, but this one had gone too far. "Are you mad because I use words you don't understand or because I couldn't help reading just a teensy bit during the boring part of a funeral?"

"Both. We don't have anything in common."

"But . . . but we've been dating for nearly a year and—" I stopped before blurting out that everyone considered us a couple or that our parents expected us to marry.

"The only thing you ever want to talk about is the plot of the latest book you're reading. I know more about your favorite characters than I do about you. And now I find out that you'd rather read about some made-up person than listen to the final tributes for a real man. You live in a dream world, Alice, not this one."

"I do not!"

"Remember the time you were reading a book instead of watching where you were going and you walked into a lamppost? You ended up with a lump on your forehead the size of a doorknob. You were nearly knocked out cold."

"That wasn't my fault. I was trying to finish the book on my way to work because it was due back at the library that day. There was a long waiting list for it. I'm not the only person who likes to read, you know."

"You're lucky you didn't step in front of a streetcar." He paused to offer his arm to an elderly woman, helping her to her car before returning to me. "And remember how you set your mother's kitchen on fire because you were trying to read and fry chicken at the same time?"

"A dish towel. I set a dish towel on fire." I laughed as I tried to make light of it but Gordon stared me down, forcing me to admit the truth. "Okay . . . I suppose the fire did spread to the kitchen curtains—but that could have happened to anyone."

"I give up." He lifted his palms in defeat, then let them fall, slapping against his thighs.

"So you'll forgive me for reading at the funeral?" I asked, standing very close to him, looking up at him. "I only read a chapter—maybe a chapter and a half."

"I don't think we should see each other anymore."

"Gordon!"

"I'm sorry." He turned away.

I couldn't believe it. I sputtered for something to say. "Well! If that's the way you feel, then good! I feel the same way!" I spoke with an air of triumph, but it was an act. With my fair complexion, my cheeks easily betrayed my emotions and they burned now with humiliation. How dare he break up with me?

I strode the three blocks home in a rage, my bag with the troublesome book bumping against my side. I could hear my mother puttering around in the kitchen and I smelled onions sautéing, but I marched up the stairs to my room and closed the door. Mother no longer asked me to help her cook.

Just to spite Gordon, I sat down on my bed and opened the book, continuing where I had left off during the funeral. My anger had a chance to cool as I lost myself in someone else's drama for the next hour or so. In the end, the hero saved the heroine and the story ended happily ever after. I closed the book with a sigh of contentment. A moment later my father arrived home and Mother called us to dinner.

I didn't mention the argument to my parents. I was certain that Gordon would get over it in a day or two. Besides, I couldn't imagine asking them for advice. They seemed perfectly suited to each other and never argued. I also had a feeling that Mother would take Gordon's side. She still was upset with me for starting the fire. She'd nearly had a fit during those first few panicked moments as she'd tried to douse the oily flames and keep them from spreading. And when the next-door neighbor saw the smoke pouring from the window and called the fire department, Mother had been mortified. Her reputation as a cook had been sullied. That was my word, not hers—but a good one, I thought. *Besmirched* would have described her reputation nicely, too.

"You're very quiet tonight," Mother said as we did the supper dishes together. I was drying them with one of the new dish towels she'd been forced to buy. We had ruined several of them trying to beat out the flames. Mother had been angry about the towels, too: *"Don't you know that this country is in a depression, Alice? No one has money to spare for new household goods, including our family. Your father gives away every spare cent we have to the poor parishioners in his church, and here you are wasting good money."*

"Gordon and I had a fight," I told her. "That's why I'm so quiet. He hurt my feelings. He said that I read too much, and he accused me of living in a dream world."

"Hmm. Imagine that." I saw her roll her eyes. She was supposed to be consoling me, not taking Gordon's side. I wanted a poultice lovingly applied over my aching heart, not sarcasm. Well, my heart wasn't really aching, yet. I didn't believe that Gordon had meant what he'd said.

I decided to walk next door after Mother and I finished the dishes to see my best friend, Freddy Fiore. Her real name was Frederica, like a princess in an Italian love story, but everyone called her Freddy. We had attended school together since first grade, and after graduating from high school we enrolled in the Cook County Normal School to become teachers. Neither of us had a steady boyfriend back then or any marriage prospects, so we decided to continue our education.

Freddy turned out to be a marvelous teacher—the kind that every child remembers fondly for the rest of her life. My teaching career proved disastrous. I quickly discovered that I was not at all suited to the profession with my "dreamy" personality and a soft-spoken voice. The students ignored me completely. Besides, I'm only five-feet-two-inches tall and many of the boys in the one-room schoolhouse where I practiced teaching towered over me, running roughshod over all of my attempts to maintain order.

My friend Freddy, who is nearly as tall as Gordon, grew up in a household with four brothers and had no problem at all commanding respect. She received glowing recommendations and a job as a second grade teacher at our old elementary school. The Normal School faculty delicately suggested that I eschew teaching and recommended me for a position at our town's public library. It was a perfect fit for me.

I knocked on Freddy's back door, then let myself inside, as usual. She was in the living room, reading a book to her mother, who suffered from a mysterious muscle weakness. Freddy's father had passed away a few years ago. I waited impatiently for Freddy to finish the chapter, my heart bursting to pour out my woes.

"Can I talk to you for a minute?" I asked when she closed the book.

"Sure." She found a radio station for her mother to listen to and we went out to the kitchen to sit at the table. Few people served tea or coffee during these hard economic times. I hadn't wept over my breakup with Gordon, but this was Freddy, my warm, compassionate friend sitting across the table from me. My tears finally began to fall.

"Allie, what is it? What's wrong?"

"Gordon broke up with me!"

"Why? What happened?"

"We had an argument, and he ended it by saying we shouldn't see each other anymore."

"He wasn't serious, was he? You've had spats before and he's gotten over them. Remember the time you kept calling him by the wrong name? It was the name of the hero in the book you were reading, wasn't it?"

"That was an honest mistake. Anyone could have made it."

Freddy arched one eyebrow at me. "I thought Gordon displayed uncommon patience."

"I guess so . . . But he wasn't very patient today. He brought up the incident with the fire. And the time I nearly got a concussion from walking into a lamppost." I pulled my handkerchief from my sleeve and dabbed my eyes. "He shouldn't hold all these things against me. Aren't we supposed to forgive and forget?"

"Do you want me to go over to the funeral home and talk to him?" Freddy asked. I could always count on her to come to my rescue.

"Would you?"

"Sure. When would be a good time?"

"Tonight. I'll stay with your mother, if you want me to. Gordon doesn't have any wakes scheduled tonight so he and I were supposed to see a movie, but then he . . . he broke up with me!" I ended with a sob. Freddy squeezed my hand, then stood and put on her coat.

"I'll do my best."

She was gone for nearly three hours. Her mother had fallen asleep in the rocking chair by the time Freddy returned home, but I didn't know if I should help her to bed or not. I never knew how to help ailing people.

"What took so long?" I asked the moment Freddy stepped through the door. "What did Gordon say?" Once again we went into the kitchen to talk.

"Gordon didn't want to talk about you at all, at first. I think he's pretty mad. He was just leaving for the movie theater by himself when I got to the funeral parlor, so I asked him if I could tag along. I figured if I spent a little time with him, maybe he'd talk about you afterward."

"Good idea. So you went to the movies with him?"

"Well, first he made me promise that I wouldn't cause a scene in the theater like you did last week."

"See? He blows everything out of proportion. I didn't cause a scene. I don't know why the usher asked us to leave."

"Gordon said it was because you started talking very loudly in the middle of the movie, saying that it wasn't at all like the original book, and when everyone started shushing you—including Gordon—the usher got involved. Gordon is still mad because he didn't get to see how the film ended."

"He didn't need to see the end. I told him how the book ended and it was so much better than the movie. They changed everything in the movie, including the hero's motivation. Can you imagine? That movie was such a travesty that I couldn't help getting upset."

"Well, Gordon is still upset about it, too. But he said the last straw was seeing you reading a book at Elmer Watson's funeral."

"Poor Mr. Watson. He always loved *National Geographic* magazines. I know he wouldn't have minded at all that I read a novel at his funeral. The eulogies did go on and on."

Freddy reached across the table to take both of my hands. "The thing is—and please understand that I'm on your side, Allie. We've been best friends forever, you know that. But the way Gordon explained it as we walked home . . . well, he just isn't sure that things are going to work out for the two of you. He and his family are in the funeral parlor business. And that means you'll be in the business, too, if he asks you to marry him."

"We aren't even engaged, yet."

"I know. But he understands all of the unspoken rules in the funeral trade, and he says that you crossed a line. Wouldn't you be upset if someone came into your library and did something that you thought was disrespectful?"

"You mean like folding down the corner of the page instead of using a bookmark?"

"I don't think the two would be *quite* the same . . . at least not in Gordon's mind."

"Okay. You can tell him that from now on, I promise I will never read a book at a funeral for as long as I live. Will that make him happy?"

"I don't know . . . He says you don't seem very sympathetic to people's feelings during their time of grief."

"Just because I read one measly chapter at a funeral?"

Freddy released my hands. She looked uncomfortable, as if the wooden chair had splinters. "It wasn't only that. He told me about your book scheme. How you wanted him to ask the families of the deceased to donate their loved ones' books to your Kentucky Project when they came in to arrange a funeral."

"Is that so unreasonable? I'm sure most people would be happy to do it." I had read an article in *Life* magazine that told how people in the backwoods of Kentucky needed books and magazines to read. When I showed it to the head librarian, she let me put a collection box near the check-out desk for patrons who wanted to donate their used books. "Seriously, Freddy. Why not collect them at the funeral parlor, too? Do you think that's such a bad idea?"

"I have to tell you the truth, Allie—it's a terrible idea."

"Why?"

"When my father died, it was hard enough to cope with my grief and try to plan a nice funeral. It was much too early to think about giving away his books."

"But those people in Kentucky have nothing to read. Can you imagine such a horrible life? Who needs books after they're dead? Why not give them away so they can help living people?"

"I know, I know. But it's just a little . . . insensitive . . . to ask someone about it when they're planning a funeral."

"Mr. Watson loved maps," I mused aloud. "He owned a wonderful atlas. If I had known he was about to die, I could have asked him ahead of time to donate his books in his will."

Freddy cleared her throat. "Let's get back to Gordon. I'm really sorry, but I don't think I was able to change his mind. It sounded like he has been storing up all these grievances for quite some time."

"Wait. Doesn't he know it's wrong to hold grudges? Did you tell him that?"

"It's not a grudge, Allie. He said that when he started adding it all together, he began to realize that maybe you and he weren't very well-suited for each other."

Tears sprang to my eyes again. "He really means it? He's really breaking up with me? For good?" Freddy nodded. "Can't you do something to help me patch things up?" I begged.

"I can try again—if you're sure that's what you really want."

"What do you mean? Why wouldn't I want it? Gordon and I have been together for almost a year."

"Gordon has some legitimate complaints that you'll need to think about. Are you willing to stop reading so much in order to stay together? And I know you've complained about his faults, like the fact that he never reads anything at all, even the newspaper. These things would all have to be worked out. You'd have to make some compromises."

"Why?"

"I'm told that's what marriage is all about—being willing to make changes for the person you love. Suppose you had to choose between never reading again or losing Gordon. Which would you pick?"

"I could never give up reading!" The thought appalled me. "I love books, Freddy! Maybe I could agree not to bring books to the funeral parlor, but we're talking about two entirely different kinds of love—my love of books and my love for Gordon. Don't you love what you do? How could you choose between teaching or marriage?"

"If I met a man I loved, I would gladly give up teaching for him," she said, pulling herself to her feet. "Listen, Allie. Go home and sleep on it. It's late. Maybe Gordon will see things differently tomorrow."

"Will you go back and talk to him again? I'll stay with your mother tomorrow night, too."

"Of course."

I went home and got ready for bed, unable to imagine breaking up with Gordon. Everyone said that he was a real catch. He wasn't particularly handsome, but he had a very good job, unaffected by the Depression. People continued to die whether the stock market crashed or soared.

Gordon and I had been together for so long that people in Blue Island thought of us as a couple. We attended library functions and picnics together, stood on Main Street and watched the Fourth of July parade together. I would be so embarrassed when everyone started whispering and speculating behind my back or asking me, *Where's Gordon? Why aren't you with Gordon?* What would I say?

And church! Everyone at my father's church knew I was dating Gordon. He sat beside me every Sunday. How could I ever face the other parishioners or hold up my head again?

I had a hard time falling asleep that night. And to make matters worse, I had finished my book, and now I had nothing to read.

CHAPTER 2

I arrived for work the next morning tired and foggy-brained from lack of sleep. I could say that I had been awake half the night crying my eyes out over Gordon, but it wouldn't be true. I had gone downstairs and borrowed my father's Sherlock Holmes anthology and ended up reading until nearly one o'clock in the morning. There's nothing like a dastardly crime and the challenge of matching wits with a clever detective to take a person's mind off her problems.

Before the library opened for the day, our head librarian, Mrs. Beasley, gathered the staff together at one of the conference tables. "Would everyone take a seat, please? Quickly? We need to have a short meeting."

I sat down with the other ladies on our staff, yawning as I waited for the meeting to begin. Mrs. Beasley looked staid and unsmiling, but that wasn't unusual. Librarians are serious people, seldom given to idle jocularity. The reason for this, I believe, is because we are overwhelmed by the enormous number of good books waiting to be read, leaving little time for frivolity. My personal list of must-read books presents a daunting challenge; I can't even imagine the pressure that our head librarian must be under.

Mrs. Beasley resembled a sturdy little bulldog, complete with jowls. But judging by the way that many of our patrons seemed to fear her, she might have resembled a German shepherd guard dog. I never understood why people reacted to her this way.

"Are you kidding?" Freddy said when I asked her about it. "Mrs. Beasley acts as if all of the library books belong to her and she begrudges loaning them out. You'd think the library was sacred ground and she was the high priestess the way everyone tiptoes around and speaks in hushed tones." I disagreed with Freddy's assessment. Beneath our head librarian's bulldog exterior was a wise, well-read woman. I didn't blame her in the least for feeling protective of our books. The way some people abused them was a crime.

Today Mrs. Beasley began by clearing her throat. Again, this wasn't a worrisome sign. Librarians are not overly talkative so our throats can get froggy from lack of use. "I met with the library's board of directors last night," she began, "and I'm afraid I have some very upsetting news. The board has announced that the library must cut operating costs."

Everyone stared. There were no dramatic gasps or sobs. We are a stoic, reserved bunch who hide our emotions well—except when reading a terribly sad or poignant story, of course. I have been known to sob aloud at a tragic ending.

"The board said that this prolonged economic depression has made cost cutting necessary. With so many homes in our community in foreclosure, there simply isn't as much revenue from property taxes as there was a few years ago. Businesses are closing, too. Every day we see another empty storefront downtown, so the city is losing tax revenue there, as well. People all over the country have been forced to cut back to the bare necessities, and so we must cut back to the essentials, too."

"But books *are* essential!" the children's librarian, Mrs. Davidson, said. I had been thinking the same thing.

"I know. I agree," Mrs. Beasley said. "And I let the board know my opinion, too."

"People will need our library now more than ever," Mrs. Davidson continued, "especially if they're unemployed and can't afford to purchase books. Where else can you find free entertainment nowadays? We should be *expanding* during the economic crisis and buying even *more* books, not cutting back."

Mrs. Beasley nodded, jowls jiggling. "That is exactly what I told them. But the board believes that the library already has enough books for everyone in town to read if they choose to. They said that our patrons would just have to adjust to shorter library hours. They also announced that some of our personnel will have to be let go."

"Who? Who?" Mrs. Davidson asked, sounding very much like an owl.

"I'm afraid that the last one hired will be the first one to go."

"That's me!" I said with a squeak. "I was the last one hired!"

"Yes, Miss Ripley. I'm so sorry."

I wanted to stand up and shout that this was unfair, but loud voices were not permitted in the library.

"The cost cutting will affect all of us, not just Miss Ripley. With reduced hours, we all will be working less and receiving smaller paychecks."

I had heard about the Depression, of course. I'd seen pictures in the newspapers of shantytowns and Hoovervilles and read about factories closing and men out of work. Several houses on our street stood vacant, including one that had belonged to the Simmons family. Freddy and I had gone to school with their daughters, but when Mr. Simmons lost his job, the bank foreclosed on their mortgage and tossed them and all of their belongings into the street. I wasn't ignorant of unemployment and breadlines and soup kitchens, but aside from the hoboes who showed up at our back door asking for a handout, I never imagined that the Depression would touch my life. Now I was unemployed.

Of course, I wouldn't starve or be homeless since I lived in the parsonage with my parents. My father, safely employed as a minister, heard hard luck stories every day, but my family was warm and well fed. My two older sisters—more sensible than me, according to my parents—had married farmers and lived out in the country several miles south of Blue Island. Their farms supplied us with plenty of eggs, butter, fruit, and vegetables.

I turned my attention back to Mrs. Beasley. "Let's all hope and pray that the changes are only temporary," she was saying. "Perhaps one of President Roosevelt's social assistance programs will come to our rescue. In the meantime, the library will be open only two evenings a week from now on, and half days on Wednesday, Saturday . . ."

Blah, blah, blah. I stopped listening. The new hours wouldn't matter to me. I was unemployed. The news that I no longer had to work every Friday night would make Gordon happy, because we could spend more time together—but then I remembered that Gordon no longer wanted to spend any time at all with me. The accumulated shock of all this bad news was too much. I felt as if I had just collided with another lamppost.

"When will all these changes begin?" Mrs. Davidson asked.

"The last day of this month. We'll need to post the library's new hours right away and give our patrons time to adjust."

"That's this week!" I shouted, forgetting to use my library voice. There would be little hope of finding another job with so many other people unemployed. Besides, I didn't want to be a store clerk or a teacher or a telephone operator. I loved my job. "This is awful," I moaned. I didn't realize that I had spoken out loud until Mrs. Beasley rested her hand on my shoulder.

"I know, Miss Ripley. And I'm so very sorry. I fought for you, for all of us. I really did. But times are hard all across the country."

It was time to unlock the door and get to work. Library patrons had congregated on the front steps and beneath the pillared porch, stamping slushy snow off their feet. Mrs. Beasley dismissed the meeting. "And let's try not to have any long faces, ladies. We owe it to our patrons to be cheerful. After all, our reduced hours will be hard on them, as well."

I usually spent the first half hour at work "shelf-reading," making sure the books were in alphabetical order and the Dewey decimal numbers all aligned. Some patrons have a terrible habit of pulling out a book, then shoving it back in the wrong place—sometimes on the wrong shelf! I started straightening the fiction section, but I simply couldn't concentrate. It was hard to think alphabetically after losing my job *and* my boyfriend. What was left?

I switched to typing catalogue cards. I loved this job because it enabled me to peruse all of the new books, straight from the printing press. I could be the first person to open them—and to sign them out and read them, too, if I wanted. The books were stiff and spotlessly clean, with that incomparable new-book fragrance. Is there anything like it in the whole world? I've been known to open new books and inhale the aroma like perfume.

I fed a crisp white catalogue card into my typewriter, then picked up the first book and opened it to the title page, careful not to crack the spine. I am a very orderly person who enjoys typing the required information on the card, neatly and precisely. Where else but the library could I find work that used my special gifts and talents?

I must admit I wasted a lot of time that morning staring off into space, trying not to cry and splotch the typewriter ink. When I got home from work and told my mother the news, she dried her hands on her apron and wrapped her arms around me. "What a shame, Alice. I know how much you loved your job."

"How much longer is this stupid Depression going to last?" I asked.

"I'm afraid no one knows, honey."

My tears gushed when I went next door to Freddy's house later that night and told her the terrible news. "Will you please try to talk to Gordon again?" I begged. "Maybe he'll feel sorry for me when he hears what happened at the library. Maybe he'll change his mind about breaking up with me."

I expected as much. I expected Gordon to come straight over to console me the moment Freddy told him my tragic news. But an hour went by. Then two hours. I couldn't concentrate on the radio program that Freddy's mother was listening to. I saw a pile of spelling tests on the table and picked up a red pencil and graded them for Freddy. It was the least I could do since she had sacrificed her evening for my sake. She still wasn't home when I finished the tests, so I started correcting a pile of arithmetic homework. The tedious work made me grateful that I hadn't become a teacher. If I had to grade boring papers every night for the rest of my life, I wouldn't have any time to read.

When Freddy finally arrived home, I knew that her news wasn't good. I could see that she had been raking her fingers through her thick curly hair the way she always did when she was frustrated.

"What happened?" I asked.

"I'm sorry, Allie. I tried, I really did."

"Isn't Gordon ever going to forgive me?"

"He's not mad at you, Allie. He just doesn't want to date you anymore. But he said to tell you that he's sorry about your job."

Freddy let me sob on her shoulder. "Can't you talk to him some more?" I begged. "Please?"

"I . . . um . . . I don't think I should do that."

"Why not?"

She released me and backed up a few steps as if trying to put distance between us. "Well . . . when we finished our milk shakes and I got ready to come home, Gordon started saying how much he had enjoyed talking to me, and . . . well . . . he asked if I wanted to go to a movie with him next week."

"What!" I panicked, just like I had when I'd seen the flames racing out of control in my mother's kitchen. Now it was my life that was out of control.

"Of course I refused," Freddy said quickly. "Honestly, he had a lot of nerve. I'm your best friend, for heaven's sake."

"I'm going home." I grabbed my coat and stuck my arms into the sleeves.

"Please don't be mad at me, Allie. I told Gordon that he was a cad for dumping you and an even bigger cad for asking me out. I wouldn't have talked to him at all if you hadn't begged me to."

"I'm not mad." And I wasn't. I was jealous. "I need to go home and lie down." It felt like the world was using my heart for a punching bag, and it couldn't take any more blows.

"Let's do something fun this weekend, okay, Allie? Just the two of us?"

There weren't many fun things to do in Blue Island, Illinois, but I agreed. I hugged Freddy good-bye to show her that we were still friends and went home to sulk.

On my last day of work, everyone was sad to see me go. "But we won't say good-bye," Mrs. Beasley insisted. "I'm sure you'll be back to borrow books. And you're going to continue to collect books for Kentucky, aren't you?" She gestured to the overflowing box of donated books near the check-out desk. There were four more boxes just like it in the back room, along with three bags of used magazines. "When are you planning to ship these to Kentucky?" she asked.

"Soon, I guess. I'm not really sure." I had lost my enthusiasm for the project, not to mention my reason to get out of bed every morning. As a parting gift, Mrs. Beasley let me check out one of the brand-new books I had catalogued that day. It would be the last time that I would ever have that privilege.

On Sunday I sat with my mother in church instead of with Gordon for the first time in nearly a year. Everyone in town would know about our breakup now. All around me, I could see the gossip mill starting to grind as heads bent close, whispering, nodding, tilting in my direction. It was unbearable. The moment my father pronounced the benediction, I fled into the vestry, my cheeks betraying my embarrassment, and ran out through the back door.

My parents gave me a week to mope around and feel sorry for myself and sleep late every morning. By the second week they'd had enough. Mother breezed into my bedroom at seven o'clock on Monday morning and rolled up the window shades, flooding the room with light.

"It's time to stop moping, Alice. I know you've had some difficult losses, but you won't get over them by sleeping late and reading books all day."

"There's nothing else to do," I mumbled, my face buried in the pillow.

"There's plenty to do. Your father and I have drawn up a list."

This was terrible news. My parents were veteran list-makers, believing that every problem in life could be solved with an adequate list. No matter how daunting the task, they believed the impossible could be accomplished by breaking it down into items and checking them off, one by one. If my parents had drawn up one of their lists for President Roosevelt, the Depression would have ended by now.

"Put on your robe, Alice, and come down to breakfast."

I did as I was told. Did I have a choice?

"Your mother told me about your rift with Gordon," my father said as I slouched into my chair at the kitchen table. "I was sorry to hear it. Would you like me to talk to—"

"No!" My father and Gordon's father were friends, being close associates in the death and grieving business. I suspected that they had conspired to put Gordon and me together in the first place. "Don't talk to anyone about us. Please!"

He sighed and gave me his soft-eyed, pastoral gaze. "If that is your wish, Alice. But—"

"Please, Daddy. I can handle this on my own."

He munched on his toast for a few moments, shaking his head sadly before saying, "Your mother and I have compiled a list."

It was a declaration of war. He would try to recruit me for one of his Christian good-deed tasks—always a high priority on any of his lists. I had to avoid those at all costs.

"I can make up my own list. I'll have it on your desk by noon. I promise."

He didn't seem to hear me. "Now that you're no longer working at the library, I know of many unfortunate people in our community who could use your help."

"I don't like working with unfortunate people. They make me uncomfortable."

"Alice Grace!" Mother said with a gasp. "What a thing to say."

"I'm sorry, but the way they look at me with their big sad eyes makes me uneasy, as if it's my fault that I have everything and they have nothing. I don't know what to do or what to say."

I could tell by my father's drumming fingers that he was running out of patience. "How long do you plan on wallowing in self-pity, Alice?"

I gulped down my glass of orange juice and stood. "I'm all done wallowing. I'm fine now. Really." His drumming fingers stopped, and I could see that he was about to preach a sermon on how self-pity was one of the Seven Deadly Sins. If I added up all of the sins that my father claimed were part of the Deadly Seven, there would be seven hundred of them. I was fairly certain that self-pity wasn't on the original list, but if I challenged him on it, he would make up something flowery and philosophical-sounding, like, *Self-pity is the younger sister of sloth, dining on the same bitter foods, sleeping in the same sordid bed . . .* or some such wisdom.

"Here is our list," Father said, handing it to me before I could escape. "You might want to use it as the basis for your own. And since your mother and I are both going out on errands today, we have agreed that you should accompany one of us. No more lying around all day."

I took the list from him and folded it in half without looking at it. "Where are you going?" I asked him, dreading his reply.

"I'm delivering donated food and clothing to Chicago's near West Side. They're calling the area 'Floptown' since so many people are forced to live on the street."

I quickly turned to my mother. "And where are you going?"

"I promised your aunt Lydia I would pay her a visit before she leaves."

"Where is she off to this time? Patagonia? Bora Bora?" Mother's younger sister was as odd as a cat with feathers. A visit with Aunt Lydia was like an hour spent in a windstorm, and I usually avoided it at all costs. But today it seemed like a better choice than a place called Floptown. At least I could bring along a book to read.

"I'll go with you, Mom."

CHAPTER 3

W hen we finished the breakfast dishes, Mother put on her visiting hat and a pair of clean white gloves and we rode the streetcar to Aunt Lydia's house. I brought along an empty bag. These days, you couldn't travel two blocks without running into a poor person selling apples on the street, and I knew that by the time we traveled to my aunt's house and back, my softhearted mother would have purchased enough fruit to make a dozen apple pies.

Aunt Lydia and Uncle Cecil had no children—and the world should be thankful for that. They lived in an enormous house in the fashionable Beverly neighborhood and had vaults and vaults of money, even during this Depression. No one seemed to know what line of work Uncle Cecil was in or where all his money came from. I was convinced that he was mixed up with one of Chicago's notorious gangsters.

Mother always referred to her sister as "fragile." To me, Lydia was as jumpy as a cricket in a chicken yard. I never understood how my grandparents had managed to produce two daughters as drastically different as my saintly mother and my loony aunt Lydia.

A maid answered the door and led us inside Aunt Lydia's house. Her décor was a wild jumble of expensive, tasteful pieces of furniture perched alongside outrageous souvenirs and gewgaws from the many places she had traveled. In the sunny morning room where we sat down to chat, for instance, she had hung a stuffed moose head from the wilds of Canada above an antique Louis XIV writing desk. The moose, as glassy-eyed as my aunt, wore an embroidered scarf from Morocco tied around its head like an immigrant woman in a kerchief.

We chatted and sipped coffee for a while before Aunt Lydia announced her latest travel plans. "We're going to a spa in the Appalachian Mountains. The fresh mountain air is supposed to be *marvelous* for the lungs. So invigorating." My aunt carried a cut-glass tumbler of golden liquid in her hand at all times, ice cubes tinkling as she gestured. On the rare occasion when she wasn't holding the glass, she looked naked.

"Don't people usually go to the mountains in the summertime?" I asked. "Won't it be cold there in March?"

"Oh, but we simply *must* get away. The spa has a hot spring. I'll be taking a water cure."

"Drinking it or bathing in it?" I asked. Mother poked me with her elbow in warning, but I ignored the hint.

"Why, both, of course. They have a *very* rigorous schedule at the spa—we'll be eating a special diet, taking exercise, communing with nature. Cecil and I are looking forward to it *immensely*."

"Cecil is going, too?" Mother asked.

"Yes, we're driving down there together. He needs to get away as badly as I do."

I pictured a mob of gangsters chasing after him, car tires squealing, tommy guns rattling.

"We'll be driving down through Kentucky," she continued, and the moment I heard the word *Kentucky*, an idea struck me like a gong at the carnival after someone swings a big hammer and hits the target. Why not ride to Kentucky with my aunt and uncle and deliver the donated books I had collected, in person? My uncle's car was the size of a small steamship, with a trunk large enough to stash a couple of dead bodies. Surely it would hold my five boxes of books and the magazines. Best of all, I could get away from Blue Island—the gossip and humiliation. I could disappear!

"May I go with you, Aunt Lydia?"

She and my mother stared at me in unison.

"Alice Grace Ripley!" Mother said, when she finally found her voice. Her outrage could be measured by how many of my names she used. If I had been given a fourth name, she would have used it now. "You know better than to invite yourself. And you also know that we can't afford to send you to a spa." I'm sure she would have added that we weren't the sort of irresponsible people who frittered away money on useless luxuries like water cures and hot springs, but she would never insult my aunt to her face.

"If you need to get away," Mother continued, "why not spend some time on the farm with one of your sisters? I'm sure they would have plenty for you to do."

I made a face. "They'll make me chase their kids and round up their chickens. Besides, there's not a decent library for miles and miles out where they live."

"What has gotten into you?" Mother asked.

I looked down at the polished parquet floor, tears stinging my eyes. "As you may recall, I've been laid off work at the library because of the Depression."

"Then why not marry that strapping young beau of yours?" Aunt Lydia asked. "A rollicking good honeymoon will cheer you up in no time."

Mother's face turned the color of a ripe tomato at the mention of such a taboo subject as a rollicking honeymoon. My cheeks felt sun-warmed, too. "Alice and her young man have had a falling out," Mother said in a whisper—although I don't know why she needed to whisper. Aunt Lydia's maid didn't understand English and the rest of the world already knew about my breakup with Gordon, thanks to the diligent ladies in my father's congregation.

"Oh, that's too bad, darling," Aunt Lydia said. "Have you thought about taking a lover?"

Mother's face went from red to white in an astonishingly short time. Her ability to speak vanished completely. "It's a little too soon to look for another beau," I said quickly.

"Who said anything about a beau?" Aunt Lydia said with a wink. "What you need is—"

"Lydia, please!" Mother begged.

"Well, it sounds to me like Alice could use a few days at a spa. Of course she can come with us. Cheers, darling!" She lifted her glass in salute.

"I wouldn't be going to the spa," I explained, "just to Kentucky. I've been collecting used books and magazines for the poor people down there, and since you and Uncle Cecil are going that way, I thought maybe I could tag along and deliver the books in person."

"How would you get home again?" Mother asked, being annoyingly practical.

"I don't know. Maybe I'll just stay there, and Uncle Cecil can pick me up on the way home. I've been corresponding with a librarian down there, and I'm sure she must have some volunteer work for me to do while Aunt Lydia is taking her cure. I could help her catalogue all the donated books."

"I still think you'd enjoy the spa more," Aunt Lydia said, winking at me again. "But of course you're welcome to ride along, Alice. A nice road trip will cheer you up in no time."

I wondered if I might regret my rash decision later. Uncle Cecil's cigars smelled like burning tires, and for all I knew, nasty men with prison records might be chasing him all the way to Kentucky. But how wonderful it would be to simply vanish, leaving everyone to wonder where I'd gone.

On a cold, misty morning in March, my road trip to Kentucky began. We would travel the Dixie Highway, which ran all the way from Chicago to Miami and passed right through my hometown of Blue Island. I had been eager to leave, wanting to get away from the pitying looks and prove to Gordon that I didn't care about him anymore—although I had no idea how leaving town would actually prove anything. But the moment Uncle Cecil's car arrived at the parsonage and I saw Mother's tears and Father's worried frown, I knew I had made a terrible mistake. I felt homesick, and I hadn't even left home. I had never traveled far from home before and had never been separated from my best friend, Freddy, for more than a week. My parents didn't take vacations.

Before I could stop them or say that I'd changed my mind, my father and Uncle Cecil had shoehorned the donated books and my one measly traveling bag into the car's trunk alongside Aunt

Lydia's countless suitcases and hatboxes. "Lydia packed her entire wardrobe," Uncle Cecil grumbled.

"I heard that!" my aunt said. "Why do you always exaggerate, Cecil?"

I had forgotten how much they bickered. My parents never bickered; they simply exchanged lists.

Mother kissed me good-bye. Father rested his hand on my shoulder and said, "Remember who you are, Alice." It was one of his favorite admonitions. The answer he had drummed into me was, "I am a child of God"—and therefore I needed to act like one. But aside from that rote reply, who was I really? I used to be able to say, *I'm Gordon Walters' girlfriend* and *I'm a librarian at the Blue Island Public Library.* I could no longer say either of those things. I swallowed the lump in my throat and climbed into the car. The door slammed shut behind me, sealing me in like a pickle in a canning jar when the lid sucks shut with a *pop.* I gazed straight ahead so my parents wouldn't see my tears and I wouldn't see theirs. Uncle Cecil gunned the engine and headed south.

I had been eager for a change of scene, but unfortunately the scene never changed, mile after mile, hour after hour. We drove through scattered farming communities like Steger and Grant Park and Watseka, Illinois, and they all looked numbingly alike, their brick storefronts lined up like boxers facing each other across Main Street. Identical-looking filling stations and diners and roadside motels seemed to follow us like pushy salesmen, disappearing in the rearview mirror, then popping up again farther down the highway. And in between each town, farmland stretched endlessly as far as the eye could see. As the stench of cow manure filled the air, I nearly begged Uncle Cecil to light one of his cigars.

I couldn't recall reading any good novels that featured rural Illinois or Indiana as their setting, and no wonder. The book would be much too boring. Interesting plots were inspired by interesting surroundings, and who could be inspired by farmland? This probably explained why my life had been dull and uneventful so far. I lived in a boring state.

Rain spat from the clouds onto Uncle Cecil's windshield. The dull sky and gray pavement were the color of dingy dish towels.

My uncle turned on his head lamps so he could see through the fog, and I feared our overloaded trunk would make the headlights shine up into the sky instead of down onto the road.

The terrain might have looked boring to me, but it became more fanciful and enchanted for Aunt Lydia the farther we drove. She had brought along her tumbler of golden liquid, pasted to her hand even at this early hour, ice cubes rattling like bones until they finally melted just outside of Danville. I saw her sipping from it, but I never saw her refilling it—and yet the glass never emptied. It was magical, like a sorcerer's trick.

"Look, darlings! A herd of buffalo!" she said, pointing to a dozen dairy cows huddling in the fog. My uncle and I exchanged glances in the rearview mirror. "And doesn't that castle over there remind you of the ones we saw in Germany, Cecil?"

"For crying out loud, Lydia, that's a barn!"

At this rate, she would be seeing leprechauns and unicorns before we reached Indianapolis. Uncle Cecil stomped the accelerator and *whooshed* past a slow-moving car as if in a hurry to deliver Aunt Lydia to her water cure as quickly as possible. I pulled a book out of my bag and began to read, praying that we wouldn't get into a head-on collision in the fog.

We stopped for lunch at a roadside diner, ingesting enough grease to lubricate a locomotive before getting under way again. I hadn't noticed any gangsters chasing us, but my uncle drove as if carloads of them were speeding after us. I continued to read my book, becoming the main character, living her life. It was so much better than my own.

The storm clouds lifted as the afternoon progressed, and every time I looked up from my book I noticed more and more hills—and more and more signs of the economic depression. Men in tattered clothing stood alongside the highway, thumbing for a ride. Entire families camped in makeshift tents beside the road, their laundry sagging on ropes strung between the trees. Overloaded cars waddled down the Dixie Highway like tortoises, with piles of possessions lashed onto their roofs in tottering bundles. We also passed crews of unemployed men who had been put to work by the president's Civilian Conservation Corps, laboring on the roads, stringing telephone lines or repairing bridges.

We stopped in Lexington, Kentucky, for the night and started driving again early the next day. By now I was so engrossed in my novel that I couldn't have described what any of my real surroundings looked like. I was nearing the end of the story. The main character was achieving her goals, accomplishing something important, becoming stronger and more courageous. She was about to live happily ever after with the story's handsome hero when a very loud *Bang!* suddenly interrupted my reading.

Aunt Lydia screamed. "They're shooting at us!"

I knew it. The gangsters had caught up with us. Uncle Cecil wrestled with the steering wheel as he tried to bring the swerving car to a halt. He negotiated a curve, and we finally managed to stop alongside a gray weather-beaten barn. He leaned back against his seat, breathing hard. "No one is shooting, Lydia. I had a blowout."

"What did you do that for? We could have been killed!"

"I didn't do it on purpose. Tires blow all the time."

"Well, you must have been doing something wrong for it to explode like that. You weren't driving correctly."

He got out, shaking his head, and walked around to the back of the car. I heard the trunk groan open, then heard Uncle Cecil thumping around, moving books and suitcases as he searched for his spare tire. Aunt Lydia rolled down her window. "Are you going to tip the car up in the air? I hate sitting in the car when it's all tipsy."

"The only thing tipsy is you," he mumbled. He dropped the car jack and tire iron on the ground with a clang. "Yes, I'm going to jack it up." My aunt leaped out of the car as if it was on fire, so I leaped out, too.

We had stopped in a narrow valley surrounded by tree-covered mountains. I didn't see any houses, just the dilapidated barn. A faded sign painted on the front of it read: *Church of the Holy Fire. Sunday Worship 10 A.M. Sinners Welcome.* Uncle Cecil put the jack in place and turned the crank, grunting and straining. The heavy car rose and tilted as the rear wheel slowly lifted off the ground.

I heard a low growling sound, and a moment later a huge black dog hurtled toward us from behind the barn, barking and snarling. Before I had time to scream, it reached the end of its chain and choked to a stop. But it continued to lunge and bark at us, straining the rusted chain. Aunt Lydia gripped my hand.

"We have to leave, Cecil. Right now. This place you picked to have your blowout is unacceptable."

"I didn't pick this place; it's where the tire blew."

"Well, put the car down. Go farther up the road and change it."

"I'm not driving on a flat tire." He unscrewed the lug nuts and yanked off the tire. Dirt smudged his forehead and white shirt.

Aunt Lydia huddled close beside me as the dog continued to growl and bark and pace. "If that animal gets loose, he'll kill all three of us," she said.

"I told you to stay in the car, but you wouldn't listen."

"Well, we can't get in the car now. It's up in the air!" My aunt's fear was contagious, and we huddled beside each other, trembling. It seemed to take forever, but at last Uncle Cecil tightened the last lug nut and pumped the jack handle, lowering the car. The dog sounded hoarse from barking, but his chain had held tight.

"That was a terrifying experience!" Aunt Lydia said as we climbed back into the car.

"What are you talking about? We had a flat tire. That's life, Lydia. A tire blows, you fix it, you move on."

Uncle Cecil's words seemed profound to me. As my racing heart slowed and we continued on our way, I felt ashamed of how I had reacted. No one had been shooting at us. The dog hadn't been a rabid beast, just an ordinary black dog on a very long chain. I realized that I was as out of touch with the real world as Aunt Lydia was, my imagination out of control from all of the books I had read. Is this what Gordon had meant when he'd said I lived in a dream world?

I didn't want to end up like my aunt. I made up my mind that from now on, I was going to wake up and pay attention to the world around me. I would put all of my problems behind me—tossing them into the trunk of my car, so to speak, like a worn-out tire. I would move on just as my uncle had done. I would go to Acorn, Kentucky, and be a heroine to all those poor people who needed my books. My life would have meaning and purpose again.

We drove for another hour or so, up and down a road that snaked into the mountains, following greenish rivers and rocky creeks. Trees surrounded us on all sides, and we plunged deeper and deeper into the woods as if entering the land of fairy tales. Not the nice, happily-ever-after kind, but the lost-in-the-woods-among-wolves kind. My newfound courage began to drain away.

"Where is this town, anyway?" Aunt Lydia asked at one point. "And why did they put it in the middle of nowhere?"

"There's lumber and coal up in here," Uncle Cecil replied.

"At least the roads are paved," I said, trying to sound positive. "There must be a town around here somewhere."

"These roads weren't built for the towns," Uncle Cecil said. "They were built to get the coal out."

In spite of my resolve to be heroic, the woods frightened me. What if we got lost and wandered in these woods forever? I decided to escape to the safer world of make-believe, and I hunched down in the backseat to finish reading my book.

Around midday, Uncle Cecil announced that we were coming to a town. I looked up from reading and saw a handful of houses wedged into a narrow valley between two mountains. Wherever there was a flat strip of land on either mountainside, someone had built a house or a building. If people came out of their front doors too fast, it looked as though they would tumble right down the hill.

"Is this the place we're looking for?" Aunt Lydia asked. I searched for a sign and spotted one on the side of a flat-roofed hut: *U.S. Post Office, Acorn, Kentucky.*

"Yes! There's the post office! This is it!" I assumed we were entering the outskirts of Acorn and that we'd eventually see a larger cluster of buildings when we reached the center of town, but Uncle Cecil drove straight through the village and out the other side before any of us could blink. He had to make a U-turn and go back, driving slower this time. I had thought Blue Island was small, but Acorn didn't deserve to be called a town.

On our second ride-through, I spotted a hand-painted sign in front of a shabby two-story house: *Acorn Public Library.* A smaller red, white, and blue sign identified the library as a project of the WPA, President Roosevelt's Works Project Administration.

We parked in front and I climbed out. The library sat very close to the street with no sidewalk and only a narrow patch of dirt for a lawn. According to the hours posted on the sign, the library was supposed to be open now, but when I tried the door it was locked. I knocked, then peeked through the front window. There were no lights, no signs of life, no response to my knock. I pounded harder, rattling the ancient door on its hinges.

The third time I used my fist.

An upstairs window slid open above my head and a wooly-looking man whom I nearly mistook for a bear peered out. "Hey! You trying to break the door down? What do you want?" His growl resembled a bear's, as well.

I shaded my eyes and looked up at him. "Do you know where I might find the librarian, Leslie MacDougal?"

"Who are you?"

"Alice Grace Ripley from Blue Island, Illinois. I have some books that I'd like to donate to her library."

"Just a minute." The window slammed shut.

"Well!" Aunt Lydia huffed. "The people aren't very friendly around here. Are you sure you don't want to come to the spa with us, darling?"

I had to admit that I was having second thoughts. This poky village and run-down library weren't at all what I had expected. But given the choice between spending a week in a library or taking a water cure—whatever that was—I would choose a library every time, no matter how tiny it was. I could be useful here. More important, there were books here.

"I'll be fine, Aunt Lydia. I've been corresponding with the librarian, and she sounded very kind in her letters. She was very enthused about the donated books and I told her in my last letter that I would stay and help her catalogue them." I didn't mention the fact that the librarian had never answered my last letter, nor had she officially invited me to stay. "This looks like a nice little town, doesn't it?" I added.

"What town, dear? I don't see a town. Where are the hat shops and the shoe stores?"

"They have a library," I said.

Meanwhile, Uncle Cecil had opened the trunk and was unloading the books, piling the boxes beside the library steps. "That's the last one," he said, patting the top of it. He was in a hurry to be on his way, and I didn't blame him. Aunt Lydia had insisted she'd seen a dead monkey in the road a few miles back, so I understood his urgency to get her to the spa. I pulled my suitcase from the trunk and set it down beside the car. "Thanks for bringing me. See you in about two weeks?"

"Right." He slammed the trunk just as the shaggy man emerged through the front door, blinking in the sunlight like a bear that had awakened too early from hibernation. He had buttoned his shirt crookedly and fastened only one strap of his bib overalls. And he was barefooted. I approached him as cautiously as I would a genuine bear.

"I'm sorry to bother you, but I'm looking for Leslie MacDougal. I've been corresponding with her about these books that I've collected for her library." He gave a curt nod, lifted the first box, and carried it inside. I picked up a bag of magazines and followed him. "She's expecting me. I told her that I would be delivering them sometime this week."

He nodded again, dropped the box on the floor in the foyer where the library patrons would surely trip over it, and returned for another one. I followed him in and out, carrying the magazines and chattering away about our library in Illinois and how much I looked forward to meeting Acorn's librarian. Why wouldn't he answer my question and tell me where she was? Was he deaf, dim-witted, or simply ill-mannered?

When we'd hauled the last box and bag inside, I cleared my throat and spoke loudly and clearly, covering all three possibilities. "Would you kindly tell me where I might find the librarian, Leslie MacDougal?"

"That's me."

"You can't be her. You're a man!"

"What gave it away, lady? The beard?"

"But . . . but I've come to help her. I planned to stay here and—"

"Stay? You can't stay!" At that moment, we both heard the accelerating engine, the crunch of loose gravel beneath the huge car's tires. We looked out the open door in time to see Uncle

Cecil's car driving away. "Hey! Where's he going? He can't leave you here!"

The bear-man raced out of the door, nearly tripping over my suitcase, and sprinted up the road behind the car, shouting and waving his arms. "Wait! Stop!" He ran quite fast considering that he was barefooted. With his wild-looking hair and angry shouts, he appeared to be chasing the car away, rather than trying to stop it. I hurried after him, panicked at the thought of being marooned with this wooly lunatic. But my uncle's huge automobile, as sound-proof as a casket, disappeared around a curve and vanished in a cloud of dust.

CHAPTER 4

As the dust from Uncle Cecil's car swirled and settled, Leslie MacDougal turned and walked toward me, looking as sinister as a vaudeville villain. He held one hand against his side, panting from his useless sprint. "When is he coming back for you?"

"In two weeks."

"Two weeks!"

I knew it might be longer, considering my aunt's fragile condition, but why make matters worse? I lifted my chin to look up at him, since he was at least a foot taller than me. "I wrote to you and mentioned that I planned to stay and volunteer—"

"And I wrote to you and told you not to come."

"I never received your letter."

"But you came anyway? Without an invitation?"

"I thought you were . . . I mean, your name is Leslie . . . and most librarians are women." And much friendlier and better groomed, I wanted to add as he strode past me, heading toward the house.

"I'm not a woman," he hollered over his shoulder. "That's why I told you to stay home and just ship the books to me."

I cleared my throat and tried to summon a measure of dignity as I followed him back to the library. "I apologize for the misunderstanding, Mr. MacDougal, even though it wasn't entirely my fault." If anyone was to blame, it was this man's parents for giving him a woman's name. I took a deep breath and exhaled. "If you will kindly direct me to the nearest hotel, I'll gladly get out of your . . . hair." He halted on the front porch and turned to face me.

"A hotel?—Ha! Where do you think you are, lady? Back in Chicago?" He shook his head and went inside, leaving the library door wide open.

It seemed that I had baked myself into a jam tart, as Mother would say. What in the world was I going to do? If I had been reading about this disastrous misunderstanding in a book, I would have flipped to the last chapter to see how everything turned out. But it wasn't a story, it was my life—and I had no idea what to do. After gazing down the road for several minutes, praying in vain that my uncle's car would miraculously reappear, I picked up my suitcase and followed Leslie MacDougal into the foyer.

Bookshelves filled the rooms to my right and my left, confirming that what looked like a house from the outside was indeed a library—the tiniest library I had ever seen. I felt like Alice in Wonderland after she had grown to a very large size. The rooms lacked the wonderful bookish aroma of our library back home. Instead, they smelled like fried chicken.

Mr. MacDougal sat cross-legged on the hall floor and was busily unpacking the first box of books. "Wow!" he said when he came to the nearly new *World Atlas*.

"Isn't it wonderful?" I said. "That atlas came from the collection of a very kind gentleman named Elmer Watson, who used to patronize our library back home. He passed away recently, so I took the liberty of speaking with his widow and she very kindly agreed to donate it to your library."

Mr. MacDougal didn't reply. He didn't even nod his head.

The memory of Mr. Watson's funeral and how it had led to my breakup with Gordon made me teary-eyed. When I'd lost my job the following day, I had wanted to get as far away as possible from a town where I was no longer needed or wanted. Instead, I had simply relocated to another town where I wasn't needed or wanted. *"Out of the chicken coop and into the stewpot,"* my mother would say. I did feel as though I'd been wrung, plucked, and scalded.

Mr. MacDougal continued to unpack the books, perusing their contents, piling them haphazardly all around him. He was so absorbed that he seemed to have forgotten me. I watched his face and saw the appreciation in his eyes—what little I could see of his eyes beneath his shaggy hair. He ran his hand over the covers the way a man in love might caress his beloved's face, and he even opened one or two of the newer books to inhale their scent before piling them on the floor with the others. I felt justified for the trouble I'd taken to deliver them, even if my arrival had been unexpected and unwelcome.

It was hard to tell how old Mr. MacDougal was, but his hands weren't wrinkled and his brown hair and beard didn't have any gray in them. He had lifted the heavy boxes effortlessly and had run pretty fast as he'd chased Uncle Cecil's car, so I judged him to be around thirty. He might be good-looking with a shave and a haircut. And a bath. And a decent suit of clothes. As it was, he looked like one of the raggedy, down-on-their-luck men we had seen along the way, except that Mr. MacDougal had no excuse since he was gainfully employed. I cleared my throat. He looked up, frowning as if annoyed by the interruption.

"I think you'll agree that there are some very nice books in those boxes."

"Very nice. Thanks." He sighed as if I had broken a magic spell and began repacking the books.

"Look, I'm sorry about your name, Mr. MacDougal."

"I've been sorry all my life, but I was too young to object to the name when my parents saddled me with it."

I felt a breeze behind me. We had left the door wide open. "Why was the library closed when it's supposed to be open?" I asked as I turned to shut the door. "The hours on the sign say—"

"I know what the sign says. I'm the one who painted it."

"But it wasn't open when I arrived. The door was locked."

"I got busy."

"But suppose one of your patrons had wanted a book or—"

"You the library police, lady?"

"No . . . and my name is Alice Grace Ripley."

"You see any people lining up out there waiting for books, Alice Grace Ripley?"

"Well, no . . ." He stood and carried one of the boxes into the parlor. I followed him. "Oh, my!" I said when I saw the main desk. At least I assumed there was a main desk buried beneath all of the books and papers. What in the world did this man do all day? He certainly wasn't keeping the library in order.

"Looks like you could use some help," I said.

"Looks like."

He carried in the rest of the boxes, glancing up the stairs each time he passed them as if eager to return to whatever he had been doing up there. When he finished, he stared at me, hands on his hips. From his expression, he might have been waiting for me to say, *Well, I'll be going now*. But of course I had no place to go. He had already made it clear that the town didn't have a hotel.

"I believe it's lunchtime," I finally said. "If you would be kind enough to direct me to a café or a diner, I'll leave you alone."

He attempted a smile, but it was closer to a smirk. "Sure. There's a four-star restaurant down the street, right next door to our swanky four-star hotel. You can buy a four-course gourmet meal. Will that suit you?"

"You don't have to be sarcastic."

He lifted his arms in exasperation and let them slap against his sides. Dust puffed from his pants. "I'm just not prepared to deal with you, that's all."

"You've made that perfectly clear."

He glanced up the stairs again. Sighed again. "Let me see what I can rustle up for lunch. Come on."

He led the way through a door and into a kitchen that looked as though it had been tacked onto the back of the house as an afterthought. Flies buzzed and swarmed around a towering sink full of dishes. More flies encrusted two yellowing strips of flypaper hanging above it. Behind the cookstove, a plaid shirt and two pairs of men's long underdrawers hung on a sagging rope. And judging by the smell, Mr. MacDougal was either manufacturing Limburger cheese or his milk had soured several weeks ago. If he had a wife, she had probably left him. I didn't blame her.

"Excuse the mess," he mumbled. He cleared a place to eat on the round wooden table and motioned to a chair. "Sit down." The chair creaked like a sack of kindling wood as I reluctantly obeyed.

My host took a loaf of homemade bread from the bread box and sawed off several thick, crumbling slices. Then he opened a can of pork and beans and spread the contents on three slices of bread, topping each of them with another slice to make sandwiches. I had never heard of a baked bean sandwich before, but I was hardly in a position to complain. He opened a cupboard door as if searching for a clean plate, then gave up and pushed one of the sandwiches across the bare table to me.

"Thank you," I said, remembering my manners.

"You want coffee?" he asked. "It's mixed with chicory, so it's kind of bitter."

"No thank you." I briefly bowed my head to pray while he poured himself a cup of coffee—and never before had I been so keenly aware of the need for the Almighty to bless a meal. Then I lifted the sandwich, careful not to spill the beans, and took a tentative bite. It was actually very tasty, if a bit unusual.

We ate in silence. Outside, birds chirped and sang and called to each other, and the sound of rushing water gurgled continually as if someone had left a huge tap running. When a train whistle wailed in the far-off distance, it gave me an idea. "Um . . . when does the next bus or passenger train come through town?"

He laughed out loud and continued laughing until I felt my cheeks burn. "Well, excuse me," I said, "but I've never visited such an uncivilized place before."

"Did you have your eyes closed on your way here?"

"No . . . I was reading a book. A very good one, in fact." If Gordon had been here, he would have rolled his eyes and shaken his head in exasperation. "Listen, Mr. MacDougal, it looks as though I'm going to be stuck here for a while, and I want you to know that I'm willing to pay for my room and board."

"I should hope so. Folks don't have much to spare now that the mines are closed."

We finished eating in silence. When he'd gulped down the last of his coffee, he stood and picked up the extra sandwich. "I need to take this upstairs to Lillie."

Who in the world was Lillie, and why hadn't she come down and introduced herself? How often did people around here get company from Illinois, for goodness' sake? Whatever her reason for staying hidden, I figured she might be as strange as Leslie MacDougal, and the sooner I got out of their way the better. I stood as well, wishing for a napkin to wipe the bean juice off my fingers. He had licked his.

"Thank you very much for lunch, Mr. MacDougal. If you would kindly direct me . . . somewhere . . . I will leave you to your work."

"Look, Miss Ripley. I have no idea what to do with you. My traveling librarians might have an idea, but they're out delivering books."

"What's a traveling librarian?"

"Just what it sounds like. It's not easy for folks around here to get to town, so our librarians deliver the books to the people."

"In a bookmobile?"

"On horseback."

"*Horse*back? You're kidding." I tried to imagine Mrs. Beasley or Mrs. Davidson or myself, for that matter, galloping around Blue Island on horses, distributing books like Pony Express riders. I nearly laughed out loud. But Mr. MacDougal was perfectly serious.

"Alma usually rides a mule," he said, "but Marjorie, Cora, and Faye all ride horses."

I had never heard of such a crazy idea. This was 1936, not pioneer days. Again, I felt like Alice in Wonderland, except that when I'd fallen into this rabbit hole I'd ended up in Acorn, Kentucky, with the Mad Hatter. "How far do the librarians travel? And for how long?" I asked, hoping they would return soon.

"Just a day's ride. They'll start coming back in two or three hours."

I had no intention of sitting around and doing nothing for that long. I stood and smoothed my skirt. "Well. I did come here to volunteer, Mr. MacDougal, so if you will kindly give me a quick tour of your library, I'll be happy to get to work."

"You want to work?" He said it as if I had offered to do cartwheels down Main Street.

"Yes, work. It's better than standing here feeling useless. I am an experienced librarian, after all. I can card and shelve books, catalogue the new ones—whatever needs to be done." And from the looks of this place, plenty needed to be done. "Or, if you don't want my help, I'll be content to sit and read a book all afternoon. It's up to you."

"No, it isn't. Do whatever you want, lady."

45

He went out into the hallway and up the squeaking stairs, taking the third baked bean sandwich and a cup of coffee with him. I went into the main room and looked around. Leslie MacDougal was a disgrace to the library profession. There was no excuse for a library this tiny to be in such a mess.

I didn't need a tour. I easily found the fiction section, the tiny collection of reference books, the even smaller shelf of children's books. The leaning pile of books on the main desk obviously needed to be carded and shelved, so I located the wooden box of cards that had been filed according to their due dates. The messy mound of cards that hadn't been filed must belong to books that were checked out. I went to work, forgetting my uncomfortable predicament, and soon lost myself in the familiar, satisfying task of putting the library in order. Each card I filed represented a book that someone might be reading and enjoying this very minute, transporting him or her to a different place and time. I forgot all about Leslie MacDougal until the creaking stairs announced his return a few hours later.

"Where is everyone?" I asked. "Not a single patron has come in for a book. The town looked deserted when we drove through it."

"The Depression hit us hard down here. Most families depend on coal, one way or another. They lost their jobs in the mines when the factories up north closed."

"Did all the people leave town?"

"Some of the men went on the bum, looking for work. The younger ones signed up for the Civilian Conservation Corps to make a few bucks a day. They send money home whenever they can."

"I saw the WPA sign on the library door. Is this one of their projects?"

He nodded. "Mr. Roosevelt pays Faye and Cora and the other girls to deliver books. Nobody around here wants to go on the dole, but they're willing to do an honest day's work, if they can get it."

"Don't they have husbands?"

"Some do, some don't."

He didn't have a thick Southern accent like other people I'd met from the South, but he had a way of stretching out certain words as if he was sighing in the middle of them. *Library* sounded like *lah-brary* and *sign* was *sah-n* and *I* became *ahhh*.

46

"How long have you been the librarian here, Mr. MacDougal?"

"My name is Mack. And you ask too many questions. You're a flatlander. People don't like flatlanders very much to begin with, especially ones who talk us to death and pester us with questions. When you meet Cora and the others, I advise you to mind your own business, not theirs."

"I'm simply making polite conversation."

"There's nothing polite about nosy questions."

"Well. I have one more question and then I'll leave you alone. Where is your card catalogue?"

"Up here," he said, tapping his forehead. "I know every book in this place." He turned his back on me and disappeared up the stairs again, taking them two at a time.

The afternoon passed quickly. About the time I was starting to see the wooden desktop, I heard horses plodding up the road and halting out front. The front door squeaked open, and women's voices and laughter echoed in the foyer. The traveling librarians had returned.

A moment later, two women walked into the room, and when they saw me sitting behind the desk they halted as if they'd run into a glass wall. "Who are you?" the taller one asked.

"I'm Alice Grace Ripley from Illinois." They stared as if they'd never seen a stranger before. Maybe they hadn't.

"Well, what are you doing in our library?" The taller one looked ready to grab me by the arm and toss me out the front door. Luckily, Mack sauntered down the stairs just then.

"She's okay, girls. Miss Ripley's helping us out."

The glass wall vanished and they resumed their conversation without a word of welcome or how-do-you-do, as if I had vanished, too. They unpacked all the books from their bags—one woman had a pair of leather saddlebags, the other a couple of burlap sacks—and piled them on the newly cleared desk.

"Hey, Cora. Did you get up to the school today?" Mack asked the burlap-bag lady.

"It's on my route for tomorrow."

"Good. Wait until you see what I have for the kids." He pulled out Elmer Watson's atlas with a grin and a flourish.

"Where did you get that?"

"Pretty nice, huh?"

I might have been invisible. It galled me that he was taking all the credit for Mr. Watson's wonderful atlas as if he had printed and bound it himself while they had been out riding their horses.

"*I* brought it with me," I said loudly. "From Illinois. We had a book drive at the library where I work and one of our patrons donated it."

Mack gestured to the woman with the atlas. "This is Cora. And she's Marjorie."

"It's nice to meet you." I smiled my friendliest smile. The ladies nodded absently.

"Here are the rest of the books," Mack told them. "Look through them and take whatever you want for your routes."

His words horrified me. "Wait! Those books haven't been processed and catalogued yet!" They ignored my protests and knelt down to rummage through the boxes. I heard more horses outside, stomping and sneezing, and two more women came inside to unload their books. Mack introduced them as Alma and Faye, and they weren't any friendlier than the first two women had been. I quickly forgot who was who as they milled around, looking through the boxes of new books, deciding which of their patrons would enjoy them.

"Um . . . I really think you should catalogue the books first," I said again. "They don't even have cards or pockets yet." Everyone ignored me.

Eventually the women made their selections and started to leave. I cleared my throat to get Mr. MacDougal's attention, and he finally recalled my predicament. "Hey, any of you girls know where Miss Ripley can spend the night?" They gazed at me as if I were a stray cat—pitiful but unwanted—then mumbled their excuses.

"Gosh, I don't know, Mack."

"We're full up at my place."

"I don't have a bed to spare now that Lloyd's mamaw is here to stay."

"You know I got a passel of kids."

And so on. They said their good-byes and left. Mr. MacDougal wouldn't put me out in the street, would he?

I worked behind the desk until suppertime, valiantly holding back tears. He served scrambled eggs and corn bread for dinner. "I guess you'll have to stay here tonight," he said as we ate our supper in the kitchen. He had gone to the trouble of washing two plates and a cast-iron frying pan to cook the eggs. The kitchen sink had a hand pump and running water, but I learned that the toilet facilities were outside. When it got dark, he lit several kerosene lamps since the house didn't have electricity.

At bedtime, Mr. MacDougal led me up the creaking stairs to what must have been his own bedroom. He kicked a few stray pieces of clothing under the bed, then yanked off the sheets. They looked as though they hadn't been changed in years. I pushed aside thoughts of bedbugs as he rummaged through a closet in the hallway and found a folded pair of limp, gray sheets. He handed them to me.

"These are clean."

"Thank you. I'll make the bed myself, no need to bother."

"Wasn't planning to." He showed me where to find the chamber pot, but I decided that I would allow my insides to burst before I would use it. I had loved reading Willa Cather's trilogy about primitive life on the American prairie but had never imagined that I would have to live that way myself with no electricity or running water. I closed the bedroom door after he left and quietly slid a chair in front of it.

The bedroom was dark and creepy in the dim lamplight. I know what they say about looking gift horses in the mouth, but I couldn't help being critical. The sinister wallpaper was peeling off. The floor seemed to slant downhill. Cobwebs festooned the ceiling, and where there were cobwebs there were certain to be spiders. I put the sheets on the bed, changed into my nightgown, and recited my prayers. I usually prayed after climbing into bed, but that night I felt compelled to kneel beside the bed and beseech the Almighty for help. Perhaps my humble position might prompt Him to reply quickly.

I said "Amen" and gingerly climbed into bed. Earlier that day I had picked out an interesting-looking book from the return pile called *Appalachian Folk Tales*. I settled back against the pillow to read it by lamplight. Too late I discovered that folks in Appalachia were very fond of ghost stories. I would not recommend reading such dark tales in a strange man's gloomy bedroom, but I didn't think it was wise to leave the relative safety of my room and prowl around in the dark to find another book. I read until I was thoroughly terrified, then blew out the lamp and tried, in vain, to sleep.

The house creaked and groaned. I heard mysterious scratching sounds in the walls and the pattering of feet above my head. Not only did the house moan as though it were haunted, but I heard a continuous rushing of water outside that should have been soothing but wasn't. Then an army of frogs began to belch and bellow and *gronk* until I wanted to scream.

I slept a scant hour or two. A maniacal rooster awakened me at dawn, and I dressed and went downstairs to use the outhouse. It was morning, but deep purple shadows blanketed the backyard. Unlike the flat Midwest where the sun pops above the horizon within a matter of minutes, Acorn, Kentucky, wasn't going to see the sun until it climbed above the mountaintops several hours from now. I finished my business and walked down to the creek—the source of the rushing water I'd been listening to all night—as I pondered what to do.

My life had no plot. The main character in every novel I'd ever read always knew what she wanted, and in spite of numerous obstacles she would move forward toward that goal. The action would reach a climax as she struggled to succeed and then the story would resolve—sometimes tragically if she had a fatal flaw, but usually happily ever after. The murder would be solved, the romance would end in marriage, victory would be won, and the main characters would have a brand-new start. I knew that real life wasn't exactly like a book, but why did everyone else's life seem to hum along with a sensible plot and realistic goals, and mine didn't?

What did I want in life?

I would like my library job back. I wasn't sure if I wanted Gordon back. Aside from that, I had no other goals. Running away to Kentucky had offered a diversion, but sooner or later—hopefully sooner—I would return to Illinois, and then what? Should I become a farmer's wife like my two sisters?

I tossed a pebble into the stream—it was what people in books always did for mysterious, symbolic reasons. I sighed and turned to go back inside. It was too chilly and too early in the morning to stand by a creek and feel sorry for myself. Halfway to the back door, I heard a loud bang, like a gunshot. It startled me as well as a flock of birds that rose up in flight from a nearby tree. Two more booms sounded in quick succession, speeding me the rest of the way to the back door. I fled inside and leaned against the door to catch my breath, my heart fluttering and flapping like the birds' wings. I had been wishing that something would happen, but I hadn't expected gunfire!

Then I noticed the deer antlers mounted above the door in the library, and I felt very foolish. Of course. People around here went hunting. Someone must be shooting his breakfast or dinner. That's what poor people did for food, right? Hopefully no one had noticed my undignified sprint.

I was gazing at the pile of dishes in the sink, thinking that a courteous guest would wash them for her host, when the front door slammed shut, rattling the windows. I tiptoed cautiously into the library and peeked around the corner into the shadowy foyer. Mr. MacDougal was leaning against the front door. He held his right hand above his heart as if he was about to say the Pledge of Allegiance. He wore a dark glove and beneath his hand was a stain that hadn't been on his bib overalls yesterday. He looked up and saw me in the doorway.

"Help . . ." he breathed. His eyes looked round and wide and very scared. "Help me . . ." His knees buckled, and he slid down the wall to the floor. I ran to him.

"Mr. MacDougal! What's wrong? What happened?"

He was breathing hard, gasping. "I've been shot . . ." He lifted his hand, and he wasn't wearing a glove after all. His palm was dark with blood.

"W-what should I do? I don't know what to do!"

He stared at me, and the skin visible around his eyes and lips drained from pink to white. He slowly blinked his eyes as if he was falling asleep.

"Should I call a doctor? An ambulance? Where's the hospital?" Stupid questions. There was nothing in this ridiculous town.

"Get Lillie," he murmured. Then his eyes closed and he slumped sideways to the floor like a pile of rags.

CHAPTER 5

Get Lillie? The only thing I knew about Lillie was that she had been upstairs yesterday when I arrived. Mack had brought her a baked bean sandwich. Lillie could be his wife or his dog or his maiden aunt, for all I knew.

I sprinted up the creaking stairs, taking them two at a time. Three doors opened off the narrow hallway; one led to the room where I had slept, one stood partially open, and the third was closed. I peeked inside the open door and found a witch's workroom, tiny and dark. It smelled like rotten eggs and dead grass. Bunches of dried herbs and flowers hung from the slanted ceiling, and various-sized jars and bottles and baskets lay scattered everywhere, filled with witchy-looking things. There was even a black iron cauldron and a wooden mortar and pestle. Mack's pillow and bedsheets lay heaped on the floor, where he must have slept.

I backed out and knocked on the closed door. "Lillie . . . ?"

No reply. I waited and knocked again—then came to my senses. What in the world was I waiting for? This was no time to be polite! I turned the knob and went inside.

"Lillie?"

A brass bed stood against one wall in the darkened room, covered with a patchwork quilt. A small lump in the middle of the bed shifted and rolled over, and an elderly Negro woman squinted at me in the dark. She was so tiny that I would have thought she was a child, but her coffee brown face was as furrowed as a relief map of the Rocky Mountains. Feathery white hair stuck out in tufts around her head.

"Are you Lillie?"

"Yes . . . Who in the blazes are you?"

"Alice Grace Ripley from Illinois. I'm sorry to bother you, but Mack has been shot and I don't know what to do!"

"Shot?"

"Yes! He's downstairs and . . . and he's bleeding!" The woman unwound the covers and slowly swung her heron-like legs over the edge of the bed.

"You'll have to help me, girl," she said. "I been feeling poorly these past few weeks and ain't been outta bed in a while." Her voice sounded faint and rusty, like a radio program with too much static. I helped her to her feet and we shuffled to the door. She was as thin as a stalk of wheat in a long white nightgown, as weightless as a bag of cotton balls.

"You're shaking, girl," she said as I helped her slowly descend the stairs.

"I can't help it! Somebody shot Mack!" I could barely think, let alone speak. Shock had scared all of the thoughts right out of my head. Watching blood pour from a real wounded man was quite different from imagining it in a book.

It took a hundred years to help Lillie hobble downstairs and over to where Mack lay, but at last she knelt down and gently patted his furry cheek. "Can you hear me, Mack, honey?" Apparently not. He lay stone still. "Help me lay him down flat," Lillie said. She seemed very calm, as if people arrived wounded and bleeding at the library door every day. I watched her carefully unbutton his overall straps and shirt with her tiny wrinkled fingers. Why didn't she work faster? But my own fingers trembled so badly I couldn't have unbuttoned anything.

"Should I call a doctor?" I asked.

"Ain't one for miles. Go out in the kitchen and fetch me some clean dish towels."

Clean? Had she seen the kitchen lately? I ransacked every drawer and cupboard but found no dish towels, clean or otherwise. Two pairs of woolen long johns still hung on the clothesline behind the stove, so I yanked them down, figuring they were clean, and ran to Lillie with them. She had bared Mack's chest, which was as wooly as the rest of him.

"Them ain't dish towels," she said when she saw what I had brought her.

"I couldn't find anything else."

"I guess they'll have to do, then," she said with a sigh. "Let's see what we got here." She used one leg of the long johns to mop up the blood, and I saw a bluish hole just below Mack's collarbone. When a spurt of blood pulsed from it, I closed my eyes for a moment to keep from fainting.

Lillie wadded up the other leg and used it to press hard against the bullet hole to stop the bleeding, using both hands and all of her sparrow-like weight. Before long, Mack's blood had soaked the cloth and Lillie's hands and stained her white nightgown. What I could see of his face beneath his hair and beard was whiter than the gown.

"Help me roll him over on his side," Lillie said. I knelt to help her, then watched as she pulled down his shirt and mopped the blood off his back. I saw another hole, larger than the one in front, and nearly passed out again. Lillie didn't seem fazed. "Least there's no bullet left inside him," she said. "Here, you press this against his back and I'll keep on pressing the front."

"I-I'm going to faint. . . ."

"Oh, no you ain't. Come on—whoever you are—I ain't strong enough to stop the bleeding on both sides."

"I-I-I . . ."

"Take deep breaths, girl. Get some air into your brain. You want him to die on us?"

"No, ma'am."

"Then push hard. We got to stop the bleeding."

I did as I was told. When I pushed the cloth against his back, Mack moaned.

"Stay with us, Mack," Lillie coaxed. Her voice was soothing and calm. "Don't you dare go a-dying on me now, you hear?"

I held the cloth tightly against Mack's shoulder. The blood felt warm, like something alive on my hand. I closed my eyes.

54

Maybe I was dreaming. This was the sort of dream people had when they read frightening stories before bed. Any minute now I would wake up and the morning would start all over again, only this time no one would get shot. I opened my eyes when the dizziness passed, but I was still in the Acorn Public Library, holding a bloody towel to the librarian's gunshot wound.

I averted my gaze and focused on a shelf of books nearby, reading the titles and silently alphabetizing them by the authors' last names to get my mind off all the blood. And the dying man. And the ancient woman with the wispy white hair. Why couldn't I be as calm as she was? Why couldn't I think of something practical to do?

"I-if there's no doctor in town, w-what do people do when they're hurt or sick?" I asked.

"They come and see me. I'm known as a healer round here. . . . You know how to pray, girl?"

"My father is a minister."

"Well, unless he's hiding out in the next room, he ain't gonna be any help to us, is he? We best get praying." She closed her eyes and lifted her chin in the air, yelling out a prayer as if the Almighty was stone-deaf. "O Lord, you see this boy laying here. You see he's bleeding hard. He has no help but you, Lord. You know how we all depend on Mack, and so I'm begging you to stop the bleeding and spare his life." She went on that way for several minutes before ending with, "In Jesus' precious name. Amen."

She opened her eyes and gazed at me, waiting. I glanced down at Mack, and he was so deathly pale and there was so much blood that the only thing I could think of to say was, "Oh, dear God . . . please . . . please . . . please . . ." I had never watched anyone die before and it looked as though I was about to. Tears choked off my words.

"Ain't much of a prayer," Lillie grumbled.

"I'm sorry, I'm sorry . . . I-I could say the Lord's Prayer . . ."

"No thanks. I'm thinking the Good Lord has that one about memorized by now. He don't need to hear it again."

"Should we call the police?"

"Ain't no police way out here. County sheriff might show up if Mack dies on us, but we don't want that."

I wondered if she meant we didn't want the sheriff to show up or we didn't want Mack to die. "Who would want to shoot him?" I asked.

"Oh, I can name a couple people who mighta shot him. Mack is—" She stopped and glared sharply at me as if suddenly realizing she was about to tell a secret to a stranger. "I think you better tell me who you are again, and what you're doing in my house."

"I'm Alice Grace Ripley. I came yesterday with five boxes of books to donate to the library." Yesterday. It seemed like a million years ago. "Didn't Mr. MacDougal—Mack—tell you?"

"No, ma'am, he certainly did not. Where'd you say you was from?"

"Illinois—Blue Island, Illinois."

"I never heard of no islands in Illinois. And I sure ain't never heard of a blue one."

"Well, the town isn't really blue . . . and it isn't an island, either. I think it was the waving grass or the hazy sky or—" I stopped, unable to remember the story our third grade teacher had told us about how the town got its name. But why in the world did she need an explanation at a time like this? Why were we even having this conversation? Mack could be dying. What kind of a town had no doctor and no policemen—especially if people were in the habit of shooting each other first thing in the morning?

"Please . . . can't we do something for him?" I begged. "He's bleeding!"

"Don't I know it," she said, holding up her bloody hand. "Hole goes clear through him. But I suppose that's better than having to dig around inside him and try and find the bullet."

I felt faint again. I closed my eyes. My heart had never pounded this hard in my life, even when I'd set our kitchen on fire.

"Deep breaths, girl. Take deep breaths." How could she be so calm?

When the dizziness passed, I opened my eyes in time to see Lillie lift the bloodied cloth and look at the hole on her side of him.

"Blood's starting to clot," she said. "Better keep holding tight, though, just to be sure." I quickly closed my eyes again.

Eventually, Lillie told me I could let go and she would hold the compresses on both wounds for a moment. "Run upstairs and pull a sheet off my bed to use for bandages."

I did as I was told, except that I gave her a sheet from my bed, figuring it was cleaner. I was relieved to see that Mack had regained consciousness and was talking to Lillie in a breathy voice when I returned.

"Some crazy fool tried to kill me . . ."

"They just might get their wish, honey. You ain't outta the woods yet."

"Let them think they killed me, Lillie . . . Safer that way."

Lillie pondered his words for a moment before saying, "You might be right. If they come back to finish you off, you're a sitting duck. Or a laying-down duck, I should say." She gave a cackling laugh, then looked up at me. I held the bedsheets in my shaking, bloody hands. "You know how to rip bandages, girl?" I shook my head. I had trained to be a schoolteacher and a librarian, not a nurse. "Take over this job, then, and I'll rip." I knelt down and pressed the blood-soaked underwear against Mack's wounds while Lillie tore up the sheets.

"Listen, Lillie . . ." Mack breathed. "Have my funeral. Let them think they killed me."

"How am I gonna fake a funeral all by myself, honey? I'll be needing a casket and everything."

He tilted his chin, gesturing to me. "She can help us."

"That girl? She ain't much use to nobody, far as I can tell."

Mack's eyes met mine. "Will you help me?"

I couldn't reply. I felt like I'd been pushed onto the stage in the middle of a very bad play and didn't know any of my lines. I would have run for the hills if I knew which hill to run to. And if someone out there wasn't shooting at people.

"Please, Miss Ripley?" I was surprised that Mack remembered my name. All I could do was stammer.

"But I-I-I . . ."

"Killer could come back and shoot all three of us," Lillie said matter-of-factly. "You want that?"

I shook my head. I had to be dreaming. I had eaten a baked bean sandwich yesterday. I had indigestion. This was a nightmare, that's all. I looked around and tried to draw comfort from my surroundings. I was in a library, for heaven's sake, my familiar world of books and overdue notices and card catalogues. People didn't get shot in libraries. Who would want to kill a librarian? We were nice people. Harmless people. This was a dream. A very bad dream. But until I woke up, I would be wise to play along with these crazy people and do whatever they said.

"W-what do you want me to do?"

Lillie and Mack exchanged looks. "Go upstairs and fetch Mack's rifle," she said.

"I don't know how to shoot a gun!"

"Nobody's asking you to shoot it, girl, just go get it." I knew where the rifle was. I had stared at the gun rack hanging on the bedroom wall all night, hoping I wouldn't need to use it myself.

Lillie and I traded places again, and I went upstairs while she began wrapping up Mack like a mummy. My hands trembled so badly I could barely lift down the heavy rifle. I had never held one in my life. I carried it downstairs as if it might go off in my hands. If Lillie told me to point it at somebody, I would faint dead away.

"Here it is," I told her, "but I—"

"Listen to me, girl." She took it from me and laid it by Mack's side. "Cora and the others will be coming to work soon. We gonna tell them Mack went out hunting this morning and had a accident."

"You want me to *lie*?"

"No, I want you to keep your trap shut and don't say a word. Understand?"

I nodded vigorously. Lillie might be twig-thin, but she looked as though she knew how to use the rifle. In fact, I nodded so hard it's a wonder my head didn't come loose.

"In the meantime, we're keeping the gun handy in case the shooter comes back to finish the job."

I continued to nod, but she may as well have been talking gibberish.

I was still sitting in a daze beside Mack and Lillie when the other librarians arrived. They halted in shock at the sight of Mack lying in the foyer, a bloodied mess.

"What happened, Miss Lillie?"

"Hunting accident."

"Oh, Mack!"

"Is he going to be all right?"

"Don't know yet. He lost a lot a blood. He might of got home too late."

The women wept, prayed, held Mack's hands. Three of them went upstairs and hauled down the mattress from his bed—my bed—and gently lifted him onto it. The shock and pain from being moved made Mack moan, then pass out again.

"What can we do, Miss Lillie?" they all asked. "Give us something to do."

"Not much you can do. He's in the Lord's hands now. You all just go about your work like you always do. People waiting for their books, ain't they? Tell the believing ones to be praying for Mack. Then we just have to wait and see."

"Isn't there some way we can help?"

Lillie gestured to me. "New girl says she'll help out."

All four of them eyed me dubiously. Cora spoke for the group. "Are you sure you don't want us to stay with you, Miss Lillie?"

"President Roosevelt's paying you to work, ain't he?"

"Yes, ma'am."

"Then you best get working."

Everyone hugged Lillie, consoling her. I heard one of them say, "Poor Lillie. You've lived through so much already, and now this?"

By the time the librarians loaded the books on their horses and rode away, Lillie looked exhausted. I remembered that she had been sick. "Are you all right?" I asked her. "Do you want me to help you upstairs to bed?"

"No, I need to stay here beside Mack. You can get me a chair to set on, though." I dragged over an armchair from the non-fiction section, and Lillie sank onto it with a sigh. "He ain't outta the woods, you know. Next few days are the most important."

I nodded. I had no idea what to say. Lillie studied me as if she still wasn't quite sure who I was and what I was doing here. I wasn't entirely certain myself.

"You know how to cook?" she finally asked.

I started to say yes, then recalled how Mother had banished me from the kitchen after setting fire to it. "Not very well, I'm afraid."

"Well, I ain't strong enough to wait on all of us, so you better get on out there and do the best you can."

"Yes, ma'am." First I would have to wash all the blood off my hands. If the stains on my clothes didn't come out, I would have to throw them away. Mother would scold me for my wastefulness: *Don't you know this country is in an economic depression?* And how could I reply? *I'm sorry, but someone tried to kill the librarian, and he bled all over me.* No one would believe it.

I walked out to the tacked-on kitchen to clean up and make breakfast. I would have to figure out how to build a fire in the woodstove before I could cook anything. I gazed around at the empty woodbox, the cold stove, the flies, and the dishes festering in the sink, and I sank down at the kitchen table and sobbed.

CHAPTER 6

"I f Mack's gonna live, he's gonna need some medicine." Lillie gave me that piece of news as we ate our breakfast of cold corn bread and strawberry preserves. It was all I could find to eat in the disheveled kitchen, and besides, the stove wouldn't stay lit for more than two minutes. I didn't like the way Lillie said "we" every time she decided something needed to be done. Considering how frail she was, "we" probably meant me. But Mack looked as though he might die any minute, and I didn't want his death on my conscience.

Yesterday I would have asked Lillie where the nearest pharmacy was. Today I was wise enough to know that if Acorn, Kentucky, didn't have a hotel, a café, a police department, a doctor, or a hospital, the town probably didn't have a pharmacy, either. "Where would you like me to go for the medicine?" I asked, dreading her reply.

"We gonna need some willow bark and some elm bark and maybe some green peach tree leaves, if we can find them this time a year. If Mack's gonna pull through this, he'll be needing a poultice to draw out the poison and something to take down his fever." She seemed to be talking to herself more than to me so I kept quiet. "But the first thing we need to take care of is the pain. Quickest thing is to make do with some tansy. I believe there's some up in my workroom."

"Wait. What's tansy?"

Lillie tried to describe what it looked like, and after three trips up to the storeroom and back, I finally found the correct bunch of dried-up leaves among the many bunches hanging from the ceiling. "Now what?" I asked.

"Now you fix the tea, and we try and get Mack to swallow it."

I felt completely inept. I had to admit to Lillie that I didn't know how to make tansy tea. She explained the process, then dozed in her armchair while I struggled to start a fire in the cookstove and keep it going long enough to boil water. I would have asked her how to build a fire, too, but I didn't want to disturb her.

By the time the water boiled and the tea was ready, I smelled like a smoked ham. Lillie told me to lift Mack's head onto my lap and spoon the liquid into his mouth. He moaned in pain when I moved him. I prayed that I wouldn't kill him.

Mack eventually choked down most of the tea. It was past time for the library to open and I longed to do something normal, like sit at the desk and process books, but I seemed to have my hands full with two patients to care for. Lillie lay curled in the armchair like a withered crane on her nest, and Mack lay on the mattress in the middle of the foyer where patrons were certain to trip over him. While the two of them dozed, I returned to the mess in the kitchen. It was going to take hours to swat all the flies, haul firewood, then pump and boil enough water to clean the kitchen and wash the dishes. I rolled up my sleeves and went to work.

It turned out that preparing the tansy tea was only the beginning as far as Lillie was concerned. After lunch I helped her climb the stairs to her witch's workroom, and she soon had me grinding and brewing and concocting all sorts of strange things to make poultices. I wished in vain for a clean, sanitary hospital. Sometime during the afternoon, she stopped calling me "girl" and started calling me "honey." I figured we were now friends. Meanwhile, not a single patron had come into the library for a book.

Mack was still alive when the packhorse librarians returned in the afternoon, but he was too weak to talk and couldn't remain awake for more than a few minutes. Cora arrived first. She was the oldest of the ladies, around my mother's age, I guessed. She reminded me of my mother with her calm, no-nonsense manner and quick, competent hands. But I couldn't imagine my mother wearing trousers and riding all over these mountains on a horse the way Cora did. As soon as Lillie's back was turned, Cora grabbed my arm and pulled me into the fiction section, whispering like a schoolgirl with a secret.

"Listen. When I told my brother Clint about Mack's accident, he gave me this." She opened her jacket and pulled out a pint Mason jar filled with liquid.

"What is it?"

"Shh! Miss Lillie's dead set against strong drink, but moonshine is the best painkiller I know of, and Clint makes the best in the county. Don't tell Miss Lillie I gave it to you or she'll make you dump it out. Ask Mack if he wants some when Lillie ain't around, okay? Then add it to one of her potions when she ain't looking."

More secrets. I was now knee-deep in them.

Marjorie returned to the library next. "You need help with Miss Lillie's horse?" she asked me. "When I rode in I noticed that Belle wasn't out in the pasture."

"Horse? What horse?"

"Belle is Miss Lillie's mare. Mack usually lets her out of the shed during the day."

"I don't know anything about horses. I didn't even know Mack had a shed."

She looked at me with pity. "What'd they say your name was again?"

"Alice Grace. My friends call me Allie." And right now, I could use a friend. If only Freddy was here. She had always been the sensible, competent one, taking charge in every crisis. She had taken care of me ever since the day I fell and skinned my knees while roller-skating when we were seven years old. She used to help baby birds when they fell from their nests and rescue lost puppies from the middle of the street. She would know exactly what to do.

"Are you a city girl, Allie?" Marjorie asked. I nodded. Compared to Acorn, Blue Island qualified as a city. "Well, come on then. I'll show you what you need to do to keep the farm running."

Farm? I hated farms. How had I ended up running one? She

linked her arm through mine, and I already felt stronger. "Thanks, Marjorie. I appreciate your help."

"You're welcome. But I'm Faye. Marjorie is my sister."

"Oh, I'm so sorry!" Faye and Marjorie were the youngest of the four women and might have been twins. Like Tweedle-dee and Tweedle-dum, I thought, remembering Alice in Wonderland again. They both wore navy wool jackets and knitted stocking caps and tall leather boots that laced up the front. They were both very pretty in a simple, unadorned way, like fashionable dresses made from homespun instead of silk.

"That's okay," Faye said. "I can tell that Mack's accident has you addle-rattled. We're all pretty shook up, too, to tell you the truth. We've been so worried that Miss Lillie might pass away any day, so we never dreamed that anything could happen to Mack."

She pulled me into the kitchen—I was disappointed when she didn't comment on how clean it looked—then led me out through the back door. Sure enough, there was a shed down by the creek with a very annoyed-looking horse penned up inside it. Faye turned the animal loose and told me I should lock it up again at dusk. I was about to ask how I was supposed to catch the horse when she said, "You know you need to lock up the chickens at night too, right?"

"Chickens? Mack has chickens?"

She laughed and pointed to a coop and rudely fenced-in yard that I hadn't noticed, either. "If you don't lock them up, the foxes will have chicken for dinner and you won't. I think Mack usually lets them out when he collects the eggs every morning. Some of the hens don't like to give up their eggs without a fight, but just shove them off their nests and show them who's boss."

The hens would know very well who was boss.

"Are you going to be cooking for Mack and Miss Lillie until they're better?"

"I . . . um . . . I guess so. But there aren't very many groceries in the house." Or a refrigerator to keep them in.

"Did you look in the basement? Most folks store their home-canned tomatoes and vegetables down there."

"Oh. And where can I buy more bread? We're all out."

She smiled, and I could see that she was trying not to laugh. "We don't buy it, we bake it ourselves. You want me to show you the root cellar while we're out here?"

I nodded. I had read about root cellars in books but had never seen a real one. We had a Frigidaire back home. "Doesn't anyone have electricity?"

"Rich folks do. The post office has it, of course. I don't see much need for it, myself. Besides, you know what you get along with a bunch of ugly old electric wires dangling all over town?"

My first reaction was to say, *You get light! And modern conveniences like stoves that stay hot and refrigerators that stay cold.* But I shook my head and said, "No, what?"

"You get a bunch of bills that you can't pay 'cause the mine's shut down. If you asked most folks, they'd tell you they'd rather sit in the dark with food in their bellies than have their house all lit up and their stomach growling like a wildcat."

She walked to a lumpy hill near the shed and opened a pair of cellar doors that led inside it. We went down a short set of stairs into an underground hole—like a grave, I thought with a shiver. We ducked our heads, and as my eyes adjusted to the darkness I saw piles of potatoes, baskets of carrots and beets, a few squashes spotted with mold. And cobwebs everywhere. I clung to Faye's arm, frantic at the thought of being locked in here.

"See how cool it is down here?" she asked. "We don't need an icebox even in August."

"Does anyone in Acorn have a telephone?" I asked when we'd climbed out again. From the expression on Faye's face, I might have asked if anyone owned an ostrich.

"Why would we need a telephone and more foolish bills to pay? If we want to talk to somebody, we just walk over to their house. The coal mine offices have telephones. And I think a few people have them over in Pottsville."

"Is that a town? How far away is it?" Maybe I could walk there and get help for Mack—and a ride home for myself.

Faye looked puzzled, as if she didn't understand the question. "How far? Depends on your horse, I guess. Mine could make it there in about . . . oh . . . three or four hours. Sooner if I pushed her. But if you ride Miss Lillie's horse, it's going to take you a lot longer. She lags going uphill."

"How many miles is it?"

Faye answered with a shrug. "Nobody counts miles around here. A place can be a few miles away as the crow flies, but if there's a hill or a creek in the way, you have to wind your way all around to get there."

"Is there a doctor in Pottsville? Or a hospital? I'm really worried about Mack."

She huffed. "Miss Lillie knows plenty more than any doctor, let me tell you. If she can't fix him up, then nobody can."

I thought about the dried herbs and gooey poultices Lillie had cooked up, and I feared for Mack's life. But did I dare walk to the next town and fetch a doctor? And I *would* have to walk. I had never been on a horse in my life and that wasn't about to change. The mere thought of catching Lillie's horse later tonight and leading it back to the shed put me in a panic.

Faye gave my arm a comforting squeeze, then let go as we walked toward the house. "Anything else I can show you?"

I glanced at the wood piled neatly against the side of the house. "Well . . . I feel stupid for asking, but . . . can you show me how to keep a fire going in the stove? Lillie seems to need a lot of boiling water and the fire keeps going out after a minute or two."

Faye laughed again. "Sure. But if you don't mind me being nosy, do you have a pile of servants back home to do all this work for you?"

"No, but things are easier in the city. We have an electric refrigerator and a coal furnace and a stove that runs on gas. You just light a match to it and the oven stays hot until you turn it off again."

"I seen those things in magazines."

Faye showed me how to light and stoke the fire, adding coal from the bin to keep it burning longer. I grabbed a piece of paper and wrote down everything. "Okay?" she asked when she finished. "I got to get on home, Allie. My kids will be wanting their dinner."

"You have children?" She didn't look any older than I was.

"Yep, four little rascals. All boys."

"Four! How old are you?" I knew it was a nosy question but I couldn't help asking.

"Twenty-three. How old are you?"

"I'm twenty-two."

"And you ain't even married yet? Gosh, folks would call you an old maid around here. I married Lloyd when I was sixteen and we had Lloyd Junior ten months later. Then Bobby, Clyde, and little Roger, all in a row."

"It must be hard to leave them every day to go to work."

"Their mamaw watches them. She lives with us. I thank the Good Lord every day that Mack set up this library and got the WPA to hire us. Otherwise, I don't know how we would get by. Lloyd ain't had work since the mine shut down . . . Poor Mack. We need him around here. He and Miss Lillie hold this whole town together."

"Did Mack grow up here?"

"The Good Lord sent him back to us just in time, and I sure hope He don't take him away yet."

"Sent him from where?"

Faye didn't reply. I had noticed that people around here ignored any question they didn't want to answer.

"I got to go. See you tomorrow, Allie."

When a curtain of shadows settled over the valley, I knew it was time to put the horse back into the shed for the night. But Lillie's horse hated me, I could tell. Every time I got close to the animal, it rolled its eyes and snorted like a dragon as it sidled away from me. I admit that I was scared to death of it. It was so big! My head barely reached its back. We danced around the yard for a while as I tried to get behind it and shoo it inside, but I finally gave up and decided to try my luck with the chickens.

Feathers everywhere! I never knew that chickens would shed feathers like a snowstorm when they were upset. You would think from the way they squawked and flapped around their yard that I was trying to catch one of them for the stewpot, not put them to bed. Every time I got three of them inside the coop, one would fly out again. And the rooster was as mean as a buzzard, flapping his wings at me as if he wanted to peck out my eyes. I was about to give up. If the foxes wanted to eat these ornery birds, they were welcome to them. Then I heard a shout.

"Hey there!"

I turned around. Lillie stood in the kitchen doorway with her hands on her hips. How she had managed to walk that far by herself was a mystery, but I left the chickens to fend for themselves and ran up to the house, praying that Mack hadn't died.

"What's wrong? What happened?" I asked breathlessly.

"That's what I want to know. I hear my hens cackling and carrying on like there's a fox in the coop. Turns out it's you."

"I'm trying to get them inside for the night."

"You're gonna scramble them eggs before they're laid, that's what you're gonna do."

"I'm sorry, but I don't know anything about chickens."

"Leave them alone, for heaven's sake. They go inside on their own when it gets dark."

That was a relief. "What about the horse? I can't get him to go back inside, either."

"Belle's a mare, not a 'him.' Can't you see the difference?" I shook my head. My cheeks felt as warm as the fire Faye had helped me kindle. "Well, just pour a little feed in her bucket and give it a shake. Should be a bag of feed in the shed."

Could it be that easy? Sure enough, I filled the bucket and rattled it, and the stupid horse walked right into the shed all by itself.

CHAPTER 7

"W e done all we can for Mack," Lillie told me later that night. "You go on to bed now, honey. I'll keep the death watch tonight."

"Is he . . . do you think he's going to die?" I whispered the question even though Mack was asleep and probably couldn't hear me. It seemed like tempting fate to ask out loud. Considering all of the ridiculous things we had poured in him and on him today, I didn't see how he could possibly live. The man had a bullet hole that went straight in one side of him and out the other! I shuddered at the memory of all that blood gushing out.

Lillie patted my arm as if to comfort me. "Only the Good Lord knows if he's gonna live or die."

What worried me the most were the secret gulps of moonshine I had given Mack to drink. I had shown him Cora's Mason jar when Lillie wasn't around and asked if he wanted some.

"Depends . . . Who made it?" he'd breathed.

"Who made it? I don't remember . . . One of the packhorse ladies, the tall one with the broad shoulders, told me that her brother made it. What difference does it make?"

"Cora's brother, Clint?"

"I think so."

"Okay, give me some." The liquor had made Mack cough and

choke, and his face turned very red. Then he'd fallen into a deep sleep. He still hadn't awakened. Guilt plagued me for interfering with Lillie's crazy remedies.

"Run up and get me a blanket from off my bed," Lillie said, interrupting my thoughts. "And you better get me some extra bullets for this gun. Mack keeps them in his dresser drawer."

I didn't want to ask why she needed a loaded gun. I did as I was told, then went upstairs to sleep in Mack's room for the second night. Was it really only yesterday that my aunt and uncle had dropped me off? They planned to be at the spa for two weeks—fourteen long, excruciating days. If someone had tried to murder the town librarian on my first full day here, what might I expect tomorrow?

My shoulders ached from pumping water and hauling coal and firewood. This rustic life left me so exhausted that I expected to fall asleep as soon as I lay down on top of the box springs in Mack's bedroom—he was using the mattress downstairs. For the first time in my life I didn't feel like reading a book before bedtime. How could I concentrate on a made-up story after plunging into such an unbelievable real-life drama?

I tried to get comfortable without being poked by an errant bedspring and listened to the rush of the creek outside and the incessant croak of frogs. They were singing a round like a choir of hoarse old men, taking up the refrain where the first frog left off, echoing back and forth. Instead of counting sheep, I decided to compile a mental list of all the comforts and conveniences that I took for granted back home. If that didn't work, I would try to come up with a plan for what I would do with my life after I returned to Blue Island.

I had my eyes closed, imagining Mrs. Beasley's retirement and being named head librarian in her place when something whirred past my face. I opened my eyes and saw a dark shape fluttering around my room. Was it a bird? How had a bird gotten into the house? It flew past again, swooping and dipping erratically as if it had been sipping from Mack's jar of moonshine. Wait! It wasn't a drunken bird, it was a bat! I grabbed my pillow to shield my head and ran downstairs, whimpering as I tried very hard not to scream. Lillie sat bolt upright in her chair when I stumbled into the foyer, her eyes wide.

"Who's there?" She reached for Mack's gun.

"It's me, Lillie. Alice Ripley. Th-there's a bat flying around my room!"

She sighed and leaned back, closing her eyes. "Goodness' sakes, girl, I thought you were the angel of death, coming for Mack and me."

"Sorry . . . sorry . . . but there's a *bat* in my room!"

"They're creatures of the night, honey. They always come out after dark."

"Yes. Yes, I know they do."

"Well then . . . ?" She wrapped the blanket around herself and curled up in her armchair as if no further explanation was needed.

"Lillie, how am I supposed to sleep with a bat flying around the room all night?"

"Same way he sleeps during the day with you flying all around the room. Just tuck your head under your wing and close your eyes."

"But—"

"He won't hurt you none. Get some sleep, honey. We got a lot to do tomorrow."

I crept back upstairs with the pillow over my head. I lifted the covers and checked every inch of my bed thoroughly before climbing in. As I lay there trying in vain to sleep, I wasn't sure if it would be better to actually see the bat flying around again and know for certain where it was, or not to see it and wonder.

I didn't want to cry. Tears wouldn't accomplish anything and would only make my pillow soggy. I decided to recite the Lord's Prayer and any other Bible verses I could remember. I drifted off to sleep somewhere in the middle of the Twenty-third Psalm and the valley of the shadow of death.

The room was still dark when the rooster woke me up in the morning. He probably needed to be fed or let out of his coop or something, but I didn't want to move from beneath the warm covers. I had worked harder yesterday than I'd ever worked in my life, cooking all the meals, washing the blood out of our clothes, cleaning the kitchen, feeding the chickens, taking care of the dumb horse—not to mention cooking up crazy teas and potions for Lillie and tending the library for Mack. Books went in and out at a steady rate with four packhorse librarians making deliveries every day, but not a soul in Acorn, Kentucky, seemed capable of walking into the library and checking out a book for himself.

I could tell that Lillie was much weaker than she let on and probably needed my help as much as Mack did. She'd had an initial burst of strength right after Mack had been shot, but had barely moved from her chair since then. She didn't eat enough to keep a chicken alive. I hoped it wasn't my cooking. She had poured what little energy she did have into saving Mack's life. All day yesterday, she had told me which herbs and roots to gather or boil or grind, then she had fallen asleep in her chair while I tried to follow her instructions. What if I went downstairs this morning and found both of them dead in the middle of the library floor?

I lay in bed a while longer, considering my options and fighting the need to use the outhouse. I finally came to the unhappy conclusion that all three of us would die of hunger if I didn't get my sorry self out of bed and make breakfast. I put on my clothes—shaking them vigorously to make sure that the bat hadn't made a nest inside them—then crept downstairs.

I peeked into the library first. Both Mack and Lillie were alive and asleep. Good. I went outside through the back door to use the outhouse and remembered to let the horse out of the shed. The spring morning was misty and cold, the surrounding hills sleeping beneath a gray blanket of clouds. The creek sounded louder than it had yesterday as it rushed through the backyard and into the woods on the edge of the property. I wondered what the name of it was. By the time I had faced down the chickens and managed to gather a few eggs, my shoes and socks were soaked from walking through the wet grass. The eggs weren't nearly as clean as the ones Mother bought in the store.

Back in the kitchen, I consulted Faye's list of instructions on how to build a fire in the stove and I managed to keep it hot enough to scramble a frying pan full of eggs. By the time they were cooked, my two patients had awakened and we ate the eggs and the last of the bread for our breakfast. I dreaded the thought of having to bake more. The only thing I knew about bread was that it came from a bakery. Sliced.

Before long, the packhorse librarians trooped in. Marjorie handed me a loaf of bread wrapped in a dish towel. It was still warm. "This is for Mack and Miss Lillie. I heard theirs got all eaten up and that you didn't know how to make more." Her tone was filled with wonder, as if I had two perfectly good legs but didn't know how to walk on them. I accepted gratefully, not caring if I had been insulted.

The women commiserated with Lillie over Mack's condition, then decided to drag Mack and his mattress out of the foyer and into the non-fiction section—formerly the dining room—to get him out of the way. "Now he'll have a nice, quiet place to either die or get well," Cora whispered to me. They visited with Mack for a while, then filled their sacks and saddlebags with books and rode off, following the creek up into the misty hills.

"We got some hard work to do," Lillie informed me after they were gone. And for the rest of the morning she had me collecting pine knots out of the woodpile so we could extract the pitch, then boiling the sticky sap with water in the black iron cauldron. My blond hair frizzed and curled in the steamy kitchen until I looked like a character from a silent horror movie. The kitchen smelled like Christmas trees.

"Lord musta known Mack and me would need some help," Lillie told me when she came out to the kitchen to check my progress. "That's why He sent you to us."

I was skeptical. I had come to Kentucky to deliver books and help catalogue them, not to boil pitch and grind leaves like a sorcerer's apprentice. Besides, I didn't believe the Almighty moved people around like pieces on a chessboard. "If God could make people do whatever He wanted them to," I asked her, "why didn't He warn Mack not to go outside yesterday? Then he never would have gotten shot in the first place."

Lillie took the wooden spoon from my hand, shaking her head, and stirred the mixture herself, watching the liquid stream off the spoon. "The Good Lord works in mysterious ways, honey."

I had heard this platitude all my life, so I decided to change the subject. "Is it ready yet? Can we stop boiling it?"

"Not quite. It needs to get thicker and glassy-looking."

I shoved more coal into the fire and took back the spoon, continuing to stir. "What are we going to do with this goo when it's done?"

"We gonna mix it with some lard to make a poultice."

"And put it on an open wound?" The thought made me cringe.

While we were waiting for the mixture to finish cooking, Lillie told me to take out another pot and pour in a couple of canning jars of tomatoes and green beans from the basement, along with carrots, potatoes, and onions from the root cellar. "What are we making this time?" I asked as I pared the vegetables and collected the peelings in a pan for the chickens.

Lillie grinned at me as if I was the village idiot. "Lunch, honey. This here's gonna be our lunch."

The sticky concoction of pine pitch and lard was still warm when Lillie removed Mack's bandages and laid the first poultice on his chest wound. Mack cried out in agony. "Arghh! What are you doing, Lillie? Trying to kill me? That burns like hellfire!"

"Shh . . . shh . . . don't rile yourself, honey. Only make things worse."

"They can't possibly get any worse!"

I tried to back quietly out of the room as she got ready to put another wad of goop on his shoulder, but she motioned me forward. "Go ahead and give him some of that moonshine, honey." I stared at her. "Come on, I know you have it and I know you been sneaking him some. This old body of mine might be breaking down, but my nose still works good as new."

I sat down beside the mattress and held the cup to Mack's lips. He guzzled it greedily. It made him cough and sputter, but eventually his breathing slowed and he drifted to sleep. "Do you think Mack's going to live?" I asked Lillie again. If it wasn't for the slow rising and falling of his chest, I would have thought he was already dead.

"Hard to say. It's up to the Good Lord." I wished she would stop telling me that. She sank back in her chair with a sigh. Her brown skin looked pale, like coffee with a lot of cream in it. Her lined face sagged with exhaustion.

"What about you, Lillie? Are you feeling okay? Is there something we can cook up to give you more strength?"

"Honey, if I knew a secret to give a hundred-year-old woman more strength, I'd be the richest woman in Kentucky."

"You're one hundred years old?"

She smiled her gap-toothed grin. "I'll be a hundred and one this Fourth of July."

That meant she must have been born in 1835. Had she been a slave? She would have been a grown woman in 1865 when the War Between the States ended and the slaves were emancipated. I had read the novel *Uncle Tom's Cabin*, which told about the horrors of slavery. I wondered if Lillie had lived through some of those horrors. I wasn't supposed to ask nosy questions, but I wanted to know what her long life had been like.

"Were you born here in Kentucky, Lillie?"

"Nope, across the state line in Virginia."

"Were you ever a slave?"

"I've been many, many things in this sorry life of mine, and a slave is just one of them."

"It must have been a terrible life."

"Lord knows it was."

"Did you live on a plantation?"

She nodded slowly. "My mama and me were field hands. Don't know anything about my daddy. But there was an old granny on the plantation who delivered all the babies and knew all kinds of tonics and potions to help people. She decided one day that she's gonna pass her knowing on to me. That's how I learnt. Pretty soon we was in big demand all over the county. Anybody got a sick slave or a baby doesn't want to be born, they send for us. Massa make a lot of money off us."

"What happened when the war started? Were you near any of the battles?"

"Talk about battles—I seen more suffering than I ever hope to see again. Too much for one lifetime. They send me out after the fighting's over to help patch those poor boys up again. They didn't use nice little bullets either, like the one that went through Mack. No sir. They had great big balls of metal that tear up your arm or leg when they hit you. Umm, umm, them's bad times. But even worse than them broken bodies were the broken hearts."

"What do you mean?"

"Folks get set on having their own way, and they end up with their hearts broken when it don't happen. God's the one who's deciding what's going to be and what ain't. He knows what's best even if we're too stubborn to realize it sometimes. We're like little kids fighting over the wishbone, squabbling about who's gonna get his wish. Bible says that even though we make lots of plans, it's the Lord who's gonna have His way."

She closed her eyes, and I thought she might be falling asleep. But then she opened them again and said, "What's your story, honey?"

"My story? I don't have one."

"Mmm, mmm. No story? That's the saddest thing I ever heard."

Her reaction made me mad. "Of course I have a story—everyone does. Just not a very exciting one. I grew up in Illinois. I worked as a librarian . . ." I paused so I could maintain my composure. "I love books, so when I heard that your library needed some, I held a book drive in our town. Then I came down here to deliver them and help out."

She studied me as if my skin were transparent and she could see what was going on inside me, watching my heart beat and the blood whoosh through my veins. Her scrutiny made me uneasy.

"You ever been in love?" she asked. The abruptness of her question startled me.

"Me? I had a boyfriend, but we broke up. That's one of the reasons I came here. I needed to get away for a while."

"I ain't asking if you had a boyfriend. I ask if you ever been in love."

"It's the same thing."

"Oh no, it ain't." She laughed out loud, and it made me angry. I wanted to justify myself but something stopped me. I thought of all the love stories I'd read over the years, and the way the lovers in those books thought about each other day and night; the way they confided in each other, doted on each other. Was true love really the way authors portrayed it in books?

I was sitting on the floor beside the mattress, and when I didn't reply, Lillie gently laid her hand on my head, a mother soothing her child. "What'd you like about this boyfriend a yours?"

The first thing that came to mind was that Gordon was a good catch. He was even-tempered and reliable and had a good job. Until he'd broken up with me, he had been as logical and predictable as the Dewey decimal system. I opened my mouth to say those things, then quickly closed it again. Lovers in romance stories never mentioned the Dewey decimal system when describing their beloved.

"Ah ha! See, honey?"

"See what? I haven't answered your question yet."

"No, but your face says it all. When a person's in love, all you gotta do is mention her lover and her face starts glowing like a harvest moon."

I shrugged, wanting to avoid the subject, but Lillie wouldn't let me. "This boyfriend got a name?"

"Gordon. Gordon Walters."

"See? Most people smile when they speak the name of the man they love. And you ain't smiling."

"Well, I'm very angry with him. I told you, he broke up with me. He isn't my boyfriend anymore."

"You want him back?"

I thought for a minute, then shrugged again. "I don't know. I don't think so."

"Now, why ain't you heartbroken, honey-girl? You ain't shedding a single tear when I'm asking about him."

"I don't cry very easily, that's all."

"No? And why's that?"

Again I opened my mouth to reply but nothing came out. I could cry buckets of tears when reading books with sad endings—and sometimes I cried over happy endings, too. Why didn't I feel those emotions in real life? I gaped at Lillie, speechless, as she nodded her head. "Um hmm, um hmm. See now?"

"No. I don't see anything." Why was she asking me all these questions? What business was it of hers? I thought people in Appalachia didn't ask nosy questions. I decided to turn the tables on her.

"Have you ever been in love, Lillie?"

Whether it was an act or not, I didn't know, but her face did seem to glow as she broke into a wide gap-toothed smile. Even as she smiled, tears pooled in the creases around her eyes. "Oh my, yes, honey-girl. I sure was in love once. I reckon we only get one great love in a lifetime, and Sam was mine."

"How did you meet him?"

"That story's gonna take a long time to tell."

"I don't mind. We have plenty of time." I loved stories. I could get lost in a good story and easily forget everything else. And right now I had a lot I wanted to forget. "Please tell me, Lillie."

"Maybe another day, honey. I'm real tired right now. I think I need a little rest."

Lillie closed her eyes and fell asleep as quick as a cat. I pulled the blanket around her shoulders and tiptoed over to the library desk to card books. I couldn't stop thinking about Gordon and me, until at last I came to the conclusion that if true love really was the way people described it in books, then no, I never had been in love with Gordon or he with me. But why hadn't I ever realized it before?

I was shelving books after lunch when I heard voices outside and footsteps clattering up the porch steps. Were patrons finally paying a visit to the library? I hurried to the door and swung it open to find a middle-aged woman and four little boys. "We come to hear the story," the oldest boy said. The three younger ones ducked under my arm and squeezed through the door before I could stop them. Their faces were white, but their bare feet were as brown as Lillie's.

"Wait! Mr. MacDougal is sleeping and—"

"Mamaw wouldn't let us come yesterday 'cause we didn't behave," the oldest boy told me somberly. He pointed to the woman who I assumed was Mamaw. She was barefooted, too. "But she said we could come today."

"Never did see kids get into as much trouble as these young ones," Mamaw said, shaking her head. "But like Little Lloyd says, they been minding themselves all morning so I brung them here for the story." She moved past me to follow the boys inside. I closed the door and hurried after them, afraid they would disturb Mack and Lillie. I found the group gathered around the mattress, gazing down at Mack in his bloody overalls as if looking at an exotic animal in the Lincoln Park Zoo.

"All that blood come from him?" one of them asked. His brother nudged him.

"'Course it did, stupid. He got shot with a gun, remember? Ma said so."

"Is he going to die, Miss Lillie?"

"He might," she said matter-of-factly. "Too soon to tell."

"Who's going to read the story to us if he dies? Mamaw can't read."

I glanced at Mamaw and she lifted her palms, sadly shaking her head. I heard a moan as Mack shifted positions and opened one eye. He closed it again and said, "Hey, boys. Missed you yesterday. You fellas been acting up again?"

"It was Bobby's fault. He's the one who caught the cat."

"Yeah, but Clyde dared me."

"Did not! Lloyd did!"

I recognized the names—these must be Faye's boys. They were raggedy little urchins scarcely old enough for school, but they looked as wise and battle worn as old men. The youngest one, about three years old, already mimicked the swagger and toughness of his older brothers.

"We don't need to know the gory details," Lillie told them. "Just as well you didn't come yesterday. Mack here has been under the weather."

"He shot himself, didn't he?"

"Let that be a lesson to you," Lillie said, shaking her withered finger. "Don't you go fooling with your daddy's rifle again—you hear me, Clyde?"

"What about the story?"

"And the pirates?"

"Maybe Miss Ripley will read to you today."

"That yellow-haired lady?" Little Lloyd pointed to me. "Can she read?"

"Yes, of course I can—" Before I could say more, they plopped down in a tidy row on the floor in front of me, oldest to youngest, and gazed up at me expectantly.

"*Treasure Island*," Mack murmured. "The book's in my top desk drawer." He smiled at me, and for the first time since I'd met him, I felt like smiling back. Mamaw pulled up two chairs from the library table, one for each of us, while I fetched the book.

My audience sat completely spellbound as I read, the way kids back home would sit in front of the radio for hours listening to *Buck Rogers* or *The Lone Ranger*. When I finished the chapter, Mamaw poked my arm with her elbow and smiled. She didn't have any teeth. "Then what happened?" she asked.

I read the next chapter, and I had never felt happier being a librarian than I did in that moment. We were all engrossed in the story when we heard a sound outside. It took me a moment to recognize it as a car engine. Bobby jumped up and peered out the front window. "Holy cow, it's the sheriff!" Before I could move, all four boys scrambled to their feet and scurried out of the library like rabbits disappearing into the underbrush. Mamaw followed them.

I looked over at Lillie who was now wide awake. "Don't you say a word, honey." We heard boots tromping up the steps, the door squealing open, footsteps in the hallway. A mountain-sized man in a tan uniform halted in the doorway to the non-fiction section, looking all around. He removed his hat to reveal graying black hair and a receding hairline. Lillie acted as wary as a cat with a big dog sniffing around. I could see their mutual distrust and wondered what was behind it. I was quite sure he hadn't come in to check out a book.

"Afternoon, Miss Lillie." He nodded slightly.

"Afternoon, Sheriff. This here's Alice from up in Illinois. She come to help out in the library."

"So I heard."

How in the world had he heard?

"Also heard you had a little hunting accident down here. Came to see how Mack was doing."

I longed to jump up and plead with the sheriff to drive Mack to a hospital where he could get proper medical attention instead of enduring sticky homemade poultices and tansy tea with moonshine, but something about the man made me as uneasy as Lillie.

"Tell you the truth, I'm thinking he may not pull through," Lillie said softly.

That was news to me—and probably to Mack who had been awake a moment ago and now was faking unconsciousness.

"I'll know more in a couple of days," she said.

"I need to talk to him when he wakes up," the sheriff said. Lillie didn't reply. "Anything I can do for him?"

"You saying your prayers, Sheriff? Prayer never hurts and always helps."

He smiled without giving a reply, a smile that went no deeper than the skin on his face. "You ladies need anything?"

This might be my only chance to get to a telephone or a train station and back to civilization, but I hesitated. I had an instinctive dislike for this man, something deep in my gut that I couldn't explain. And I knew from reading mystery stories that the heroine always ended up in worse trouble when she didn't follow her gut instincts. Even so, I might have asked the sheriff for help and fled Acorn for good if it hadn't been for Mamaw and those boys. But during the past hour when I had been carried away to Treasure Island, something had changed inside me. In spite of the hard work and the uncooperative farm animals, in spite of my misgivings as a sorcerer's apprentice—or maybe her accomplice—in spite of everything about this crazy, bat-infested library, I decided in that moment to keep quiet. I would stay here and work. And help.

"Can't think of anything we need, Sheriff," Lillie said with a shrug. She shook her head—and so did I.

"Well, I'll be on my way then. Afternoon, ladies." He tipped his hat to us as he placed it back on his head. His heavy boots made the floorboards groan as he left the house.

Lillie gripped my arm the moment the door closed, clutching it hard enough to hurt. "That man's a snake," she whispered to me. "A snake!"

Her words rattled me. Maybe my gut instinct had been right. But the sheriff was the good guy in most stories, rescuing people from the bad guys. Why was everything in this town turned upside down?

CHAPTER 8

Three days later, when Lillie was sure that Mack would live, she started planning his funeral. She announced this news at breakfast, and I couldn't believe my ears. "You mean you're going to *lie* to everyone and say that he *died*?"

"It's for the best, honey." The three of us were eating together in the non-fiction section. It was the first time that Mack had been able to sit up and feed himself since the morning he'd been shot. He wore his arm in a sling made from an old tablecloth, and he had to lean against the bookshelf to stay upright, but evidently his condition had improved so much that Lillie had decided he was ready to die and be buried.

I put down my plate and stared at Mack, waiting for an explanation. He was eating tiny bites of his pancake as if it really was going to be his last meal. "You make these pancakes all by yourself, Miss Ripley?" he asked.

"Yes. I decided to cook something different for a change. Why?"

"They're . . . interesting. I don't believe I've ever had pancakes that were deep-fried before."

I may have used a little too much oil. But that didn't change the fact that these people owed me an explanation. I knew quite a lot about funerals after dating Gordon Walters for nearly a year, and I didn't see how in the world you could fake someone's death.

"Funerals are long, drawn-out affairs," I told him, "with a wake and a memorial service and a burial. How are you going to lay here and play dead for two or three days?"

Lillie waved her twig-like hand as if shooing away my concerns like flies. "We don't have fancy funeral parlors around here, so the corpse starts stinking to high heaven pretty fast, especially in warm weather. We try and get folks in the ground as quick as we can, before that happens."

"But you can't bury him! He isn't dead!" Although I had to admit that he could easily play the part of a corpse. Compared to the bear of a man who had answered the door five days ago, he looked pale and sickly. And no wonder, after bleeding the way he had and then lying around on his mattress enduring Lillie's remedies and Cora's homemade moonshine.

"Well, we can thank the Good Lord that he ain't dead," Lillie said. "Jesus answered all our prayers. Now, first thing we gotta do is get Lloyd Hayes to build us a casket. I'll talk to Faye about it when she comes in this morning."

I had lived with Lillie long enough to know it was useless to try to reason with her. I turned to plead with Mack. "Is this what you really want her to do?"

He nodded somberly. "Otherwise, the shooter might come back and finish me off."

"But it's deceitful! We would have to tell a hundred lies and—"

Lillie laid her hand on my arm to soothe me. "No one's asking you to lie, honey. Just keep your sweet little mouth shut."

I stared at her, then at Mack. He looked up at me with eyes as dark and soulful as a cocker spaniel's. "Please, Miss Ripley?"

I exhaled in frustration. "What will you do if I say no?"

Lillie tightened her grip on my arm. "Don't say no, honey." It sounded like a threat. She looked at me for a long moment, smiling her gap-toothed smile, then finally let go. "Second thing we gotta do is mix up a potion to put Mack into a deep sleep. I know just how to do it, too. He'll be so far gone, folks can poke pins in his toes and he'll never feel it."

I shivered at the thought. "Haven't you people ever read *Romeo and Juliet*? Don't you know what can happen when people try to pretend they're dead?"

Mack gave me an irritating grin. "I read it. But I'm not Romeo and there's no Juliet to die along with me—unless you're volunteering for the part."

I crossed my arms and huffed. "I don't want any part of this. How far is it to the nearest railroad station?" I made up my mind to pack my suitcase and walk to the next town if I had to, then take the first passenger train back to Chicago.

"How far?" Mack repeated. "Well, I guess that depends on which horse you're planning to ride. Belle doesn't like to go very fast so it would take her a couple of hours—"

"You people infuriate me! I asked how many *miles* it was, not how many *hours* it takes. Doesn't anyone around here know about *miles?*"

"Sure, but it depends on which creek bed you plan to follow and whether or not it's flood season. It floods a lot this time of year, and sometimes the bridges wash away and—"

I didn't wait to hear the rest. I gathered up our dishes and carried them out to the kitchen. I would have slammed the kitchen door behind me for dramatic effect, but my hands were full. I could hear their mumbled voices in the other room as they conspired together, planning Mack's demise. I stayed out of it.

Later, I was seated behind the library desk, attacking the piles of returned books, when Faye arrived for work. She peeked into the dining room to check on Mack, who was doing a stellar performance of a man hovering at death's door. Lillie shooed her away.

"He took a turn for the worse last night," Lillie said in a stage whisper. "Now he's running a real high fever." She hobbled into the foyer and made a big show of closing the dining room door as she pulled Faye aside to ask, "Can you get Lloyd to build us a casket, honey? Tell him he can take wood from my shed, if he needs to."

Faye's hands flew to her mouth. "A casket? Oh, Miss Lillie! Don't tell me—"

"I'm afraid so, honey. I done all I can for Mack, but I don't think he's gonna make it."

"No! He can't die!"

"Only a matter of days now," Lillie said, shaking her head. "Maybe hours. I see the life draining outta him bit by bit, and ain't nothing I can do to stop it."

Faye covered her face and wept. I pictured Mack in the next room faking unconsciousness, and I wanted to kick his carcass off the mattress and onto the floor. Lillie mustered a few tears of her own. "Truth is, honey, I may not be too far behind him."

"Lillie, no! I can't bear to lose either one of you!" Faye threw her arms around Lillie, nearly knocking her over, sobbing as she rocked Lillie in her arms. I couldn't bear to watch this scene play out three more times when the other librarians arrived, so I grabbed my sweater and left the house to go for a walk.

I had been slowly exploring the town whenever I needed to get away, first walking up the road to the post office to mail a long letter to my friend Freddy. I had described all of the events that had happened to me so far, and I could imagine Freddy's reaction as she read about them. My story was so unbelievable that she would wonder if I was writing a novel of my own. Or maybe she'd think I really had lost my mind and had gone to the spa with my aunt to take a water cure. Hadn't Gordon accused me of living in a dream world? I would have to write to Freddy again and assure her that this town and my trials were all very real.

The tiny post office also seemed to serve as the gathering place for Acorn's elderly men. I heard the mumble of voices as I walked up the steps, but the conversation halted abruptly as I opened the door. Half a dozen pairs of eyes glared at me from wrinkled faces as if I had interrupted a conspiracy instead of a poker game. Four of the men seated around a rickety card table clutched their fan of playing cards to their chests, as if worried that I would see how many aces they had.

"Excuse me, but I would like to buy a stamp please. I need to mail a letter." Silence. "You do sell stamps here . . . ?"

One of the men at the card table—the oldest one from the look of him—laid his playing cards facedown and slowly pulled himself to his feet. He grabbed his cane, hobbled over to a chest of drawers that served as the countertop, and pulled out a tattered envelope. His hands trembled as he removed a single stamp and handed it to me. I paid him, licked the stamp, and stuck it on the envelope, then looked around in vain for anything resembling a mail slot.

"Um . . . where's your mailbox?" He took the letter from my

hand and dropped it into the same drawer where the stamps had been. He nodded slightly as he closed the drawer.

"Oh . . . well . . . thank you. Good day to you." I had no confidence at all that my letter would ever reach its destination.

The houses in Acorn were pitiful and bedraggled, the library a mansion in comparison—and it was run-down and in need of a good coat of paint. I wondered which houses belonged to Faye and the other packhorse ladies. Laundry sagged on clotheslines, goats and chickens scratched around barren yards, skinny hound dogs howled at me as I walked past. There seemed to be a lot of trash and pieces of rusty metal piled everywhere. I saw a gaunt old man tending a weedy garden patch, attacking clods of earth with a hoe as he prepared for spring planting. I waved, but he returned my greeting with a stare. These people were poor. Dirt poor. There were no other words for it. The town had a defeated look as if it had been beaten and left for dead on the side of the road.

The second time I ventured out I followed the creek behind the library upstream as it wound past boulders and fences and disappeared into the woods. I meant to ask Lillie if the stream had a name, but I kept forgetting. The bank was soggy with spring rain and the mud tugged at my shoes, trying to suck them off my feet. When I grew winded from the steep climb and spooked by all of the vague rustlings in the forest, I turned around and followed the creek back home.

This morning I decided to walk in the opposite direction from the post office, following the road that my uncle had taken as he'd sped away. I reached the place where he had turned around that first day, but I continued walking, passing a cemetery on my left, perched on the side of a very steep hill. It was the first cemetery I'd ever seen that wasn't on a flat patch of land. Tombstones climbed all the way up the slope like spectators on bleachers, jockeying for the best view. The corpses must be standing upright in their caskets. I looked away, remembering Mack and Lillie and their dastardly funeral plans.

Eventually I came to a side road and a sign that said *Jupiter Coal Company—Acorn Mine*. I decided to walk down the road toward the mine, and I soon reached a clearing on a narrow strip of level ground. The mining camp looked deserted. One end of the camp had been the business end, with railroad tracks, a tall clapboard structure on stilts, and a lot of mysterious scaffolding. A small sign on the side of a squat one-story building said *Mine Office*. A tangle of wires connected it to the outside world—my world—but whether the wires were for telephones or electricity, I didn't know. I didn't see anything that looked like a mine entrance and wondered if it was underground somewhere or dug into the side of the mountain.

I turned and walked the opposite way toward a row of shacks where the miners must have lived. Each tiny building had two doors and presumably housed two families, even though the huts were scarcely bigger than the shed where Lillie kept her horse. Several of the windows had been smashed, and shards of glass glittered in the sunlight beneath the empty window frames. The drab, barren houses reminded me of photographs I had seen of slaves' quarters before the emancipation. I halted when I reached a barrier across the road with a *No Trespassing* sign tacked onto it.

Sadness hung over this camp like fog. A closed mine meant men without jobs, families going hungry. But it struck me that this may have been a place of misery even when the mine had been operating. I imagined men in miners' caps plunging into a dangerous, claustrophobic shaft six days a week and emerging, black-faced, twelve hours later. I imagined anxious families scratching out a living in these colorless shacks, worrying about explosions or cave-ins. Sons would have little choice but to follow their fathers into the mines, never getting any further ahead, generation after generation. I finally turned around and walked back to the library, carrying the sadness with me like a hobo with his belongings slung over his shoulder.

The library was quiet again. The packhorse ladies had all ridden off and the crying over Mack's approaching death had finally ended. I peeked into the dining room and saw him sitting up again, reading a book. Lillie had curled up in her chair and fallen asleep, exhausted by her performance, no doubt. Mack beckoned to me when he saw me. "Can I talk to you?"

I shrugged, then folded my arms across my chest as I leaned against the doorframe.

"Listen, it should be pretty clear that someone wants me dead. If you don't help us . . . Well, do you really want my blood on your hands?"

"*My* hands? It's not my fault that somebody's trying to kill you. For all I know, you deserve it."

"Maybe I do . . . But Lillie can't handle this alone. She needs your help."

"How can you play such a mean trick on those women? You must have heard how grief-stricken Faye was. What a cruel lie to tell!"

Lillie shifted in her chair and stretched as my raised voice awakened her. "Those gals might be sad now," she said with a yawn, "but just think how happy they'll all be when we resurrect Mack from the dead. It'll be just like Easter morning around here."

"This is unbelievable!" I recalled Gordon's angry words to me on the day of Elmer Watson's memorial service—how funerals were a once-in-a-lifetime event and that poor Mr. Watson would never be buried again. Gordon's family should open a funeral parlor in Acorn, Kentucky. They could make twice as much money.

"Won't you at least think about helping us?" Mack pleaded.

I walked away without giving a reply. If I had read about this plot in a novel, I would have slammed the book shut and declared it highly improbable. It strained credibility to think that two intelligent, God-fearing people would try to fake a man's death and deceive an entire community. But then everything that had happened here during the past week had seemed preposterous. I might be powerless to stop these events, but I didn't have to participate in them. I vowed to simply stand by and watch them unfold in angry silence.

The only bright spot in my day was when Faye's boys came in with Mamaw for the next installment of their story. By then my temper had cooled and I could greet the little ones with a smile. "Are you here for the next chapter?" I asked. They returned my good cheer with somber faces.

"Mack's gonna die, ain't he?" little Clyde asked.

"Well . . . that's what Miss Lillie is saying." I spoke through clenched teeth.

"Our pa's building him a casket."

"Hmm. I see."

"When Mack's dead and buried, will you finish the story for us?"

"Yeah, will you?"

"We've been real good," Little Lloyd said. His brother elbowed him and he amended it to, "Well, we ain't been *too* bad."

"I'll be happy to read to you," I said. I would gladly lose myself in *Treasure Island,* the saga of treachery and betrayal and buried treasure.

"Time to cook up that potion, now," Lillie told me after the boys went home.

"You mean the one that's going to put Mack to sleep?"

"Um hmm. If you'd kindly help me get upstairs to my workroom, I'll mix it up and we can get it cooking on the stove. Now, I know you ain't real happy about helping us, honey. Tell you the truth, I'd rather you didn't see what all goes in it. You understand, right?"

"Believe me, I have no intention of stealing your magic formula."

Mack "died" that afternoon. It was too wet and rainy to bury him that night so they scheduled his funeral for the next morning. Once word of Mack's death spread, everyone in town pitched in to help. Faye's husband delivered the casket—a roughhewn box that looked as though it had been made out of old packing crates. Cora tacked a tattered blanket inside for a lining. Several men volunteered to dig a grave for him in the cemetery on the edge of town.

Lillie's knockout potion was so powerful that I feared she really had killed him. Mack fell into such a deep sleep that he never even twitched a muscle as the packhorse ladies lifted him into his coffin. They bawled their eyes out as Alma lowered the lid into place. She wiped her eyes on her sleeve, then picked up a hammer and a handful of ten-penny nails.

"Don't nail him in yet," Lillie said. "I need to say good-bye first. In private." Somehow she produced a few genuine tears, and the ladies quietly slipped away into the night.

"Now what?" I asked, hands on hips. "You aren't going to let them bury Mack alive, are you?"

"'Course not. We need to go out to the shed and gather up a half-dozen empty feed sacks. Then we're gonna fill them up with dirt and rocks so we can put them in the coffin instead of Mack."

She kept saying *we*, but I knew whom she meant. Lillie didn't have the strength to carry the shovel, much less dig with it—and Mack looked as dead as he was supposed to be. From what I could see, the only person who could shovel dirt and lift rocks was me. I put on Mack's old woolen jacket and went to work down by the creek, digging and loading in the dark of night, carrying each heavy sack up to the house and piling it by the casket.

"Nope, still not heavy enough," Lillie would inform me each time. And back I would go, out into the drenching rain, for another load.

"This is the last thing I'm going to do for these people," I muttered as I worked. "No more potions. No more lies. No more insane schemes in the dead of night. I'm finished! Done! I'll take care of the library books and read stories to the kids, but that's it until my two weeks are up!"

Mack was still dead to the world when Lillie finally decided I had shoveled and hauled enough ballast. My arms and legs trembled with fatigue from the unaccustomed labor. I longed for a hot bath to wash off the filth but had to make do with a kettle of hot water and a sponge bath in the kitchen sink. Since neither Lillie nor I could move Mack, he slept in that awful casket all night, just like a real dead man. It served him right.

Mack was as groggy as Rip Van Winkle the next morning. He could hardly get his legs underneath him to climb out of the box. "Wow! Have I got a headache! Did somebody drop a rock on my head while I was asleep?" he asked as I helped him to his feet.

"I wish I had thought of it," I mumbled. "Do you know how many pounds of dirt and rocks I shoveled for you last night? In the rain?"

He smiled sheepishly. "About a hundred and seventy-five? Maybe one-eighty?" When I didn't smile back, Mack fixed me with his soulful eyes. "I'm indebted to you, Miss Ripley."

"You bet you are! I'm still exhausted." He leaned on me as I helped him stagger up the stairs so he could hide in Lillie's workroom during his funeral. Then I hefted the rocks and bulging feed sacks into the casket and nailed it shut, venting my fury with each whack of the hammer. It took forever. I had never wielded a hammer before and I kept missing the nails.

Faye's husband, Lloyd, and five other men volunteered as

pallbearers to carry the coffin to the cemetery on the hillside. At least the rain had stopped. Barefooted children had combed the woods and fields to gather wildflowers while women in feed-sack dresses and knitted shawls had prepared the funeral luncheon. Lillie changed into a long black dress that might have fit her fifty years and a hundred pounds ago but now it billowed around her frail body like a feed sack on a broom handle. She stuck a black hat with a mourning veil on top of her wispy white hair and leaned on my arm as we followed the casket outside. Someone—probably the packhorse ladies—had draped the library porch in black crepe. The entire town, some eighty or ninety people, from babes in arms to gray-haired old-timers, gathered in front of the library for the funeral procession to the cemetery.

"Who's going to conduct the service?" I asked Lillie as I helped her descend the porch steps. "I don't suppose this town has a preacher?"

"I'm gonna do it."

"You're a preacher, too?"

She answered with a grin. I couldn't imagine my father or any other minister telling as many lies as she had or orchestrating this terrible charade.

An elderly man, whom I recognized as the village postmaster, hobbled up to us. "Too far for you to walk, Miss Lillie, so we fetched you a ride." The crowd parted to reveal a two-wheeled cart, pulled by a goat! The animal wore a black bandana around his neck—presumably to convey his grief—and someone had wound black mourning crepe around the spokes of the cart's wheels.

"You're kidding!" I blurted. It was such a ludicrous sight that I had to put my hand over my mouth to keep from laughing. I tried to imagine Gordon and his father escorting grieving mourners to the Blue Island Cemetery in goat carts.

The postmaster helped Lillie climb aboard, then she turned to me, patting the seat beside her. "You wanna ride with me, honey?"

"No, thanks. I'll walk." I might be exhausted from shoveling dirt for half the night, but I still clung to my dignity. A goat cart, indeed! The postmaster scowled at me, clearly insulted. The goat added a rude *bleah* to my refusal. The man turned away and proudly herded his goat up the road, leading the funeral procession.

91

They buried Mack near the bottom of the cemetery out of respect for Lillie. She couldn't climb the steep hill, and I don't think the goat could have made it up the slope either, even though Miss Lillie didn't weigh much more than a bag of feathers. The mourners began to sing "Safe in the Arms of Jesus" as everyone gathered around the gravesite, but there was such an odd assortment of musical instruments—guitar, banjo, harmonica, and fiddle—that it sounded more like a square dance than a funeral. Children tossed spring flowers onto the lowered coffin. The packhorse ladies cried and wailed. Mamaw and the boys were sniffling, too, leaving tear tracks down their dirty faces. This was cruel. Just plain cruel.

The sheriff's car pulled up as we were partway through the second hymn, "He Hideth My Soul in the Cleft of the Rock." I wondered if he was going to pry open the casket and view Mack's corpse for himself. Was it against the law to help fake someone's death? Could I be arrested as an accomplice? My heart began to gallop with guilt when the sheriff climbed out of his car, but he simply removed his hat in respect and stood watching from the edge of the road, away from the knot of mourners.

Lillie pulled a black-edged handkerchief from her sleeve and wiped her tears as she prepared to deliver her sermon. "Our friend Mack was a good man, and we're sure gonna miss him. He brought books and stories to this town and set up the library for us. I know we'll always remember and be grateful for what he done. There's so many things in this life we just don't understand—why we have hard times and trials, why we gotta lose people we love. But God has a plan. Yessir, He always has a plan. It's up to us to decide every day if we're gonna be part of it or not. Are we gonna do His will and build His kingdom? Or are we too busy making our own plans?"

I looked down at my shoes as she talked, scuffing the dirt with my toe. I wasn't following any plan at all, God's or my own. What was wrong with me? Maybe I should start making a list like my father always did. But what would I put on it? Did God write lists for us? Would He give me a peek at mine if I asked Him?

I didn't pay much attention to the rest of Lillie's sermon as I thought about the sorry state of my life. She finished with a prayer and everyone sang "Pass Me Not, O Gentle Savior," which seemed more appropriate for a revival than a funeral. Then everyone drifted back to the library. A couple of the men carried the mattress back upstairs to make room as the entire town crowded inside the house. I saw people roaming through the library, pulling books off of the shelves and gazing at them in wonder as if Mack had written each and every word himself. I would have to straighten the shelves after everyone left.

The musicians gathered on the front porch to play a medley of lively gospel songs as if we were at a barn dance. I saw some of the men from the post office passing around jars of what looked like moonshine. The women loaded down the library table with food, simple dishes like beans and corn bread, homemade pickles and dev-iled eggs. I knew it was a sacrificial offering since these people didn't have much to eat themselves, and it made me angry all over again.

I waited until all of the guests were fed before filling a plate for myself. After looking around for a vacant place to sit down, I ended up sitting behind the library desk. I had just taken a bite of hard-boiled egg when the fiddle player sauntered over with his instrument in one hand and a plate of food in the other. He was about my age and had the unusual combination of dark brown eyes and straw-colored hair, a good-looking man in shabby clothes and worn-out shoes. They were probably his Sunday best.

"Hey there. Mind if I sit here?" he asked. I did mind, but with-out waiting for my reply, he laid his fiddle and bow in front of me and sat down on a corner of my desk. "I'm Ike Arnett," he said, extending his hand. "You must be our visitor from up north."

I quickly finished chewing and swallowed as I shook his hand. "Yes, I'm Alice Ripley from Illinois."

"I knew you was the flatlander everyone's talking about 'cause you're so pretty. Girls from up north are a whole lot prettier than the ones down here. And you're just about the prettiest gal I ever did see."

The last thing I needed was the flirtatious attention of a hill-billy fiddle player. I looked down at my plate, not at him, pushing beans around with my fork. Then I realized that I was being rude. I looked up again and said, "Thank you." With a decent haircut and fashionable clothes, Ike Arnett could be handsome. His cocky grin told me that he already knew it, so I didn't return his compliment.

"The music you've been playing out on the porch is very interesting," I told him. "I've never heard hymns played quite like that before—especially at a funeral."

"Ever been to Kentucky before?"

"No, this is my first time."

"Well, that explains it." He smiled and there wasn't a girl in the world who could have resisted smiling back.

I continued to eat and he continued to stare at me until the silence became uncomfortable. "Um . . . does your little band play together very often?"

"We're not really a band. Just some folks from town who got together to pay our respects to Mack."

"Oh. Well, you sounded very good."

"Thanks. I have a lot of time to practice now that the mine is closed and most of the dance halls have shut down. But I been getting by, doing a little of this and that. And every so often I get work playing my fiddle." He raked his fingers through his hair, but it flopped back onto his forehead just like before, hanging into one of his eyes. "When times were good, I played in a band every weekend. We traveled all over the place, even up to Ohio and West Virginia. I had a girl in every town."

"I assume you aren't married, then?"

"Why settle down when you can have a good time?" He winked at me. I couldn't believe it! Oh yes, Ike Arnett knew he was good-looking.

"Life on the road's no good for a family man," he continued. "I guess I could settle down now that I ain't traveling as much, but I haven't found the right girl." He waited for me to look up at him, then added, "Yet."

I remained deadpan, refusing to swallow the bait. "Where did you learn how to play the fiddle like that?"

He shrugged. "Fiddling's been passed down in our family for years and years. I been sitting on our porch, listening to my grand-daddy and uncles play for as long as I can remember. So one day I took the fiddle off the mantel when my chores was done and started fiddling around with it myself. I took a real shine to it."

"That's very interesting." And it was. How could anyone play as skillfully and artistically as Ike did without ever studying music or taking lessons from a teacher?

He changed the subject and began to talk about Mack while he ate, chattering on and on about what a great friend Mack had been and how much he would miss him. I confess that I tuned out Ike's words as if changing radio stations. His affection for Mack seemed genuine, which made me feel even guiltier for playing a part in this huge deception. I was beginning to wonder how I would ever get Ike Arnett off my desk again when the banjo player sauntered over.

"Quit your flirting, Ike. We got work to do."

Ike shoveled the last few bites of food into his mouth and stood. He picked up his violin and winked at me again. "See you around, Alice."

The day's events took all the starch out of Lillie, and late in the afternoon, Faye and Marjorie helped her up to bed. When the last mourner left and the packhorse ladies had finished helping me clean up, I went upstairs to see if she was all right. She had a lamp burning, and I took a good look at her room for the first time. It was very neat and tidy, considering that she had been sick in bed before I arrived. Frilly white curtains hung on the windows and a beautiful patchwork quilt covered her bed. Framed pictures decorated the walls, and an embroidered sampler hung at the head of her bed. I moved closer to read it: *"There is a friend who sticketh closer than a brother." Proverbs 18:24.*

Mack limped into the bedroom to see her, too, and sat on the edge of her bed. I glared at him, making sure he knew exactly how I felt about him.

"It was a very nice funeral, honey," Lillie told him. "You should've been there to see how well-liked you were."

"Did the sheriff come?"

"Yessir, he was there, making sure you was dead and buried. I think you're safe for now, honey."

"Maybe. But I'm worried that someone will see me. I'll have to go outside to . . . you know . . ."

"You could move up to the cabin until your work is finished."

"What work?" I asked. They ignored my question.

"I can't leave you, Lillie. Who'll take care of you if I'm not here?"

"Honey-girl's been helping me. She'll take care of both of us."

It took me a moment to realize who Lillie meant.

"Wait . . . me? . . . Listen, I won't be here much longer. My aunt and uncle are coming for me next week." They continued to talk, ignoring me completely.

"How about tomorrow night, after dark?" Lillie said. "That'll give you time to pack some food and things. Think you're strong enough to travel up there?"

"I guess we'll find out." He bent over the tiny woman and kissed her forehead, then tucked the covers around her with his good arm. "Good night, Lillie. We'll talk more tomorrow." And before I could stop him, Mack limped into his old bedroom where I had been sleeping and closed the door.

"Hey! That's my room. Where am I supposed to sleep?"

No one replied.

CHAPTER 9

The next day I had the library all to myself. Mack and Lillie both stayed in their rooms, and the only time I saw them was when I brought their meals upstairs. I didn't even have to cook since we had plenty of leftovers from Mack's funeral. Faye's boys must have been naughty again, because they didn't come in to hear the next chapter of *Treasure Island*. It was just as well, for I could hear Mack thumping around in his bedroom all afternoon, and the boys would have heard him, too.

When I brought dinner upstairs, Mack had changed out of his bloodstained clothes for the first time and was sitting on Lillie's bed, talking quietly to her. Their whispered discussion halted when I walked in with the supper tray.

"Don't stop on my account," I said. "I'll just leave this here and eat downstairs."

"Now, now, honey-girl. I know you're feeling peeved with us."

I pinched my lips shut and didn't reply. Who wouldn't be out of sorts after sleeping in Lillie's chair in the non-fiction section all night? I still had a kink in my neck from my uncomfortable night's rest. At least there hadn't been any bats flying around downstairs.

Mack tilted his head to one side and gave me his puppy-eyed look. "You came here to help out, Miss Ripley, and you've been an enormous help to us. Maybe not in the ways you intended, but—"

"But the Good Lord knows we couldn't of done any of this without you," Lillie finished.

"I get no satisfaction in knowing that I've aided in a terrible, deceitful conspiracy against an entire town."

Mack grinned. "Very nicely and dramatically put, Miss Ripley. A bit melodramatic, perhaps . . ."

I wanted to punch him, but Lillie held up her hand. "Truth is, Mack would probably be dead for good if you hadn't helped him. And I'd be knocking on the pearly gates right behind him."

"This town has a lot of secrets," Mack added, "and I'm afraid you stumbled right into the middle of them."

I rolled my eyes. "Now who's being melodramatic?"

Mack and Lillie exchanged glances.

"We just wanted to let you know how grateful we are for all your help," Mack said. "Now, please sit down and eat dinner with us. Let's let bygones be bygones."

I sat down on a spindly chair beside Lillie's bed and ate. The worst was over, I decided, so why not make peace? There would be no more need for potions or secrets or lies. I could concentrate on my work in the library while I waited for my aunt and uncle to return. Maybe I could invite a few more children from town to come to our story time with Faye's boys.

We had finished eating and I was collecting the dishes when Lillie said, "There's just one more *tiny* little thing we're gonna need your help with, honey."

My shoulders sagged. A sound escaped from my throat, something closer to a whimper or a groan than a sigh. "Now what?"

"I could use some help getting ready to leave," Mack said.

"Leave? Where are you going?"

"To a cabin I know of up behind the town. I need to leave tonight, after dark."

"How are you getting there? You can barely stand up, let alone walk. You want me to borrow the postmaster's goat cart?" It irritated me that they would dare to ask another favor, and I made no attempt to hide it.

"I plan to ride Belle. I might need a little help getting her ready."

"This is the twentieth century! Don't you know anyone with a car?"

"The manager of the coal mine has a big, shiny black car, Miss Ripley. So does the sheriff. But I doubt they'd be willing to give me a lift, seeing as they think I'm dead. Besides, there's no road up to the cabin. So will you help me? . . . Please?"

"It depends. What do I have to do?"

Mack stood and moved toward the door. "Can you help me get packed?"

"I suppose so."

I followed him into his room, which now looked as though Ali Baba and his forty thieves had ransacked it. A pair of saddlebags lay on his bed, and I helped him stuff various belongings and toiletries into the leather bags, then rolled up a couple of quilts and tied them into a bedroll. Mack's arm was in a sling and he had to do everything one-handed. I could see that his shoulder still gave him a lot of pain and that the slightest activity left him exhausted. He already had packed a bulging burlap sack, but I didn't want to know what that might contain, and he didn't seem inclined to tell me.

"I guess I'll have to leave my typewriter here for another trip," he said, glancing around when we finished.

"What typewriter? What do you need a typewriter for?"

"Don't ask questions, Miss Ripley. You won't like the answers."

I made two trips up and down the stairs, piling everything by the back door. Then I helped Mack hobble down to the kitchen. He directed me as I filled an empty feed sack with food supplies.

The night turned out to be dark and cloudy with no moon or stars. "Perfect," Mack decided. *Creepy,* I thought. Sparse spring branches creaked and rasped as they blew in the wind. A hint of rain still fogged the damp air. Mack leaned on me as he limped down to the shed, where I was supposed to help him saddle the horse. The saddle was so heavy I had to stand on a crate in order to lift it onto the animal's back. And the beast kept moving around, refusing to stand still for me. By the time I managed to heft the saddle into place, I was panting. Mack pointed to a strap dangling under the horse's belly.

"Make sure you cinch that up real tight."

"Wait. You can't possibly expect me to crawl underneath that animal and fasten that buckle."

"If you don't, I'll be on my rear end in the creek before Belle takes a dozen steps."

"Lead me not into temptation . . ." I mumbled, imagining the scene.

"Pardon?"

"The horse is enormous! Can't you buckle the strap yourself?"

"Not with one hand."

"What if she lies down on top of me while I'm under there?"

"She won't. Horses seldom lie down. Come on, I'll make sure Belle won't kick you."

Kick me? I worked fast, glancing at Mack and at the horse's hind legs.

"Now the bridle," Mack said. "Just slip it over her head and get her to open her mouth so you can put the bit in place." I stared at him. "What's wrong?" he asked.

"You expect me to put my fingers into the horse's mouth?"

"Belle won't mind. She's used to it."

"Well, I'm not used to it! I've never been this . . . intimate . . . with an animal before—under its belly, in its mouth—especially a beast that's three times my size."

I heard him mumble something about melodrama, but I chose to ignore him. Between the two of us, we finally got the bridle on and the horse was ready to go. As we led it from the shed to the back door where we'd piled Mack's saddlebags and bedroll, I could tell the horse wasn't too happy about going out for a midnight ride. It stomped its feet and snorted, acting as sulky as I felt.

The last thing Mack had me do after tying on all his belongings was drag a wooden bench over from beside the back door and help him climb up, since he was too weak to swing up into the saddle the regular way—especially with only one arm. As it was, he half crawled onto Belle's back, stomach first. He was sweating and wincing by the time he was astride, even though the night air was cool. I was about to wish him well—and good riddance—when he extended his good hand to me. "Grab on, Miss Ripley, and I'll pull you up behind me."

"What?"

"You have to come along."

"Oh, no I don't!" I backed away from him.

"How else will Belle get home again?"

"I don't care. That's not my problem."

He beckoned to me again. "Come on, hurry up before someone sees us."

I crossed my arms. "No. This is the limit. I . . . I refuse."

"I thought you agreed to help me."

"I've done all sorts of things to help you, including crouching beneath a horse, hauling sacks of dirt, telling a pack of lies, and committing fraud. But now I'm done. Finished. No more. You and Lillie got along fine before I arrived, and from now on you'll just have to spin your web of deceit without me."

"Listen, this will only take a few minutes. You'll be back home and tucked up in bed within the hour."

"No! I've never been on a horse in my life, and I'm not going to get on one tonight."

"Come on . . . it's easy. Little children do it. Climb on the bench and give me your hand." He reached his good arm out to me again. I backed even farther away from him.

"No, I can't . . . and I won't!"

I heard a clicking-sliding noise behind me, metal on metal. I turned and saw Lillie standing in the doorway in her nightgown, holding Mack's rifle.

"Go ahead and get on the horse, honey," she said sweetly. "I come to think of you as my own daughter, so I sure would hate to shoot you."

Shoot me?

"Come on, Miss Ripley," Mack coaxed, smiling, extending his hand.

Did I have a choice? Lillie was holding a gun. A gun! She probably wouldn't *really* shoot me, but then again maybe she would. Mack was living proof that people around here didn't think twice about shooting each other.

"Climb on, honey," Lillie urged.

My knees trembled with a mixture of anger and terror as I climbed onto the tottering bench. Mack grabbed my hand and hauled me up onto the horse. I had to wrap my arms around his waist to keep from falling off, and that made me angrier still. He shook the reins and Belle began to move, clomping and swaying over the lumpy ground. I remembered the saddle strap I had cinched and prayed that I had pulled it tight enough so we both wouldn't land in the creek.

I had begun to feel a mild fondness for Mack as I'd helped Lillie save his life, but those feelings were gone now. Tonight I hated him. Even so, I clung to him against my will, terrified of falling off the horse. The ground was such a long way down! We ambled across the yard and down to the creek in the dark, then Mack turned the horse to the right and we followed the narrow bank of the creek like a trail up into the hills.

"Do you care at all that I've just been coerced at gunpoint? Against my will? And don't you dare tell me I'm being melodramatic."

"You've really never been on a horse before?"

"Never! Horses belong in novels about the Wild West. We drive *cars* where I come from. Cars!"

"Well, you're not home now, are you?"

I felt his ribs quivering and I had the infuriating feeling that he was laughing at me. "Are you *laughing*, Mr. MacDougal?"

"No, ma'am. I'm trying real hard not to laugh." But he couldn't hold it in, and before long he was sputtering and chuckling. I even saw him wipe his eyes.

"This isn't funny!"

"No, ma'am. It truly isn't. But just think how exciting it will sound when you tell all your friends back home that you went on a midnight horseback ride with a dead man. Kind of spooky . . . like *The Legend of Sleepy Hollow*, don't you think?"

"I have no idea who shot you, Mr. MacDougal, but he now has my complete support and encouragement."

He laughed even harder.

We rode for several minutes as the horse plodded uphill. I gripped Mack's waist, swaying atop the horse's hips, ducking beneath low-hanging branches that dripped icy water down my back. Then I had another thought. "How am I supposed to find my way home all alone in the dark? Do you care at all that I might get lost?"

"Belle knows the way. It isn't far. Just follow the creek."

"If the horse knows the way back, then why did I have to come?"

"So you'd know where the cabin is. I'll have to depend on you to bring me food and things for a while."

"Wait. You said this was the very last thing I would have to do for you."

"Actually, I believe Miss Lillie told you that. And you know how she likes to exaggerate."

"Is she going to point a gun at me again?"

"I guess that's up to you, Miss Ripley. Lillie does whatever she needs to do to get the job done."

I had the same stomach-sinking feeling that all hostages must feel when they realize there is no way out. Then I thought of one. "What are you going to do next week after my aunt and uncle come back for me?"

"Shhh . . . Stop talking, Miss Ripley. You're going to have every dog in the hollow barking."

We rode for twenty minutes more, the forest growing darker and thicker as we climbed higher and higher. Every sound spooked me, and I was certain I could hear creatures scurrying around, rustling through the underbrush below us and in the tree branches above. The horse huffed and snorted as it climbed, its hooves skidding on the mud at times. Then it pulled up short and stopped walking altogether, for no reason that I could see. It danced in place as if standing on a bed of hot coals.

"What's wrong?" I whispered. "Why is the horse acting so jittery?" I was afraid it had decided we were too heavy and was about to rear back and throw us off.

"Shhh!"

"Why is he stopping? What's wrong with him?"

"It's not a him, Miss Ripley. Belle's a mare." We stood still for a long moment, and I could hear Mack sniffing the air. "Smell that?" he asked. "There's a cat around here somewhere. Belle smells it, too."

"A cat? Doesn't she like cats?"

"We're not talking about your grandma's tabby cat. We have big cats in these woods. Lynx. Wildcats."

This news was too much for me. I leaned my forehead against

Mack's back and cried like a little girl. My nerves were so jumbled from everything I had endured that I would need a month at Aunt Lydia's spa to straighten them out.

"Hey, hey," he soothed. "Don't cry." He made a clicking sound and urged the horse forward again. "We'll be fine. I didn't mean to scare you."

"No? What did you mean to do? You've already forced me to get on this stupid horse at gunpoint, and now you're telling me there are wildcats stalking us? That's my choice? Get shot or get eaten by wildcats? Who wouldn't be scared?"

"Don't worry, cats usually go for smaller game. They'd have to be plenty hungry to go after Belle."

"Wonderful. What about going after me?"

He laughed, and it made me so angry I wanted to push him off the horse and let the wildcat eat him. "Stop laughing! It's not funny!"

"I'm sorry. But if you ever got into a tussle with a wildcat, Miss Ripley, I'd put my money on you."

I decided not to say another word to this horrible man and seethed in silence the rest of the way. Ten minutes later—although it seemed like ten years—Mack veered away from the creek and urged the horse straight up a steep incline on our right. "Hang on tight," he said.

"Wait! I'm going to slide off the back!"

"You'll be fine. Lift your bottom a little and lean forward."

The nerve of the man, telling me what to do with my bottom! But I closed my eyes and hung on to Mack for dear life. I didn't open them again until we halted. In the gloom among the trees, I could barely make out the bones of a tiny cabin, perched on an impossibly small square of flat land. A jumbled tangle of vines and tree branches engulfed it as if the cabin were having a wrestling match with Mother Nature. The cabin was clearly losing. The tumbledown structure not only looked uninhabited, it looked uninhabitable. I didn't care. I was so furious that all I wanted to do was climb down off this horse and go home. I would take my chances with the wildcats just to be rid of Mack.

He steered Belle as close to the cabin as he could get without going inside and slid off with a grunt onto the tiny porch. I extended my hand to him. "Help me down, please." I would have jumped off, but the horse had legs like a giraffe's and the ground looked very far away.

"Hand me the saddlebags first," Mack said. I complied. "Thanks. Can you untie the bedroll . . . and that burlap sack? Good. Now slide forward into the saddle."

I did what he said, sliding onto the hard leather seat. "Will you please help me down now?" I asked politely.

Mack shook his head. "The trip will go faster on the way back. It's downhill most of the way. Belle will be eager to get home. Don't let her gallop, though, or you might fall off."

"How am I supposed to stop her?"

"Hang on with your legs. Keep the reins tight. But don't pull too hard or she'll buck and throw you off."

"Throw me off! Wait—!"

"Just keep following Wonderland Creek down the hill."

"*Wonderland?* Is that the name of this creek?"

"Yeah."

"You're kidding."

"No, that's what it's called. Why?"

"Never mind. Please, Mack. Help me down. I want to walk home."

"You can't walk. It's too dark. How will you see where you're going? Listen, Belle knows the way home and she's very sure-footed. She'll have you there in twenty minutes. She moves faster downhill."

"No, wait! That's what I'm afraid of! I don't want her to run!"

"Lean back on the way down. Hang on with your legs. And don't forget to take her saddle and bridle off when you get home."

"Please don't leave me out here in these woods all alone!"

"You're not alone. You have Belle. Good night, Miss Ripley. Thanks for your help." Mack gave the horse a gentle slap on her rear end and off we went.

I would have screamed, but fear had driven all of the air from my lungs. I closed my eyes, then remembered I needed to watch for low-hanging branches. The slope was so steep that I felt like I was going to tumble right over the horse's head. She was grunting and snorting as she negotiated the rocky slope. Maybe she was as scared as I was. What if she really didn't know the way home and we wandered around in these creepy woods all night? But Belle quickly reached the stream and turned downhill, following the creek bed. Wonderland Creek indeed.

It might have taken only twenty minutes to get home, but it seemed like an eternity as Belle and I bounced and jostled downhill through the ink-black forest. I clung to the reins and the little horn on the front of the saddle, whimpering like an abandoned kitten. I didn't stop whimpering until I felt the ground start to level off and I knew we were almost there. My vision blurred with tears of joy and relief when I saw the dark outline of the library in the distance. Lillie had left a lantern glowing in the kitchen window.

The horse went straight into the shed, and if I hadn't remembered to duck in time, I would have been knocked to the ground. I gratefully slid off her back when she stopped. My legs were so weak from fear and exhaustion that they crumpled beneath me and I landed in a heap in the hay and manure. I figured as long as I was down there, I may as well reach beneath her belly to unbuckle the saddle.

"Nice horsey, good horsey . . ." I murmured as my fingers fumbled in the dark. "Please don't kick me."

I scrambled to my feet when she started stomping hers and I quickly slid the saddle off her back. Then I pulled the bridle off her head and hung it on a hook. I was done. Finished. I latched the shed door behind me and staggered up to the house.

Everything was quiet. There was no sign of Lillie or her rifle. I took the lantern from the kitchen window and carried it upstairs to Mack's bedroom. At least I had a bed to sleep in again. I looked in the mirror above the dresser and saw a crazed woman with straw sticking out of her hair and eyes as wide and glassy as Aunt Lydia's stuffed moose. *It's okay,* I told the girl in the mirror. *You're home now where it's safe. Everything's going to be okay.*

No sooner were the words out of my mouth than the bat whizzed past my head. This was too much. It was all too much!

I dove into Mack's bed and pulled the covers over my head, crying myself to sleep as the bat swooped around the room, diving and darting as if having the time of its life.

CHAPTER 10

An odd sound outside below my bedroom window awakened me the next morning. *Whack, thwap! Whack, thwap!* I parted the curtains and looked down to see Ike Arnett, the fiddle player, splitting wood with an axe and stacking it in our woodpile. I had been growing worried as I'd watched the pile diminishing day after day, fearing that I soon would have to chop wood, too. Mack had stacked a large pile of logs down by Belle's shed, but they needed to be split before they'd fit into the cookstove.

I dressed quickly and hurried down to the backyard. "Good morning, Ike."

"Hey, Alice. How you doing?" He paused to rest, wiping his brow with the back of his hand.

"I'm doing fine, thank you. How are you?"

"Great. Working up a sweat." He propped his axe against the stump and unbuttoned his flannel shirt. As he shrugged it off, he seemed to choreograph every move in order to display his impressive set of muscles. Ike resembled every hero in every romance novel I had ever read—not that I read those kinds of books on a regular basis, of course.

He caught me watching him and grinned. I had to say something. "It's so nice of you to do this for us . . . to help out this way."

"That's what neighbors are for. I saw that your woodpile was getting low."

"Yes. Thank you."

"How's Miss Lillie doing? I guess she took Mack's death pretty hard, huh?"

"I guess." I couldn't say more without sounding sarcastic, so I thanked Ike again and went inside, carrying an armful of freshly split wood.

Miss Lillie was already awake and sitting up in bed when I brought in her breakfast tray. She looked small and frail and helpless as she leaned against the pillows, but I knew better. She greeted me with a shy smile. "Didn't mean to scare you with the gun last night, honey."

"No? What did you mean to do?"

She thought for a long moment, then said, "Get you moving."

I laid the breakfast tray on her lap. "Do you need anything else?" I backed toward the door.

"Yes, honey-girl. I need you to sit down and talk to me while I eat." She patted the edge of the bed and beckoned to me. "Come on, I won't bite."

I did as she said. Reluctantly. And with more than a twinge of fear.

Lillie picked up her fork and poked at her eggs. I wanted to remind her of all the hard work I had done to get those eggs onto her plate—braving the damp morning air and the pecking, flapping chaos of the henhouse, hauling firewood and coaxing the flames to stay lit long enough to scramble the eggs and bake the biscuits. I had to admit that the biscuits hadn't turned out very well, and any leftover ones could be used as cobblestones, but at least I had tried.

"I used to teach school a long, long time ago," Lillie said, "and I learnt that most youngsters can do what you ask them to do—even if they don't think so. They just need a little push sometimes to get them moving, that's all. So over the years I learnt to give a little push in the right direction when I had to."

"Did you point a rifle at your students, too?"

"'Course not," she said, smiling. "But listen now, honey. You shouldn't be holding grudges against people. I did what needed to be done last night, and so did you. And it wasn't so bad, was it? Once I got you moving?"

"It was horrible."

"But you learnt something, right?"

108

I held my tongue, resisting the urge to say I had learned not to trust a word that she or Mack said. *Six more days,* I told myself. *Five, after today.* I had been here for nine days, and with any luck my aunt and uncle would come to my rescue very soon.

"So can we be friends again, honey?"

I sighed. Nodded. Lillie was not someone you'd want for an enemy. I decided to make polite conversation while she nibbled her eggs. "Did you teach school here in town, Miss Lillie?"

"No. I was teaching a long, long time ago down in Virginia, right after the war ended. That's where I met my Sam, the man I come to love more than anyone in the whole world—except for Jesus, of course. Mmm hmm he's a fine man." Her face beamed. That was the only word for it. But whether she was smiling because of Sam or Jesus, I couldn't be sure.

"Was Sam a teacher, too?" I asked.

Lillie laughed. "No, honey-girl, he was one of my students! Before Mr. Lincoln come along, nobody's allowed to teach slaves to read and write. So Sam didn't know how to do either one till the war set us free, even though he's a grown man. I already learnt how to read back on the plantation—in secret, of course. That's so I could write down everything Old Granny was teaching me about how to heal folks. Massa would've tanned all the skin off my hide if he'd known I could read and write. Had to be real careful, you know."

"How did you become a teacher after the war?" I imagined Lillie attending classes at the Normal School like Freddy and I had.

"You know what they say, 'In the land of the blind, the man with one eye is king.' Since I'm the only one who can read, they made me the teacher at the new colored folks' school. My Sam, he was real smart, though. He learnt how to read in no time. And along the way we fell in love."

"Did you marry him?"

"Couldn't marry him, honey, much as I wanted to. I was already married. I jumped the broom with a field hand named Charley when I was still on the plantation. Big handsome fellow with skin like a moonless night. We had us a little baby boy named Buster." Lillie smiled, remembering. "Trouble is, Massa sold Charley down South, and I didn't know what become of him."

Her story horrified me. I had read about such atrocities in Frederick Douglass's slave narrative and in novels like *Uncle Tom's Cabin*, but I had never met a real live slave before. "Why did your master sell him?"

"Massa didn't need no reason. He sold my son, too, right after the war started and Buster was still a boy. So when the war was over, I was hanging around close to Massa's old place and teaching school, waiting to find out if I still had a husband and a son. Ain't nothing Sam and me could do but wait."

I was intrigued now by Lillie's tragic story. "What happened?"

Instead of replying, Lillie sat up straight in bed, her head tilted to one side, listening. "Did you unlock the door downstairs, honey? Ain't it about time for the other gals to get here?"

"I'll go unlock it." I hurried downstairs, intending to come right back and hear the rest of Lillie's story, but I saw Marjorie outside, tying her horse to the porch railing. She carried the burlap sacks she used to tote books and also an old, worn-out pair of tall lace-up boots, the kind that all of the women wore on their delivery routes. I held the door open for her.

"Here's the boots you asked me about, Miss Lillie."

I whirled around and sure enough, there was Lillie, standing at the bottom of the steps, grinning. "Thanks, honey."

Marjorie handed the boots to me, not to Lillie. "Try them on, Alice. See if they fit you."

"Me? . . . Thanks, but I already have shoes."

"Yes you do, honey," Lillie said, "and they're real nice ones, too. Ain't much good for riding horses, though." She took my arm as she spoke and guided me over to the stairs, then motioned for me to sit down. "Go ahead and try them on now, seeing as Marjorie was nice enough to bring them."

I felt the hair rise on the back of my neck as I sat down and did as I was told. I already had one boot on when the front door opened and the other three women came in. They gathered in front of the stairs, watching me pull on the second boot and lace it up as if they'd never seen such a sight before.

"Looks like they're gonna fit her real good," Alma said with a smile. The others nodded. Any minute they might applaud. I didn't know what was going on, but I had a bad feeling about it. After all, Lillie was capable of staging a person's funeral and convincing everyone he was dead.

I gulped as Lillie laid her hands on my shoulders like a queen about to bestow her blessing. "Now, we know you come down here outta the goodness of your heart, honey, to help us out. Right, gals? So we was discussing it at Mack's funeral, and we decided that the best way you can help—and honor Mack's memory—is if we was to give you a library route like all the other gals have."

My heart began to pound. I wondered what they would do if I pushed them aside and ran out the front door. "You mean . . . on a *horse?*"

"Them books get pretty heavy otherwise, especially when you're walking uphill. And there's an awful lot of hills around here."

"I-I don't know how to ride a horse, Miss Lillie."

"Cora will teach you, won't you, honey?"

"Sure. I'd be glad to."

"We'll all help," Faye added. This was a lynch mob, leading me to the hanging tree.

"Cora says she'll take you out on her route today and show you the way. Hers is the easiest one. She's been wanting to start a new route further up where some folks are living on Potter's Creek. Ain't that right, Cora? Remember how Mack used to talk about that? Them folks on Potter's Creek ain't hardly ever seen a book."

The women were all smiling and nodding. Alma had tears in her eyes. "Mack was always thinking of other people instead of himself," she said.

"We wouldn't even have jobs if it weren't for Mack," Marjorie added. Everyone agreed.

How long had Lillie been plotting this little scheme of hers? Was Mack in on it, too? I wanted to dig in my heels, throw a temper tantrum, and refuse to do a single thing Lillie said. But I still got chills when I remembered how she had stood in the kitchen doorway last night, cocking Mack's gun. She knew how to make potions, too. She might be a frail little thing, but I was scared to death of her. And she was pairing me up with Cora, the tallest and heftiest of the four women, with shoulders as broad as Mack's. Cora could probably pick me up by the scruff of the neck and plop me onto the horse's back without breaking into a sweat.

"Now, I know you gals want to get on your way," Lillie said. "Go on down and get Belle saddled up for her, would you, Cora? I'll help honey-girl pack her lunch."

After the others left, I confronted Lillie. "Why are you making me do this? I can't deliver books like they do. I don't know anything about horses."

"Oh, that don't matter. You can learn. Little kids ride horses around here all the time. Bareback, no less. Them women are paying you a big honor, honey, accepting you like one a their own and letting you ride with them." Lillie took my arm and started pulling me toward the kitchen as she spoke. I dragged my feet like a condemned woman.

"But . . . but I don't want the honor." Memories of last night's ride were still much too fresh—and so were the bruises on my backside. I had long since given up hope that this was a nightmare and that I might wake up. This was too unbelievable to be a nightmare. I wanted to go home. "Please tell the ladies thank-you for me, but I don't know how to ride—and I don't think I can learn."

"Listen, honey." She lowered her voice to a whisper. "We got to bring food and things up to Mack without people getting suspicious. If you ride a route like all them other gals, you can check on him every day or so."

"Please don't make me get on a horse again. *Please!*" My tears did no good.

"You're the one who helped Mack get up there, so why do you want to leave him up there all alone to starve to death?"

"But I helped him pack some food—"

"Besides, while you're out on your route, you can do some poking around for us."

"Poking around?"

"Um hmm. Try to figure out who shot Mack and why."

"I thought you knew who shot him."

"Well, it turns out there are several folks who mighta done it, and we got to figure out which one it was for sure."

"How could there be more than one suspect? What did Mack

do to make people want to murder him?" Although I could have cheerfully murdered him myself.

"It happens, honey. People get riled up, start feuding . . ."

"But what if the killer finds out that I'm helping Mack and decides to shoot me, too?"

"That's why it's best if you pretend to be one of the library gals, taking books to people. Folks around here get real suspicious of flatlanders riding around in the hills and hollows, especially when she comes outta nowhere like you done. Those boots fit you all right, honey?"

Would this ever end?

I leaned my head against the kitchen doorframe, wishing I had never gotten out of bed this morning. Or out of Uncle Cecil's car nine days ago. "Isn't there any other way?"

"Not that I can think of. Listen, I know you're feeling mighty peeved with me, but can't you find it in your heart to help out these poor gals and their families? Fact is, between the four of them, they're supporting nearly every family in Acorn. Everybody is kin to everybody else up in these hills, and we're falling on some real hard times around here. Sure would be a shame if something happened to bring out the truth about Mack and these gals had to lose their livelihood, wouldn't it?"

I closed my eyes, at a loss as to how to answer.

"Here's your lunch, honey." She handed me a small bundle wrapped in a dish towel and tied with string.

"When did you make this?"

"Last night. While you was out. Go on now. Cora probably has Belle all saddled up and waiting for you."

"Are you going to threaten me with the rifle again if I don't go?"

She smiled. "Don't you worry none about that. Just have yourself a real nice ride."

I was about to become a packhorse librarian whether I wanted to or not.

CHAPTER 11

The horse didn't seem any happier about going for a ride this morning than she had last night. Belle snorted and stomped her feet like a petulant child as Cora led her up to the back door where her own horse was waiting. I knew exactly how Belle felt.

"I don't think Mack has ridden her in a while," Cora said. "Seems like she's not used to being bossed around."

"Maybe I shouldn't ride her, then. I don't know anything about horses. I've never even been on one before." Except for last night, of course, but I couldn't tell Cora about that ride.

"Really? No kidding?" Cora stared at me as if I'd told her I usually rode dragons instead of horses. "Well, I'll give you a quick lesson. First, you always mount on the horse's left side."

"You do? Why?" I was stalling for time.

"Just put your left foot in that left stirrup there, and swing your right leg up and over." But before I could even get close to Belle, she backed away from me, shaking her head as if trying to shake off her bridle.

"I don't think the horse likes me very much," I said. And the feeling was mutual.

"She doesn't know you, that's all. You gotta win her trust. Horses are basically afraid of people. See how her eyes are on the sides of her head and yours and mine are in front? That's so she can look all around and see her enemies coming. She's the kind of animal that gets hunted by other animals. And we're the kind of animal that does the hunting. You gotta convince her that you ain't a threat to her."

"Oh, believe me, I'm not a threat. I'm terrified of her!"

"But you can't let her know that. Show her who's in control."

"How do I do that?"

Cora gave me a quick riding lesson, explaining how to use my legs and which way to tug the reins when I wanted the horse to turn or stop. She may as well have been speaking another language. I was so frightened that her words of advice fell all around me without sinking in, as forgotten as raindrops in the creek.

"Okay, climb on," she said when she was finished. I had to drag the bench over from beside the back door, and even then Cora had to give me a boost before I made it up into the saddle. "You sure are a little bit of a thing, ain't you?" she said. I knew it was impossible to ever do this on my own the way Lillie expected me to.

Cora mounted her own horse and motioned toward the creek, leading the way. "Okay, turn her this way . . . no, not that way, this way . . ."

"I'm trying to go that way, but she won't do it!" I flapped the reins and managed to turn us around in a complete circle before Belle gave up trying to obey me and headed back toward her shed.

"Make her stop, Alice. Pull back on the reins a little."

"Whoa!" I begged. "Whoa!" My efforts did no good. Belle refused to cooperate and nothing would change her mind. Cora finally trotted her horse down to the shed behind us and grabbed Belle's bridle. It took some tugging, but she managed to get us turned around and headed in the right direction. We rode side by side up the path beside the stream.

"Now, the creek is your main road," Cora said. She sounded weary and the day had just begun. "All you gotta do is ride up Wonderland Creek on the way out in the morning and follow it back home at night. There are a few turnoffs along the way, so you'll have to learn to watch for the landmarks. There ain't any signposts up this way. But your route always comes back to Wonderland Creek. You can't get lost."

Want to bet?

When the path we were following narrowed and started to climb up the hill, Cora pulled in front and led the way. Thirty minutes later we reached the cabin where Mack was hiding. The trip had seemed to take much longer last night. Once I was on my own, I would have to stop here and deliver things to him. I'd like to deliver him a punch in the nose. The cabin looked even more weather-beaten in daylight, as if the forest was doing its best to squash the ramshackle structure and reclaim that patch of land for itself. Knee-high weeds sprouted through cracks in the porch floor. A sapling peeked out of the front window through the broken pane of glass. A thick layer of fuzzy moss claimed the cabin's roof.

"See that cabin?" Cora pointed to it and my heart began to thump.

"Um . . . yes?" Had I given Mack away by staring at it? Had Belle left hoofprints in the mud last night? My traitorous horse suddenly turned toward the incline as if ready to climb up to the cabin again and pay Mack a visit. I tugged desperately on the reins. "Whoa, horsey! Whoa!"

"When you get here," Cora said, "start watching for the trail to the Larkin place. The turnoff will be on your left, across the creek. It's just a little ways up."

Cora turned her horse toward the creek again and got it moving as effortlessly as Uncle Cecil steered his huge car. I jiggled Belle's reins, but she didn't budge. "Come on, horsey . . . Giddyup . . . please . . . ?" Belle finally started to move, but she turned the opposite way and headed downhill toward home. "Whoa! Whoa!" I begged. She ignored me. "Cora! Help!"

She turned her own horse around and caught up to us, leaning over to grab Belle's bridle again. "Hey! Behave yourself now!" I didn't know if she meant Belle or me. Cora offered me another quick riding lesson, explaining how much slack I should leave in the reins and how I shouldn't let them get too tight or too loose, and how to use my legs to help steer. "You'll get used to each other before long," she said. I doubted it. I already hated and feared this horse every bit as much as I despised and feared her owners.

When we'd traveled a short distance past Mack's cabin, Cora stopped to show me where there was a ford in the creek. "This is where we cross over to the opposite bank and head up that trail to the Larkin place."

"What trail? There's a trail over there?"

"You'll see it in a minute. Now, it'll be even harder to see it in wintertime when the snow hides it. I can tie a rag around one of the tree trunks if you want, so you can find it better."

I started to explain that I would be leaving next week, long before summer began, let alone winter, but I decided to keep my mouth shut. No one in this town listened to a word I said anyway, including my horse. I squeezed Belle's sides with my legs and urged her across the rock-strewn creek behind Cora. The water looked clear and cold. On the other side, we followed a narrow dirt trail that led back into the woods. The trees linked arms above us, crowding close, blocking out the sky.

Five minutes later we reached a log cabin in a clearing. A crude picket fence surrounded the house, and chickens flapped and squawked and chased each other inside the enclosure. Everything was a dull brown color—the cabin, the fence, the dirt yard. Even the chickens were brown and probably laid brown eggs. But alongside the house, a fruit tree of some kind was about to bloom, its vulnerable pink buds offering a blink of color in the otherwise bland landscape. Something about the cabin, constructed from rough squared-off logs, looked odd. It took me a moment to realize that it didn't have any windows. A door in front and another one on the side both stood wide open. At the edge of the property I saw a man with a mule and an old-fashioned plow, tilling a patch of brown soil.

Before we reached the picket fence, a dog tore around from behind the house and raced straight toward us, barking and snarling. The sound echoed off the surrounding hills as if there was an entire pack of dogs. Belle halted, dancing in place the way she had last night when she'd smelled the wildcat. A young girl—bone thin and very pregnant—came out onto the porch and yelled for him to shut up. Her hair was the flaming red color of maple leaves in the fall.

"Hey, June Ann. How you doing?" Cora called above the din.

"Pretty good . . . Rex! Shut up!"

Cora leaned over in her saddle, unlatched the gate, and rode inside the yard. I tried to follow her, but Belle wouldn't budge, spooked by the barking dog. June Ann waddled down off the porch and caught the dog by the scruff of its neck. "Hush now, Rex!" The dog finally obeyed, and June Ann beckoned to me, "It's okay. He won't hurt you none. Come on in."

Cora turned around in her saddle, and I thought I saw her roll her eyes at the sight of me and my disobedient horse, frozen in place. "Give her a kick, Alice. Kick her hard!" I kicked as hard as I dared, aware that Belle might seek revenge and try to kick me in return the next time I unbuckled her saddle. But she finally began to move again. We clomped into the yard behind Cora, who introduced me to June Ann Larkin.

"So nice to meet you, Alice. Can I get you ladies some coffee or something?"

I exhaled. "Yes, please. I'm dying of thirst. And I need to get off this horse and rest my backside for a while . . . if that's okay."

Cora frowned at me and I knew I'd said something wrong. "Water will be just fine," she told June Ann. "For both of us. We can't stay long."

"You sure?"

"Yes. Don't fuss on our account." Cora dismounted as June Ann went into the house, then she helped me down off my horse. "They always offer you things," she whispered, "but they're just being polite. They'll give you their last crust of bread or drop of coffee if you let them."

June Ann was back in a minute with two mismatched glasses of water. She had her library book tucked under her arm. "I finished reading it in one day," she said. "So I read it all over again."

"I figured you would like it," Cora said. "I brought you another one by the same writer." Cora set her water on glass on the porch railing and began digging through her library bags.

"When is your baby due, June Ann?" I asked.

"Any day."

It looked more like any minute to me. June Ann was no taller than I was and stick thin. She couldn't be more than fifteen or sixteen years old—much too young to be married and pregnant. But I remembered Faye saying that she had been married at age sixteen.

I already knew there was no doctor or hospital in town to deliver June Ann's baby. Women back in Illinois often had their babies at home, but they could at least telephone a doctor and he would drive over to the house and deliver them. The only way a doctor could get up to June Ann's house was by horseback. I knew better than to ask nosy questions, but I couldn't help myself.

"What will you do when your time comes? Are you all alone out here?"

"My husband, Wayne, will ride down and fetch one of the midwives. I sure wish Miss Lillie could come up and birth my baby, but I guess she's getting on in years. Miss Lillie birthed me and all my brothers and sisters. She birthed my mama, too. In fact, she birthed pretty near everybody in the county."

"Yep, me too," Cora said. I couldn't picture it. If you put two Lillies together, you still wouldn't have a woman as tall and sturdy as Cora. Nor could I imagine Cora as a newborn.

"I guess Lillie trained the two midwives, Sadie and Ida," June Ann said with a sigh, "so I suppose they'll be just as good."

June Ann seemed sad to me, not at all like other expectant mothers I'd seen. My two sisters had been as round and jolly as St. Nicholas when they were ready to deliver their first babies. June Ann looked tired and weary, as if she'd already been staying up nights with a cranky newborn. She was barely a woman, yet she seemed as old and frail as the men who had been playing cards in the post office. I sipped my water, watching Wayne Larkin and his mule wrestling dark clods of earth. There was a sadness here in this little clearing, the same melancholy I had felt at the deserted mining camp.

Then Cora handed June Ann a book from her saddlebag and the girl smiled faintly for the first time. "I really enjoyed the last one," she said. "Hope this new one is just as good."

"They're both written by the same person, Grace Livingston Hill. You didn't read this one already, did you?"

"Nope. And even if I did, I wouldn't mind reading it again." She caressed the worn cover and smiled faintly again. I knew the anticipation June Ann felt as she was about to open a book and lose herself in the story, living a more interesting, colorful life along with the characters. That's when I realized that I hadn't read a single novel since the night I had arrived in Acorn and had tried to read the book of ghost stories before bed.

"I also brought you these." Cora handed June Ann a small pile of magazines and booklets. "They got some good pieces in there about taking care of babies. If you like them, we'll bring some more."

"Thanks. Maybe next time you come my baby will be here." She caressed the front of her bulging dress the same way she had caressed the book. But this time she didn't smile.

"It won't be me coming next time, June Ann. Alice is gonna be taking over my route from now on. I'm showing her around today."

"My friends call me Allie," I said.

"Okay . . . Allie," she said shyly. "I guess I'll see you next week." But she wouldn't see me again, of course. My aunt and uncle were coming back for me next week. I felt like a sneaky snake-oil salesman, making promises and telling fibs.

Long before my backside stopped aching, Cora told me it was time to leave. "Good luck with your little one," I called as I waved good-bye. I caught myself smiling and wishing I could see June Ann again. I recognized a kindred spirit in her love of books. It would be nice to come every week and bring a little happiness into what must be a hard and lonely life. But I was going home to Illinois, not riding a book route.

Cora and I headed down the trail through the woods the way we had come, back to Wonderland Creek. Once again, Belle tried to turn the opposite way and go downhill toward home. "Hey! Wrong way!" Cora shouted.

"I can't help it. She went this way all by herself." Belle finally stopped when I tugged hard on the reins. But then she wouldn't move at all. I would never be able to wrestle this ornery horse up Wonderland Creek all by myself. When we returned to the library today, Cora and I would have to explain to Lillie that it simply couldn't be done. Lillie would have to trust somebody else to bring supplies to Mack.

Cora splashed down to where I'd halted and grabbed Belle's bridle, turning her around. "This way, Belle. You behave yourself. We got a long way to go to the Sawyer place."

A long way? I tried not to groan. My hip joints ached and my rear end already felt like I'd been paddled with a two-by-four.

120

We followed the creek upstream for nearly half an hour to the next house on Cora's route. Once again it was tucked into a clearing among the hills, a few minutes' ride from the creek. She showed me the landmark: a huge pine tree growing out from between two large rocks—as if the tree had split the rock in two.

The moment we rode into the clearing, a swarm of children poured out of the cabin, surging toward us like bees out of a hive. They didn't stand still long enough for me to count them, but they all had the same straw-colored hair. I figured if someone lined them up, they'd probably look like stair steps. Their mother must have delivered one baby in the morning, then gotten pregnant again right after supper. But what a happy sight they made as they ran barefoot to meet us, whooping and hollering. "Here she comes! Here comes Miss Cora!" I hadn't seen this much excitement since the circus came to Blue Island.

"Did you bring us more stories to read?"

"Do you got more books for me?"

The boys wore ragged overalls and the little girls were in print dresses. I recognized the calico pattern—it was the same one as the feed sacks I'd filled with dirt and buried in Mack's coffin. The children followed our horses up to the house as if Cora were the Pied Piper.

"Can I please get down and rest again?" I begged.

"Sure. The young ones like it when I stop awhile."

"You gonna read to us today, Miss Cora?" one of the boys asked when he saw her dismounting.

"How about if Miss Alice reads to you? She's gonna be bringing books to you from now on, so I'm showing her how to get up here to your place."

Cora had to help me get down, and I heard the children chuckling and snickering at the ungainly way I slid to the ground, then tripped over my own feet and landed on my aching backside.

But the giggles and good-natured shoving settled into stillness as Cora opened her bag and unpacked the books. The children stared in such wide-eyed fascination that we might have been bringing toys and candy like Santa Claus. Cora handed me one of the books. "Here, why don't you read this one to them?"

The children clung to me like burs on a dog as I made my way to the porch steps and sat down. I could hear each child breathing as the group gathered in a tight circle around me, waiting for me to begin. Their mother came to the doorway in her apron to listen, too. The children took turns turning the pages for me, and they couldn't seem to resist running their hands across the pictures as if they could feel the colors and shapes. That explained why the pages of all of the children's books in Acorn's library had looked so grubby. But the loving caresses weren't meant to deface the books.

"You talk funny, Miss Alice," one of them said after I'd read a few pages.

"That's because Miss Alice comes from up in Illinois." Cora pronounced it like *Ill-a-noise*.

"Where's that?"

"Maybe I'll bring a book with maps to show you the next time I come."

I couldn't believe what I'd just said! Why was I talking as if I'd be coming back? I had told June Ann I would be back, too. Again I felt torn. Part of me wanted to have the privilege of bringing books to people who cherished them as much as I did, yet I knew I could never be a real packhorse librarian, especially on my own. I hated riding, hated Belle—yet these dear people had quickly found a place in my heart. I felt a kinship with them. Maybe if I could travel here by car or walk—but not riding that stupid horse! Yet the children's hunger for books brought tears to my eyes. Life up here on this farm must be so difficult, and a simple story brought such joy.

I was almost to the end of the book when one of the smaller boys interrupted me, tugging on my sleeve. "Miss Alice? Miss Alice?"

"Yes?"

"Where's your horse going off to?"

I looked up in time to see Belle's hindquarters disappearing down the path into the woods. I had forgotten to tie her up. "Oh no! Stop her! Stop her!"

I scrambled to my feet and took off after her, with all nine children—I had managed to count them once they sat still—chasing after Belle along with me. They were laughing and shouting as if we were playing the greatest game in the world. I remembered how far Cora and I had ridden already and I wanted to weep at the thought of walking all the way home.

The two oldest boys outraced everyone else and managed to catch Belle, who wasn't moving very fast, lucky for me. If she had decided to trot home, we never would have caught her.

"That was fun!"

"Can we chase her again the next time you come?"

"You're coming back again, ain't you?"

I didn't know what to say.

Later that afternoon, Cora and I stopped beside the creek to eat our lunch. Sunlight dappled through the tree branches like silver coins as a gentle wind rustled through them. It was peaceful here with the creek gurgling and the birds chirping in the treetops. Crows called to each other and the sound of their cawing echoed through the hills. Every now and then the birds would grow quiet, and I had never experienced such stillness. Without realizing it, I let out a soft sigh.

"It's even nicer when the weather warms up and the leaves finish coming out," Cora said. "But I think fall's my favorite time. All the colors in the leaves, and the way they rustle under the horse's feet . . . it's real nice."

I would be long gone before fall. Before summer, even. Five more days, after today. I opened the lunch Lillie had packed for me and found a sandwich made from dinner rolls and leftover chicken from the funeral, a dill pickle wrapped in brown paper, and an apple. "Are you married?" I asked Cora after taking my first bite of the sandwich.

"Yeah, but my husband ain't around no more. When the mine shut down he went on the bum, trying to find work. Ain't been home since. Lots of people around here have lost kin one way or another."

"I walked up to the Acorn Mine outside of town the other day. How long has it been closed?"

"About three years or so. They say the folks up north don't need our coal anymore with all the factories shutting down. You know if that's true? We can't believe a word the coal company says."

"Well, in this case I'm afraid it is true. People are having a hard time all across the country. I lost my job, too, because they had to cut back on costs."

"Where'd you work?"

"In a library. I'm a librarian like Mr. MacDougal."

"Mack? He weren't really a librarian. But I suppose folks called him one because he got the library going here in town and got jobs for us."

"Is Mack from around here?"

She didn't answer right away. I didn't know if it was due to grief or a reluctance to answer my nosy question. "Folks around here don't usually like to talk about each other," she finally said. "We don't care much for gossip. Even a tiny pinch of it has been known to get folks feuding. But seeing as Mack's gone, I don't suppose it matters much." She bit off a piece of corn bread and took a moment to chew.

"Mack grew up here. His daddy worked the mines like all the rest of ours did. But Mack never was like everybody else. Always was different, and not just because his folks died and left him an orphan when he was real little. Miss Lillie once told me that she knew Mack would turn out different because he was born backwards, feet first. When most boys his age would be out catching fish or swimming in the creek, he'd be off by himself with his nose in a book. All them books in the library? They all belong to him and Lillie. The house belongs to them, too, but they let the town use it for a library."

This intriguing information raised even more questions in my mind. But now that Cora had begun talking I was afraid to interrupt and ask them, fearing she would think I was being nosy and would stop. Of course I was being nosy. I wanted to know more about Mack. He looked like everyone else in Acorn, but something about him had seemed different from all of the others, including the way he talked. I tried to think of a very general question to get her going again.

"So how long has Mack been running the library in Acorn?"

Cora glanced up at me and frowned. I felt a moment of panic when I realized I had spoken of Mack in the present tense, not in the past. But then she looked away again, shaking her head.

"Guess it's been a couple a years now. He left home and went away to Berea College, where they take poor people who can't pay for it. He could have been free and clear of this place—and he did work up north in Ohio for a while. But then he came back. I won't go into all the reasons why, because they're none of my business or yours. But he and Lillie always wanted to make things better for folks around here. And now they'll never get the chance." She paused and looked up at me. "Tell you the truth, I don't think Miss Lillie is long for this world."

"She told me that she's one hundred years old."

"Well, she's real lucky that you came along when you did to help her out. Especially now that Mack is gone."

I couldn't reply. Surely someone else would take care of her after I went home, wouldn't they?

Cora rose to her feet, stretching her shoulders and neck muscles. "If you stop to eat here by the creek again, make sure you look around for snakes before you sit yourself down." I leaped up as if I'd been bitten by one. Cora nodded and said, "They like to sun themselves on the warm stones."

"Thanks. I'll try to remember that."

"And don't forget to tie your horse up real good or she'll head home and leave you every time." The barest hint of a smile flickered on Cora's lips, the first I had seen. Then she turned away again. She helped me mount Belle and we rode farther up the creek—after I did a lot of nudging and kicking to get the horse going in the right direction, that is.

"Folks in this next cabin are kin to me," Cora said as we arrived in another clearing. "Sometimes I stay and visit awhile."

This time no one came out to meet us. We dismounted and Cora led the way inside. "Gladys . . . Clint?" she shouted from the front porch. "You got visitors." The cabin had only one room. A field-stone fireplace took up one wall, and in the dim light I saw a woman about Cora's age tending the fire. I couldn't believe that people still cooked on an open hearth instead of a stove. I smelled bread baking but didn't know how that was possible without an oven.

As my eyes adjusted to the dim light, I saw a toothless granny smiling at me as she rocked in front of the fire. She held a smoking corncob pipe clenched between her gums. Across the room a man who looked very much like a bearded version of Cora lay beneath the blankets in an iron-framed bed. Yellowing newspapers covered all of the cabin's walls, but whether they were for decoration, insulation or reading material, I couldn't tell. Perhaps all three.

Cora introduced me. "This here's the new packhorse lady, Miss Alice. That's my brother Clint"—she gestured to the man in bed—"his wife, Gladys, and that's our granny. Have a seat." She gestured to a table and chairs near the fireplace, and I sat down. Cora gave her grandmother a small pile of *Life* magazines to read, then pulled a chair over to the bed and sat down to read the newspaper to Clint. When Gladys finished tending the fire, she sat down on the edge of Clint's bed to listen, too. The newspaper was at least a month old with news items I had heard about before I left home. But it must have been news to Clint and Gladys, who shook their heads and clicked their tongues in dismay as Cora read aloud to them. Granny sat in her rocking chair, puffing smoke and staring at the pages of the magazines as if she was required to memorize them.

"Does that paper say if they're gonna get the mine started up again?" Clint asked when Cora paused to turn the page.

"Nobody's saying anything about the mine. But Miss Alice says the coal company might be telling the truth when they say the whole country's poor and out of work. It ain't just us."

"Well, that's bad news," Clint drawled. "Can't you bring us any good news?"

"I wish I could, but there just ain't any good news to bring." She turned to me. "Miss Alice, you just come from the city a week ago, didn't you? You know of any good news?"

"Me? . . . No, sorry . . . I never pay much attention to the news." They stared at me as if to ask, *Why not?* I could almost hear Gordon saying, *"You always have your nose in a book and your head in the clouds."*

Gladys must have noticed my embarrassment because she changed the subject. "Your husband come home yet, Cora?" she asked.

"Ain't heard a word from him."

"You still doing okay?"

"I manage. This here's a real good job, delivering books. I'm getting me a new route up Potter's Creek next week, so Miss Alice will be coming up to see you from now on." Cora paused and gestured to her grandmother. "Our granny can't read a single word, Miss Alice, but she sure does love looking at the pictures. See how she's smiling?" It was true. The older woman was grinning so widely that she'd had to take the pipe out of her mouth. I felt uneasy talking about Granny within earshot, but Cora said, "Don't worry. She's as deaf as a stone."

We stayed for about an hour, then mounted our horses again. "Do your brother and his wife have children?" I asked when we were on our way.

"A whole peck of them—six or seven at last count. Some are grown, the rest are in school. We'll head up to the schoolhouse on our next trip."

I wondered where the children slept—and where Granny slept for that matter. I'd only seen one bed. "Has your brother been sick long?" I asked, making conversation.

"I'll tell you what happened but don't go spreading it all around. He has a still back in the woods. Makes moonshine. Everybody up in these hills drinks it, makes it, sells it, or runs it. But Clint got into a tangle with the revenuers a few weeks ago and ended up getting shot."

"Shot? I didn't know government agents would shoot at people. They repealed Prohibition more than two years ago, you know."

"It was Clint's own fault. He started shooting first. The revenuers busted up his still, but he's gonna build another one when he's feeling better. At least they didn't throw him in jail again. Couldn't catch him, I guess."

Cora led us back to Wonderland Creek, and we headed downstream toward home. Belle cooperated for once, as eager to return as I was. About an hour later we halted in front of Mack's cabin again. I tried not to glance over at it.

"Have you been memorizing all the landmarks that I showed you today?"

"Yes. I think so." I planned to write everything down as soon as I got back to town—although I didn't know why I should bother. I would never be riding this way alone.

"Today we delivered books to the folks on the west side of Wonderland Creek," Cora said. "Tomorrow we go back up and deliver to the folks on the east side. The Howard clan lives way back up in the hills. Then there's Maggie Coots and Miss Opal. And the school's up in there, too."

"Are all of these people as excited about getting books as the people were today?"

"Oh yes, ma'am. Even the ones who can't read a word."

At last we arrived at the library. Home again. I would have loved to soak my tired bones in a hot bath, but since I hadn't seen anything resembling a tub in the house, I knew there was little chance of that happening. We unsaddled Belle and walked inside the library just as Faye and Marjorie returned. Everyone chatted as they emptied their bags, and I felt a sense of camaraderie and satisfaction that I hadn't felt in a long, long time. How wonderful to be among people who loved books as much as I did, even if they were poor and illiterate—and a little trigger-happy.

CHAPTER 12

The next day, Cora took me to the shed so she could teach me how to get Belle saddled up and ready to go. "The girls and I will still help you out, but you never know when you might need to saddle Belle by yourself when we ain't around."

I nodded, unable to imagine a time when I would get on any horse voluntarily, let alone this one. As soon as Belle saw Cora and me, she started throwing a horse tantrum. Cora tried to soothe her. "For goodness' sakes, Belle. What's gotten into you?"

"Isn't there another horse in town I could ride? One that's a little better behaved than this one?"

"I don't know of any other horses. In fact, Alma's kin is going to need the mule to do the plowing, and then she'll be without a mount. I don't know what's wrong with Belle. Maybe she misses Mack as much as we all do. Horses can be funny that way."

I knew what was wrong with her—she hated me. And the feeling was mutual.

We got Belle saddled, but as I led her up to the back door where Cora's horse and the bags of books were waiting, I noticed she was walking funny. "Cora, look . . . I think Belle is limping." I knew I sounded happy, not concerned. Cora had just said there were no more horses in town, so if Belle was injured it would be an answer to my prayers.

"Have you been cleaning her hooves every day?"

"Cleaning her hooves? No . . . I didn't know I was supposed to. And besides, I don't know how."

"Let me get the tool out of the shed and I'll show you." I watched Cora work, knowing I would never, ever, have the nerve to lift a horse's hoof in the air and clean it with a scraper. "You should give her a regular brushing, too," Cora said when she finished. I knew I couldn't do that, either. Mack would have to take care of the horse when I brought his supplies to him.

"You're going to have to show her who's boss today, Alice," Cora said as she fastened on the saddlebags. "Make her mind you."

"But she's a lot bigger than I am."

"That don't matter. Sometimes there's a kid in school who's bigger than the teacher is, but she still has to make him mind."

"Oh . . . well, you see, I never did figure out how to do that, either. I was supposed to be a teacher, but I had the same problem with some of the children that I have with Belle. They wouldn't do a thing I said."

Cora motioned for me to climb onto the bench and gave me a boost up into the saddle. Every ache and pain from yesterday throbbed in protest.

"What you need is some gumption, Miss Alice."

"What do you mean?"

"Are you this quiet and timid back home? Afraid of your own shadow?"

"I-I never thought I was. But things are so much different back home. I work in a town where we don't need to ride horses because I can take the streetcar." I wanted to add that people back home didn't get shot at, either, unless they were gangsters. And no one back home complicated my life the way Mack and Lillie had.

"What do you do with yourself back there in Illinois when you ain't working in a library?"

I had to think about it. "Well . . . I like to read books. That's mostly what I do."

"All day? That ain't living." It was the same thing Gordon had told me. I was starting to think he might have been right. Cora swung up into her own saddle and rode off toward the creek. "Come on, make Belle follow me," she called over her shoulder.

"Giddy-up," I said, nudging Belle with my knees. She didn't move. "Go! Come on now! Giddy-up!" I jiggled the reins and kicked her until she finally began to move. But she walked toward her shed, not the creek. "No! Bad horse! Not that way! Whoa!" I tried to remember everything Cora had taught me and tightened the slack in the reins to make her stop. I used my legs as I pulled the reins in the right direction. Belle's head swiveled toward the creek. "That's it. Go that way. Move!" For the first time she did what I told her to do and we soon caught up to Cora. She gave me a nod and a faint smile.

"I see you found yourself some gumption."

We rode up the creek and into the hills past Mack's cabin, which looked quiet and deserted. I wondered how he was faring without Lillie's potions and remedies. I also wondered what he had brought along in his mysterious burlap bag, and what the "work" was that he and Lillie mentioned. Cora had said the two of them were trying to make things better for the people in Acorn, but as far as I could tell, they still had a long way to go. Belle halted when she saw the cabin. She whinnied softly as if calling to Mack. I urged her forward again.

Our first stop was the Howard farm. It looked prosperous compared to some of the others, with a cow and mule and small log barn to put the animals in at night. I saw a man, a woman, and three children out in the field, busting up the clods of black earth with a plow, pitchforks, and hoes. It looked like backbreaking work. They waved when they saw us, and the smallest of the children, a ragged brown-haired boy, ran over to greet us.

"Pa says we can't have a story today, Miss Cora, 'cause there's too much work to do."

"Okay. Maybe next time, Joe-Bob. But tell your folks that this here is Miss Alice. She'll be bringing your books from now on."

"Hi, Miss Alice." He gave me a shy wave. "We finished reading all the books you brung us the last time, Miss Cora. Want me to go get them?"

I longed to tell him to please wash his hands first, which were as grubby and black as the soil. But he already had disappeared inside. Cora pulled out the new books she'd brought, and we made the exchange and moved on.

It took us the rest of the morning to get to our next stop, which was the schoolhouse. The children must have been expecting us, because they rushed out of the one-room building to greet us. The teacher stood in the doorway, smiling. Boys and girls of all ages and sizes peppered Cora with excited comments and questions, but they talked so fast that it sounded like gibberish.

"This new atlas has been a godsend," the teacher told us when we went inside the small, stone building. I felt a surge of pride when she held up Elmer Watson's prized book. "See what they've been making?" She gestured to the walls, which the children had decorated with hand-drawn maps of various countries and continents.

"This here is Miss Alice," Cora told the children, "and she's the one who brought that book here all the way from Ill-a-noise." The children applauded. They applauded! I felt like a storybook heroine.

"I don't know how we can ever thank you," the teacher said.

"No need," I said, sniffling. I silently vowed to start another book drive as soon as I got home.

The schoolhouse looked new, so I asked about it. "The government built it a year or two ago," Cora said. "It was one of those make-work projects the president is always going on and on about. What do they call it? It's the same outfit that pays us to deliver books."

"You mean the WPA? The Works Progress Administration?"

"That's it."

"The school should have a lot more students," the teacher added, "but we've been having trouble getting the parents to send us their children. Some folks think there must be a catch to it, and that they'll have to pay us money. Others don't see a need for an education since the boys will all work in the mines someday. And some folks need their children to stay home and help out with the farm work."

"Gotta get that corn in the ground," Cora added for my benefit.

We stayed for a few minutes, and I watched the teacher settle her class down to work. It amazed me that she could accomplish so much with barely any textbooks or materials. I had seen school districts back home toss out texts that were in better shape than the ones she had, and I vowed to talk to our school superintendent about donating our used ones.

Our last stop for the day was at a cabin and farmyard down the hill, not too far from the school. Most of the cabins I'd seen looked run-down, but this one was different. Spring flowers bloomed in an overflowing garden below the front porch. The yard was tidy and free from the usual piles of trash and rusting metal, the cabin windows clean. The firewood had been neatly stacked outside, and even the henhouse had a coat of white paint. A cow and several goats grazed in a spring-green pasture behind a rail fence.

The pretty dark-haired woman who came out to greet us looked as neat and well-groomed as her house and yard. Her dress and shoes would have been right in style back home in Blue Island. I guessed her age to be around thirty.

"I've been waiting for you, Cora," she said. "Do you have time for a visit?" She spoke without a Kentucky accent.

I looked to Cora for direction and she nodded. "Sure, Maggie. We got time to set a spell."

We tied up our horses and followed the woman inside. I was getting much better at climbing on and off my horse and rarely tumbled to the ground anymore when dismounting. I even remembered to use the horse's left side to get on and off.

The house was just as light and cheerful on the inside as on the outside. Muslin curtains hung over the windows, colorful rag rugs warmed the floor, and a vase of flowers brightened the table. But the cabin's most striking features were the shelves and shelves of books. I wanted to peruse them and maybe pick one or two to read, but Cora was introducing me.

"Maggie, this here is Miss Alice Ripley. She's come all the way from Ill-a-noise to help us out and is going to be bringing your books from now on."

"It's so nice to meet you, Alice. I'm Maggie Coots."

"Please, call me Allie."

As we shook hands, I heard a terrible, wracking cough coming from the next room. "That's my mother-in-law, Opal Coots," Maggie said, lowering her voice. "She isn't feeling well today, or

I would introduce you. But she's been waiting all day for her new book. She likes me to read to her in the evening. Would you like some tea, Allie? I'll pour us some."

I started to protest, remembering Cora's warning, but Maggie insisted. "Please. I would love it if you would stay so we could get to know each other." Maggie cooked on a cast-iron stove like the one in Lillie's kitchen, instead of the open hearth, and she deftly moved the kettle to a hot spot to bring it to a boil. A wooden frame in one corner of the room had an unfinished multicolored quilt stretched out on it. The cabin walls were finished on the inside, not covered with newspapers, and decorated with framed pictures. I was dying to know what made Maggie so different from the other people I had met, but didn't dare ask.

"I heard you've been staying with Miss Lillie," Maggie said as she set out matching cups and saucers and a blue china teapot. She must have seen my surprise because she smiled and added, "News travels fast around here, especially when it concerns a flatlander. How's Miss Lillie doing without Mack?"

"She's . . . she's holding up." I wanted to say that she was the same as always, tough as an old shoe.

"I have a feeling that Mack's passing will be the death of Lillie," Cora said. "You know how much that boy meant to her. It might have been one bullet, but it will kill two people."

Maggie looked away for a moment as if to control her grief. Emotion thickened her voice when she spoke again. "I was so sorry that I didn't get down for his funeral. I heard it was lovely." Then she regained control and changed the subject. "What books did you bring me today, Cora? And, Allie, you can go ahead and look through my collection if you want." She must have seen me eyeing the shelves.

"Thanks. Maybe I will." I stood and walked to the first bookshelf, tilting my head to read the spines.

"If you see one you like, you're welcome to borrow it. How long will you be staying in Acorn?"

"I-I'm not sure." It was the closest I could come to an honest answer. I quickly moved to the next bookshelf to escape Maggie's scrutiny. When the water boiled, we sat and talked about our favorite novels and authors as we sipped our tea. I liked Maggie Coots a lot and hated to leave when Cora said it was time to go. But even though Maggie's home had been gracious and cheerful, I still sensed the same aching sadness I'd felt in so many of the other places we'd stopped.

"Maggie seems different from the other people I've met," I told Cora on the way home, hoping to get her talking.

"She's a flatlander like you—no offense."

"Why is she living here?"

"She came with a group of church folks from up north. Do-gooders. You know the type. But she fell for Hank Coots, a local boy, and they ended up getting married. He died in an accident at the mine. He and Mack were best friends—and now they're both gone."

"Her cabin was very pretty inside."

"It's the only one up in these hills that has a road leading up to it. It's just a dirt road, but that's how they were able to haul the stove and the glass windows and all them other things way up here. Folks say Maggie has money from her kin up north. Never seen any of her kin down here visiting, though."

"I wonder why she stays here, now that she's widowed?"

"She takes care of her mother-in-law, Opal Coots."

"Why doesn't she take her to a hospital back home for medical treatment?"

"Ain't no cure for what Miss Opal's got. Besides, Opal won't go. Says she was born here, and she plans to die here and be buried with her kin. I give Maggie credit for not running off and leaving her."

"Can you get to Maggie's cabin by road, then? Instead of going up through the woods?"

"Sure. The road is just outside of town, a little ways past the coal company and the old mining town. But I always come this way. It's prettier."

By the time I reached home, I was certain I would never be able to sit down again. I unlaced my boots and dropped them by the kitchen door, never to be worn again. Lillie had a pot of something simmering on the stove, and I lifted the lid to take a peek. It looked like chicken stew. I hoped she had killed and plucked the ornery white chicken that pecked at my ankles every morning when I collected the eggs.

After I'd washed and changed out of my horse-scented clothes, I decided to catch up on some of the work piling up in the library. I pushed the desk chair aside, too sore to sit, and worked standing up. Lillie dozed in her usual chair in the non-fiction section. I let her sleep. The less we said to each other the better. I would be going home in a few more days, and I had no intention of getting mixed up in any more of her schemes. I glanced at the calendar on the desk and sighed, longing to cross off another day.

I was happily engrossed in my work when Lillie's voice startled me. "Where'd you ride to today, honey?" There she stood, alongside my desk. She could move around as quietly as a cat, even with her cane.

"We went up to the Howard farm—I think that was their name. The whole family was out working in the field. Then we went to the schoolhouse." I found myself smiling as I remembered being lauded as a heroine for bringing the new books.

"What about Maggie Coots? You stop and see her?"

"Yes, we stopped there, too. She asked about you, Lillie. She seemed very worried about you now that Mack is *gone*." Lillie couldn't have missed the bite in my tone, but she didn't comment on it.

"Maggie say anything else? Maybe something that sounded funny to you?"

"What do you mean? . . . No, she was very nice. She even invited us to come inside for tea."

"She ask you anything else about Mack?"

"She said she was sorry she missed his funeral."

"It figures."

"Why are you scowling like that, Miss Lillie? *What* figures?" Lillie didn't reply, and I couldn't help scowling at her in return. "I liked Maggie. We have the same taste in books. I wouldn't mind visiting her again."

Lillie laid her hand on my arm as if I was leaving this very minute to go visit her and she needed to stop me. "You be careful around Maggie Coots, honey."

"Why?"

"That's all I'm saying." She gave my arm a squeeze and released it.

"Wait. You can't give me a warning like that and not tell me why."

"Sure I can. I just did." Lillie hobbled off to the kitchen to check on her stew.

"I like Maggie!" I shouted after her. I would have stomped my foot if I thought it would do any good.

We ate supper at the kitchen table for the first time since Mack and I had eaten lunch there that first day. The fresh air and exercise must have given me a voracious appetite, because I gobbled down two bowls of Lillie's stew. "It's delicious," I told her. "Which chicken was this? I hope it was that mean little white one who pecks me all the time."

"We only eat chicken on special occasions, honey."

I stopped eating, the spoon frozen halfway to my mouth. "Is this a special occasion?"

"Nope."

"What am I eating, then?"

"Squirrel."

I dropped the spoon into my bowl with a clatter. *Squirrel?* Those cute, furry little creatures with the bushy tails? I had eaten a *squirrel?* I clamped my hand over my mouth and pushed back my chair as I felt my gorge rise.

"Where you going, honey?"

I couldn't reply. I was about to lose my supper but I didn't want to be sick. I would only have to clean it up. I tried desperately to think of something else—anything else—to clear my mind. Lillie was pulling my leg, wasn't she? How could a one-hundred-year-old woman kill and clean a squirrel? They were so small! She would have to be a very good shot. That thought was not a comforting one.

"I need some air," I mumbled. I hurried through the back door and stood outside, gulping deep breaths of fresh spring air. I tried to take my mind off food, but I couldn't help remembering Mack's funeral luncheon and all those casseroles the women had made. What else had I unknowingly eaten that day?

I decided to walk down to the shed and feed Belle, then put her to bed for the night. Dusk had fallen. I would close up the chicken coop, too—and maybe I would count them just to be sure Lillie wasn't teasing me.

My stomach had a chance to settle as I walked through the damp grass, listening to the water rushing past in the creek. Wonderland Creek. I heard a crow or maybe a blue jay scolding me in the tree above my head, and I looked up. It wasn't a blue jay. It was a fluffy gray squirrel chattering angrily as it glared at me with beady, accusing eyes.

CHAPTER 13

All day Saturday I worked in the library, carding the books
that had accumulated from everyone's routes and returning
them to their proper shelves. I thought about the people I had met
during the past two days, and I found myself choosing books in my
mind that I thought each of them might like—even though I knew
I would never ride up there to see any of them again.

Mack was on my mind, too. I had gotten used to seeing him
sprawled on the mattress in the non-fiction section, and the room
looked bare without him. Three days had passed since I had dropped
him off at the cabin in the middle of the night, and I knew he must
be running low on food. Maybe I should walk up there and bring
him some more—and remind him that he would have to make other
plans after my uncle came to take me home this week.

My thoughts were a million miles away when I heard the front
door open and close. I peeked into the hallway and saw Ike Arnett,
the fiddle player, grinning at me. "Hey there, pretty lady. You open
for business?"

I had no idea what the official library hours were. Our only walk-
in patrons had been Mamaw and her grandsons. But I shrugged
and said, "Of course. What can I do for you?"

"Can you recommend a good book to read?"

Was this another attempt to flirt with me? Ike Arnett did not
seem like the type of man who read books. But then neither

did most of the people on my route. Perhaps I was judging Ike unfairly.

"I'll be happy to help you. What types of books do you enjoy?"

"I like the kind where you can learn things. Especially about nature or about America. Mack used to pick out books for me all the time."

I led the way into the non-fiction area, hiding my surprise. "How about one of these?" I asked, pointing to a shelf of books on American history. He tipped his head, reading the titles.

"I already read this one . . . it was real good. And this one, too." He pulled a third book from the shelf and flipped through it. "Maybe I'll try this one . . . if you think I'd like it."

"I'm sorry, but I've never read that book."

"Oh. Well, I'll take it anyway and if I don't like it, I'll bring it back." He followed me to the desk like a puppy dog, and I helped him check out the book. When we were finished, he stood looking at me for a long moment. "There's something else I been meaning to ask. I know you and Miss Lillie could probably use some help around here and . . . well . . . I'd be willing to go through Mack's clothes and things for you. Take them off your hands. It must be hard for Miss Lillie to see reminders of him all over the place."

"It's very considerate of you to offer to help." But of course Mack still needed his clothes. He wasn't dead. "I-I'll ask Miss Lillie about it." I retreated to the foyer to avoid Ike's gaze, aware that I'm a terrible liar. He followed close on my heels.

"I know it might seem cruel to ask about it just a few days after Mack's funeral," he said, "but there's some folks around here who can really use some new jackets and things. I'll make sure his clothes go to good homes."

"That's very kind of you, but it might be a bit too soon . . ." My voice trailed off as I recalled the plan I had tried to concoct with Gordon, asking mourners to donate their deceased relatives' books as they planned their funerals. What had I been thinking? "I'll talk to Lillie, but she might need a little more time to grieve."

"No problem. And by the way, I know Miss Lillie has Alma and Cora and the Wireman sisters helping her—"

"The Wireman sisters?" It sounded like a singing quartet on the radio.

"Yeah, Faye and Marjorie. But if you ever need a man's help, you just let me know, okay? I'll come right over."

"Thank you. I'll do that."

I overslept on Sunday morning. In my exhaustion, I no longer noticed the rooster screeching at dawn. At home I used to awaken to the sound of tolling bells every Sunday, from my father's church next door and from the other churches scattered throughout Blue Island. It hardly seemed like Sunday without bells. Sunlight poured into my room, and when I realized how late it must be, I leaped out of bed and quickly scrambled some eggs and leftover potatoes together, determined not to let Lillie cook for me anymore.

"Is there a church nearby that I could attend?" I asked when I brought her breakfast upstairs. "I feel like I should go. After all, I missed last week because of Mack getting shot and everything."

Lillie gave me a sharp look. "Why'd you say it that way—you feel like you should go?"

"Well . . . it's Sunday. That's what we do back home. We go to church."

"Why?"

Did she really not know the answer or was she being ornery? I had a feeling it was the latter, but I sat down in the chair beside her bed and explained it to her, just in case. "It says in the Bible that we should remember the Sabbath day to keep it holy. It's one of the Ten Commandments. We're supposed to take a day off from work and go to church on Sunday."

"So that's why you go? Because you're supposed to?"

"Well, yes. Why else would people go?"

"To worship God."

"Well, of course to worship God. That goes without saying."

"No, it don't. I think it should be said. Otherwise, if people go to church because that's what they always do on Sunday, or because they think they're supposed to go, then they're going for the wrong reasons."

Lillie was being contrary, and I didn't want to argue with her. I stood up, ready to leave. "Is there a church here in Acorn or not? I didn't see a steeple when I was out exploring the town, but maybe I missed it."

"Acorn don't have a church like the one you're looking for," Lillie said. I wasn't surprised.

"Is there a church nearby that I could go to?"

"There's one over in Pottstown with a pretty white steeple, and it even has colored windows, too."

"How far away is Pottstown?"

"Well now, that depends on which horse you ride . . ." I looked up at the ceiling, praying for patience as Lillie continued. "It would take Belle a couple of hours to get you there—"

"I wasn't planning on riding Belle. I thought I would walk."

"Honey, if you're gonna walk all the way to Pottstown, then you shoulda left yesterday."

I didn't know why, but I felt like crying. "How am I supposed to go to church around here?"

"You want a little white building with a steeple and wooden pews and all that?"

"Yes—a church! Where people worship God." I nearly stomped my foot in frustration. I'd been tempted to stomp a lot lately—just like Belle.

"Don't know why you need a steeple to worship God," she mumbled as she ate a forkful of food.

"Because . . . that's what churches look like back home. Listen, just forget it. I don't need to go to church."

"I thought you just told me you was *supposed* to go."

"My father is a minister. I haven't missed a church service in my entire life, until now."

"You think God is keeping track in His big black book up there in heaven? He gonna mark you absent?" She grinned, and I knew she was mocking me. I went into my own room and closed the door.

I spent the day writing letters and reading the book Maggie Coots had let me borrow, but I had trouble concentrating on it. With luck, Uncle Cecil would arrive in two days and take me home. I pictured myself back in the parsonage, soaking in a steaming bathtub, devouring my mother's chicken and dumplings, sleeping on clean sheets. I would wallow in luxury and never take electricity or indoor plumbing for granted again. I would talk on the telephone, listen to the radio, and best of all, read books!

Realistically, I knew my life of luxury would last only a day or two before my father would present me with one of his lists. He would insist that I find productive work to do or join him and my mother in their charity projects. I wanted to start another book drive, of course, and see about getting some used textbooks for Acorn's school. But then what? The empty days that loomed ahead depressed me.

I also couldn't help wondering what would happen here in Acorn after I was gone. Who would read the last few chapters of *Treasure Island* to Faye's boys? How would Mack process and catalogue all the new books I was going to send him if he was living up in the cabin, playing dead? Did Faye and the other ladies know how to run a library? Lillie certainly couldn't do it all alone. Maggie Coots would make a perfect librarian, but then who would take care of Opal Coots all day? And why didn't Lillie trust Maggie?

These problems were not mine to worry about, I told myself. Yet I couldn't stop worrying about them.

That evening, Lillie offered to teach me how to make corn bread. "It'll go real good with the pot of beans I got cooking," she told me. "We'll have us a real nice supper." Lillie sat at the kitchen table coaching me as I mixed the cornmeal and flour and lard.

"What ingredients did you put in the beans?" I tried to ask nonchalantly. She couldn't blame me for being suspicious after she'd fed me squirrel.

"You want the recipe?"

"Sure."

"First you gotta boil the beans so they get nice and soft. Then I add onions, some home-canned tomatoes, and just a spoonful of sorghum. That's my secret ingredient. Sorghum."

"No meat?"

"A little chunk of salted meat for flavor, if you got it. Why you asking? You thinking of cooking up a batch for your folks when you get home?"

"Maybe . . ." I didn't dare look at her, afraid she would see that I was fibbing.

"If you want, I can give you my recipe for squirrel stew, too."

I could hear the laughter in her voice and felt my cheeks grow warm. "No, thank you. People back home don't eat squirrel."

"Honey, if people get hungry enough, they'll eat anything."

"Is this batter mixed enough?" I asked. I was desperate to change the subject. "Should I put it in the pan now? How hot does the oven need to be?"

"Hot enough to bake it," she said, laughing at my embarrassment. "Yes, it's ready, honey. Go on and put it in the oven."

The oven door opened with a creak and I bent to shove the pan inside. A rush of hot air made my face even redder. Sometimes I hated being a fair-skinned blonde. People could read my distress like a thermometer as the color filled or drained from my cheeks. I closed the door again and sat down across the table from Lillie to wait for the bread to bake.

"You started to tell me the other day about Sam and your husband and your son. Did you ever find your family again?"

"Didn't I finish that story?"

"No. We have time now while the corn bread bakes. I'd really like to hear it."

Lillie gazed off into the distance for a moment, as if waiting for a ship to return. Then she sighed and said, "Well, honey, it's like this. After the war ended, I waited and waited for Charley and Buster, but they never came home. Now, my old massa had three boys. One of them come home from the war okay, one come back without an arm, and one got killed up in the north someplace. Maryland, I think. He was Massa's oldest boy, so I figured Massa should know how I'm missing my own son. So I walk on over to the old plantation, and I ask him to help me find my family. But his heart's just as hard and cold as a big old stone. He won't tell me where he sold them off to. I knew he wrote it all down in that big ledger book of his. Massa wrote everything in there."

"Why wouldn't he tell you?"

"Massa and his friends lost everything they had because of that war, and they're blaming us Negro slaves for causing it. They think we shoulda been content with our life the way it was, instead of getting the folks up north all riled up about setting us free."

144

"Wasn't there another way to find out about your family?"

"Yes, I asked the Good Lord to help me find them. And a few months later, old Massa got sick. Doctors tell him they can't help him no more, so they send for me. Well, it ain't them who come for me, it's the missus. She always used to send for me when her boys was little and one of them was sick with a fever or something. Missus used to treat me real nice when Massa ain't looking. Anyway, she come all the way out to the colored town where I'm teaching school, driving the wagon herself, and she ask if I won't please come back and see what I can do for my old massa."

Lillie paused, gazing off into the distance again. I didn't know if she was going to finish her story or if she had lost her train of thought. I waited as long as I could before asking, "Did you go with her?"

"Of course I went, honey-girl."

"You helped your old master, even though he had been so mean to you?"

"Ain't I been trying to tell you that you can't be holding grudges against people? Didn't you hear me say that? What do you think Jesus is gonna say if we come walking up to those pearly gates carrying a whole sackful of grievances and grudges on our backs? Jesus is gonna ask, What's that you toting there on your back? Do you want to be opening that sack and showing Him all those ugly things? He's dressed all in white and shining like the sun, and you're coming in with a load of hate in your arms? Umm hmm. I can't imagine doing that."

I felt my cheeks growing warm again and didn't know why.

"Jesus tells us to be praying, 'Forgive us our debts just like we're forgiving others,' because He knows if we don't pray for that every single day and remind ourselves to forgive, we ain't gonna be doing it. And I need His help, honey-girl. Without it, I surely can't forgive all the people who wronged me. And unless Jesus helps me, I for sure can't forgive the man who sold my husband and my son and never will tell me where they're gone to. Umm hmm, no ma'am."

I could smell the corn bread baking, so I stood and rattled through the cupboards and drawers as I got out bowls and spoons to set the table for our dinner. By the time I sat down again, I was sure that Lillie would have forgotten our conversation and her impromptu sermon, but she started up again without coaxing.

"Yes, I know I have to forgive Massa, whether I feel like it or not, because that's what the Bible says to do. So I get into that wagon with my old missus, and I go on back to that plantation. Place looking terrible now that the war's over and ain't nobody left to take care of it like they should. Flower garden's all overgrowed with weeds, house needs paint. Inside don't hardly look like anyone's cleaned it in a while."

I nodded, imagining that it might have looked a lot like this kitchen on the day I arrived.

"Missus took me into the room where Massa lay dying, and I could see he's been all eaten up inside with disease. That's what happens when you hang on to bitterness and hatred, honey-girl. It eats you right up from the inside, just like a cancer. Massa sees me come in, and he ain't so full of vinegar and bluster no more. All the fight's gone clean out of him, and he ain't the same man. He says, 'You got something in your bag of tricks to make me well, Lillie?' So I look him all over, and I see how yellow his skin look, like he's been rubbing dandelions over himself. And I told him, 'No sir, ain't no cure for what you got, but I can fix you something to stop the pain in your bones so you can rest.' He closed his eyes and didn't say another word. He's too proud to ask a slave like me for anything else."

"Too proud? Even though he was dying?"

"Pride has a way of turning our hearts hard over the years unless we let God soften them up again. That's why God puts all kinds of troubles in our path, hoping they'll do the trick—just like cooking them beans in hot water all day turns them soft. Our trials are supposed to turn us toward God, but we whine and complain and wish someone would turn down the fire so we could have our old life back the way it was."

She paused again and I didn't prod her to continue her story. I had the feeling her sermon was meant for me, and I didn't want to hear it. I got up and peeked in the oven again. The corn bread was nearly done. "Shall I dish up the beans now?" I asked. "That way they can cool a little before we eat them."

She smiled at me. "Sure, go ahead, honey."

I took my time ladling the beans into our bowls, pumping water to fill our glasses, rinsing the bowl I had used to mix the corn bread. All that time, Lillie watched me in serene silence. "I think the bread is done," I said, peeking at it again. I took it out and set the hot pan on the table, then got out a knife to cut it.

"Let's say grace," Lillie said when I sat down again. I bowed my head but didn't hear a word of her prayer. I wanted to hear the end of Lillie's story and find out if she ever found her husband and son again, but not if she was going to preach to me.

"Bread's real good," she said after taking a bite. "Anyway, the missus pulled me aside after I left Massa's room, and she begged me to help him. She say he ain't been sleeping nights, he's in so much pain. 'I'll pay any price you ask, Lillie,' she says. So I tell her the only price I want is to know where Massa sold my Charley and little Buster. 'It's all written down in that book of his,' I tell her. 'Buster must be twelve years old by now and maybe he forgot all about me, but I still want to see him.' "

Lillie ate a few spoonfuls of her beans and another bite of corn bread. "So, the missus and I, we made a deal. Next time I come out to the plantation, I brung some of that same potion I gave Mack—only not near as strong. And Missus gave me a piece of paper all folded up that tells me where Charley and Buster was sold." Lillie returned to her dinner.

I waited until I could no longer stand the suspense. "Where were they? Were they close by? Did you find them?"

She chewed the last of her corn bread and swallowed. "That was mighty delicious, honey. I'm as stuffed as a possum." She grinned at me in a strange, mischievous way.

Possum? Was Lillie hinting that the salted meat had been possum? I wanted to know—yet I didn't want to know. The meal would sit much better in my stomach if I didn't know the truth. Lillie watched me, waiting. When I didn't question her, she yawned and said, "I'm so tired I can hardly keep my eyes open. Will you help me upstairs, honey?"

Her voice had been slowing down as she'd told her story, and her tiny body sagged lower and lower in the chair. I let her lean on me as we went up to her bedroom. She was already wearing her nightgown—sometimes she wore it all day. I sat on the edge of her bed after she had climbed in, hoping to hear the rest of her story.

"Don't be hanging on to hard feelings, honey," she said instead. "Make sure you empty that sack every night before you go to bed. That's what the Good Book says, you know. Don't let the sun go down while you're still angry."

"Aren't you going to tell me more of your story? Did you find your family?"

"Another day, honey. I'll tell you that story another day."

I cleaned up the kitchen and went up to bed early. I tried to read Maggie's novel by lamplight, but I couldn't stop thinking about Lillie's words of advice. I didn't want to be carrying a sackful of old hurts and grievances when I arrived at the pearly gates to meet Jesus. I knew I had to forgive Lillie and Mack for all the trials they had put me through. And I also knew that I hadn't been very kind to my best friend, Freddy.

She had never dated very much and never had a steady boyfriend. Her father had been ill the entire time we were in high school. Then shortly before he died, her mother had become ill. Freddy was always helping other people, including me, yet she'd never seemed jealous when I'd started dating Gordon, even though she didn't have a boyfriend. I regretted acting like a spoiled child just because Gordon had invited Freddy to the movies.

I laid my book aside and sat up in bed to write a letter to Freddy, even though I would probably arrive home before my letter did. Some things were easier to say in a letter than face-to-face.

Dear Freddy,

I've had time to think about a lot of things while I've been away, and I no longer have any hard feelings toward Gordon for breaking up with me. You and he were both right; we never did have very much in common. And I know that I've done some things to hurt his feelings—like calling him by the wrong name, for instance, and getting us thrown out of the movie theater.

I want you to know that I still think Gordon is a really nice person, and he deserves a sweet girlfriend like you. If you would like to accept his invitation and go to the movies with him sometime, I wouldn't be mad at either one of you. I honestly don't mind, Freddy. The truth is, I've come to realize that I never was in love with him—not in the way that people describe love in all the novels I've read. And when I do fall in love someday, that's how I want to feel about the man I marry—the same way women in all of my favorite books feel. You deserve to find a good man like Gordon. In fact, I think you and he would be great for each other. Please accept his invitation and go to the movies with him, Freddy. I would love to see both of you live happily ever after.

Your dearest friend always,

Allie

Tears ran down my face as I folded the letter and put it in the envelope. I was crying, and I didn't know why.

CHAPTER 14

I fixed breakfast on Monday morning with a smile on my face. Only two more days until I headed home. I was mixing flour and lard to make biscuits when Lillie suddenly appeared in the kitchen doorway. "You're up awfully early," I said to her. "Are you feeling all right?"

"I come down to help you pack some food and things for Mack before the other gals get here. And I need you to give him this letter from me when you see him today." I quickly wiped my hands on my apron as she handed me a sealed envelope.

"Today? But I'm not going anywhere today except to the post office. Cora said she only rides up Wonderland Creek twice a week and I was just up there on Friday—"

"You're going today, honey. Mack will be all out a food by now. Besides, I need to know if he's okay. You never know what might happen with gunshot wounds. They don't always heal up like they're supposed to. Anything can happen."

I opened my mouth to ask if she was in the habit of treating gunshot wounds on a regular basis, then decided not to. For all I knew, she might be the one inflicting them on people, waving that rifle around the way she did.

"Listen, Lillie. I can't ride a horse up into the woods by myself. I don't think I'm ready—"

"Now, now . . . you're as ready as you'll ever be. You go on out to the shed and fetch me an empty sack to put Mack's food in. I'll scramble the eggs this morning."

"I'm in the middle of making biscuits—"

"Honey, I don't need any more of your biscuits. I only have half a dozen teeth left in my head, and I need to hang on to them as long as I can."

I would have been insulted, but I knew she was right. I had bent a knife while trying to cut into one of my biscuits to put butter on it. I untied my apron and went down to the shed in search of a feed sack, scheming for a way to talk Lillie out of this. Belle stomped and kicked as soon as she saw me, throwing her little horse fit even after I dumped a huge portion of grain into her trough to empty the sack.

"Miserable animal . . ." I mumbled as I carried the bag up to Lillie. She stood at the stove, frying eggs and issuing orders as I filled the bag with onions and potatoes and a couple of Mason jars of canned goods. Just because I was filling the sack didn't mean I intended to deliver it on horseback. All through breakfast I found myself wondering how long it would take me to walk up to Mack's cabin carrying the heavy sack. I was cleaning up the breakfast dishes when the packhorse ladies arrived. Lillie hobbled into the library to greet them.

"Morning, gals," I heard her say. "Honey-girl decided she wants to ride on her own today. Could you all help her pick out some books to take? And, Faye, can you get Belle saddled up for her?"

I sank down at the kitchen table with my head in my hands as I heard them agree. Faye patted my back and said, "Good for you, Allie," on her way through the kitchen and out to the shed.

"Better get your boots laced up," Lillie said when she shuffled into the kitchen again and saw me sitting there.

"I can't do this, Lillie."

"Of course you can."

I shook my head, no longer caring if she pulled out a rifle and shot me.

"What's the matter, honey? You looking awful pale, even for a white gal. You about to faint on me?"

"Yes! Can't you see that I'm terrified? That stupid horse gives me nothing but trouble, even when Cora is with me, and I'm scared to death to be out there in the woods with that animal all by myself. What if she won't obey me? What if she goes the wrong way and we get lost? What if she throws me off? I can't do it, Lillie. I can't!"

"Now, now . . . you dry them tears, honey." She handed me a dish towel. "Did you pray this morning and ask the Good Lord to watch over you? Help you in all your ways?"

"No. I didn't know you were going to make me go anywhere." Besides, it seemed presumptuous to expect a great big God to care about that ridiculous horse and me. God had much bigger things to worry about—like homeless people and the Great Depression.

"Come on, then. Let's pray." Lillie took both of my hands in hers, gripping them tightly as if trying to squeeze all the fear out of me like juice from an orange. She closed her eyes and shouted up at the ceiling, "Oh, *Lord*! Remove this child's *fear* in *Jesus'* name! In *Jesus'* name give her the *courage* she needs and the *faith* she needs to *believe* in you and in your *power*, Lord Jesus!" With each word that Lillie punctuated, she squeezed my hands tighter and tighter until I could feel my bones crunching together and my blood vessels closing off. "Show her that she's your *child*, Lord. And that she can do *all* things through Christ, who gives her *strength*!"

If she didn't stop praying soon, I'd be too crippled to hold the reins. "Amen," I breathed. "Amen."

She opened her eyes and looked down at me in surprise. "You all prayed up already?"

"Yes . . . yes! I'm ready." I would have said anything to get Lillie to release her death grip. She gave my hands a final squeeze and released them. They flopped into my lap, as limp as damp laundry. I could see no way out of this task. Lillie had trapped me again. Like it or not, I would be forced to ride up Wonderland Creek on my own for the first time.

"I got a feeling the Good Lord has a special job for you today, back in those hills," she said.

The hair on my arms rose. "A job? What kind of job?"

"I don't know, but I'm thinking He wants you to be a blessing to somebody today."

152

I stared at her. I had no idea what she was talking about.

"Okay now," Lillie said with a grin. "I'm gonna go on out and have a little talk with my horse. Belle is my horse, you know."

"What do you need a horse for? You're a hundred years old."

"I use to ride all through these hills on horseback, delivering babies and tending folks. Not on Belle, though. Somebody give Belle to me a few years back to thank me for saving his life."

"Some thank-you. She's as mean as a snake."

"Mean? No . . . Mack says she's as sweet as can be. I never did get to ride her, though. Now, if I had me a wagon, I suppose I could hitch her up to it . . ."

"She hates me."

"Horses don't know how to hate, honey. Only people are that stupid. But come on. Let's go outside, and I'll have a talk with her."

Faye and the others had Belle all saddled up, loaded with books and ready to go. They had ridden off to make their own deliveries and had tied Belle to the post near the back door. The horse snorted and pranced as usual when she saw me, but the moment Lillie limped through the kitchen door, Belle stilled. Lillie stretched out her bony hand, and Belle lowered her head as if bowing to her. She let Lillie stroke the long white blaze down the middle of her muzzle and rub her ears.

"Belle, honey? I need you to be a good girl today and mind what honey-girl says." Lillie spoke so softly I had to lean close to hear her. "Me and Mack need her help, so I need you to treat her just as nice as can be, okay?"

Belle kept her head bowed, blinking her huge brown eyes as if she really were listening to Lillie's words. The contrast between the tiny, frail, old woman and the enormous horse couldn't have been greater. Lillie could have fastened the strap beneath Belle's belly without bending over. "Yes, now . . ." she soothed. "That's a good girl. You're my good girl, ain't you, Belle?"

By the time she gave Belle's shoulder a final pat and turned to me, the horse was standing so still and calm, she might have just returned from the taxidermist. Could this really work? I didn't trust Belle. She probably would resort to her usual tricks as soon as Lillie was out of sight.

"Belle promised me she'll be on her best behavior today," Lillie said.

"You speak horse language, too, besides all your other talents?" Fear made me sarcastic, but Lillie didn't seem to notice.

"I can teach you to talk to her, if you want. A horse will do whatever you ask if she knows what you're asking. And if she knows you're listening to what she has to say." I stood with my hands on my hips, certain that Lillie was making this up. "For instance," she continued, "when a horse flattens both ears back on her head, she's irritated."

"She does that a lot."

"When she blinks her eyes like she been doing just now, that means she's thinking things over. And see how she's got her hind leg cocked up? That tells you she's relaxed. But you gotta watch out. If her leg is cocked *and* her ears go back, she's getting ready to kick you."

I took a step backward, just in case.

"And if she starts pawing the ground, she's going down—and taking you with her if you're on her back."

"What do I do then?"

"Don't worry. Belle promised she'd behave for you. Horses are simple creatures, honey. They can go forward and backward, left and right, up hills and down hills. You just gotta tell them which one you want."

I had my doubts. And as Lillie looked me in the eye, I was certain that she could read all of them. "It's time, honey," she said quietly. "Go ahead and climb on."

I moved the bench around to Belle's left side. My arms and legs trembled so badly I could barely pull myself up and onto her back. Lillie untied the reins and handed them to me, then passed the sack of food up to me.

"You'll be fine, honey. The Good Lord's gonna watch over both of you today. You gonna be a blessing to somebody, I just know it." She grinned, watching from the doorway as Belle started to move—in the right direction, for once—toward the creek. So far, so good. Belle found the trail and walked slowly up the creek bank, exactly like I wanted her to. I glanced over my shoulder just before the woods swallowed up the trail and saw Lillie waving at me. I didn't dare let go of the reins to wave in return.

154

This was crazy! I was on a horse all by myself, riding into the woods, alone. Alone! Freddy and my family would never believe me when I told them about this—I barely believed it myself! At home the streets and sidewalks bustled with traffic and streetcars, and there were always other people around. Out here, there were only birds twittering and branches rustling—and the deep silence of the trees.

Part of me was terrified and a little angry at how I'd been coerced into this. But at the same time, I saw a side of myself that I hadn't known existed. For the first time in my life I was having an adventure, not reading about one in a book. I was actually doing it! And all of the emotions that I used to feel when reading an exciting story—fear, suspense, dread, exhilaration—were intensified a hundred times in real life.

Belle plodded up the hill, going deeper into the forest. The woods seemed huge and empty. Every bad thing that could happen in a fairy tale happened in the woods. But as much as I feared the forest, I was much more afraid of Belle. What would I do if the stupid horse decided to give me a hard time now that Lillie and Cora weren't around to help me? I had been riding for only two days, hardly enough time to get the hang of it. But I comforted myself with the thought that this was the last time I would have to ride Belle. Tomorrow or the next day my uncle would arrive and take me home. Today all I had to do was deliver the books, then stop and have a talk with Mack. I'd tell him he would have to make other arrangements. In fact, he should ride back to the library with me and take care of Lillie and Belle and all of his books himself.

Belle paused when we reached Mack's cabin at the top of the hill as if she wanted to pay him a visit. I let her catch her breath. "We'll stop on the way home," I promised her. "People don't like it when we're late with their books." Belle shook her head, then started walking again.

I was beginning to relax a little when I remembered how the horse had scented the wildcat on the night Mack and I rode up here. A chill shivered through me. Wildcats lived in these woods. Cora had mentioned snakes, too. I had been afraid to ask if there were bears, fearing her answer. Did wild animals come out to hunt in the daytime? What would I do if Belle smelled a wildcat again and halted? It didn't take me long to answer my own question: I would let her turn around and gallop home!

I began to feel more and more frightened. I didn't know if Belle sensed my fear or not, but she suddenly stopped. "What's wrong?" I whispered. She snorted in return. I looked all around. I sniffed the air the way that Mack had. I listened. The only sounds were the wind in the trees and a crow cawing. I nudged Belle's sides and jiggled the reins. "Come on, girl. Let's go." She wouldn't move forward. I was about to panic when I realized that we were at the ford. We were supposed to cross the creek here and take the trail to June Ann Larkin's cabin.

"You're right," I said aloud. "I'm sorry . . . thank you for noticing." I turned her to the left, and she plodded across the creek and up the trail to the Larkin place. I shook my head, embarrassed with myself. Not only was the horse smarter than me, but now I was talking to her the way Lillie did.

Before long, the cabin came into sight. Four days had passed since I'd been here and I wondered if June Ann's baby had been born. As soon as we came into the clearing, her dog bolted out from behind the house, barking and snarling. Belle halted. As Rex flung himself at the rickety fence, trying to reach us, June Ann came to the door and called him back. She was still very pregnant. I rode up to the gate and slid to the ground, remembering to tie up Belle. June Ann waddled forward to meet me and gave me an awkward hug.

"Oh, thank the Good Lord you're here, Allie. I'm all alone and I'm scared half to death!" A shiver went through me. Her eyes were red-rimmed, and she sniffled as if she'd been crying. There was no sign of Wayne or the mule out in the field.

"Why? What's wrong?" If something had scared June Ann, what in the world could I do about it? I was more terrified of these woods than she was and more of a stranger to them. I didn't know how to shoot a gun. I glanced around nervously but didn't see any imminent danger. "What's wrong?" I asked again.

She didn't reply. Instead, she doubled over, holding her stomach and uttering the most heartrending moan I had ever heard. My heart slithered down my chest and dropped into my stomach. I knew what was wrong, and now we both had a good reason to be terrified. "June Ann? Are you having the baby?"

"I reckon so . . . Oh, it hurts so bad!"

"Where's your husband?"

The pain finally seemed to ease. June Ann stopped moaning and stood a little straighter. She lifted her apron and wiped the sweat from her face. "He rode off on the mule to fetch the midwife. You didn't pass him on the way up, did you?"

"No. I didn't see anybody."

"Well, thank heaven you're here. I was so scared, being here all by myself. You can't even imagine how much it hurts! Like I'm about to *die*! Please stay with me. *Please*, Allie?"

"Okay . . . okay . . . I'll stay. But I should warn you, I don't know anything at all about having babies. Back home they always chased the unmarried girls away whenever it was a woman's time so we wouldn't see what goes on. I think they were afraid we'd never want to get married or have children if we found out what it's like." I didn't tell June Ann, but in my experience, the secrecy only made girls like me even more frightened of the whole mysterious process.

"Oh, I seen babies birthed before," she said with a wave of her hand. "My mama had eight kids and I was the oldest. It ain't that I don't know how it's done. But it just hurts so bad! No wonder my mama used to scream like she was being torn in two. And my baby ain't even coming out yet."

Thank heaven for that.

"Maybe we should go inside," I said. "Don't you want to lie down or something?" I was afraid that June Ann might double over in pain again any minute.

"Okay. Come on in."

I followed her inside, but it was so dark and dreary and smoky in the windowless cabin that I was immediately sorry for suggesting it. As near as I could tell in the gloom, the house was much like Cora's brother's cabin with an open hearth and simple furnishings. An iron-framed bed stood in one corner.

"Do you want me to light a lamp?" I asked her.

"We can't waste lamp oil. Wayne was saving up for glass windows, but then the mine shut down. I told him never mind. The cabin stays warmer in the winter without windows. There ain't as many drafts."

I stood in the middle of the dark room feeling helpless. "Is there anything I can do? I don't know what to do. How far away does the midwife live? Will it take her very long to get here?"

"Well, it depends on which horse she's riding—"

Before I could stop myself, I groaned. I should have been used to that answer by now, but I wasn't. It frustrated me every time.

"What's wrong?" June Ann asked.

"Nothing . . . Do you think they'll get here soon?"

"Wayne says it might be a while because our mule don't like to be ridden. He might have to walk a spell if it starts acting up."

"How long ago did he leave?"

She shrugged. "I don't know. At least an hour. Wayne should be pretty near to Ida's place by now, but if she ain't there, he'll have to go fetch Sadie, and who knows how long that'll take."

My knees went weak. I needed to sit down even if June Ann didn't want to. I groped my way to the table and pulled out a chair, not waiting to be invited. June Ann stood beside me.

"They say the first baby takes a long time, but my pains started about sunrise and I'm already hurting real bad."

"Do you have any neighbors I could fetch? The other day I brought books to a family a little ways up the creek, and they had a whole pile of kids."

"You mean the Sawyers?"

"Yes, that's the name. Mrs. Sawyer must know a lot more about giving birth than I do. I could ride up there and be back in a half hour or so."

June Ann gripped my arm. "Please don't leave me all alone!"

"H-how about your family? Do they live nearby? My mother always stays with my sisters and helps them out when they're expecting." Fear was making me babble. Surely June Ann's mother would have come by now, if that were possible.

"Wayne won't let me ask my mama, because his kin and mine are feuding."

"What are they feuding about?" I wasn't supposed to ask nosy questions, but it was all I could think of to say as I tried to stay calm and pass the time. June Ann was making me very nervous as she stood beside me, swaying back and forth and holding her belly as if rocking without a chair.

"Well, the story is that the feud started over money. My great-granddaddy and Wayne's great-granddaddy was best friends. They came upon a whole pile of money, but they buried it in the ground and never said where. When they both died, each family accused the other family of stealing it instead of sharing. There's been a lot of fighting over the years, and the families stopped talking to each other. Their children weren't supposed to marry each other, but Wayne and me did get married and now everyone turns their backs on us. We was doing okay without their help until they had all that trouble and the mine had to shut down."

"What trouble?"

"You know, when Hank Coots got killed and . . ." She paused, and I saw the color wash out of her face as if lifting a drain stopper. She started panting as though she had just run up a steep hill. Then she doubled over again, moaning and groaning like it was the end of the world.

I leaped to my feet, terrified. Should I rub her back? Hold her hand? I began to pray, silently crying out for help, meaning every word of it for once. I had been forced to do so many ridiculous things since coming here, but please, God, *please*, don't make me deliver a baby!

At last June Ann's pain eased. She stopped moaning and gave a heavy sigh. "Sorry. The booklet Cora brought me says that you can tell when the baby's coming by how close together the pains get."

"How close are they?"

She shrugged. "I don't know. I don't have a clock or anything. How long you been here?" She looked at me and broke into a smile. "Goodness' sakes, you look as scared as I am, Allie. Look at you! You're as white as a sack of flour. I'm the one having the baby. You better sit down again." I did.

"I am nervous, June Ann, I'll admit it. I've been trying to remember everything I've read in novels about delivering babies. Aren't we supposed to boil water or something?"

"I don't know. Go ahead and boil some if you think it'll help."

It also seemed to me that a lot of women in novels died in childbirth, but I didn't mention that to June Ann. "I'll get some water if you tell me where it is."

"The well's out back. You can fill that kettle there on the hook."

June Ann already had a fire going in the fireplace, but I stoked it and added more wood, then grabbed the cast-iron kettle. It wasn't hard to find the pump out back, but it was impossible to get any water to come out of it. I worked the handle up and down, up and down, until my arm felt like it might pull out of its socket. At last the water began to trickle, then gush. I filled the kettle and hauled it back inside, turning the fire hook so the kettle would hang over the flames. I prayed the entire time I worked. Really prayed, talking to God the way my father did when he beseeched His help.

Done. The water was heating on the fire. I had no idea what I was supposed to do with it once it boiled, but at least it would be ready when the midwife got here. *Please, God, get the midwife here! Soon!* June Ann watched me in mild amusement. I wondered what to do next.

"How about if I read a book to you?" I asked. "It might take your mind off everything."

Her eyes brightened. "Did you bring me another book?"

"As a matter of fact, I did." I got it out of my saddlebags, and since June Ann couldn't afford to light a lamp, I dragged one of the chairs over to the open door and sat down to read. June Ann couldn't stay seated, nor did she want to lie down on the bed. She paced back and forth as I read to her, stopping every now and then to double over and moan.

"Go on. Keep reading," she would say after the pain faded away.

By the time I reached chapter three, I figured it must be lunchtime. I was hungry. I had brought a sandwich with me, so I got it out of my saddlebag and offered half of it to June Ann.

"No thanks. I don't feel so good." No sooner had she spoken than another labor pain struck and she doubled over, gripping her stomach. All of a sudden water began to gush as if she had dumped a kettle full of it on the floor. I jumped aside as some of it splashed onto my boots.

"What's happening? June Ann! Is it . . . is it the baby? Is the baby coming?" I held my breath, waiting while she continued to grit her teeth and groan.

"Oh, Lord! It hurts, it hurts! Make it stop!"

But I had a feeling that the only time the pain would stop was when the baby arrived, and I certainly didn't want to pray for that. She finally stopped moaning. June Ann swayed in place and leaned against the table as if she felt dizzy. I grabbed her arm and eased her onto a chair.

"What happened? Are you okay?"

"Sorry, Allie. I'm so sorry. I don't reckon the baby's coming yet, but my sack of waters just broke."

"What does that mean?"

"Means the baby's gonna come for sure now. But look at this mess!" She started to rise.

"No, stay there. You need to sit down. I'll clean it up. Tell me where the mop is and I'll do it. Do you want to change your clothes? And don't you want to lie down?"

"I don't have any other clothes . . . and it hurts too much to lay down." I managed to mop up the water with some rags, then June Ann asked me to continue reading. It was a short book, and if the midwife didn't come soon, I'd be reading "the end" with a baby on my lap. Every time I turned a page I prayed that the midwife would arrive before the baby did.

Finally, June Ann's dog started to bark. I heard horses galloping up to the cabin. "Thank God!" I breathed. And I meant it. Wayne Larkin hurried into the cabin with Miss Ida, the midwife, and I was so relieved I wanted to hug them both.

The midwife made June Ann lie down so she could look her over, feeling her bulging belly. "It ain't time yet," Ida said, looking at me. "May as well be on your way."

I went to June Ann's bedside to say good-bye. "Thanks for staying with me," she said. "I'm so glad we're friends. You don't know how much it means to me to have a friend. You'll come back again, won't you?"

Guilt squeezed my heart when I remembered that I would be returning to Illinois soon. I didn't have the courage to tell her.

"Sure, June Ann. I'll stop by on my way home today. Maybe I'll get to see your new baby."

By now it was afternoon. I couldn't decide whether to continue with my route or head home. I was too rattled to think straight. But when I got to the creek, Belle surprised me by turning upstream. Twenty minutes later, I recognized the trail marker—the pine tree and two rocks—and headed up to the Sawyers' cabin.

"You're back! You're back!" the children shouted when they saw me. They insisted that I dismount and read from the storybook I had brought them. I explained to Mrs. Sawyer why I was so late, but she didn't seem to take much interest in her young neighbor. I didn't ask why.

My last stop was at the home of Cora's brother Clint and his wife, Gladys. He was still bedridden. "Got any news today?" he asked. I knew that the other librarians not only brought books but also news of the outside world. Yet I had to be careful, as Cora had said, not to be nosy or spread gossip.

"Do you know June Ann Larkin?" I asked.

"Her clan is kin to me," Gladys said.

"Well, she's having her baby today. Her husband, Wayne, just arrived with the midwife." Gladys seemed as disinterested as Mrs. Sawyer had been. She clamped her lips shut and didn't say another word. I had half a mind to give her Lillie's speech about holding grudges. Didn't anyone care that June Ann was lonely living way up in the woods? How could their families possibly allow a feud over money to separate them from their children?

By the time I turned toward home, my hips ached, my tailbone felt bruised, and my legs were weary from hanging on to the big horse's sides. But Belle never once gave me a rough time, even when we reached the lower ford and I urged her across the creek to return to June Ann's house.

Wayne was out in the field busting clods again. Rex tore out of the house to snarl at me in greeting, but the midwife called him back. "June Ann had a baby girl," she called out to me. "It went pretty quick for her first one. Healthy baby, too. I'd say about seven pounds. Want to see her?"

I climbed down and went inside the cabin. "Oh my!" I breathed when I saw the newborn lying at June Ann's side. She was so tiny yet so perfect, with a halo of reddish fuzz encircling her head, the same color as June Ann's hair. And I had played a tiny part in her birth. June Ann looked flushed and exhausted. "How are you?" I asked.

"Tired. I feel like somebody turned me inside out."

"She's beautiful, June Ann. What are you going to name her?"

"Wayne ain't made up his mind yet. He ain't too happy about her."

"Why not? She's perfect."

"He wanted a boy to help out with the farm. I told him I'll try and do better next time." She wiped a tear from her eyes. I wanted to walk out to the field and punch Wayne Larkin in the nose.

"Don't cry, June Ann. She's beautiful."

"Yeah, I guess."

The midwife offered me a cup of chamomile tea from the water I had thoughtfully pumped and boiled, but I shook my head. "It's getting late. I need to go. And June Ann needs to rest."

"You're gonna come back and finish reading the story to me, ain't you?" she asked.

I nodded, aware that I was lying. I was returning home to Blue Island. I would never see June Ann and her baby again. My heart ached for her. She wasn't much more than a child herself and too young to be a mother. But if she followed the example of the other women in these hills, she would be pregnant again by next week.

"Thanks for staying with me, Allie."

"You're welcome. I'm glad I could help." And very glad the baby hadn't come while I'd been alone with her.

I told her good-bye and tiptoed out.

CHAPTER 15

The sun had dipped below the hills, lengthening the shadows, when I left the Larkin farm. I'd noticed that twilight—that beautiful, purple time of day when the glaring sun is gone but the stars have yet to come out—lasted longer here than it did back home. In the flat Midwest, the sun could sink below the prairie horizon within moments. But here in the mountains, twilight—my favorite time of day—lingered like a good story, well told.

Belle headed through the woods to the creek, then turned all by herself and climbed the steep hill to Mack's cabin. I was much later than I should have been, and I wondered if Mack and Lillie were worried about me. It would serve them right if they were, especially after all of the "favors" they had forced me to do. I decided not to get off the horse. I would hand Mack the bag of food, remind him that my aunt and uncle were coming any day, and ride back to the library.

Belle took me right up to the porch. She might have gone up the steps and through the open door if I hadn't stopped her.

"Mack?" I called. "Mack, it's me, Allie."

No answer, no sign of life. The spooky cabin was dark inside. Had Mack starved to death or died of his gunshot wound since I'd dropped him off? The last thing I wanted to see was his real dead body, but I knew that Lillie would send me right back up the creek if I didn't investigate. I slid off the horse, tied her to the porch railing, and called out again. "Mack? . . . Mack, are you here?"

I heard rustling noises, then a voice coming from somewhere in the woods. "Shh! Don't call my name. Are you crazy?" A shadowy figure emerged from the bushes alongside of the cabin. I was relieved to see him alive, but did he have to be so rude?

"*Sorry.* I keep forgetting that you're *dead.*"

"If you aren't careful, I might be."

I was tempted to say, *Good,* but then remembered Lillie's warning about holding a grudge. "Sorry," I mumbled again.

Mack came closer, and I barely recognized him at first. He had cut his long hair and shaved his beard and mustache. He looked ten years younger. In fact, he looked quite civilized.

"You look so different! I never would have recognized you."

"That's the whole idea. I'm glad it worked." He grinned, and in the fading light I noticed an endearing dimple in his cheek that made him look like a schoolboy. Belle whinnied when she saw him and snuggled up to him like a long-lost lover. He stroked her neck as he stood looking at me. "I was starting to get worried about you. I saw you go upstream this morning all alone and figured you should have been heading back this way a long time ago. You get lost?"

"Of course not. I've been working. June Ann Larkin had her baby today, and I stayed with her until the midwife came so she wouldn't be alone. Then I delivered the rest of my books." I was proud of myself for sounding poised and professional, not at all like the shivering, fearful girl whom Lillie had prayed for this morning.

"That was nice of you. Is June Ann okay?"

"I just stopped by the Larkin place a few minutes ago and saw the baby. She had a little girl and—" I stopped. Mack was looking at me the way children look at puppies. "What? Why are you looking at me that way?"

"You're smiling, Miss Ripley. I don't think I've seen you smile once since the day you arrived."

"Well, is it any wonder? How could anyone smile after all of the ridiculous things you and Lillie have put me through?"

Mack backed away, holding up his hands. "Sorry I mentioned it. It's just that . . . you're awfully pretty when you smile."

"Well, thanks. That's just what I needed to complete my day—a backhanded compliment from a dead man. Here's the food Lillie packed. And she sent you a letter." I untied the bag, pulled out the sealed letter, and handed it to him.

"Do you mind if I read this now?" he asked, holding it up.

"Go ahead. Far be it from me to ask nosy questions."

He tore open the envelope and pulled out a single sheet of lined paper. I couldn't read what it said in the dusky light, but I could see that the message was brief. When he finished, he tucked the letter and envelope into his shirt pocket and gave me a weak smile. "Leave it to Lillie to figure out a plan."

"Do I dare ask what she's plotting this time?"

He looked away as if unable to meet my gaze. "Don't worry, Lillie's plans always work out for the best."

"Good. Well . . . I want to get home before dark." I set the food sack on the porch, then untied Belle and walked around to her left side. I had every intention of getting on my horse and riding into the sunset, just like the heroines did in all of the Western novels I'd read. But no matter how hard I tried, I couldn't stretch my foot high enough to reach the stirrup. I glanced around for a tree stump or a chair, but of course there weren't any. The porch step wasn't high enough.

"Alice, wait. Don't go yet. Stay and talk to me for a while. It gets awfully lonely up here with no one to talk to all day."

"You should have thought of that before you decided to stage your own funeral. Haven't you ever noticed how lonely most cemeteries are?"

"Please stay." Mack stood beside Belle, stroking her neck and shoulder. The horse leaned into him adoringly, like a melting chocolate bar. My rear end needed a rest, and besides, I would have to find something to stand on before trying to make a dignified exit.

"I guess I could stay a few minutes."

"Good. I was just getting ready to cook up a batch of morels when you arrived. You're welcome to share them with me."

"A batch of what?" I remembered eating squirrel—and possibly possum—and suddenly had trouble swallowing.

"Morels. They're mushrooms. You ever try them?"

"No. And I'm not about to." I had no intention of eating anything that might drug me or turn out to be poisonous. I once read a crime novel in which the villain drugged someone senseless with mushrooms. I looked at the wreck of a cabin in front of me and asked, "How are you able to cook anything in that hovel?"

"I don't cook in there. I can't risk anyone seeing smoke coming from the chimney. I built a fire back in the woods. Come on, I'll show you. It'll only take a minute." He turned toward the bushes, motioning for me to follow him. I didn't move. "What's the matter?" he asked when he looked back and saw that I hadn't budged.

"The truth is . . . I don't quite trust you."

"I'm devastated, Miss Ripley." He tried not to smile but couldn't help himself. "I assure you, I have nothing up my sleeve . . . either one. Come on, the morels are all washed and waiting to be cooked."

"Where do you get clean water way out here?"

"There's a whole creek full of it down there." He walked toward me and reached for my hand. "Come on, I won't bite."

My heart began to beat in a way that it never had before. Mack's hand was much rougher than my boyfriend Gordon's had been, but then Gordon worked in an office and didn't have to forage around in the woods all day. I wasn't afraid of Mack in the usual sense. He didn't seem like a dishonorable man—if I could ignore the fact that he had faked his own death and that someone hated him enough to try to kill him. I wasn't frightened of him, but I was wary of being tricked. What new surprises might be in store for me now that I was letting Mack tow me deeper into the forest?

Sticks and brush crunched beneath my feet as we hiked. Belle followed us like a huge brown shadow. I smelled the campfire before I saw it, hidden in a gully, surrounded by rocks. Mack had collected a pile of wood, and the campfire glowed with hot coals. The little glade formed a natural room with stones to sit on and a large flat rock that served as table. On it were a cast-iron frying pan and a tin plate containing the ugliest mushrooms I had ever seen. They were like something from a fairy tale with wrinkly cone-shaped tops that looked like rumpled velvet.

"Have a seat." Mack motioned to a rock close to the stone table. I watched as he put a lump of lard in the pan and held it over the fire until it melted, then added the mushrooms. I could tell by the way he winced with every motion that his wounded shoulder still bothered him.

"They taste better when you use butter," he said, "but I'm all out." The mushrooms sizzled and steamed as he propped the pan above the coals. A delicious aroma filled the glade. I was hungry, but I wouldn't have eaten those mushrooms if I were starving.

"Aren't you afraid someone will see the smoke and figure out that you're here?" I asked.

"Folks are used to seeing smoke back in these woods. It usually means someone has a still going and is making moonshine. People can get pretty testy if you get too close to their operations. They might even take a potshot at you. Most people know enough to steer clear and mind their own business when they see campfires in the woods."

"What about government revenue agents?"

"Now, they're the ones who do follow the smoke signals. But they'll be disappointed if they come here and see that it's just an ordinary campfire."

A few minutes later, Mack pulled the pan from the fire and set it on the stone table. He speared a forkful of mushrooms, blew on them to cool them off and then sampled a bite. He closed his eyes in pleasure. "Mmm, delicious. Morels are the best mushrooms in the world." He handed me the fork. "You sure you don't want to try them?"

"I'm quite sure." The squirrel stew had been delicious, too, until I'd learned what it was.

"How's Lillie?" Mack asked after eating a few more bites. "Is she feeling all right?"

"She seems to find enough strength to do the things she wants to do—like point a gun at me or shoot unsuspecting squirrels. She came outside this morning to have a talk with Belle. Lillie told her to be a good horse and to do whatever I said."

Mack laughed. "And has Belle been behaving for you?"

"Yes, surprisingly enough, she has been."

"Good girl," he said, patting Belle's shoulder. The horse had parked herself very close to his side. She lowered her head and nudged his shoulder as he petted her. Any minute now, they were going to kiss each other.

"Tell me the truth, Mack. Did you know about this plot of Lillie's to get me out here on a horse, delivering books and bringing your food?"

"Desperate times call for desperate measures."

"I've done a lot of favors for you and Lillie, and I think you owe me the courtesy of answering a few questions in return."

"No promises, but you can go ahead and ask."

I took a deep breath, trying to decide where to begin. "Lillie said there might be more than one person who wanted to kill you. Can you at least tell me why? What did you do to deserve getting shot at?"

"Can't answer that one yet. Sorry."

"Does it have to do with this 'work' you mentioned? What are you and Lillie up to?"

He pondered for a moment while he chewed. "How much do you know about the coal strikes here in eastern Kentucky? Ever hear of 'Bloody Harlan'?"

"No, but it sounds dangerous."

"It is dangerous, especially if you're a coal miner trying to fight for better working conditions and decent housing and fair pay for all the hard work you do." He spoke with passion in his voice.

"And you're involved with all of that?"

"In a roundabout way . . . but not over in Harlan County."

I waited for him to say more, but he didn't. Instead, he ate two more forkfuls of mushrooms. I rose to my feet. "I need to go."

"Alice, listen. I know I gave you a hard time when you first arrived, and I'm sorry. I was right in the middle of something, and I knew it might be dangerous, so I was annoyed with you for coming here when I told you to stay away."

"But I never received your letter."

"Most people wait for an invitation before they come knocking on a stranger's door, suitcase in hand."

"*Most* people don't arrive with five boxes of very nice books all the way from Illinois—at their own expense!"

"Hey, come on. Don't get all riled up. I'm trying to say I'm sorry for everything that I put you through. Including this." He made a vague gesture, taking in the woods and the hills and the horse. "But as Lillie said, the Good Lord must have known we'd need your help. And I'm grateful. Now, do you think we could sign a truce? Become friends?"

It irked me to do it, but I agreed. We shook hands. "It's about time you asked for a simple thing like my friendship, seeing as I've been at your beck and call for nearly two weeks."

"Has it been that long?"

"Yes. And that reminds me. My aunt and uncle will be returning for me any day. In fact, I think you'd better ride down into town with me tonight. I won't be around to bring your food up here much longer. And I don't think Lillie can do it after I'm gone."

"Your visit to Acorn, Kentucky, is really over, huh?"

"Yes. In some ways, it's been the longest two weeks of my life. But at the same time, I have to say that it has been . . . interesting. I've learned a lot."

He stopped eating and set the frying pan on the rock table. "Wow. Those two weeks sure went by fast."

"Can't you confide in one of the other packhorse ladies? Cora or—"

"No! And whatever you do, don't tell any of them the truth."

"Why not? I thought you were close to them. That you trusted them."

"I can't explain it right now, but we can't let any of them know that I'm still alive. It's too dangerous."

"Can't you hide out in the library after I'm gone?"

"Too risky . . . I'll be fine up here."

"Good. Well, I want to get home before dark."

"No, wait. I feel bad that I haven't answered all your questions. Try asking another one."

I thought for a moment. "I met Maggie Coots, and she seemed very nice." He nodded vaguely and scooped up more mushrooms from the pan. They were nearly gone.

"But Lillie told me to be careful around Maggie. Why would she say that? Does Maggie run around shooting people or something? What am I supposed to be careful about?"

"Who knows? I can't read Lillie's mind. It's hard to figure out why she says the things she does. But I do know that Lillie is usually right about people. She has a certain instinct about them. Almost as if she can read their minds. Or their hearts."

"She called the sheriff a snake. All he did was stop by the library and ask if he could help. Why is he a snake?"

"The sheriff is controlled by the coal company. He does whatever they tell him to do, instead of what's just and fair. As for Maggie, you have to understand that she's a flatlander. People around here naturally distrust them."

"Your friend Hank seemed to trust her."

"Who told you about Hank?"

"Cora did. She said he was your best friend, but that Hank died in a mining accident. June Ann mentioned Hank, too."

"We were friends. We grew up together, and he liked books almost as much as I did. We were supposed to go to Berea College together, but Hank never got to go. His father died, and Hank had to go to work in the mines to support his family. I sent him my textbooks so he could keep studying, but . . ." Mack ended the story with a shrug.

"How did Hank meet Maggie and fall in love with her?"

Mack got a funny look on his face. He stared at the ground, not at me, frowning. I wondered if Mack had been in love with Maggie himself. It happened all the time in novels—the hero falling in love with his best friend's girl. "I'm not sure how," he mumbled. "I didn't live here at the time."

"Can you think of any reason why Lillie would say to be careful around Maggie?"

"No." He still wouldn't meet my gaze.

I decided to leave. I was never going to get a straight answer to any of my questions. Besides, what difference did it make if Mack told me what he was up to or not? I was going home.

"I want to get back before dark," I said. "Can you show me the way to the creek?"

"Sure." He reached for my hand again, then made a clicking sound in his cheek. Belle stopped munching on weeds and lifted her head to look at him. "Come on. This way." The horse followed both of us through the woods like a trained dog.

"Are you sure you don't want to ride back to the library with me?" I asked when the dilapidated cabin came into view. "I feel funny leaving you way out here by yourself now that I'm going home to Illinois."

"I told you, I'll be fine."

We stopped beside the front porch. I could hear the creek gurgling below us. "Well, Mack . . . I probably won't see you again. It's been . . ." I searched for the right word, remembering the bear of a man who had shouted at me from the second-story window that first day. I couldn't say, in all honesty, that it had been a *pleasure* to meet him. "It has been quite an experience," I finished.

He released my hand, which he still had been holding. "I'm glad we met, Alice. And thank you for bringing all the new books."

It would have been a dramatic and novel-worthy ending if I could have swung up into the saddle and galloped away, but no matter how hard I tried, I couldn't get my left foot high enough to reach the stirrup. I even maneuvered Belle closer to the steps to make it easier, but I still wasn't tall enough. In the end, Mack had to give my rear end a boost before I finally made it up into the saddle.

He was laughing at me, I knew he was, even though he didn't dare to make a sound. I felt the imprint of his hand on my backside all the way down Wonderland Creek, my face burning like the coals of Mack's campfire.

Lillie was sitting at the kitchen table with bowls of food all laid out, waiting for me when I arrived. I thought she might ask why I was so late, but instead she asked, "Who did you bless today, honey?"

I had forgotten all about Lillie's prediction. My mouth fell open in surprise when I remembered helping June Ann. "How—how did you know?"

"You had a light shining all around you like you was an angel. That's how I knew. Now, who got the benefit of that blessing?"

"Do you know the Larkins? June Ann and Wayne?"

"Of course I do. Sweet little redheaded gal. Too bad she's all tangled up in the middle of that awful feud."

"Well, June Ann had her baby today. A little girl. She was all alone when I got there, so I stayed with her until the midwife came."

"See? You were a blessing, just like I knew you would be."

"No, really. How did you know? I didn't see any lights shining—on me or anyone else."

"The Good Lord told me all about it when I was praying for you. That's why I knew you just had to go up that creek today, whether you wanted to or not."

"You talk to God as well as horses?"

"Sure. Don't you?"

I shook my head. I didn't believe that Lillie could talk to either one—even though I had seen what might be proof that she had communicated with both. It had to be a trick. "How does God speak to you, Miss Lillie? Is it an audible voice?" My father spoke of hearing from God, but I didn't think he ever heard a voice.

Lillie gestured to the empty chair across the table from where she sat. "Come on, honey. Sit down and eat your supper. I warmed up the beans from last night."

"Aren't you going to tell me how you knew?"

"There are some things—like falling in love—that you just can't explain."

CHAPTER 16

The next morning I awoke with the same feeling I got when I came to the last chapter of a book: a little sorry to see it end, but anticipating the start of a new story. Aunt Lydia and Uncle Cecil would arrive today. My suitcase was packed and ready. My ordeal in Acorn had been grueling at times, but I had done a good deed by bringing the books to Kentucky. I could go home knowing that I had made a difference.

I put on my traveling dress, combed my hair, and carried my suitcase downstairs to set beside the front door. It would be wonderful to wash all my dirty clothes in an electric washing machine when I got home, instead of rinsing them by hand. Last night before falling asleep I had watched the bat dart around my room and had wrestled with what to say to the other packhorse ladies. Should I give a formal farewell or simply disappear as unexpectedly as I had arrived? I was afraid they would be mad at me and would reproach me for deserting them when they needed my help, especially with taking care of Miss Lillie. They had trusted me and treated me like one of their own, even though I was a flatlander. I hated to lose that trust, but in the end I decided that telling the truth would be best.

"I may not be here when you come back this afternoon," I said when they had all assembled. "I'm returning to Illinois."

"So soon?"

"I only planned to stay for two weeks, and my time is up. My aunt and uncle are coming for me today. I'm really sorry to leave, but my family needs me at home." That wasn't quite true. No one needed me, and I still didn't have a real purpose to fulfill at home. Maybe one would magically appear.

As I feared, all four women glared at me accusingly. "You're leaving? Just like that?" Cora asked.

"Yes, I'm so sorry. But I wanted to tell you how wonderful it was to meet all of you, and thank you for being so kind to me. You've been good friends to me and I'll never forget any of you."

"Who's gonna take care of Miss Lillie?"

"And Belle?"

"And that coop full of chickens?"

"Who's gonna bring the mountain folks their books?"

"I-I don't know. Doesn't Lillie have a family we could contact?"

"Mack was her family."

I watched as they loaded their book bags, and it seemed like they were erecting thick walls between us again, like the ones that had been in place when I arrived. Faye frowned sternly, as if sorry that she had ever taken her wall down.

"You'll hear from me again," I said. "I'll write to all of you. And I'm going to collect more books for you—children's books and schoolbooks. I know how badly you need them."

"Who's gonna run the library?" Alma asked. But she wasn't asking me—they were asking each other. As far as they were concerned, I had already deserted them.

I wished I could explain that I wasn't the one who had deserted the library and Miss Lillie and all of them—Mack was. They should be mad at him.

I waited for my aunt and uncle all morning. Then I waited all afternoon. Lillie wasn't feeling well and stayed upstairs in bed. I tidied the library, making sure the work was finished and every shelf was neat and in order. But not a single car rolled through Acorn that day, including my uncle's. What could have happened to them? Were they lost? Was Aunt Lydia's condition worse than anyone had thought? I worried and paced, watching the road in vain.

"I see you're still here," Faye said when she returned that afternoon.

"Yes . . . I guess my aunt and uncle were delayed. I'm sure they'll come tomorrow." The others didn't react to my presence at all. They came in, chatted amongst themselves, dropped off their books, and left, just as they had on my first day. I carried my suitcase upstairs at bedtime and unpacked my pajamas.

I didn't repeat my heartfelt farewell the second day. I simply told them once again that it had been a pleasure to meet them and thanked them for letting me visit. Then I sat and stared out the front window, waiting and worrying the entire day.

"You're still here," Faye said when she returned that afternoon. It was more like an accusation than a question.

"I-I don't know what could be taking my uncle so long." Alma rolled her eyes.

On the third morning, Cora confronted me, her burly arms crossed on her impressive chest. "You gonna go on up and do your route today, like you promised me? I hate to keep them schoolkids waiting for their books. But now them folks up on Potter's Creek are waiting for me, too, and I can't be in both places at once."

"I-I'm afraid to leave . . . My aunt and uncle are certain to come today. Probably this afternoon."

"If you leave right now and don't dawdle, you can be back by this afternoon."

"But—"

Lillie interrupted my protests. "I'll keep them entertained until you get here, honey." I turned in surprise and saw her grinning at me as she descended the stairs, miraculously well again. I hesitated, wondering what Lillie could possibly do to entertain Uncle Cecil. He would have no interest at all in the ramblings of a hundred-year-old folk-healer and would be angry at the delay. And who knew what Aunt Lydia would find to do in my absence.

Lillie crooked her finger, beckoning me closer. I bent so she could whisper in my ear. "While you're up there, you can feed poor Mack. He must be running low on food again by now."

I didn't care about Mack. He was able to forage for his own food. But I would like to see June Ann again. She needed a friend so badly. And I wanted to return Maggie's book to her and thank her for it, even though I'd been too distracted to read it. In fact, I hadn't read a single book in two weeks and I usually finished one in two days.

"You want me to saddle up your horse?" Cora asked.

"Sure. I-I guess so." I was still a little afraid of Cora. Besides, I couldn't bear the thought of sitting here for a third day, waiting, doing nothing. I turned to Lillie. "Promise me you'll ask my uncle to wait for me?"

She lifted her right hand as if taking an oath. "If your uncle comes today, honey, I promise to keep him here if I have to knock him down and sit on him."

That I'd like to see. A strong wind would blow Lillie over.

As I rode Belle all the way up to the Howard farm, my mind raced with ideas about how I could fix things here in Acorn before I left for good. Maybe Maggie Coots could visit June Ann once in a while and read books to her. I knew I was meddling, but if I told Maggie the truth about Mack, surely she would keep his secret. Her husband had been his best friend. Who knew, maybe a romance would develop between her and Mack. After all, they had Hank in common and they both loved books.

I made a quick stop at the schoolhouse after visiting the Howards, then headed down the hill to see Maggie. She greeted me warmly, like an old friend, and we sat at her table to sip tea. She seemed truly sorry to hear that I would be going home soon. "What about Miss Lillie?" she asked. "Who will take care of her now that Mack is . . . ?" She couldn't seem to say the word *dead*.

"I was hoping you knew something about Lillie's family. I would gladly contact them if I knew how. And who."

Maggie shook her head. "I don't know any more than you do. I'm an outsider, a flatlander just like you. I came down here from Boston to teach school—against my parents' wishes, I should add. How did your parents feel about you coming here?"

"They didn't mind. I was doing charity work, after all, and my father is a minister. He encourages me to do things like this. And it was only for two weeks."

"My father is a businessman, and he thought I was out of my mind when I told him I was leaving civilization to come here. But I was so tired of living a useless life, you know? Running around to social events, spending money on worthless things. I wanted to do something to make a difference, so I came down here to be a teacher."

Her words about living a useless life made me uncomfortable. "How did you meet your husband?" I asked, wanting to change the subject.

"At a parent-teacher conference, of all things." She smiled, remembering. "Hank had to support his family after his father died, including several rambunctious younger brothers. I called him up to the schoolhouse to talk about discipline. He was very antagonistic, at first. Then . . . we fell in love."

"I admire you for staying here and living in such primitive conditions."

"It has never been a sacrifice, Allie. By the time Hank and I married, I had fallen in love with the people down here and these beautiful Kentucky hills."

"Do you think you'll ever move home again?"

"I don't know. All my memories of Hank are here, so this is where I want to be."

"What about teaching? Might you teach again?"

"I've thought about it."

"Or you could start a library. You have plenty of books."

"You mean like Mack's library? . . . I don't know. For now, I need to stay close to home. Hank's mother needs me." I was surprised that she referred to this cabin as "home" instead of Massachusetts.

"Do you know June Ann Larkin and her husband, Wayne?"

"Not really."

"They live down the creek a few miles from here. June Ann just had a baby and she's very lonely. But she loves to read. I thought . . . I thought that maybe you could visit her once in a while. Become friends." To my surprise, Maggie shook her head. Her eyes filled with tears. "Did I say something wrong, Maggie?"

"No . . . excuse me," she said, wiping her eyes. "It's just . . . I'm not the right person to ask." She brushed away another tear. "And I can't leave Mama Opal."

So much for my schemes. "Listen, Maggie, can I give you my address back home in Illinois in case . . . I don't know, in case you want to write to me? I would love to hear from you."

More tears rolled down her cheeks as I gave her a piece of paper with my address on it. "Do you have to go?" she asked.

"I do. I'm so sorry. In fact, my family is probably down in Acorn right now, waiting for me." We hugged good-bye. I hated to leave.

It wasn't my day to visit June Ann, but I decided to make a quick side trip to see her, hoping she had cheered up, hoping her husband had gotten over his disappointment by now and had accepted their baby daughter. But I could tell by June Ann's sad, red-rimmed eyes that nothing had changed.

"I can only stay a few minutes," I told her as she invited me inside. "How are you?"

She blew her nose and wiped her eyes. "I guess I got the blues today."

"June Ann, isn't there anyone who can come and stay with you? I'll talk to your family if you tell me where to find them."

"Don't bother. They won't come."

I looked down at the baby, asleep in a homemade wooden cradle that looked like something Daniel Boone might have carved. "Does she have a name yet?"

"Wayne still can't decide. I've been calling her Feather, because she's as soft and light as one." Her tears started to fall again. I was making matters worse, not better, for everyone I visited. I hugged June Ann good-bye a few minutes later and rode down to Mack's cabin. He didn't seem surprised to see me.

"Can you stay for a while?" he asked.

"No, sorry. I'm not getting off this horse." I still blushed at the humiliating memory of his hand on my backside as he had given me a boost. "I just came to drop off more food, then I have to get back. My family will be coming for me any minute. They might even be waiting for me."

"Weren't they supposed to be here by now?"

"Yes. I'm getting very worried about them. Listen, are you sure you don't want to ride back with me and hide out at the library?"

"It's not safe for me to ride anywhere in broad daylight."

I needed to leave. Belle was acting restless, as if she wanted me to either get off or go home. But I couldn't stop thinking about the people I was leaving behind and the problems that my leaving had created. "Listen, Mack. Everyone I talk to is worried about Lillie. She'll have no one to take care of her after I leave."

"Lillie will be fine."

"She won't be fine; she's one hundred years old! Doesn't she have a family we can contact?"

"Trust me. She'll be fine." His lack of concern for the frail old woman angered me. But then he might well ask why I wasn't concerned enough to stay with her.

"I'm worried about June Ann Larkin, too," I said, remembering her tears.

"That's a lot of worrying for someone who's leaving and never coming back."

"I guess I made some friends."

"Around here, we usually mind our own business and don't meddle."

"Well, while I'm meddling, you should know that I'm also worried about Maggie Coots. She seems depressed. You should have seen how she cried today when I told her I was leaving. If you and her husband were once friends, you should be concerned about her, too."

Mack turned away, but not before I saw that odd look on his face again—guilt or grief or maybe longing. I couldn't identify it.

"I have to go," I said again. "I would hate to keep my family waiting. Good-bye, Mack."

"Yeah . . . Bye, Alice."

Belle and I were back at the library by two o'clock. I expected to see Uncle Cecil and Aunt Lydia chatting with Lillie in the non-fiction section, listening to glowing reports about all my hard work and what a wonderful job I had done. Instead, I found Lillie asleep in her chair, alone.

"They're still not here?" I asked when she awoke and saw me.

"Guess they ain't coming today, honey."

All day Friday, I paced the creaking wooden floors, staring out of the library's front window, waiting. On Saturday, Ike Arnett came to return his book. Had he really finished it in only a week? I decided it would be rude to ask. He tossed it down on the desk in front of me and said, "I hear you're leaving us. Is that true?" He wasn't smiling, for once.

"Yes, it's true. I only planned to stay for two weeks and it's been nearly three."

"Why can't you stay longer? You got a boyfriend back home waiting for you?"

"No, I don't have a boyfriend." I was surprised to discover that it no longer hurt to admit it. "Would you like to check out another book?"

"What I'd like is for you to stay." He had been holding one hand behind his back all this time, and he caught me by surprise when he whipped his hand around to reveal what he'd been hiding—a bouquet of flowers. "These are for you, Alice."

"Oh! They're beautiful!"

"Just like you." His magnificent smile returned. Ike was doing his best to be sweet and charming—and he was succeeding. Gordon had never brought me flowers. Or called me beautiful. I held the blossoms to my nose to inhale their scent.

"Thank you! I don't know what to say."

"Say that you'll stay. I'm going to be fiddling over in Pottstown next Saturday and I'd love for you to come with me."

"I'm sorry, Ike, but I can't. My aunt and uncle will be coming to take me home any day." He looked so dejected that I quickly added, "But if it weren't for that, I'd love to come and hear you play."

He didn't seem to know what to say next—and neither did I—so I walked around from behind the desk to search for a vase for the flowers. The library didn't have one, so I went out to the kitchen to look for an empty Mason jar.

Ike followed me, sighing in disappointment. "They say our Arnett clan is jinxed, and I'm starting to believe it. Just when I find the prettiest girl in Kentucky, she up and leaves me."

Ike's last name, Arnett, registered with me for the first time. The Arnetts were feuding with the Larkins. That meant June Ann must be related to the Arnetts. I turned around to face Ike so quickly that I ended up walking right into his arms. I blushed as he held me for a moment, then I scrambled backward out of his embrace.

"Sorry, Ike. I didn't mean to bump into you—"

"I ain't sorry in the least!" he said, laughing.

"But I wanted to ask, do you know June Ann Larkin?"

"Sure. She's my cousin. Why?"

"I met her when I was delivering books up along Wonderland Creek. She just had a beautiful baby girl, but she's so lonely up there. Isn't there anyone from your family who would be willing to forget this stupid feud and pay her a visit?"

His smile wavered for just a moment, and he frowned slightly. "I'd like to help, but you know how it is . . ."

"Actually, I have no idea how it is. I can't understand what this feud is really all about."

"You'll get a different answer depending on which side you ask. But the truth is, them Larkins are a bunch of liars and thieves. As far as the Arnetts are concerned, our great-granddaddy died without telling us where the treasure was buried. His no-good Larkin partner died a few days later, so you can guess who ended up with the map and all the money."

I wondered if he was joking. Buried treasure? A map? But the look on Ike's face told me that he believed this crazy tale. I decided to drop it. I filled a Mason jar with water for the flowers and thanked him again.

Sunday was a magnificent day. The weather was warm and the trees were sprouting leaves. Spring had arrived in Acorn, but my aunt and uncle had not. If only there was some way to get in touch with them. Were they lost? Had Aunt Lydia's condition deteriorated? After all, she had been seeing monkeys and castles on the trip here. I had feared I would need a water cure myself after the trauma I had endured, but instead, the ordeal had made me stronger in a lot of ways. I remembered worrying that I was more like my flimsy aunt than my strong, self-assured mother. At least my visit to Acorn had settled that issue in my mind. I was stronger than I thought I was, capable of coping with some very trying experiences. But now it was time to go home.

I decided to get up early on Monday morning and ride my route so I could stop and see Mack on the way back. He must know where I could find a telephone. I had to call home and find out what was taking so long. I made Lillie swear again that she would watch for my family and ask them to wait for me. "I'll tie them to a chair if I have to," she promised. "You go on, honey. And don't worry."

June Ann looked happy to see me in spite of her tears. "I been praying all morning that you would come," she said, "and here you are. Can you set down and talk awhile?" I tied up Belle and followed June Ann into the dreary cabin. "The baby and I are all alone up here," she said as we sat by the hearth.

"Alone? Where's Wayne?" I hoped the stupid oaf hadn't left her because she'd failed to give him a son.

"He got all the crops in and decided to go look for work. They say the government will pay a couple dollars a day for that conversation corpse."

I had to smile. "You mean the Civilian Conservation Corps?"

"I guess. Feather and I get really lonely up here now that he's gone." She pushed the baby's cradle with her bare foot to rock it. The baby didn't stir. She looked like a little angel with her sweet, round face and halo of fuzzy red hair.

"Why don't you come down to Acorn with me and stay in town?" I asked on impulse. "That way, you won't be all alone up here." Maybe June Ann could take care of Lillie after I went home.

"I can't. I have to look after the animals. I can't leave them. But I been waiting and waiting for you to come back. I'm so glad we're friends."

By the time I left, guilt weighed me down like a heavy, wet overcoat. I was surprised Belle's back didn't bow in the middle from the load. Instead, she behaved so well for me that Lillie might have traded her in for a different horse.

I rode up to the Sawyer place and read the children a story. Then I stopped to see Gladys and Clint and their pipe-smoking granny. I knew better than to meddle, but since I was leaving soon, I threw caution to the wind. Who cared what anyone thought of me? I sat Gladys down for a little talk.

"Listen, you said you were related to June Ann Larkin? Well, I was just at her place and she's so lonesome she's in tears. Her husband, Wayne, went out to find work, and she's all alone with a beautiful new baby. Couldn't you find it in your heart to visit her once in a while? She could use some company."

Gladys glared at me as if I had asked her for the deed to her cabin and all of her livestock. At gunpoint. "You should be asking that Larkin clan, not me. June Ann's made her bed with them, and now she'll have to lie in it. She's a Larkin now."

"I would ask one of them if I knew who to ask."

"We don't mention any of them Larkins by name. There's bad blood between us."

"Yes, I know but—"

"When you see Cora, tell her we said howdy." Gladys stood and opened the door for me.

I fumed all the way down the mountain to Mack's cabin. Belle took me right up to the porch. "Mack!" I hissed, afraid to raise my voice. "Mack, where are you?" I waited, reluctant to climb off Belle. But when several minutes passed and there was no sign of him, I had to dismount. I tied her to the porch railing and went inside.

The cabin's interior was even creepier than I had imagined, dark and shadowy and stinking of mildew and rotting wood. Cobwebs festooned the rafters, dead leaves littered the floor. I expected to see the empty feed sacks I had used to deliver Mack's food or at least the empty Mason jars, but there wasn't a single clue that Mack or anyone else had ever lived here. When a mouse skittered across the floor, I yelped and hurried outside again.

"Stay here," I told Belle. "I'm going to look for Mack." She was tied to the railing and couldn't have gone anywhere, but I needed to talk to someone in the eerie silence. I followed the narrow path through the trees to the glade where Mack's campfire had been. The pile of firewood was gone and the ashes spread out as if Mack had never cooked mushrooms there a few days ago. He was nowhere in sight. I called his name as loud as I dared. Waited. Called again. Mack had vanished.

Belle was waiting patiently for me when I returned. I had to perform a circus act to get on her back, balancing on the rickety porch railing like a tightrope walker, but I made it into the saddle without falling or breaking any bones.

I muttered beneath my breath as we ambled down the hill toward the library.

"Stupid man! Stupid, stupid man!"

CHAPTER 17

M y family still hasn't come?" I asked Lillie when I reached
the library. I found her sitting at the kitchen table, peeling potatoes.

"No sign of them today, honey."

I paced in front of the sink, feeling desperate. "I need to get to
a telephone. Do you know where I can find one?"

"Now, what do you need a telephone for?"

"I need to call home and find out if my parents have heard from
my aunt and uncle. They were supposed to return for me a week
ago. I'm worried sick about them."

"Worrying don't do no good. You just get yourself all worked
up for nothing."

I continued to pace and to worry, watching Lillie remove a potato
peel in one long, thin spiral. "What about the post office?" I asked.
"Do they have a telephone up at the post office?"

"Why would they be needing a telephone to deliver the mail?"

"I just thought . . . since it was a government office . . ."

"You could always send your folks a letter."

"Letters take too long. I'm very worried, Lillie. My parents
must be worried, too."

"Now, why would they be worried? They know where you are,
don't they?" She laid down the knife and pushed the little pile of

potatoes across the table toward me. "Chop these up for me, would you, honey? We're gonna make us some soup for dinner."

"In a minute. I'm trying to think . . ." I paced some more. "How do I get to the sheriff's office? He must have a telephone."

"Maybe he does and maybe he doesn't. I ain't never had a reason to go there and find out."

"Is it far? Could I ride there on Belle?"

"Sit down, honey. You're gonna wear out my floorboards."

"I can't sit. I need to find a telephone!"

"No, you need to sit down."

There was something about the way she said it that made the hair on my arms stand up. I'd had the same sensation once before when I accidentally touched a live wire on a frayed plug. "Why do I need to sit?"

"Something I got to tell you, honey." I pulled out a chair and sat, afraid to breathe. "Those relations of yours that you been waiting for? They come by when you was out delivering books last week."

"Last *week*? But you promised you would make them wait! You swore to me!"

"No, by the time I swore to you, they'd already come and gone. Seems they arrived a day earlier than you was expecting. The day June Ann had her baby, in fact. No, by the time I made all them promises to you, honey, they'd already been here and gone again."

"But . . . but . . . where did they go?"

"Home. They decided to go on home when they heard you was busy helping out here."

I leaped to my feet. "*What?*"

"I told them all about the tragic accident that our librarian had, and how you was kind enough to step forward and take his place. I told them the library needs you—which is the gospel truth, honey. The gospel truth."

"But . . . I know my uncle. He would have waited until I came back. He would have talked to me and made certain—"

"I explained to him that I'm one hundred years old, and that I'm all alone here with no one to help me and no one to take care of all these books except you. I told him that you've been making new friends, and that these friends are counting on you, too. It's the truth, honey, ain't it? So, once your kinfolk saw how much we needed you, they agreed that it was very sweet and kind of you to stay a little longer."

I sank onto the chair again and lowered my face in my hands. "No . . . no . . ." My moans sounded like June Ann's when she'd been in labor. Lillie got up and came around the table to pat my shoulder.

"Your aunt asked if you'd met any nice young men, so I told her that a fiddle-player named Ike Arnett was sweet on you. She's the one who decided they should go on home without you. She told your uncle, 'Let poor Alice have an adventure for once. She doesn't have a job or a beau back home.' I promised that city uncle of yours that we would make sure you got home safe and sound, just as soon as we got somebody else to help out."

I couldn't stop my tears. "You kidnapped me! You're forcing me to stay here when you knew I wanted to go home!"

Lillie stopped patting and put her arm around my shoulders. "We won't make you stay if you don't want to. But the truth is, we do need your help, honey. Mack and me, we need your help real bad. I can't cook and clean and take care of this library all by myself. And who's gonna keep feeding Mack?"

"How long are you going to hold me captive?"

"Just till things get straightened out."

Did I want to know what things needed straightening? Or how long that might take? I wiped my tears, angry for losing control, and looked Lillie in the eye. "I know I'm not supposed to ask nosy questions, but since I've ended up in the middle of these 'things,' I think I deserve to know what's going on."

"Mack's got himself in a lot of trouble, honey. He came back here to try and fix things and ended up making them a whole lot worse. He meant well, but some folks don't see it that way."

"Has he broken any laws? Because if he's in trouble with the law, he needs to know that I have no intention of going to jail with him. I refuse to become another Bonnie and Clyde."

"Who are they, honey?"

"Never mind. But tell me the truth. Is Mack breaking the law?"

"Not that I know of."

I huffed in frustration. "Why should I believe a word you say? You lied to this entire town when you told them Mack was dead."

"That had to be done, honey. Otherwise, he really would be dead by now. Listen, I can see that you're peeved with me again, and I'm real sorry about it."

"Oh, I'm more than peeved. I'm furious! Did you ever think to ask me if I wanted to stay and help you?"

"Of course not. I knew you was itching to go home. You woulda told me no."

She was right, of course. But that was beside the point. I knew I'd never get a straight answer out of Lillie. I needed to talk to Mack. But where was he?

"Where did Mack go?" I asked. "I stopped by his cabin today and he wasn't there. There was no sign of him."

"I'm sure he's there. Dead men don't leave any signs—and Mack is supposed to be a dead man, remember?"

"So he was hiding somewhere? He deliberately avoided me?"

"If you was as riled up as you are right now, I don't blame him for hiding. Do you?"

I slammed out of the back door and walked down to the creek to think. What options did I have? I could write a letter to my parents, begging them to come and rescue me or send me train fare, but that would take time—and the postmaster was Lillie's friend. Who knew if he would even send my letter to them? I could walk to the sheriff's office—if someone would tell me where it was and how to get there. But could I trust the sheriff? Lillie had called him a snake and I hadn't liked him, either. I would have confided in Maggie Coots, a flatlander like myself, except that Lillie had warned me to be careful of Maggie. Then again, Lillie certainly couldn't be trusted. I didn't know whom to trust or what to do.

Eventually, when my temper had a chance to cool, I went inside and helped Lillie finish making supper. I was hungry, and if I didn't watch her carefully, I might be eating squirrels again.

"How much longer might you and Mack need my help?" I asked as we finished making the soup together.

"You have to ask Mack that question, not me."

I rode Belle up to the cabin after supper to do just that. Mack wasn't there, so I tied the horse to the railing, sat down on the porch, and waited. I had a lot of time to think of all the questions I wanted to ask Mack before he finally slithered out of the woods wearing a sheepish grin. "Are you looking for me?"

"Good guess. You're pretty smart, aren't you?"

"So I've been told." He gave Belle a good petting, murmuring affectionate nonsense to her, then sat down on the step beside me, looking as innocent as June Ann's baby.

"Did you know about this plan of Lillie's to keep me trapped here? Did you know she was going to convince my aunt and uncle to go home?"

"To be perfectly honest . . . she might have mentioned it in that letter she wrote to me. She said she had a feeling they would come early, and she asked me to keep you here as long as possible."

"I hate you!" And I did. But then he smiled, and I couldn't help noticing the boyish dimple in his cheek again.

"Hey now. I'm sorry to hear that you hate me," he said. "But you came down to Kentucky because you wanted to help out, right? And you're doing that. You're helping in more ways than you can ever imagine. Besides, who else could I get to run the library while I'm up here playing dead? You're a very good librarian, you know."

"But you didn't give me a choice! You never asked me if I would like to ride a book route or if I wanted to stay here and work. You and Lillie have schemed and connived to keep me here like . . . like a captive."

"I suppose you could look at it that way . . . but remember those pirates in *Treasure Island*? They took that young boy on an adventure against his will and look how good that story turned out."

"That's a novel. This is real life—" I stopped, shocked by my own confession. It was what Gordon had said to me. Countless times.

Mack picked up a stick and idly drew patterns in the dirt in front of us. "Would you have stayed to help or taken on a library route if we had asked you nicely?"

"Absolutely not."

"See? That's why we didn't ask. That's why we 'connived,' as you so eloquently put it. We needed your help and there was no other way to get it."

"I could have you both arrested for kidnapping, you know."

"Of course you could. But tell me, if you had gone home with your relatives last week, what would you be doing right now that's so important?"

The answer was *nothing*. I had nothing important to do back home. Which was why I had reluctantly decided during supper tonight that I might as well resign myself to staying here and helping out. I pulled the stick out of Mack's hand and tossed it aside.

"I want you to put your hand on a Bible, Mr. Leslie MacDougal, and swear to me that you aren't doing anything that's against the law—besides faking your own death, which I'm quite sure is a felony in most states."

"No jury in the world would convict me once they found out why I did it."

"Why did you do it?"

"I told you. So the shooter wouldn't come back and try again. That's why Lillie's been telling lies, too—to save my life."

"I might start taking potshots at you myself if you don't tell me the truth. Are you breaking any other laws?"

"No. And I'll swear to it on a Bible or my mama's grave or anyplace else you want me to swear." He was trying very hard to keep a straight face and not smile, or worse, laugh out loud. I wanted to kick him in the shins. "Once you get to know me, Alice, you'll see that I eschew getting into trouble with the law."

I stared at him in shock. "*What* did you say?"

"I said that I eschew getting into trouble with the law. Eschew means—"

"I know what it means!"

"Then why are you getting all riled up?"

"Because . . ." How could I explain to him that the word *eschew* had been one of the reasons my boyfriend had broken up with me? How could this annoying backwoods librarian casually use the same word in a perfectly innocent sentence? What were the chances of that happening? Did Mack read the same literary journals that I did?

"Never mind," I mumbled. "I'm just surprised that you know what *eschew* means, that's all."

190

Mack placed his hand over his heart as if I had hurt his feelings. "You cut me to the quick, Miss Ripley. I am a college graduate, you know."

I closed my eyes and waved my hands, wanting to erase this pointless conversation. "Forget all this *eschewing*. Just tell me who you think tried to kill you. Lillie said there might be more than one suspect."

"She's right, there might be." He stroked his smooth-shaven chin for a moment the way he used to stroke his beard. "Okay, I'll tell you this much. When I came back here after college and after working up north for a few years, people I'd known all my life didn't quite trust me anymore. Some of them—Cora's brother Clint, for instance—have a habit of making moonshine up in these mountains. *There's a lot of stills up in them there hills*," he said, mocking a mountain accent. "Some of those moonshiners began to think that I worked for the government. They saw me snooping around, and they may have intercepted a letter or two of mine at the post office, addressed to an official in Washington, and they decided that I was a revenue agent. A *revenuer*, as they like to call them."

"Are you a government revenue agent?"

"Of course not. But my enemies want the moonshiners to think that I am so they'll take a few potshots at me and try to run me off."

"So you think Clint or one of the other moonshiners might have tried to kill you?"

"It's a possibility. Which is why I can't let Cora or the other girls know I'm alive."

"Why are you really snooping around and sending letters to Washington?"

"Sorry. The less you know, the safer you'll be for now. But I promise I'll tell you just as soon as I can."

"Who else might be trying to kill you besides the moonshiners?"

"Remember how I told you about all the union troubles over in Harlan County? Some of us tried to pressure the coal company here in Acorn for better working conditions, too. Then when the mine shut down and all the men lost their jobs, a lot of the miners blamed me. They didn't believe that the whole nation's economy is in trouble, not just Kentucky's. They don't get newspapers here very often."

"They would kill you over a misunderstanding?"

191

"It's like this: Before I came to town they had jobs. After I came, they were all out of work."

"But . . . but weren't you the one who created the packhorse librarian jobs? Lillie says those four women support nearly every family in town."

"That's true. But for those who are suspicious of me, getting government jobs for the ladies makes me look like I have clout with the government. So maybe I *am* a revenuer, after all."

I exhaled, trying to make sense of this mess.

"Then there's the age-old family feud here in Acorn," Mack continued, "between the Larkins and the Arnetts."

"Your mean June Ann's family versus Wayne's family?"

He nodded. "It happens that my mother was a Larkin."

"Oh, for heaven's sake. Someone would kill you for that? I thought your parents died when you were young?"

"I don't want to go into all of it," he said, rubbing his eyes, "but whenever an inheritance or buried treasure is at stake, there's always the possibility of bloodshed."

I couldn't speak. Buried treasure? Were the stories true? "Ike Arnett told me a bizarre story about a treasure," I said when I could find my voice, "but I didn't believe him."

"You met Ike?"

"He came into the library to get a book to read. He played his fiddle at your funeral, too."

"He's very talented. Listen, Alice, the sooner I finish my work, the sooner you can go home. But I need your help. I'm stuck up here and can't go where I need to go."

"Where do you need to go?"

"To the Acorn Mine, to begin with. You could do me a huge favor if you went over there for me and looked around to see if they left any papers in the filing cabinets when they closed down the mine. That's all. You don't have to take anything, just look around. Will you do that for me?"

"You're crazy. It's . . . it's preposterous! I'm not a spy or a detective. I could end up in a lot of trouble."

"Not for looking around. Don't be so melodramatic. You went to the mining camp once before and looked around, didn't you?"

"Well, I'm not going again." I almost added, *especially for you.* Then I had an idea. "I *might* agree on one condition: help me get to a telephone so I can call home. I need to tell my parents what's going on. They must be very worried about me."

"You're in luck." Mack grinned. "There's a telephone in the mine office. You can kill two birds with one stone."

"Won't the phone be turned off if the mine is closed?"

"Not necessarily. You don't know how hard it is to get the telephone company to come all the way up here. It's easier for them to just keep the phone connected. In fact, that can be your legitimate reason for being there, if anyone asks. You came to use the phone."

"In the first place, who is this 'anyone' who might question me at a deserted mine office? And in the second place, why should I believe anything you say?"

"The 'anyone' was rhetorical. And why not believe me? Why trust anyone in this big bad world, when it comes right down to it? Why trust God?"

"Let's leave God out of this." I sighed. "Do these papers at the Acorn Mine have anything to do with why someone shot you?"

"Maybe . . . maybe not."

"I think I have a right to know the truth since you're asking me to snoop around for you."

"If anyone stops you, just tell them you're there to use the telephone. Period. And while you're there, see if they cleaned out the filing cabinets. It's simple."

"I'm quite certain that trespassing is against the law."

"But you look so very innocent and guileless, Alice, with your peachy complexion and curly blond hair—like the heroine in a fairy tale. You could be Little Red Riding Hood strolling innocently through the woods."

"Does that mean there's a Big Bad Wolf waiting for me?"

He didn't laugh, but whether it was because he didn't get the joke or because there really was a wolf, I couldn't tell.

"I'm sure you'll be completely believable when you explain about the telephone. It's the truth, isn't it?"

I glared at him through narrowed eyes. "I don't think you or

Lillie or anyone else in Acorn, Kentucky, would recognize the truth if it fell from the sky and hit you in the head."

Mack didn't reply. We sat side by side on the cabin step for a few minutes, listening to the creek rushing below us, feeling the warm evening breeze on our faces as I tried to decide what to do. One of the trees in front of the cabin was an apple tree, planted by a long-ago settler, and it was about to burst into bloom. The woods up in these Kentucky hills were so peaceful and serene that no one would ever imagine that feuding and loneliness and hardship were brewing beneath the surface. And secrets.

Mack slowly rose to his feet. He winced in pain as he twisted his head from side to side and rubbed his left shoulder. He had been massaging his left arm off and on while we had talked.

"Is your wound still bothering you?" I asked. "I promised Lillie I would find out how it's healing."

"Yeah, it bothers me. I think it's healing okay, but sometimes my arm and fingers go numb. I may have damaged a nerve or a muscle or something. It's going to be hard to use my typewriter."

"What are you typing?"

"Nothing at the moment. My typewriter is still at Lillie's house. But the sooner I get my book finished and to a publisher, the sooner we can both go home."

"You're writing a book? What kind of book?"

"Ever hear of a novel called *The Jungle* by Upton Sinclair?"

"Of course. It's an exposé of the meatpacking industry in Chicago. It was a bestseller. It caused a lot of ruckus, as I recall."

"My novel will be an exposé of the mining industry here in Kentucky. It isn't even finished yet and it has already caused a ruckus here."

"The mining company knows about this exposé you're writing?"

"I had to tell a couple of people about it when I first came back because I needed to do some research. On the day of Hank Coots's funeral, someone broke into the library while I was gone and stole the manuscript. All of it, including my research notes. I had to start writing it all over again."

"That must be some book if they don't want you to finish it."

"Well, when you read it, maybe you'll understand what I'm trying to do . . . what *we're* trying to do."

"You and Lillie?"

"No. You and me."

Oh, boy.

"Please, Alice, just look around in the mining office and tell me if it's cleaned out or not. The sooner I finish my work, the sooner you can go home."

"Can you give me a timeline or a date? How much longer will I need to stay in Acorn? I'm sure my parents will want to know when I finally find a telephone and call them."

"Can you give me about a month? I'll help you get home after that, Alice, I promise."

I thought of all the endless work there was to do every day, and how hard it was to do it without modern conveniences, and how tired I felt when I fell into bed at night. Another month? I couldn't help groaning. Then I thought of June Ann who needed a friend, and Maggie Coots and all the children on my route who eagerly awaited their books.

"Okay," I said with a sigh. "I'll stay for another month."

CHAPTER 18

I've decided to stay in Acorn a while longer and help out," I told the other librarians the next morning. I expected smiles and maybe even thanks. I got neither. The women didn't seem to believe me—or else they thought I was a fool who couldn't make up her mind. I packed some books and rode my route, stopping to see June Ann, the Sawyers, and Cora's brother and sister-in-law. Lillie had said I should poke around. Mack implied that if we solved the mystery of who had tried to kill him, maybe he could come out of hiding. I would begin today.

Cora's brother was finally out of bed, limping around the cabin in his long johns. As I piled books on his table and handed Granny a new *Ladies' Home Journal* to read, he squinted at me suspiciously. "I don't believe Cora ever told us why you come down here to our town in the first place."

I explained how I had collected the donated books and brought them to Kentucky. "In fact, the book I brought you today is one of the new ones." I finished with a smile, proud of my achievement. Clint's eyes narrowed even more until they formed slits.

"Where'd you say you was from again?"

"I live in a small town in Illinois, not too far from Chicago."

"Chicago? Ain't that where all them gangsters come from? That John Dillinger fella—'Public Enemy Number One'?"

My perky smile began to waver. "Chicago does have that reputation. And it's true that Dillinger was killed in Chicago."

"Well, if you brought the books already, why ain't you going home?"

"I decided to stay and help out in the library after Mack's . . . accident."

"You a good friend of that MacDougal fellow?"

Before I could reply, Gladys chimed in. "He's a Larkin, you know."

I stifled a sigh. "I never met Mack until the day I arrived to deliver the books."

Clint picked up a poker and jabbed the fire. "Sounds mighty suspicious to me. Don't get too many flatlanders around here unless they're up to something."

Great. Was he going to accuse me of being a revenuer, too? My smile vanished completely as I searched for a graceful way to exit this conversation—and this cabin. I had liked Clint a lot better when he was flat on his back, not brandishing a poker and squinting his eyes at me. I was supposed to be asking the questions, not answering them.

"Cora says you've been getting real friendly with Miss Lillie," Gladys said. "That true?"

"I'm not sure what you mean. We are friends, I suppose. We live together. Miss Lillie is all alone now that Mack is gone, and she needs someone to help her. Did you know that she's one hundred years old?"

Gladys nodded, her expression pinched with distrust. "Miss Lillie's been doctoring folks and birthing babies around here since before most of us was born. She knows everyone's secrets, and you can bet she'll use them to her advantage. I hear she took care of Great-Granddaddy Larkin before he died. Some folks believe that she and them Larkins spent all the treasure."

This conversation wearied me. I scooped up the pile of books from last week and shoved them into my bag. "Miss Lillie hasn't shared any secrets with me, Gladys. In fact, I'm trying to find out where her family is so they can come and take care of her after I leave, but she hasn't even told me that." I left a short time later, determined not to ask any more questions on my routes.

The next day, as soon the packhorse women left on their rounds,

I put on a sweater and my walking shoes and hiked up the road to the abandoned mine. I still wasn't sure if I wanted to get tangled up in everyone's feuds and mysteries, but since I had agreed to stay for another month, I wanted to call home. My parents must be frantic with no way to reach me. And they must be furious with my uncle for not waiting to talk to me in person to find out when I'd be coming home.

I walked down the road alone, as if out for a pleasant stroll with no particular destination in mind. Every time I passed a house, I imagined that people were watching me from behind their curtains, wondering what I was up to. My imagination had always been my biggest problem. I had read countless novels, and now it seemed as though this town had every type of plot: murder mysteries and lost treasure, evil mine owners and family sagas, horseback adventures and pioneer living, even a love story or two. I didn't need to read books. For the first time in my life I was living them.

The graveyard on the hill looked spooky to me, even on a sunny spring afternoon, the first day of April. I wondered how many secrets were buried there along with the bodies. I glanced at the mound of dirt over Mack's grave and knew that at least one secret was. A chill shivered through me. How could I know whether or not Mack had told me the truth, even now? He could have made up everything. I might be in cahoots with a criminal and not even know it. I was no good at snooping around—in abandoned mines or anyplace else. I wasn't cut out to be another Sherlock Holmes, yet I had been forced into the role against my will. Everything that had happened to me in Acorn had been against my will.

I reached the mine entrance and turned down the road leading to the office, ignoring the NO TRESPASSING signs. *"Look innocent,"* Mack had told me. I was innocent. I was here to use the telephone.

I arrived at the office door and found it secured with a padlock. Of course it would be locked if the mine was shut down. I sidestepped through the weeds to peer through the front window, wiping dust off the glass. The office was dark inside since most of the windows were boarded up, but I could make out a desk piled with papers and a row of filing cabinets along the back wall. Except for the lock and the boarded windows, the office looked as though someone had been here only yesterday. Maybe they had been. Maybe they were here right now. I leaped away from the window and glanced around nervously.

Silence. Nothing stirred except for a few crows and nameless insects buzzing in the tall weeds.

I looked through the window again and saw the telephone, black and modern looking, perched on a corner of the desk. I traced the wire across the floor from the desk to an outside wall. Then I tramped around the corner of the building and saw that the wire continued out of the building and up to a telephone pole. More telephone poles and wires stretched up the road into the distance, away from town. Out to the civilized world. Home.

I had felt so isolated these past few weeks, cut off from the world with no radio or daily newspaper. Now these wires would reconnect me. I had to get inside to use the phone.

I walked all the way around the building to look for a window I could open, but the front one was the only one that wasn't boarded up—and it was in plain sight of the road. I found another door in the rear, but it was latched from the inside with one of those little hooks and loops. I could see the latch through the window on the door. The window had small squares of glass, and I figured if I broke one of the panes, I could reach inside and unlatch the door. It made no sense to me that they would put a huge padlock on the front door, board up the windows, then leave the back door vulnerable to amateur sleuths like me.

I glanced around like a guilty person. I guess I was one. At least the rear of the building was more isolated than the front and not in plain view of anyone passing by on the road. No one would see me if I broke in. I picked up a rock and smashed the window, taking two tries to do it, wincing as the sound of tinkling glass broke the silence. Crows screeched at the sudden noise as if to betray me. My heart pounded. My chest hurt. I had been holding my breath and hadn't realized it. The suspenseful stories I'd read had produced these physical reactions but this was the real thing—and twice as upsetting. I ran a stick around the inside of the window frame, knocking out the rest of the glass, gritting my teeth at the sound. Then I carefully reached inside and unlatched the lock.

I was officially a criminal.

Once the door was open, I drew a deep breath and tiptoed into the room, praying the phone still worked after all of my criminal activity. The office was cold and damp. It smelled like cigarettes and mildew and my parents' coal cellar. As I waited for my eyes to adjust to the dim light, I saw the filing cabinets right beside me. Since I had already broken one law, I might as well peek into the files for Mack. The heavy drawer squeaked as I yanked it open. It was stuffed with papers. I quickly closed it again.

Fingerprints! Would someone check for my fingerprints? Forget the files. Forget Mack. I needed to use the telephone. Now. I needed to get out of here. I crossed to the phone and lifted the receiver.

Dead. No tone, no static, no operator asking if she could help me. Nothing. I had gone through all of this effort for nothing.

Should I snoop around a little more for Mack? I didn't even know what I was supposed to be looking for. Before I could decide, I heard a rustling noise outside the front door. Keys jingled in the lock. My heart stopped. I didn't have time to duck behind the desk and hide before the door swung open and there stood the sheriff. I let out a strangled shriek and clutched my chest.

"Oh! You scared me!"

He eyed me coldly. "Miss Ripley, I believe?" It sounded like a line from a cheap detective story.

"Yes! I . . . I . . . I . . ." All I could do was stammer.

"What are you doing here?"

For a very long moment, I had no idea. Then I remembered. "Th-the phone! I came to use the phone. B-but it's dead."

"That's because the mine is closed. Didn't you see all the NO TRESPASSING signs?"

"No . . . I mean, yes. I saw them . . . But I also saw that the wires were still connected and so I thought it might still work. The phone, that is. I-I need to make an important call."

He looked at me as if waiting to hear more. Give a person enough rope and she'll hang herself, they say. But I couldn't help blurting out my story.

"I've agreed to stay here in Acorn a little longer and take care of the library and Miss Lillie. She's all alone now that Mack . . . now that Mr. MacDougal . . . And so I need to call home. I live in Illinois."

He still didn't speak. From the novels I'd read, I recognized this as a typical police maneuver: say nothing and let the criminal incriminate himself—or herself, in my case. The sheriff's uniform was neatly pressed. He wore a gun in a holster on his belt. It looked menacing—but I suppose that was the point of wearing a gun in the first place. Especially if you had to deal with criminals every day. Like me.

I drew a calming breath. "Do you know where I could find a telephone that's in working order? I'll be happy to make it a collect call."

"I have one in my office. Would you like me to drive you there?"

I didn't know what to say. I could hear Lillie's voice in my head shouting, *A snake! That man is a snake!* Mack insisted that Lillie was usually right about people. Yet if I refused his offer, my behavior would seem even more suspicious. Hadn't I just said that the telephone call was important? I swallowed a knot of fear.

"That would be very nice of you, Sheriff . . . to drive me there and let me use your phone . . . If it wouldn't be an inconvenience to you, that is."

"It's an even bigger inconvenience to have flatlanders trespassing and breaking into buildings here in Acorn. It gives me the inconvenience of arresting them."

"Oh, I-I-m sorry! I'm so sorry!"

He broke into a grin. No, it was more like a smirk. "I was making a joke, Miss Ripley. I'm not going to arrest you."

I nearly crumpled to the floor in relief. "Thank you. That's very kind of you."

"Shall we go make that phone call now?"

He motioned me through the door ahead of him, and I saw a ring of keys dangling from the padlock on the front door. He closed the door and locked it again. His black car was parked by the main entrance, coated with a fine layer of dust from the dirt road. Some spy I would make. I had never even heard the car drive up the road. I wondered how he had known I was here, trespassing. Who had been watching me? I knew better than to ask.

"How far away is your office?" I asked as I climbed into the car.

"We'll be there in twenty-five minutes."

I bit my lip to keep from voicing my frustration. Didn't anyone around here compute distances in miles?

The sheriff's car smelled like engine oil and cigar smoke. He slid behind the wheel and closed his door with a heavy *thunk*. I felt trapped. My heart pounded faster. How did I know if I could trust him? He started the engine and turned the car around, creating a cloud of dust. Gravel spit and crunched beneath the heavy car's tires. He pulled out onto the main road and drove away from town.

"I don't believe I've ever heard your story, Miss Ripley."

"M-my story?"

"What brings a nice young woman like you all the way to Acorn, Kentucky?"

I knew very well that he was interrogating me. "Books! Books brought me here . . . Or rather, I-I brought books here to Acorn." I had to get control and stop blubbering. I sounded guilty and I wasn't—well, maybe just a little. "I'm a librarian back home in Illinois, and we had a book drive to collect materials to donate to your library. I volunteered to deliver them."

"What's your connection to Leslie MacDougal?"

"None! No connection! I never even met him until the day I arrived. I read about the need for books in a magazine article, and we corresponded once or twice, but that's all. I-I thought he was a woman—from his name, I mean." I laughed nervously.

"And what have you learned from your stay with us, Miss Ripley?"

Careful . . .

"I've learned that we take books and libraries for granted back home. But I've seen how grateful everyone is around here to have reading material. They'll read the same book over and over if there aren't any new ones. Do you enjoy reading, Sheriff?"

"No. Books are a waste of time."

I tried very hard not to react to such an ignorant statement. It took an enormous effort, but I kept my mouth shut. He resumed the interrogation.

"You said that you've agreed to stay. Why is that, Miss Ripley?"

The question caught me by surprise. I needed to formulate an answer that would be truthful. If my father had taught me anything, it was to tell the truth.

"Well . . . Acorn seems to be without a librarian at the moment. I have the necessary skills, so why not volunteer them?"

"And your job back home . . . ?"

"I was laid off temporarily, due to the Depression."

"I see." He took a half-smoked cigar from the ashtray and stuck it between his teeth, then drove with one hand while he maneuvered to light it. I wished he would keep both hands on the wheel. The road was narrow and twisting, with a drop-off to the river on one side, a wall of rock on the other, and no shoulders along the road where a mistake could be forgiven.

"So you've made yourself at home here, have you?" he asked, puffing smoke.

"Everyone has been very nice to me."

He threw me a sideways glance. "That's unusual. From my experience, folks around here don't take well to strangers."

"We seem to have a love of books in common." I managed a smile.

"What about Miss Lillie?"

I gulped. "What about her?"

"She's an odd one, that's for sure. She take to you, too?"

"She's all alone now that Mack is . . . gone. She needs my help until we find a way to contact her family. That's another reason I've agreed to stay."

He didn't react. This man wasn't a snake—he was a rock, and as hard to read as one. I suppose that was part of his job, especially when dealing with criminals. Like me. For all I knew, he intended to throw me in jail for trespassing and breaking and entering. I gulped again.

"Since I've agreed to stay longer, I need to let my family know my plans—which is why I need a telephone. The one in the mine office was the nearest one I could find."

He still didn't reply.

"I'm very sorry about breaking in. I'll be happy to pay for a new window."

He puffed another cloud of cigar smoke and tapped the ash in the ashtray. Since he wasn't talking, I decided that maybe I should stop talking, too. The road twisted and turned as it snaked over the mountain. It felt strange to be moving so quickly and smoothly after swaying on horseback for the past few weeks.

We passed a few houses, weaving through the woods, following a

203

river. I began to feel more and more uneasy and wished my imagination wasn't so active. I wished I hadn't read so many novels about evil villains. I wished I had never heard Miss Lillie call this man a snake. He could be taking me anywhere.

I breathed a little easier when we came to a large collection of houses and buildings. A town, at last. It wasn't laid out in a grid of streets like the towns in Illinois were, but consisted of dozens of structures jammed onto narrow patches of land. The town was much larger than Acorn. It had church steeples. Stores. A big county courthouse with the sheriff's office right beside it. We pulled up in front and stopped. I gave a huge sigh of relief, which I hoped he didn't hear.

"Follow me, Miss Ripley."

It seemed strange to see electric lights in the ceiling and hear a telephone ringing. I had only been away from civilization for three weeks, but it seemed like three years. The sheriff led me to a littered desk with a telephone on it. He motioned to a straight-backed chair.

"Have a seat."

I sat.

"Wait here."

I waited.

He disappeared into a back room. I needed a bathroom, but I was afraid to ask for one. I watched people at work all around me and tried to calm my nerves. What was I so worried about? I had wanted to use a telephone, and I was getting my wish.

I had time to think while I waited. What if the sheriff was the good guy and Lillie and Mack were the villains? What if this was my chance to escape? Surely this town had a train or a bus station. I could tell the sheriff that I had changed my mind, that I wanted to go home, that I had been tricked into staying. I could be back in Illinois in a day or two. This adventure could be behind me like a bad dream. No more outhouses. No more horse rides. No more squirrel stew. I could be home in my comfortable bed, reading novels by electric lighting and drinking refrigerated Coca-Cola to my heart's content.

Then I thought of June Ann and Maggie Coots, waiting for their books, waiting for someone to talk to. I thought of Miss Lillie and Mack. Did I believe they were telling the truth? That they

were trying to do something good for the people of Acorn, and
that men like this sheriff were trying to stop them? Or did I care
only about myself and my comforts and fears?

Whom should I believe? Whom should I trust?

Books. They were the answer to my questions. The sheriff considered them a waste of time. Mack considered them a treasure
worth sharing with people who had little else in life. I would throw
in my lot with people like Mack, like myself—people who loved a
good book. People who didn't believe reading was a waste of time.

"Are you ready, Miss Ripley?" The sheriff's voice startled me,
and I jumped.

"What? . . . Oh . . . Yes. And I'll be glad to reverse the charges
on the call."

He lifted the receiver, dialed 0 for the operator, and handed it to
me. I gave the operator my name and the number for my father's
office in the church, praying he would be there. It would upset my
mother to get a long-distance call in the daytime, and she might
become flustered. Besides, our home phone was a party line, and I
didn't want everyone in Blue Island to know my business. A collect
call from a sheriff's office in Kentucky was sure to give the town
gossips something to gab about. The switchboard would glow like
a Christmas tree.

I heard a lot of clicking and hissing coming through the wires,
then my father's deep bass voice. "Good Shepherd Church, Pastor
Ripley speaking." Tears filled my eyes.

"Hello, Daddy—?" The operator interrupted me. I had to wait
for my father to accept the collect call. I started again. "Daddy,
it's me. Alice Grace."

"What's wrong? Where are you?"

"I'm still in Kentucky. Nothing's wrong. I just thought I would
call and tell you that I'm going to stay here a while longer."

"That's what Cecil said. Frankly, your mother and I were shocked
when he arrived home without you."

"I know. I mean, I thought you might be. And maybe a little
worried."

"Of course we're worried. You've never been on your own for
so long before."

205

"Well, I'm fine. I'm working in the library here. The librarian—"
My mother would faint if she knew that the librarian had been
shot. I'd better not mention it. "They don't have a librarian at the
moment, so I agreed to stay."

"Is it safe? Are you with nice people?"

I thought of Lillie pointing her gun at me. I thought of Clint
Arnett making moonshine and shooting at revenuers, and of the
feud between the Larkins and Arnetts. I thought of all the mysterious people who seemed to have a reason to murder Mack. But I also
knew that the sheriff was listening to our conversation. He probably had tapped into the telephone line while he'd made me wait.

"Everyone has been very nice to me, Daddy. I'll write you a letter
and tell you all about it as soon as I can."

"Well. I'm glad to hear that you're being useful. But your mother
and I don't think you should stay down there indefinitely. Cecil says
it's very rustic. When do you plan to come home?"

"I'm told that they can probably find the help they need in
another month."

"A month? Certainly no longer than that, Alice. How do you
plan to get home?"

"They have trains and buses. Someone will take me to the station."

"I don't like the idea of you traveling all alone. Shall I find
someone to come and fetch you?"

"There's no need. I'll be fine." They were treating me like a child
and I resented it—even though I had been desperate to get home a
few days ago. "Listen, I'll write you a letter and explain everything.
Please give my love to Mom. And say hi to Freddy for me, okay?"

"I will. Thank you for calling, Alice. That was very thoughtful
of you. We'll plan on seeing you in a month's time. Good-bye."

"Bye, Daddy." The line went dead.

My tears started again and I didn't know why. Maybe it was
because I had just made an important decision—one of the first
big ones of my life. I had decided to stay and chosen whom I would
trust. And now I was a little afraid that I had made a mistake.

CHAPTER 19

One of the sheriff's deputies drove me back to the library—and back to the eighteenth century. I had asked to use the ladies' room before leaving his office, and as we arrived in Acorn, I already lamented my decision to forfeit indoor plumbing. But for now I had decided to stay.

I found Miss Lillie in her chair downstairs, reading a chapter of *Treasure Island* to Mamaw and Faye's boys, who were seated on the wooden floor in front of her. "There you are," Lillie said when she saw me. "You better finish reading this 'cause my eyes are getting tired. I don't see as good as I used to, you know."

She struggled up from the chair before I could protest. I was weary from everything I had been through and didn't know how I could concentrate on the story. But only a page or two remained until the end of the chapter, so I sat down to read it. My audience listened with rapt attention, including Miss Lillie, who stood in the doorway.

"Can't you read us some more?" Little Lloyd begged when I closed the book.

"We're almost to the end," Clyde added.

"Come back tomorrow—no, Friday—and we'll finish the book. I promise."

Bobby groaned. "We gotta be good until Friday?"

"That's not so long. Bye now."

As I herded them out the door, Ike Arnett, the fiddle player, bounded down the stairs from the library's second floor. What in the world had he been doing up there? He showed Lillie a red and black plaid jacket.

"Had a little trouble finding it, Miss Lillie, but thanks again for letting me have it. It means a lot to me."

"Mack would be tickled to know you're getting some use out of it."

Lillie had given him Mack's hunting jacket? I doubted if Mack would be tickled. Nor did I like the idea of Ike snooping around in the room where I slept. But Ike bounced around the foyer like a boisterous brown-eyed puppy, making it hard to stay mad at him. He halted in front of me and briefly rested his hand on my shoulder.

"Hey, Alice. Miss Lillie told me the good news."

"The news? What news?" Had she told Ike that Mack was alive?

"That you're gonna be staying in Acorn, after all."

"Oh. Right."

"I'll come by for you at two o'clock on Saturday, then." I stared at him blankly. He gave me a grin that would make most women swoon. "You said that you'd love to come with me and hear me fiddle on Saturday if only you was staying. Well, now you're staying."

Yes. I had said that. Because I'd thought I was leaving.

"So put on your prettiest party dress, and I'll be back for you at two o'clock on Saturday. See you then. Bye, Miss Lillie. And thanks again." He jogged out of the library like one of Faye's boys, only Ike was six feet tall.

"Do you think I should go with him?" I asked Lillie.

Maybe she would call Ike a snake, like the sheriff, or warn me to be careful like she had with Maggie Coots. Instead, she said, "He's a nice boy. There's no harm in going." Mack had agreed that Ike was a talented fiddle player. He had seemed to like Ike Arnett, and I did, too. He was a little too handsome for his own good, but he was sweet. And romantic. The flowers he had brought me were still flourishing in the Mason jar on my desk. As Lillie had said, I supposed there was no harm in going. I saw her watching me from the kitchen doorway with an amused grin on her face.

"Why did you let him take Mack's jacket?" I asked her.

"Because dead men don't need hunting jackets."

"But Mack isn't dead." I wondered if Lillie's memory was failing or if she was starting to believe her own lies.

"Honey, you sure enough can't keep a secret, can you? You whisper that once too many times and you gonna get Mack and us in a heap of trouble."

"I'm sorry. It's been a terrible day." I sank down in the chair behind the library desk. Work had piled up again and I could barely see Lillie over the stack of books waiting to be carded and shelved. She hobbled forward to stand in front of me.

"I see you came home in the sheriff's car. How'd that happen?"

"I went up to the mine to use the telephone—and to snoop around for Mack—and the sheriff caught me breaking into the office. He didn't press charges, thankfully, but he drove me to his office so I could use his telephone to call home."

"I hope you was careful what you said on that telephone."

"I was. I knew he might be listening."

"Did you reach your kinfolk?"

I could only nod. For some reason, the memory of my father's calm, pastoral voice brought tears to my eyes and a lump to my throat. I hadn't had time to get homesick until now. Lillie seemed to read my thoughts.

"What do you miss the most about home?" she asked quietly.

"A bathtub." I gave a shaky laugh, trying to make a joke of it. Lillie didn't laugh.

"Well, why didn't you say so? We got a bathtub, honey."

"We do?"

"Follow me and I'll show you."

Lillie led the way upstairs to her bedroom, climbing as slowly as a toddler. I followed, reluctant to get my hopes up since everything else in Acorn was as antiquated as in the pioneer days. She opened the door to her huge closet and sure enough, beneath a rod of clothes was a big copper bathtub, large enough to sit down in. In fact, it was about the same size as our bathtub back home. Lillie would drown in it. But I didn't see any water faucets.

"Where does the hot water come from?"

She bit back a smile. She must have thought I was very ignorant.

"You make a fire in the stove, honey," she said patiently, "and you heat the water as hot as you want. It works best if you bring the tub down to the kitchen and fill it halfway with well water, then add the boiling water until it's just right."

It sounded like a lot of work, but I was desperate for a good long soak in a real tub, especially if I was going out on a date with Ike Arnett. "This will be wonderful," I said. "I'll drag the tub downstairs and take my first bath on Friday night." I couldn't help smiling as I maneuvered the bulky tub out of the closet, sneezing at the dust cloud I'd raised.

"You can take a bath whenever you want to," Lillie said. "I'll even give you a sachet of lavender to put in the water so you'll smell even sweeter than you already do."

"Thank you, Lillie. That's very kind of you." I would have hugged her if she hadn't been so frail. She reminded me of a dried-up twig that would snap in two and crumble if you touched it. I was surprised to discover that I was growing fond of Lillie in spite of everything she had put me through. I sensed that underneath her conniving, gun-pointing ways, she was a fine person. And though it irked me to admit it, I could see that Mack was a good person, too.

The next day was Thursday, so I rode my usual route to the Howard farm, the school, and Maggie Coots's cabin. I could saddle Belle without too much help now, and I was getting used to climbing on and off her back several times a day. Everyone had said I could learn to ride a horse if I put my mind to it, and I guess they were right—unless Belle suddenly decided to quit listening to me, that is. I didn't kid myself that I had any control over her. She obeyed Miss Lillie's and Mack's orders, not mine. I had never known that horses were so smart, even though Freddy and I had read *Black Beauty* and every other horse story we could get our hands on as girls.

The day's ride went smoothly, and I looked forward to seeing Maggie and telling her that I had decided to stay. I knew we could become good friends. As Acorn's only flatlanders, we had a lot in common. As I neared her house, though, I suddenly heard a *crack* that sounded like gunfire. Was someone shooting at me the way they had shot at Mack? I nearly tumbled out of the saddle in fear, and the sound must have scared Belle, too, because she picked up her pace, forcing me to hunch over in the saddle and hang on for dear life. She was only trotting, but it seemed like a gallop as we thundered into Maggie's yard. I sagged in relief when I saw Maggie out by the barn, aiming her rifle at a row of tin cans. She lowered the gun when she saw us and beckoned to me. I dismounted and tied Belle to the hitching post, then sauntered over, still holding my chest to keep my wildly pounding heart inside.

"Belle and I heard shots and they scared us half to death. I'm glad it was only you. Are you doing some target practice?"

"There's a wildcat roaming around here. I saw paw prints on my property. Make sure you keep your chickens locked up, and whatever you do, don't come up into these woods at night."

My heart went from a trot to a gallop again. "Do wildcats ever hunt in the daytime?" If so, my riding days were over. Done. Finished.

"Usually not. But I'm worried the cat will come after my goats one of these nights. I have two new baby kids." Maggie reloaded the rifle, took aim, and fired. The bullet hit one of the tin cans with a metallic *plink* and knocked it over. She took aim at another can. *Boom. Plink.*

"Where did you learn to shoot like that?"

"Hank taught me when we started having all the trouble at the mine. He wanted me to be able to defend myself. He'd be worried about me now because I don't have a watchdog anymore. That's probably why the wildcat has been hanging around my place." She pointed the rifle again. *Boom. Plink.* "Want to try it?"

"No, thanks. It would be a waste of ammunition. I'd probably end up shooting myself . . . like Mack did." I was pleased that I had worked Mack's "accident" into the conversation. Lillie's accusation that I couldn't keep a secret had stung. But as soon as I'd spoken, I felt guilty for telling a fib.

When Maggie ran out of bullets, she invited me inside. We sat at her table sipping tea and talking about our favorite characters from the books we'd read. We both agreed that Jo in *Little Women* was at the top of our lists. Spending time with Maggie was like a little taste of home. I hated to leave. "But I'll be back," I promised.

I stopped to see June Ann on my way down the creek, even though it wasn't my day to visit her. I arrived to chaos. The dog was barking, the baby was crying, and so was June Ann. "Here. Hold Feather for me," she said as soon as I'd dismounted. She shoved the baby into my arms before I could refuse.

"What? . . . Why?" I clutched Feather awkwardly, unsure what to do. Her little face was crimson from crying, her tiny arms and legs stiff.

"I just need a break from her," June Ann called as she hurried down the porch steps.

"Wait! I don't know how to take care of a baby this small." But June Ann didn't seem to hear me. She jogged through the gate and up the trail into the woods. Now what?

I carried the baby inside the dreary cabin and walked the floor with her propped against my shoulder. I hummed every song I could think of to soothe her as I patted her back, but she continued to wail, her mouth uncomfortably close to my ear. Whatever was wrong with Feather, it hadn't affected her lungs.

It seemed like a very long time passed before the baby finally ran out of steam. I felt her shudder a few times as her tiny body relaxed against my shoulder and she fell asleep. I waited five more minutes to make sure she stayed asleep, then carefully laid her in the cradle and went looking for June Ann. She was sitting on a rock near the edge of the woods, far enough away, I guessed, so she couldn't hear Feather's cries. Tears still rolled down her face, leaving streaks on her dusty cheeks.

"Are you okay, June Ann?"

"I don't know. I guess so. I just had to get away from her for a while. She cries like that every day and she just won't quit. Nothing helps. She ain't hungry or wet." June Ann swiped at the tears that continued to fall.

"Do you think something's wrong with her? Is she sick?" I would have suggested a doctor, but I knew better by now.

"No, she ain't feverish or nothing. She's got the colic, I guess. But it gets on my nerves something awful when she cries like that, and then she can tell I'm upset with her and she cries even more. I love her so much, but sometimes . . . sometimes I just need her to be quiet so I can think."

"I'm sorry you're having such a hard time. I wish I knew what to do to help." I took June Ann's hand in mine and held it for a moment. She drew a deep breath, as if drawing strength from me, then let it out with a sigh.

"Thanks, Allie." She released my hand to climb off the rock, and we began walking slowly back to the cabin. "Miss Ida the midwife came up a few times to check on us. She says Feather is fine and nothing's wrong with her; she's just got the colic."

"Did Miss Ida say what to do about it?"

"She said to try rubbing her back, but that don't help. Ida's gonna ask Miss Lillie to make a potion for her."

"Good. I can bring it with me the next time I come."

"Miss Ida thinks I got the baby blues. She says they'll go away soon."

I decided to change the subject and help June Ann get her mind off the baby for a little while. Maybe her tears would stop, too. "How did you like the last book I brought you?"

"I ain't finished with it yet, but it's pretty good so far. I wish I could read when I'm up late at night with Feather, but we ain't got money for lamp oil."

I made a mental note to bring June Ann some lamp oil, too. Heaven knows I wasn't using any of it to read at night. After hauling firewood, caring for the animals, cooking breakfast and dinner every day, and rinsing out my clothes in the kitchen sink, I didn't feel like reading at night. I climbed into bed at the end of each day and slept like a dead woman, paying little attention to the bat flying all around my room.

June Ann and I talked about books for a bit, and I warned her about the wildcat roaming the woods. "Yeah, I smelled it a couple of times, so I been locking all the animals up at night. This dog of mine barks loud enough to wake the dead. He'll keep a whole clan of cats away."

On the way back to the library, I stopped to see Mack. I had to climb off Belle and sit on his porch to wait for him, but he finally crept out of the underbrush like a Cherokee sneaking up on a pioneer. I was still so jittery from the gunshots, and the screaming baby, and news of a wildcat roaming loose, that I jumped a mile when Mack said hello.

"Oh! Don't startle me like that!" I snapped.

"I'm fine. How are you?" he snapped back. He sat beside me on the steps, waiting until we both calmed down.

"I stopped by to tell you that I went to the mine office yesterday. I had to break a window to get in, and after all that trouble, the telephone was dead."

"Did you check the files for me?"

"The drawer I opened was stuffed full of papers."

"Perfect!"

"What are you planning, Mack?"

He shook his head, warning me not to ask.

"Well, while I was in there snooping around for you, the sheriff showed up."

Mack didn't seem surprised. "What did you tell him?"

"The truth. That I needed to use the telephone. He was kind enough to drive me to his office, but he asked a lot of questions while he had me in his car."

"What kind of questions?"

"Some were about you—how long I had known you, that sort of thing. He also asked about Miss Lillie. I didn't want to say too much, but I didn't want to sound like I was hiding anything, either. He drove me into town and let me call home from there."

"Hmm. That's a problem."

My temper flared again. "Why is it a problem that I called home? My parents have a right to know that I'm okay, even if I am staying with a bunch of liars and snoops and . . . and . . . who knows what else?"

He rested his hand on my arm to calm me. "I'm glad you called home, Alice. It isn't that. But the sheriff must have someone watching the mine if he showed up so quickly. *That's* the problem."

"You don't think it was a coincidence? I didn't see anyone following me along the way."

"I don't believe in coincidences where he's concerned. If he has spies watching the mine, then it's going to be a problem for me to get back in there."

"I really don't want to know what you're planning." Which was just as well because Mack didn't seem inclined to tell me. "You should also know that Cora's brother Clint has been asking me a lot of questions, too—where I'm from, what I'm doing here. When I told him I was from a town near Chicago, he got very suspicious and said that Chicago is where all the gangsters lived."

Mack laughed out loud.

"I'm glad you think it's funny. Will you be laughing when Clint takes a potshot at me, too?"

"I'm sorry." He ran his hand across his face as if to smooth away his smile. "But it's hilarious that Clint would think you're a gangster. Look at you! You're like one of those dainty porcelain dolls from Germany, with your curly blond hair and peachy skin. I don't know how Clint or the sheriff or anyone else can believe you're up to no good."

Was Mack flirting with me or making fun of me? I couldn't decide, but it reminded me of another question that I needed to ask. "Listen, tell me what you know about Ike Arnett."

"Ike? He's like a younger brother to me. Why?"

"Well, your 'younger brother' was up in your bedroom when I got home yesterday, digging around for your hunting jacket. It seemed as though he'd been up there for quite a while. He said he wanted something to remember you by. Lillie let him take it."

"That was my favorite coat. I guess it serves me right for dying."

"He also invited me to go to with him on Saturday to hear him play the fiddle with his band."

Mack rose to his feet to stroke Belle's shoulder and muzzle. I couldn't see his face when he asked, "So are you going?"

"If you think it's all right, yes. You seem to know the character of everybody in Acorn better than I do."

"Ike's fine. He could go a long way with his fiddling if he could catch a break. I was trying to help him get to Nashville . . . before I died, that is."

"Your death has been inconvenient for a lot of people, including me."

"Go with him, Alice. You'll have fun."

As soon as I got home, I went searching for Lillie. I wanted to ask her about making the potion for June Ann's baby. I found her upstairs in bed. She looked so pale and worn-out that it worried me. "Are you okay?"

"Just weary, honey. How was your day?" I told her about June

Ann and baby Feather. "Yes, Ida came by asking about medicine for the colic. If you got time tomorrow, you can help me make some. It ain't hard, but I don't think I can do it by myself."

"Sure, I'll be glad to help. I'm worried about June Ann more than the baby. It seems like she cries as much as Feather does."

"Sounds like the baby blues. Ida said June Ann might have a case of them."

"Is there anything that might help her, too? Besides someone to talk to?"

"We can fix some tonic that might help her."

"Nobody in this stupid town will visit her because of the feud. I don't suppose you have a remedy for that, do you?"

"Only Jesus can fix that mess."

The next morning, Lillie felt strong enough to get out of bed again. I was relieved. After breakfast she got out her "picking basket," and I helped her walk outside so she could show me her herb garden. "This is where I grow things to make my medicines." She pointed to an overgrown patch of sprawling plants, bordered with stones. "I ain't had the strength to pull all them weeds this spring, but there's some good plants growing in there. If I tell you what I need, think you can pick them for me?"

"Sure." I looked around for snakes first, since I had seen one slithering through the grass near the chicken coop the other day. My hesitation seemed to puzzle Lillie.

"Why you looking all around like that? Something gonna jump out and bite you?"

"I saw a snake in the grass over there," I said, shivering as I pointed.

"That's just a garter snake, honey. He won't hurt you."

"How do you know what kind of snake I saw?"

"Because I seen a whole lot of them here in my yard."

A whole lot? Her assurances failed to comfort me. I poked at the tall weeds with a stick, just to be sure, then knelt down on the damp grass with Lillie's basket. Up close, I could see borders of stones around each smaller section of plants, as well as around the entire perimeter. The garden must have been very pretty at one time.

"That there is catnip." Lillie pointed with the tip of her cane.

"We need a few leaves of that. Next to it is peppermint. Pick a few leaves and smell them."

The fragrant aroma made my mouth water. "Mmm. Like mint candy."

"If I were stronger, I'd take you into the woods to pick wild ginger and ginseng—but I ain't young anymore. We'll have to make do with dried roots for now. I still got some dried chickweed and yarrow, too, but fresh is always better."

"Maybe Mack can show me where to find what you need. He found some wild mushrooms up there in the woods."

"Um. Maybe. He has his hands full right now." She showed me a few more things to pick and then explained which plants were good and which were the weeds. "Them weeds should all be pulled up or they'll choke out the good plants. Weeds are just like hatred and greed, you know. If you ain't careful, they'll choke all the love and compassion out of a person."

"I'll come back and weed the garden for you, if I have time," I promised.

Before we went inside, Lillie pointed to a large square of earth dotted with dead leaves and more sprouting weeds. "That's supposed to be our vegetable garden, but Mack never did get around to it before he got shot. Guess we'll have to plant it ourselves if we want to keep eating."

My shoulders sagged beneath the weight of imaginary shovels and clumps of earth. I had seen Wayne Larkin and the Howard and Sawyer families plowing and planting and sweating to carve out their gardens and it had looked like backbreaking work to me. What had I gotten myself into by agreeing to stay?

When we'd picked enough herbs, I helped Lillie hobble inside again to mix up the brew in her black iron cauldron. I felt like one of the witches in *Macbeth*—"*Double, double, toil and trouble; Fire burn and cauldron bubble*"—as I stirred the finished concoction on the kitchen stove. While it cooled, Lillie gave me a mortar and pestle and instructed me to crush a handful of dried seed pods to extract the reddish-purple liquid from them.

"That juice is for June Ann," Lillie told me. "Some folks call that plant 'chase-devil' because it helps chase the sad spirits away.

Others call it St. John's Wort because you're supposed to pick it on June twenty-fourth—St. John's Day. I'm just about out of it, but maybe we can pick some more this June if I'm up to it."

I couldn't imagine Miss Lillie ever being hearty enough to roam through the woods again, the way she once had. The thought made me very sad.

We finished preparing both elixirs, and I was helping Lillie tidy up her workroom when I came upon a pile of neatly typed pages. "What's all this?" I asked, sifting through them.

"Something Mack and me was working on."

"They look like recipes."

"They are. He was helping me type up all my remedies, like the ones we made today. He said I need to pass on all the things I know about healing people. Him and me was gonna write a big book full of folk medicine and such. He even had some fancy college professor interested in it. But then Mack got shot. I been too weary to work on it by myself."

I paged through the stack of papers. Lillie was one hundred years old. When she died, all of this valuable knowledge would be lost. "I'll help you," I said. "I know how to type. I'll be glad to type these for you if you want me to."

She smiled her broad gap-toothed grin. "Honey, you don't know what a relief that would be to me."

After lunch, Lillie lay down to take a nap. I would have loved a nap, too, but I put on my oldest clothes and went outside to survey the garden patch. I knew a tiny bit about gardens, because my parents had started one behind our parsonage. For the past two summers they had grown vegetables to give away to the poor people in Blue Island, and to make soup for the hoboes who stopped by our house for something to eat as if we were running a restaurant. But now, if I wanted to eat, I would have to become a gardener along with everything else.

I knew that the first thing I had to do was turn over the soil and uproot the weeds to get the ground ready to plant. I found a spade in the shed. Like everything else in Acorn, the work would have to be done the old-fashioned way. I had labored for twenty minutes or so, breaking up a section about four feet square—and had collected a nice set of blisters on my hands—when I heard a man's voice behind me. "Need help?"

Ike Arnett strode across the yard toward me. I leaned against the shovel with a sigh. "Yes, I think I do. This work is harder than I thought it would be."

"Didn't I tell you to just ask me if you needed help? Stand still a minute—you got some dirt on your face." He swiped his thumb across my cheek. "There. Got it."

"Yes, you did say you would help, and it's very kind of you. But in this case, it seems like it would be asking a lot."

"I ain't gonna do it with a spade, that's for sure. But I'll be glad to plow it up for you. Mack had a push plow that he used every year." Ike bounced over to the shed as if he had coil springs in his shoes. He came back with a little hand plow like the one my father used, and a wide-toothed rake. He handed the rake to me. "Here. You can make it all nice and smooth after I plow it up."

"Thank you. I can't tell you how relieved I am to have help. The truth is, I don't know much about gardens. But I do know that if I don't plant one, Miss Lillie and I won't have anything to eat."

"Well, lucky for you, I've been planting gardens since I was old enough to stand up in one."

We worked side by side for the rest of the afternoon, talking and laughing about all kinds of things. Ike showed me an earthworm he'd plowed up and explained why worms were good for the garden. He knew the names of all the birds singing in the treetops along the creek, and he whistled in imitation of each one of them. He was one of the most cheerful people I had ever met, which made me realize how gloomy Gordon had always been. His family's funeral business may have been partially to blame, but Ike was as lighthearted and happy as the fiddle music he played.

Together we got the garden plowed and raked and ready to plant, but my body ached in a thousand places by suppertime. "Ask Miss Lillie to show you where her seed potatoes are," he said as we stood back to survey our work. "We can get them planted next week. She probably has some other seeds saved up, too. Alma has a bunch of tomato and pepper seedlings she started. I'll bet she'll trade you for some eggs."

219

"Should we plant corn? It seems like everybody on my book route was planting corn."

He lifted his hand to his mouth, and I could see that he was hiding a smile. "We could . . ." he said slowly. "But the corn they're planting ain't for eating. It's for making moonshine." He laughed, and I couldn't help laughing with him.

By quitting time, we had made a solid start on the garden. And I had made a good friend. "See you tomorrow at two?" he asked after putting our tools back in the shed.

"I'm looking forward to it. And thanks again for all your help."

I went inside with a tired smile on my face and began pumping water for my wonderful, glorious, long-overdue bath.

CHAPTER 20

On Saturday afternoon I was dressing for my date with Ike Arnett when I heard a terrible roar out in front of the library. It sounded as if a dragon had crawled out of the woods and was threatening to devour the entire town. I ran to the front window in Lillie's workroom and peered out. Ike had arrived in a rickety, rusty, flatbed pickup truck. It lacked a muffler, and every time he pumped the gas pedal to rev the engine, the vehicle quaked and roared. I couldn't determine the truck's original color beneath all the rust, nor could I tell the model, but it looked old enough to be the first truck off Henry Ford's assembly line thirty years ago.

He couldn't possibly expect me to ride in that wreck, could he? Maybe I should plead illness. But that hardly seemed fair after all the hard work Ike had done in Lillie's garden yesterday. I hurried into my bedroom to put on my stockings and shoes, wondering what I had gotten myself into.

"Woo-ee! Don't you look beautiful!" Ike said as I descended the library stairs.

"Thank you. You look pretty nice yourself." His handsome face was scrubbed and clean-shaven, his straw-colored hair slicked back with pomade. He wore a neatly pressed white shirt, string tie, and clean blue jeans. Ike offered me his arm as we walked out to his truck.

The vehicle looked even worse up close, the fenders missing, the front bumper attached to the frame with baling wire. Ike walked

221

me around to the passenger side and opened the door for me, taking my hand to help me up onto the seat. It lacked upholstery and padding, and was composed of pillows covered with a patchwork quilt like the one on Lillie's bed. I thought I saw a couple of springs poking between the pillows and wished I hadn't worn my good stockings.

"It ain't too pretty, but it'll get us there," Ike said. I wasn't so sure. Even if it did make it up the mountain and out of this hollow, I would be stone-deaf by the time we arrived. There was no glass in the window between the cab and the truck bed.

Ike ran around the truck and jumped in, restarting the engine with a roar. The vehicle coughed and choked as if it had swallowed a mule on the way here and the animal was stuck in its throat.

"I'm sorry it's running so rough," Ike shouted above the racket. "We don't drive it very often because we can't afford the gasoline unless I get a fiddling job." It would be impossible to talk while we drove, so I sat back to enjoy the scenery. We rode past the abandoned mine and through the town where the sheriff's office was, then continued on to a smaller town a few miles away from it.

The event turned out to be a wedding, held at a pretty little church nestled in a hollow. Ike and the pianist played "Here Comes the Bride" as she walked down the aisle. Afterward, the guests brought out casserole dishes and spread them on a table in the churchyard. It was a beautiful afternoon, and tables and chairs had been set up in the grass. The mountains made a stunning backdrop all around us.

Ike joined the other musicians who were tuning their instruments on a newly built stage, set up outside on the lawn. It smelled gloriously of fresh lumber. "How old do you think the bride and groom are?" I asked as he plucked a few strings. "They look like teenagers."

"Teenaged is about right. Folks around here usually marry before they're twenty."

"What about you, Ike? You look older than twenty."

"I'm twenty-four. But marrying would interfere with my fiddling." He gave me a wink.

"Faye told me I'd be considered an old maid if I lived here. I'm twenty-two."

He shook his head in mock dismay. "I don't know what's wrong with those flatlanders up where you come from, but if you lived in Kentucky, someone would have snapped you up a long time ago."

"Hey, let's go," the banjo player called. "We're getting paid to make music, you know."

"See you later." Ike winked again. I was growing accustomed to his winks and thought they had a certain charm.

The band began to play, and their glorious music made the event. I watched everyone dancing and clapping and tapping their toes, and I couldn't stop smiling all afternoon. Every time the band took a break, Ike sat beside me and we talked. As evening approached, Ike took a dinner break, and we ate fried chicken and sipped cider together.

"You're so talented," I told him. "Can't you get out of Acorn and go someplace where you can really get paid to play?"

"Mack always talked about helping me get up to Nashville. Said he knew people up there, but I had to turn him down."

"Why?"

"Turns out Mack's mama was a Larkin."

"Oh, for heaven's sake. You'd let a stupid thing like that stand in the way of a better life? Making music? Doing what you love?"

"You've seen how folks treat June Ann for marrying a Larkin. It would have been a one-way trip if I'd ever gone up north with Mack. The Arnetts would never let me come back. They're so sure the Larkins already found the treasure that they'd figure I was stealing part of it, too. 'Course, now that Mack's dead I guess it don't matter no more. I don't know anybody in Nashville, and I don't have the money to get there on my own."

"I guess you regret saying no to Mack's offer?"

"I guess." I had never seen Ike look so somber. He took a few gulps of his cider and said, "He was looking for the treasure map, you know."

"The treasure map? Who was?"

"Mack. He told me once that if he found it, he was gonna divide the money up between the two families and make peace around here. That would have been my ticket to Nashville for sure . . . but then he died."

"Who do you think—" I stopped short. I had almost asked him who he thought had shot Mack. I forgot it was supposed to be a hunting accident.

"Who do I think . . . what?" Ike asked.

I had to think fast. "Who do you think will take care of Lillie now that Mack is gone? I can't stay in Acorn forever, you know."

"Well, now that's too bad. We sure could use a smart, pretty gal like you to brighten up our town. What would we have to do to get you to stay longer?" He reached to take my hand, and I was glad that my long soak in the bathtub had gotten rid of the dirt beneath my fingernails. A little shiver slid through me as he gently massaged my palm. Ike was flirting with me again. I decided to cool him off by being practical.

"Well, for starters, you would have to modernize the town of Acorn. You know, put electricity and indoor plumbing in all the houses. A refrigerator and a wringer washing machine would help, too. And a real stove, the kind that doesn't need wood every five minutes to keep the food cooking. And a telephone." I would have added a real bathtub with hot water faucets, but that seemed too personal.

"Boy, that's quite a list."

"You must think I'm very spoiled for wanting all those things."

"You're being honest. Folks around here would probably like to have all them things too, but you don't miss what you never had."

"I've had to adjust to a lot of things since coming here. I miss listening to the radio, too."

"One of my uncles used to have a radio back when the mine was open, and I used to go over to his place and listen to it. Every Saturday night when I wasn't playing in a band somewhere, we'd listen to *The Grand Ole Opry* program out of Nashville. I remember hearing some red-hot fiddle playing by a group called the Fruit Jar Drinkers."

"You're making that up. That's not a real name."

"No, ma'am, I ain't making it up. It's the gospel truth. Another favorite of mine was The Possum Hunters."

I couldn't help laughing and Ike joined me. "What's your band called?"

"We've changed it a couple of times as players joined and quit. Right now we're called The Wonderland Creek Boys."

"That's a fine name. What other events do you play for?"

"Everything you can think of that needs music. If you're still here this summer, there'll be some tent revivals and baptisms and such. Barn dances, too. You'll get to hear us play a lot."

"Tent revivals? That sounds interesting." I had only read about revivals in books. My father's church was too dignified for one—although every time I saw people dozing during the Sunday services, I wondered if our church could do with a little old-fashioned reviving.

"I hope you stay, Alice. I'd love to take you along everywhere I go." I simply smiled in return, wise enough not to make any rash promises this time.

The stars were shining in the clear night sky the next time Ike took a break. He sat cross-legged on the grass in front of me and took both of my hands in his. He knew exactly how to look into a girl's eyes to make her heart forget how to beat right.

"I wish I wasn't playing so I could dance with you," he said.

What would it feel like to dance with Ike Arnett? He was so tall and strong. Just the thought of his muscular arms around me made my heart flop helplessly. I couldn't remember having heart problems when I dated Gordon, but hearts fluttered and skipped and thudded like drums all the time in the romance stories I'd read. Everything about this evening seemed to come straight out of a novel—the warm breeze, the stars winking in the sky, the silvery moon, the blissful bride and groom. Love was in the air and it made me reckless.

"Can't you ask for one song off? So we can dance?"

His smile outshone the moon. "For you, pretty lady, I'd quit the group for good!"

"No, don't do that," I laughed.

"Let me talk to Sam." He scrambled to his feet and I watched him walk over to the bearded banjo player. I could tell by the way the man grinned when he looked over at me that he was saying yes. "We're gonna play a couple of songs first," Ike told me when he returned, "then I'll come back for you. Don't dance with anybody else in the meantime. Promise?"

"I promise. I'll be waiting for you." A couple of young men had asked me to dance already, but I had pointed to Ike and said that I was with him.

I listened to the band play a few more songs, my anticipation building. Then, as they played the introduction to Stephen Foster's song, "I Dream of Jeannie with the Light Brown Hair," Ike laid down his fiddle, jumped off the platform, and swept me into his arms.

My heart forgot every normal rhythm it had ever known. I had danced with Gordon, of course, but it had never felt like this. Ike pulled me very close. My cheek rested against his chest. His warm hand gripped mine tightly. He was an excellent dancer, feeling the music in every pore of his body, and I followed him the way Belle had trotted behind Mack. There was enough electricity between us to light up Acorn and power a hundred washing machines. The crowd noticed and paused to watch us. They applauded when the song ended.

Ike bowed and kissed my hand before releasing it. "Thank you, lovely lady," he murmured in my ear. Then he jogged back to the bandstand and picked up his fiddle. I felt like I had forgotten how to walk as I made my way back to my seat. My cheeks felt oven-warmed. The tempo picked up as the band played more foot-tapping music, and I couldn't stop smiling. Watching Ike play was exhilarating. He clearly loved what he did. I recognized the same joy on his face that I felt when I was in a library, inhaling the aroma of leather and paper and fresh ink, and surrounded by books—dearly loved favorites and brand-new stories waiting to be opened and explored.

I hated for the evening to end. By the time Ike and the other musicians packed up their instruments, I could see that he was tired. His straw-colored hair, dark with sweat, had finger trails from raking his hand through it. He had removed his tie and unbuttoned his shirt collar.

"I had a wonderful time, Ike. Thanks so much for inviting me."

"Sorry I didn't get to spend more time with you."

"I know. But I wouldn't have wanted to miss hearing you play, either."

He held my hand as we walked to the truck. Once again, he opened the door for me and helped me climb in. Ike was more gallant than Gordon had been, and much more gallant than Mack had been when he'd heaved me onto the horse—and Mack was supposed to be the civilized one, college-educated no less.

Ike walked around the truck and slid behind the steering wheel. "We won't be able to talk much on the way home," he said, "so I want to tell you how nice it was to have you watching and listening to me tonight. You were the prettiest girl there, even prettier than the bride. I been hoping all night that you'd let me kiss you."

My heart started going wild again. Back home, nice girls didn't kiss on the first date. But since Ike and I had worked together on Lillie's garden for an entire afternoon, this seemed like our second date. "You may kiss me," I said. I sounded breathless.

Ike slid closer and took my face in his hands—I had always loved it in novels when the hero held the heroine's face in his hands. I had watched Ike's talented, sensitive fingers, chase up and down the fiddle strings all afternoon and they had seemed magical. Now those magical fingers were caressing my face. He leaned forward and kissed me.

Gordon's kisses had always seemed polite, even after we'd dated for nearly a year, as if he was always aware that I was the minister's daughter. Ike's kiss was not polite in the least. It was as passionate and breathtaking as his music, yet he didn't take advantage. The kiss lasted just long enough to be intriguing . . . and to leave me wanting more.

He leaned back and looked at me. "Thank you, Alice. I could let out a whoop right now, but I'd wake up the whole town."

He started the truck—which probably did wake up the whole town—and drove me home. I knew we wouldn't be able to talk to each other, so I moved closer to him on the seat. He smiled and wrapped his arm around my shoulder.

Thirty minutes later we roared into Acorn. Ike left the motor idling as he walked me to the library door. "Better not kiss you again or everyone in town will be talking about it by sunup," he said with a wink. "Can I see you again, Alice?"

"I would like that."

"Thanks! Well . . . good night."

"Good night, Ike."

I floated into the house and up the stairs to my bedroom. I knew better than to think this could be love after such a short time. But whatever it was, it was wonderful.

CHAPTER 21

I had left home to come to Kentucky nearly four weeks ago. Four weeks! It was the longest I had ever been away from home. In some ways I was homesick, but not as much as I had expected to be when I had waved good-bye to my parents in Blue Island. I missed the modern comforts of home, of course, and my mother's home-cooked meals. And I missed my friend Freddy. I longed to talk to her about everything I had experienced, including my date with Ike Arnett and his breathtaking kiss. I wrote her a long letter Sunday night as I sat in bed, but then I realized how selfish it was to describe my adventures when Freddy was stuck in Blue Island, tied down to her teaching job and her ailing mother. If I had learned anything at all during my time here, it was how exhausting it was to run a household and take care of someone who wasn't well—and on top of that, Freddy taught school all day, coping with the needs of dozens of children.

I didn't mail the letter. In the past I had been selfish when it came to my friendship with Freddy, so I decided that when I did get home, I would help her take care of her mother once in a while so Freddy could go out and have a little fun.

Ike returned on Monday to finish planting the garden with me. To my surprise, several other townspeople joined us, including Marjorie and Alma, who helped us after work that afternoon.

"Everybody loves Miss Lillie," Alma said as she tucked another one of her tomato seedlings into the ground. "The least we can do is help her."

It felt good to stand back and survey the finished garden. I felt a little sorry that I would be gone before the fall harvest came—but not sorry to miss the hard, sweaty labor of canning tomatoes and green beans.

I rode up to June Ann's cabin on Tuesday to bring the two tonics that Lillie and I had made. That was what Miss Lillie called them—tonics. "*Potion* sounds like something that witches make," she'd said, "and this here is just folk medicine, passed on from one generation to the next."

As Belle and I rode into the clearing where June Ann's cabin was, I saw her out in the field, hoeing a row of corn plants. She had the baby tied to her chest in a sling made from a crocheted shawl. June Ann waved to me in greeting when she heard the dog barking, but instead of coming to the house she continued working. I dismounted and walked out to the field to talk to her.

"You're working awfully hard, June Ann," I said when I reached her.

"Don't I know it." She continued to chop weeds with the hoe.

"We just put in Miss Lillie's garden, and I know firsthand that tending a garden this size is too much work for one person." Her plot was three times the size of Lillie's, and June Ann had just given birth two weeks ago. I was furious with the Larkins and Arnetts for not helping her.

"Well, one person is all I got," she said. I heard the weariness in her voice.

"When do you think Wayne will be back?"

"I dunno. Could be months." She removed her hat to wipe her brow. Her red hair shone as bright as flames in the sun. "He said he'd be back by harvest time, though." In the meantime, she would be forced to do all the work herself, along with spending sleepless nights with a new baby. No wonder she felt hopeless.

"Don't you want to go back to the cabin and rest? I brought you a new book to read. And Miss Lillie finished making that tonic for Feather. She made something to help you with the baby blues, too.

And I have a little present for you." I thought she might cheer up when she saw the lamp oil I had brought.

"I need to finish this row first." She bent to continue hoeing.

I could see the baby moving inside the sling, and I heard a few fitful whimpers. I pulled the hoe out of June Ann's hands. "I'll finish the row for you. I already have blisters the size of dimes. Sit down and rest for a while. It sounds like Feather is waking up."

"I can't ask you to do my work."

"You aren't asking, I'm insisting. Several people helped me with Miss Lillie's garden, so I'm just returning the favor."

"Well . . . I'm much obliged, Allie." She untied the shawl and spread it on the ground, then sat down on it to nurse her baby. When I finished hoeing the row of corn, we walked back to the cabin and fed Feather a spoonful of Lillie's tonic. June Ann took a dose of the other one.

"Phew-ee! That tastes awful! Did you try it, Allie?"

"No. But I did help Miss Lillie make it. And I brought you this, too." I gave her the container of lamp oil. I had dumped it out of the lamp in Mack's bedroom, since I was too weary to read in bed at night. "If Feather keeps you awake now, at least you'll be able to read the book I brought you."

June Ann laid her head on my shoulder and wept. "You're the only friend I have in the whole world!"

I stayed as long as I dared before continuing on my route to the Sawyer farm and the school. When I walked into the classroom, it looked half empty. "Where is everyone?" I asked the teacher.

"We always lose students once spring arrives. Their parents need help with the planting. I hear that the measles are going around, too. Have you had them?"

"Oh, yes. A long time ago." Freddy and I had been sick at the same time, and we had annoyed everyone on our party lines by talking to each other on the telephone all day.

Maggie Coots was waiting for me at her cabin with a pot of tea and a plate of biscuits and jam. We sat and talked about all kinds of things, the way Freddy and I used to do. "Do you know Ike Arnett?" I asked as she poured me a second cup of tea. "He's about my age and plays the fiddle?"

231

"I don't think so. Why?"

"I went with him on Saturday to hear his band play at a wedding."

"Ah! I can see by your smile that you had a good time."

She was right. The memory of that day did make me smile. Had it been the music or Ike—or both?

"I did have fun. He's very sweet, and he's a very talented musician. Not only that, but he likes to read."

"Look at you grinning!"

I was blushing, too. "There's so much work to do every day that it was nice to get away for a change."

"With a good-looking man?"

"Well, yes," I laughed. "With a good-looking man."

"People back home in Massachusetts were so surprised when I wrote and told them I had fallen in love with a Kentucky man. They have such ignorant ideas about the people in these hills. No one could understand how an educated woman like me could fall in love with a man who worked in a coal mine. But Hank was smart and sweet, just like your fellow. And he was handsome, too."

"Oh, I'm not falling in love," I said quickly. "Ike made it clear that he isn't looking for a wife, and I'm certainly not looking for a husband. I like working in the Acorn library, but I don't think I could ever live here all the time like you do."

Maggie wagged her finger at me. "Never say never, Alice."

My last stop was Mack's cabin, where I dropped off more food. I also brought him a letter that had arrived at the library addressed to Mr. Leslie MacDougal. It had a Washington, D.C., return address. I was curious about its contents, of course, but Mack tucked it into his pocket without commenting on it.

"You have time to stay and talk a bit?" he asked. "I'm cooking some stew on the campfire, and I need to keep an eye on it."

I dismounted and followed him back to the fire pit in the little glade. Belle followed us, too, sticking as close to Mack's side as a lover. A small black pot sat bubbling on the coals, and whatever was cooking in it smelled delicious. Mack poked the fire and expertly added another piece of wood. "Have a seat," he said, gesturing to the ring of rocks. "No, sit on this side, Alice, or the wind will blow smoke in your face."

232

I sat down and held my fingers out to the fire to warm them. Once the sun dipped behind the hills every afternoon, the woods grew chilly. Mack remained standing, giving Belle an enthusiastic brushing. I also relied on him to clean her hooves, like Cora had said to do.

"How was your date with Ike Arnett?" he asked without meeting my gaze.

"Fine . . . I'm surprised you remembered."

"You asked me for a character reference, so I wanted to make sure Ike hadn't done anything to make me regret granting my approval." He sounded as stuffy as my father did when he questioned me about boys.

"Ike was a gentleman. He played his fiddle with the band, and I listened to him. I enjoyed myself." I needed to change the subject before Mack caught me grinning or blushing the way Maggie had. "By the way, Ike told me that the reason he turned down your offer to go to Nashville was because your mother was a Larkin. Did you know that?"

"He never mentioned it." I watched Belle's antics in amusement while we talked. Every time Mack stopped brushing her, Belle nudged him with her muzzle as if coaxing him to continue. My grandmother's cat used to do the same thing when she wanted to be petted.

"Ike also told me that you were trying to find this mysterious treasure map everyone is looking for. Is that true? Do you really think one exists?"

"I don't know. All this talk about buried treasure could be just a legend. I tried searching for a while, hoping I could make peace and end the fighting. But I didn't have any luck."

"I don't understand this feud. I don't see how shunning June Ann and Wayne could possibly serve any purpose. It won't change the fact that they're married."

"The families think it will discourage other young people from crossing feud lines when they see what happened to them."

"That's ridiculous. The only person who's discouraged is poor June Ann. Why can't people get along and help each other? When Ike and I started putting in a garden for Miss Lillie, a handful of folks from town all joined in—from both clans. Meanwhile, June Ann is all alone up there, hoeing corn with her baby tied to her chest."

"That's because you and Miss Lillie aren't Larkins or Arnetts. Besides, the families will try to outdo each other to show which one of them is more caring and generous toward people outside the clan."

"They all came to your funeral, too, even though you're a Larkin."

"That's different. I was dead. The only good Larkin is a dead one—and the same goes for the Arnetts." Mack gave the horse a gentle shove, pushing her away. "Go on, Belle. That's enough. Go eat some grass or something." He crouched to stir his stew, then sat down beside me. "Those clans have been fighting for sixty years. They're not likely to make up anytime soon."

"Meanwhile, June Ann suffers from loneliness."

"Right. And the more people you tell about her, the more afraid the younger generation will be to cross family lines."

"So I'm making it worse?"

Mack shrugged. "I doubt it could get any worse." Belle sidled up behind him and nibbled his neck. He pushed her aside. "What's gotten into you? Go away or I'll tie you up!" I couldn't help laughing.

"When I was helping Lillie make a tonic for June Ann and her baby, I found the notes you typed for Lillie—her remedies and folk cures. I offered to help her type up the rest of them."

"You would really do that?"

"Sure. I'm a very good typist. Fast, too."

"That would be a huge weight off my mind, Alice. They say that when an old person dies, it's as though a library burns. I know someone at the state university who's interested in publishing her compilation. It would be an important contribution to Kentucky's history and folklore."

"I'm happy to help. But do you know where Lillie's family is? I'm worried about who will take care of her after I go home. I would like to help her contact someone."

"I was looking into that before I got shot. It's hard to get any personal information out of Lillie."

"She has told me a few stories from her past."

"Good. Maybe you can get her to tell you some more while

you're working on the book. I'd like to contact her family, too, but I hardly know where to begin."

"Do you know someone in Washington?" I asked, remembering the letter he had received. He frowned at me as if I was being nosy, so I quickly added, "If so, we could ask them to check the U.S. Census records for information. We'd have to know which state and county her son lived in, but the census might lead us to an address."

"As a matter of fact, I do have a friend who lives in that area. See if you can get Lillie to tell you more about her son, Buster. Maybe my friend can help us find him."

"Do you know if Lillie ever had other children?"

"She never talks much about herself. And the only child I've ever heard her mention is Buster. He must be in his seventies or eighties by now, if he's even alive."

"Goodness. We'd better hurry, then."

He poked the fire again and I caught a whiff of the stew.

"Mm. That smells good. What is it?"

"You want some? I think it's nearly done. As soon as the potatoes get soft, we can eat it."

I looked at him warily. "You didn't answer my question. What's in it?"

He picked up the spoon and stirred it, showing me the contents. "Potatoes and carrots . . . onions, some home-canned tomatoes . . ."

"And meat. I see chunks of meat in there. What kind is it?"

"You're awfully suspicious!" Mack broke into a wide grin. He looked so different now that his beard was gone and I could see his face. And the dimple in his cheek. The wooly man I'd first met would have looked more at home here in the woods than this nicely groomed version—and this version would look more at home behind the librarian's desk. "Haven't you ever heard the expression, 'Don't look a gift horse in the mouth'?" he asked.

"I have. But Lillie fed me squirrel the other night without telling me."

"I'll bet it tasted good. But this isn't squirrel—it's rabbit. I set a few snares." I must have made a face, because he laughed and said, "Don't look at me like that. Do you want me to starve to death up here?"

"Forget it," I said, waving my hand. "I'm not hungry. But thanks just the same . . . So, tell me, how long have you known Lillie?"

"Since the day I was born. My mother died giving birth to me. Lillie was the midwife, so I guess she felt responsible. She said my mother made her swear that she would always take care of me and never let me work a single day in the mines. Lillie kept those promises—which is why I need to finish my work and get back home. I should be taking care of Lillie myself."

"What about your father?"

"He died in a mining accident when I was three."

"And the house where the library is? Was that your parents' house? It's so much nicer than the other houses in Acorn."

"My great-grandfather Larkin built it. His son, my maternal grandfather, was still alive when I was orphaned so he let Lillie and me move in with him. Before that, we lived in the cabin where I'm staying now."

I could tell that this conversation was making Mack uncomfortable. He stood and grabbed a fork from the stone table and used it to poke one of the potatoes. "They're done. You sure you don't want to stay and have some stew?"

"Yes, I'm quite sure. I need to get back to town. Maggie Coots said it wasn't safe to roam around up here after dark because of the wildcat." I looked around for something to stand on that would make me tall enough to reach the stirrup. The stone table looked as though it would work. I grabbed Belle's bridle and led her over to it so I could climb into the saddle without Mack's help. He walked with us as far as the creek.

"See you in a few days?" he asked. Loneliness seemed to drape over him as we prepared to leave, just as it had blanketed June Ann and Maggie.

"Yes, I'll be back. Do you want me to bring you any books to read?"

"No . . . Give Lillie my love."

I didn't have to ride my route the next day so I told Lillie I would work on her book. "Not today, honey," she said from her bed. "I ain't feeling strong enough."

Her bouts of weakness worried me. She seemed to be growing frailer each day. I knew she couldn't live forever, but I didn't want her to pass away yet. Her crusty personality was growing on me, and I was determined to finish typing her book of folk remedies. I knew how much it meant to her, and I found I wanted to be part of saving something so important.

"You can stay in bed and I'll set up Mack's typewriter in my room. Once I get used to your handwriting, I can type on my own unless I need you to decipher a word."

The work was harder than I'd thought it would be. It turned out that Lillie had several notebooks, not just one, with crumbling ivory pages that were decades old. I had to be extremely careful or the paper would break off and turn to powder like dry leaves. She had written the recipes and instructions in pencil, and many of the words were smudged and faded and blurred. I found the place where Mack had stopped typing and was dismayed to see that he had gotten only as far as the first notebook.

I typed for a few hours, using the same format that Mack had used. Halfway through the morning, I encountered a word that I just couldn't figure. I tiptoed into Lillie's room, not wanting to disturb her, but she opened her eyes and asked, "What is it, honey?"

"I'm sorry, but I can't figure out this word. What does this say?"

She squinted at the page for a moment. "That says, 'Sam's liniment.' This here was his recipe. He was a carriage driver on his massa's plantation and he knew all about horses. He used to cook up a batch of this liniment whenever a horse was feeling lame. They get the rheumatism, too, you know. Just like people do."

"Was this your Sam? The man you loved?"

"Mmm hmm."

I sat down on the chair beside her bed, not wanting to miss this opportunity to hear more of her story. "Please tell me about him—and about Charley and Buster. My shoulders are stiff from typing, and I could use a break."

"Where did I leave off?"

"You told me that your former mistress gave you the addresses of where Charley and Buster had been sold."

"That's right. She sure did. So Sam and me saved our money, and when school got out for the summer, we went looking for them."

"How did you travel?"

"We walked most of the way, because a lot of the train tracks was still tore up from the war. I think we might a took a ferry down one of the rivers—I can't remember. But I know we walked a long way. And then we walked some more. We found the plantation where Charley'd been sold, but we knew better than to go there. Them white massas don't like to see colored folk walking up to their doorstep, especially Negroes they don't know. So Sam and me went to the colored town nearby. Well, I don't suppose you could call it a town. Just a bunch of shacks. Them was hard, hard times after the war. Everybody was so poor—whites and coloreds alike. At least the white folks had land so they could grow things. We didn't have nothing but the clothes on our backs."

Lillie paused to sit up and take a sip of water from her glass on the nightstand. The sun had finally climbed over the top of the mountain to the east—a process that took most of the morning—and it was chasing the cold shadows out of the room. Dust motes floated in a sunbeam before settling on Lillie's dresser. I waited, hoping she would continue her story.

"We found Charley without too much trouble. He was share-cropping on his massa's old plantation. By now so much time had passed since we'd seen each other that he'd gone ahead and married someone else, and his new wife looked like she was fixing to claw my eyes out any minute. Charley says we was already divorced so I should go ahead and marry Sam, because he was happy with his new wife. Even had a couple of kids by her. So that was that."

Lillie looked over at me and nodded, as if she had told me everything I needed to know. "Wait. What about Buster?"

"I told Charley I was looking for Buster and asked if he wanted to help. He says no, he's got four new children now. Says he has to work hard to keep food on his table and can't be running off like that. So Sam and me left and went off to find Buster."

The front door squeaked open downstairs, and I heard Mamaw call, "Anybody here?"

I sighed in frustration. "I'll be right down," I called back. I wanted to hear more of Lillie's story, but the boys wanted to hear their story, too. We had only two chapters left in *Treasure Island*. "I'll be back in an hour or so with your lunch," I told Lillie.

I went downstairs to the non-fiction section to read, and soon I was as caught up in the end of the tale as the children were. They laughed and tussled with each other after I read, "The end."

"That was real good," Bobby said.

"Can you read us another pirate story?" Clyde asked.

"I'll see what I can find. I enjoyed the book, too."

"There's buried treasure around here, you know," Lloyd said. "If we could find the treasure map, we'd be rich."

"What would you do with the money?" I asked.

They started a shouting match, telling me all the things they'd buy: a shiny new truck for their pa; a radio so Mamaw could listen to music; Clyde wanted a new horse for his ma so she could ride her route faster and get home quicker. I thought of the list I had recited to Ike with a wringer washing machine and a refrigerator and indoor plumbing. I felt very spoiled and selfish.

"They say them Larkins found the treasure and stole it already," Mamaw said.

"I'd like to hear more about this buried treasure," I said. "Will you tell me the story?"

Mamaw leaned close and the boys grew quiet, listening as intently as they had to *Treasure Island*, even though I was sure they had heard it before. "There was once two friends named Isaac Larkin and Wilbur Arnett," Mamaw began. "They came upon a great treasure when they was out hunting one day, and they buried it in the ground for safekeeping. Then they made a map of where it was buried so their families would know where to dig it up."

"Why didn't they just divide up the treasure and spend it themselves?" I asked.

"No one knows. And nobody remembers where the treasure came from, either."

"I'll bet it came from pirates!" Lloyd said.

Bobby elbowed him. "Shh!"

"Isaac and Wilbur both died," Mamaw continued, "without telling anybody where the map or the treasure was. The Arnetts—that's my clan—always figured the Larkins found the map and dug the money up and didn't share it with us. We all wondered about Mack, having money for college and all these books. He was a Larkin, you

239

know. But Miss Lillie said his college was free and that he worked for a newspaper up north for a while and made enough money to buy all the books. And some of them are Lillie's books, I guess."

"I'm surprised that Faye and the others made friends with Mack," I said, "even though he was a Larkin."

"Well, his mama was a Larkin, and she died the day Mack was born. He wasn't raised by Larkins. And Mack himself was more like a flatlander than one of us because he never worked in the mines. You see?"

No. I didn't see. I would never understand the intricacies of this feud.

CHAPTER 22

I went upstairs to check on Lillie after Mamaw and the boys left, but she was sound asleep again. I came back downstairs and had just sat down behind the library desk to catch up on my work when Ike bounded through the front door.

"Hey, Alice. Don't you look pretty today."

"Thank you." He reminded me so much of an overgrown boy that I had to resist the urge to invite him to come and listen to me read stories with Faye's boys. "Are you here to check out another book?" I asked.

"Nope." His neatly combed hair flopped into his eyes as he shook his head. "I came to take you on a lunchtime picnic. What do you say?"

"Right now? I'm supposed to be working in the library. It's supposed to be open."

"Oh, yeah? How many customers are you expecting besides me and them boys?" He smiled, obviously aware that we had no other "customers." When I didn't reply he added, "Does somebody have overdue books they're bringing back this afternoon?"

"No, I'm not expecting any patrons." I couldn't help smiling.

"Well, I know a real good picnic spot that I'm dying to show to you." He could see that my resolve was weakening. He reached for my hand, pulling me out of my chair and away from my desk. I couldn't believe I was agreeing. Back home I never would have shirked my library duties for something as frivolous as a picnic. My devotion used to annoy Gordon, who would sometimes beg me to leave early if the library was deserted. I had always refused.

"We won't be gone all day," Ike assured me. "Just for lunch. You got something we can make sandwiches out of?"

"Sandwiches? I'm sorry but I don't have any bread." He gave me a puzzled look, as if he'd never heard of running out of bread before. I felt embarrassed. "We haven't had any real bread since Mack's funeral, just corn bread or biscuits."

"Why's that?"

"Because I don't know how to bake it. Back home we buy our bread at the store."

"Oh. I guess we can make do with corn bread, then." We went out to the kitchen and put together a quick lunch. I brought a tray upstairs to Lillie and told her where I was going while Ike wrapped our lunch in a dish towel and packed it in Lillie's picking basket.

We left through the back door, carrying a blanket to sit on, and followed a path I had never taken before, downstream from the library instead of upstream. We crossed the creek by leaping from stone to stone, then followed a narrow dirt road until we came to an orchard. The fruit trees were all in bloom, flowering in delicate shades of white and pastel pink. I could hear bees buzzing, drawn by the sweet-smelling blossoms.

"Oh, Ike, this is a beautiful place!"

"You like it?"

"I love it!" I whirled in a circle like a character in a movie. I would have danced if there had been music. We spread the blanket on the ground and sat down to eat. Pastel petals showered down on us like confetti every time a breeze blew. I couldn't imagine a more romantic setting.

"I'm glad you decided to stay in Acorn," Ike said as we ate. "And not just for my sake, either. Mack worked real hard setting up that library and there wasn't anybody but you who could've run it for him."

"I know. I'm hoping to teach the packhorse ladies how to do the work so they can take over when I do have to go home."

He smiled. "I hope they're slow learners so it takes a while."

"I also want to process the non-fiction books the right way before I go, and set up a card catalogue so it'll be easier to find a book. Mack seemed to know every book by heart, but no one else does."

"Speaking of Mack, you know what never made any sense to me? His hunting accident. I went out hunting with him a couple of times before I learnt he was a Larkin, and he was always real careful around guns. I don't see how he coulda shot himself."

I felt a flush spreading up my cheeks and hoped it wouldn't give anything away. I was a terrible liar. My father could spot a fib in an instant and would "paddle the devil out of me" for it. That's exactly what he used to say, after showing me the verse in the Bible that said Satan was "the father of lies."

I swallowed the corn bread I was chewing and held up my hands in innocence. "Don't ask me, Ike. I don't know anything at all about guns. Or hunting. And I was only in town one day when it happened."

"You know what I think? I think somebody shot him."

"Who would want to shoot him?" It was the question I had been asking since the day it happened.

"The people who run the coal mine are at the top of my list."

"Why?" I had to step carefully, just as I had when hopping on the stones to cross the creek.

"They found out that Mack was writing a book, telling how they cheat all us miners. And after Hank Coots died, Mack started snooping around and asking a lot more questions. I never did believe that Hank died in an accident any more than I believe that Mack shot himself."

"Why would Mack lie about it? Wouldn't he want whoever shot Hank to go to jail?"

"Jail? Ha! The sheriff would never put the mine owners in jail. They're his friends. I think Mack lied so whoever did it wouldn't come back and shoot more people for standing up for Hank."

"But now there won't be any justice."

"There ain't no justice around here. It's every man for himself. Whoever starts snooping around might be next." His words sent a chill through me. We ate in silence for a long moment, then Ike reached for my hand.

"You know why I brought you here?"

"Because it's so beautiful with the trees in bloom? So sweet-smelling?"

"That's part of it," he said, laughing. "But I also wanted to show you this place because I think this is where the treasure is buried."

"Really?" My heart sped up, but whether it was from the idea of finding buried treasure or from the warmth of Ike's fingers as he caressed my hand, I couldn't tell. "Have you found the treasure map?"

"No. But I been doing a lot of thinking. If you draw a straight line between Isaac Larkin's house and Wilbur Arnett's house—they're the two men who buried the treasure—this orchard is smack-dab in the middle."

"Really? That's fascinating. Where are these two houses?"

"My family and I live in Great-Granddaddy Arnett's house, up there on the hill. And you're living in Great-Granddaddy Larkin's place."

"The library?"

"That's right. So I paced it all out one day, walking in a straight line from my house to Mack's, and guess what?"

"This orchard is halfway between the two?"

"Right. Now, if only I knew exactly where to dig . . ."

My excitement grew as I glanced around the orchard. Buried treasure? "Well, if I were going to bury a treasure," I said, "I would look for a landmark to use as a point of reference. You know, a big rock or a huge tree."

"That's a great idea!" But Ike's enthusiasm quickly turned to a frown. "Except that they planted this orchard about ten years ago and the treasure's been buried for more than sixty."

"What was on this property sixty years ago?" I asked.

"Far as I know, it was just woods. I remember when they cleared this land to plant the trees."

244

"Who owns the orchard? And is he an Arnett or a Larkin?"

"It belongs to the postmaster. He ain't related to either side."

"But the treasure would rightfully belong to him if it's on his property."

Ike leaned close to me. "We would have to dig it up at night," he said in a whisper.

"We?"

"Don't you want to help me? It would be an adventure, Alice. And it seems fitting that we'd be the ones to find it since you and I are living in the two great-granddaddies' houses. We could split it fifty-fifty and leave Acorn for good."

I laughed. "As exciting as a treasure hunt sounds, Ike, I don't think I want to get mixed up in this feud." Or go to jail for theft and property damage.

"Well, you think about it some more—and meanwhile, I'll try to look for a landmark." He glanced all around as if one might pop up any minute. Then he turned his attention back to me. "You won't tell anyone what I figured out, will you?"

"I promise not to say a word. Your secret is safe with me." I made a gesture of locking my lips shut with a key and throwing it over my shoulder.

He moved even closer and ran his finger over my lips. "I better make sure that secret is sealed real tight." Ike took my face in his hands and kissed me beneath the canopy of apple blossoms.

Leapin' lizards! as Little Orphan Annie would say. I could forget my own name after a kiss like that, let alone a secret. The kiss lasted longer than our previous one had, but it still ended much too soon.

"Thanks for the picnic," I murmured when I could speak. "I'd better get back to the library now." We walked hand in hand until we had to cross the creek, then parted when the library came in sight.

"Until next time," Ike said with a wink. He turned and walked back toward the orchard. I returned to the library, completely incapable of concentrating on anything.

Belle and I were following the creek on my book route early the next day when Mack stepped out of the bushes near his cabin, startling me. "Don't do that! You scared me!"

"Sorry . . . Can I talk to you?"

"What's wrong?" He hadn't shaved, and I could tell by the deep crease between his eyebrows that he was worried. He had never waylaid me on my trip upstream before, so his worry became contagious.

"Not here. Come back into the woods with me." He grabbed Belle's bridle and led us back to the glade. I had to crouch low in the saddle to keep from hitting my head on the low-hanging branches.

"Will this take long? Should I dismount?"

"Yeah. You'd better get off."

I welcomed the chance. I had been riding for three weeks, but I still wasn't used to it, and I felt chafed and saddlesore at the end of each day after riding. Mack motioned to the circle of stones and we both sat down. He hadn't built a fire in the pit, and I shivered in the cool shade.

"That letter I got from Washington?" he began. "It's from someone at the mining bureau. He's willing to take another look into Hank's death."

"That's good news . . . isn't it?"

"Yes. But he needs me to send him some new evidence before they'll reopen the case."

"Why do I have a feeling that this is going to involve me?"

"Listen, Alice. Ever since you told me the files were still in the mine office, I've been trying to figure out how I can get a look at them."

I stuck my fingers in my ears. "Don't tell me your plans. The less I know, the easier it is not to lie."

He grabbed my hands and pulled them down, holding them for a moment so I wouldn't plug my ears again. "I have to tell you some of my plans because I need your help."

"Oh no. I distinctly remember you saying that from now on, the only thing I had to do for you was bring food."

"I don't really need you—I need Belle. I'm still not strong enough to walk all the way to the mine. All you'll have to do is ride up here a week from next Tuesday night and bring her to me."

"Why that night?"

"Because the *Almanac* says there won't be a moon on April twenty-first. I need the night to be as dark as possible so I won't be seen."

"Wait. Maggie says it's dangerous to come up here at night because of the wildcat."

"Maggie worries too much."

"She saw paw prints on her property."

He made a face, waving away my concerns. "If you would bring Belle up here for me, I could ride her to the mine, get what I need, and ride back. Hopefully before dawn."

"If you expect me to sit in your creepy cabin all by myself all night, you're out of your mind!"

"You can always ride to the mine and back with me if you don't want to wait here all alone. I could use your help going through the files, but that's up to you. I won't force you to do it. Either way, I need you to bring Belle up here to the cabin on the night of the twenty-first."

"You said the sheriff has people watching the mine."

"I said 'maybe.' That's why I need to go at night."

"You're crazy! What are you going to tell him when he catches you breaking in? That you came to use the telephone?"

"I'll tell him to stop helping the Jupiter Coal Company cover up Hank's murder and put the people who were responsible for it in jail."

"You think the mine officials committed murder?"

"I'm convinced that Hank Coots's death wasn't an accident, but I need proof. That's why I need to look in those files."

"Why would they keep incriminating evidence in plain sight like that?"

"Because they're stupid, Alice. And they think they're above the law. With the sheriff in their pocket, they can get away with anything, cover up any crime."

I remembered that Ike had said the same thing, that there was no justice. And like Mack, he also thought that Hank's death hadn't been an accident. But did I want to get mixed up in this?

"Don't you see, Alice? It has taken me all this time just to find a government official in Washington who would agree to reopen the investigation. But I have to show him some new evidence. I want justice for Hank and Maggie, and this is the only way I can think of to get proof. Will you please bring Belle up here for me that night?"

I hesitated. Mack gripped my shoulders, and I could see his impatience. "I'm not asking you to help me break in or take anything. Just bring me the blasted horse! Can't you do that much? For Maggie's sake at least, if not for mine?"

"Maggie Coots is my friend, and I know she misses her husband. But if I help you and we're caught, I'll be in as much trouble as you are."

He let go of my shoulders and exhaled. "Okay. Do me a favor, then. Talk to Maggie when you see her today. Don't say a word about what I'm doing, but ask her to tell you about Hank and the work that he was involved in before he died. That's all I ask. Maybe it will help you make up your mind. But please do it soon, Alice. Because if I don't go on that night, I'll have to wait another month until there's another moonless night."

I left a few minutes later. Talking with Mack had made me late, so I didn't have time for an unscheduled visit with June Ann. I hoped Lillie's two tonics were working. Maggie's cabin was the last stop on my route that day, and it was such a warm afternoon that she and I sat outside on her porch, talking. I had no idea how to bring up the subject of her husband's death, but when she asked me how my romance with Ike was going, I saw the perfect chance.

"He took me on a picnic yesterday. He came into the library on the spur of the moment, and said 'Let's go.' He took me to somebody's orchard and it was a beautiful, romantic place with all of the apple trees in blossom." I sighed, remembering.

"Sounds like someone is getting swept off her feet."

"Maybe . . . a little. Was it like that with you and Hank?"

"Hardly! We locked horns over Hank's younger brothers for the longest time. He didn't approve of my teaching style, to say the least. But you know what they say, sparks can produce flames."

"Ike talked about Hank yesterday. He said he didn't think his death was an accident. Do you agree? That it wasn't an accident?"

"It makes no difference at all what I think. The official investigation ruled that it was an accident."

"Why would Ike say that? What was your husband involved with at the mine?"

Maggie shook her head, then took so long to reply that I didn't think she was going to talk about it. When she did, her voice sounded weary.

"Hank's father had died in a mining accident, so in the beginning, Hank was simply trying to get some safety measures in place. Then Mack came back to town and convinced him that the miners needed to form a union. I was against the idea because of all the union trouble over in Harlan County. But Hank thought that at the very least, he could pressure the mine officials to stop the practice of the short load, and set fair prices in the company store."

"What's a short load?"

"The miners' loads were measured by the long ton, which is 2,200 pounds. But the company was selling that same coal by the short ton, which is 2,000 pounds. The miners got gypped out of 200 pounds' worth of pay with every load. Not only that, but a company official weighed the coal, and if he decided there was too much rock in the load, the miners wouldn't get paid at all. There could be a ton of coal and a few pounds of rock, but the company would claim the entire load was no good. Hank was trying to demand a 'check weigh-man,' someone who worked for the miners and could verify the company's decisions."

"That seems fair."

"You probably saw the housing they built for the miners? They charged outrageous prices for those shacks and took the rent money straight from the miners' pay. Their wages were paid in scrip, not real money, forcing the miners to buy food and supplies at the company store—at inflated prices. Miners had to pay for their own lamps and fuel, too—again, with inflated prices. At the end of the workweek, most miners owed more money than they'd made. They could never get ahead. As the saying goes, they owed their souls to the company store."

"I can see why the miners would want to join together and unionize."

"When the company saw that Hank was getting everyone all fired up, they promoted him, at first—which was very strange since they usually run union organizers out of town. Hank had his 'accident' the first week on his new job."

"That does seem suspicious."

"Six months later, the mine closed when the Depression hit and the factories up north started shutting down."

"Didn't the sheriff investigate Hank's accident?" I knew the answer to my question, but I wanted to see if Maggie's reply would confirm what Mack and Ike had told me.

"Of course he did. A mine safety official came, too. But the Jupiter Coal Company controls the sheriff, so no one was surprised when the investigation concluded that it was an accident."

"That doesn't seem fair."

"You know what wasn't fair, Alice? I finally had convinced Hank to quit the mine for good and go to college like Mack had. The best way he could help his brothers and improve things in Acorn was to get an education. He had just started applying to colleges when Mack came back to town to research his book. They were friends, so . . . well, you know the rest. Mack convinced Hank to stay and try to make things better."

I was beginning to see that Mack's motivation wasn't simply for justice. He must feel guilty for the part he'd played in his friend's death. "My friend Ike doesn't think that Mack's death was an accident, either. He thinks someone from the mine shot him."

"Who knows—and what difference does it make now? They're both dead. Why are you asking me about this? Hank is gone and nothing will bring him back."

"Don't you want justice?"

Maggie gave a bitter laugh. "I used to believe in justice—and in a God of justice. But not anymore. I've seen too much injustice around here, and God doesn't seem to care one bit."

"That's not true, Maggie. The Bible says that—"

"Would you like to see Hank's grave?"

I swallowed my words. She didn't want a memorized Bible verse from me about how God watches over the sparrows. "Yes. I would like that," I said.

We walked into the woods for a short distance and reached a small clearing. Hank's grave marker was made from polished granite with his name and the date of his birth and death chiseled into it. "I didn't want him to be buried behind the church with the rest of his family," Maggie said. "I wanted him here, near me."

I expected to see only one tombstone, but there were two. Maggie drew a deep breath and said, "Our daughter is buried beside him."

The smaller granite tombstone had an angel carved on it. Rhoda Lee Coots had died at the age of two, a few months after Hank Coots had died. I couldn't speak.

"If God really cares, Allie, why does He allow innocent children to die before they have a chance to live?"

I reached to take her hand, but I still couldn't speak. I tried to think of what my father might say to Maggie, but the sight of that little tombstone left me without words.

"The coal in our state is as valuable as gold to the northern factories and power companies," Maggie said. "Yet the people who mine it all their lives have to watch their husbands and children die. Is that fair? Don't tell me that God cares."

"I'm so sorry, Maggie. I had no idea." I didn't know what else to say. If I lost my husband and child, might I lose my faith, too?

Maggie released my hand. "You'd better get going, Alice. I'll see you next week." She walked back to the cabin without waiting for me, closing the door behind her.

I grieved for Maggie as I rode down the creek toward home. As tragic as the deaths of her husband and daughter were, what saddened me the most was the death of her faith. In my naïvete, I'd known of only two types of people: those who had faith in God and went to church every Sunday, and those who didn't. I didn't know what to make of someone like Maggie Coots, who had left her privileged life behind to serve God—and now, after suffering great tragedy, no longer believed in Him. My Sunday school understanding of faith hadn't prepared me for Maggie's questions.

I had attended church all my life and had been raised as a Christian by God-fearing parents. But I realized that if the story of my own faith was made into a book, it would have nothing but a title page. Mine was a superficial Sunday morning faith, memorizing verses and parroting answers. When Lillie had asked me to pray for Mack on the morning he'd been shot, all I'd had to offer was a recitation of the Lord's Prayer. Maggie was my friend. I longed to help her—and I didn't know how.

Mack was waiting in the bushes for me in the same place he had waited this morning. This time I was expecting him. "Did you talk to Maggie?" he asked.

"Yes." I wiped my tears on my sleeve. Mack led Belle and me into the woods again and waited for me to dismount.

"Do you understand now why I have to search the mining office for information? If it was murder and not an accident, then it's my fault for stirring things up. Hank wouldn't have pushed so hard or gotten involved in the first place if it wasn't for me. I need to know the truth . . . I need to know if I caused his death."

"Yes. I do understand." And maybe if Mack got justice for Maggie, it would begin to restore her faith. "How long will it take to find what you want in those files?"

"Probably most of the night. I'll have to ride to the mine through the woods because I don't want to be seen on the road. And once I'm inside the office, there will be a lot of papers to look through."

"How will you see anything in the dark? You can't light a lamp, and the electricity is probably turned off, too."

"My father had a miner's cap. It's pretty old, but Lillie can show you where it is and how to put fuel in it."

"Is it the kind of hat with the lamp on the front?"

Mack nodded. "It's still up to you whether you want to wait here or come with me, Alice. I don't care, but I need the horse."

I didn't like either choice, especially with a wildcat roaming the woods. Mack was waiting for my answer. "Okay," I decided. "I'll bring Belle to you. But I need time to think about whether I'll stay here or not. Maybe I can come up with a third choice before then."

"Listen, I've been working on this plan ever since you told me the files were still there. I've thought it through a hundred ways, trying to figure out every possible thing that could go wrong— and trying to work it out so that I won't get you into trouble."

"The fact that you're riding Belle will link us together, won't it?"

"Hopefully everything will go smoothly and you can ride Belle home before either one of us is seen. But just in case something does happen, here's what you'll need to do. Leave the shed door open when you come up here. I'm going to leave the saddle here and ride Belle bareback to the mine, so if the sheriff does show up and I have to sneak off into the woods without Belle, you can tell everyone that someone broke in and stole her. Bring her halter, too, so it will look like she and the saddle were both stolen."

"What if they catch you?"

"If I get caught, I'll say I stole her. Either way, it won't look like you helped me."

"How will I get home from here if you get caught? And how will I know?"

"I'm sorry, but if I'm not back by dawn, you'll have to walk home without me or Belle."

"Wait. Why can't you drop me off in town before you go to the mine?"

"I can't take a chance on being seen in town. Besides, the extra trip will waste too much time. I need to ride through the woods to the mine, not on the road."

"Better yet, why can't you walk down here and steal Belle yourself?"

"I don't think I can walk that far and still have enough strength for the rest of the night. As it is, the ride is going to take all the sap out of me."

"This is crazy!" I had walked into a plot too absurd for a novel. "If you get caught, the sheriff will know that I helped fake your death and funeral. And it won't take a genius to figure out that I snooped around in the mine office for you."

"I'll get you off the hook, I promise. I'll swear that I forced you to do it, which is true enough, I suppose. The worst they will do is send you home to Illinois—and that's what you want anyway, isn't it?"

"No, the worst they could do is kill me just like they killed Hank and make it look like an accident. I wish I had more time to think about this."

"I know. But there isn't time. The night of the new moon is my only chance."

I looked at this strange, complicated man and couldn't help admiring him for his decency and courage. He had returned to Acorn determined to help his community, and now, when he could easily disappear and never return, he was willing to stay and risk his life to fight an injustice. Men like Mack were rare indeed.

I climbed onto Belle again, balancing on the stone table to do it. Mack watched but didn't offer to help. I was about to leave when he said, "Oh, and when you come that night, bring my gun. Make sure it's loaded."

CHAPTER 23

I couldn't get over the fact that my new friend Maggie had lost her faith. I longed to talk to Lillie and see what advice she could offer, but Lillie was having another weak spell, eating very little, sleeping too much. I couldn't expect a one-hundred-year-old woman to live too much longer, but she couldn't die now! I needed her advice, her wisdom.

On Friday afternoon I was working at my desk downstairs when the front door opened and in walked Ike. I could tell by the way my heart sped up at the sight of him that I was starting to have feelings for him. I could not allow that to happen.

"Hi. How are you?" I asked. My voice sounded squeaky and much too high-pitched. I cleared my throat.

"I'm good." He stopped at the parlor door and leaned against the doorframe, studying me.

I waited as long as I could for him to say something or tell me why he was here before finally breaking the silence. "Did you want something, Ike? Another book?"

"Nope."

"Another picnic?"

"Nope." He grinned like a boy with a secret.

"Did you find the treasure?" I asked in a stage whisper. He shook his head. "Well, what brings you here, then?"

He shrugged his wide shoulders. "Nothing. I just came to watch you work."

"What?"

"You watched me play my fiddle; now I'm watching you work."

I could feel my traitorous cheeks growing warm. "That was different, Ike. At least the wedding was interesting. I'm not doing anything interesting, and there's no music." I picked up the file box, fumbling as I pretended to search for a card.

"That doesn't matter. You're very nice to look at, you know."

I put down the box. "Seriously, Ike. It's hard to concentrate when you're staring at me." He walked closer, still smiling, his arms folded across his chest. I didn't know what to expect from him next, and that thought alone was disconcerting. "There must be something more productive for you to do than stand there."

"Why? You got something you need me to do around here? Like I said, I'm willing to help you go through Mack's clothes and things."

"Um . . . it's still too soon for that. I didn't realize until the other day that Miss Lillie raised Mack. He's like a son to her."

"Hmm. I see what you mean." He hadn't taken his dark brown eyes off of me for a second.

I opened the desk drawer, rifled through the pencils, closed it. I picked up a book, opened it, closed it again. Ike continued to stare, smiling slightly as if watching me was the most entertaining thing he'd done all week. I cleared my throat again.

"I need to put these books back on their proper shelves now." I stood and picked up the stack I had finished carding. I would have to walk right past him to get to the non-fiction section. Ike stopped me, resting his hand on my arm, and I felt the heat of his fingers through my sweater. "You want to go out in the kitchen where nobody will see us and kiss for a while?" he murmured.

Leaping lizards!

"As tempting as that sounds," I said, clearing my throat again, "I think I'll have to say no. I'm supposed to be on duty. And I have all these books to put away."

"Okay. How about if we kiss in there?" He tilted his head, gesturing to the non-fiction room. Was he joking?

"There are too many windows, Ike. This house isn't very private. And you never know when the packhorse ladies will return."

"Then I'll just have to sit here and stare at you some more." He followed me the way Belle had followed Mack and sank down in Lillie's chair to watch me put away the books. I couldn't imagine Gordon coming into the library to watch me work—and I certainly wouldn't have gone to the funeral parlor to watch him. Life certainly moved at a slower pace here in Acorn than it did back home.

Ike was still watching me when I put the last book on the shelf. I needed to give him a job to do. "Do you know anything about bats?" I asked, turning to him.

"Sure. I read a book once that told all about them." He jumped up from the chair as if willing to help me find it. "They're interesting animals. Did you know they eat three times their own weight in insects every night?"

"Is that right?" I took a step back as he inched closer to me. "Well, there's a bat that flies around my bedroom every night, and I want to get rid of it."

"Why? I'll bet you don't have any insects in your room, do you?"

"That's beside the point. The bat needs to live someplace else. Would you happen to know how to get rid of it?"

"Sure. I can kill it for you."

I felt a pang of remorse. The bat was annoying but it hadn't hurt me in any way. "You don't have to kill it, do you, Ike? As much as I don't like it flying around my bedroom at night, I would still hate for it to die. Couldn't you set it free somehow?"

"You flatlanders are the funniest people I ever met," he said with a chuckle. "Tell you what, I'll try and see how it's getting into your room, and maybe I can block off the opening. Then your little friend can live, okay? He just won't be able to get into your room."

"Okay."

He offered me his arm. "Let's go up and have a look around."

Ike wore such a mischievous look on his face that I froze. I had stepped into very dangerous territory. My mother always emphasized the danger of putting myself in a compromising position with a man—especially an attractive one. And Ike's kisses could easily make me forget propriety.

"Um . . . we'd better not go up there together. It wouldn't look good at all if we were seen alone in my bedroom. Besides, Lillie is sleeping up there. Can't you get rid of the bat without my help?"

"I'm trying to get you alone, Alice." He bent to nuzzle my neck the same way that Belle had nuzzled Mack's. I squirmed away, even though the shivers his lips sent down my spine were quite enjoyable.

"I know exactly what you're trying to do," I said with a nervous laugh. "You're not being very subtle about it."

"That bat is probably hanging upside down someplace right now. They like to sleep during the day. And they usually bring their whole family with them once they get inside a house. In fact, they'll have even more babies every spring. You sure you don't want to come up with me and at least see where this bat family is living and how they're getting in?"

"No. I'd rather be down here where it's nice and safe while you do what you need to do." Safe from Ike as well as from the bat. "In fact, I'd rather not be here at all when you're working. I don't think I could stand it if you chased a whole flock of bats out of hiding and they started flying all around and getting in my hair." I unconsciously hunched my shoulders and brushed at my hair as if one of them was flying above my head right now.

"You're safe, Alice." Ike smoothed down my hair and gave me a quick peck on my forehead before I could stop him. "When do you go off on your route again?"

"Not until Tuesday." I shuddered a second time because one week from Tuesday I would have to ride up into the woods at night for Mack.

"Tell you what. I'll come back while you're gone and take care of it. I'll check the attic, too. Is that okay, Miss Lillie?"

I turned around to see her hobbling into the foyer behind me. I was very glad that she hadn't caught us smooching in the nonfiction room or the kitchen.

"Is what okay, honey?" she asked.

"Alice wants me to get the bat out of her bedroom."

"We've always had bats. They don't bother nobody."

"Alice doesn't like them. She says she wants me to get rid of it."

"Do what she wants, then." Lillie shrugged and hobbled toward the kitchen, leaning on her cane.

Ike needed to leave. He was much too attractive, and I was much too attracted to him. I had work to do. "I'm going to go help Lillie now," I said, sidling away from him. "You can't watch me work anymore. Sorry."

"Yeah, I'm sorry, too. When can I see you again?"

I had been thinking about Maggie's loss of faith before Ike had arrived, and I suddenly had another thought. "Do you ever go to church, Ike?"

"I have been known to go. Why?"

"It's Easter Sunday this weekend. I would like to attend church, but I don't know where to find one. And even if I did find one, I have no way of getting there."

"I'll take you—if you don't mind riding in my truck again."

Beggars couldn't be choosers. "I don't mind. Thanks. And I'll be happy to help pay for your gasoline, too."

"How about if we go to that little church where the wedding was?"

"Wonderful. See you on Sunday?"

"Right. See you, gorgeous."

I invited Miss Lillie to come with us on Sunday, but she declined. "Big trip like that would be too much for me, honey. But you go ahead. I'll be fine."

I rose with the rooster on Sunday morning, excited about finally attending church after all these weeks. My parents would be horrified if they knew how many Sundays I had missed. Father would say that the people in Acorn had been a bad influence on me—although I would have argued that in many ways they had been a very good influence on me. I certainly had worked harder than ever before in my life, and most of the work had been for the sake of other people. And I seemed to pray more and think about God more than I did at home.

I waited on the library porch for Ike to arrive so we could make a quick getaway. He pulled me close on the seat beside him and drove through the vibrant spring-green hills and valleys with his arm around me. When we arrived, he helped me down from the truck yet didn't release my hand. "You can't hold my hand in church, Ike," I whispered as we walked toward the church door.

"Why not?"

"It isn't appropriate." I didn't want to mention that the warmth of his touch would have been much too distracting.

I would describe the simple church service as "lively" and quite unlike the stately, dignified Easter services I was accustomed to back home. It included much more singing than ours did, and the congregation might have taken the biblical command to "make a joyful noise" a bit too literally.

"I should have brought along my fiddle," Ike whispered. It wouldn't have been at all out of place in this rollicking Easter celebration.

It seemed strange to be in church after so much time. Everyone was so joyful as they praised the Lord, and I felt as though I had played hooky from school for too long and needed to catch up. I missed my father's calm, thoughtful preaching. This minister yelled his entire sermon, as if the congregation was hard of hearing. I missed my mother and the sound of her clear alto voice singing alongside me. And even though the congregation back home irritated me at times with their plodding, intrusive ways, I missed them, too. I knew all of the people in their customary pews by name. Here I was a stranger. And homesick.

"Happy Easter, Alice," Ike said afterward, when we'd climbed into his truck. "Let's celebrate." Before I could stop him, he leaned close to kiss me. I pulled away. "What's wrong?"

"I don't know . . . It just doesn't seem right or proper. We're supposed to think about God on Easter Sunday."

"I am thinking of Him. I've been thanking Him all morning that I met you." He leaned close to kiss me again, and although I knew I should have stopped him, I didn't really want to.

"Maybe we shouldn't be kissing right outside the church building," I murmured when we came up for air. "In broad daylight."

"No one knows us here." He tried to continue where we had left off, but this time I did stop him.

"We should go."

"Okay." He gave me a smile and one final kiss, then started the truck engine. He whistled all the way home. Ike Arnett had to be the most cheerful person I had ever met.

We couldn't talk much because of the noisy truck, so I sat back and enjoyed the ride. As we neared Acorn and drove past the mine, I shivered involuntarily. One more week until Mack's midnight break-in. I dreaded the ride up into the woods at night, and I worried for Mack's safety. Ike had his arm draped around my shoulder and had felt me shiver.

"What's wrong? Are you cold?"

"A little."

He pulled me closer and rubbed my arm. "Sorry. There's nothing much I can do about the missing back window. And the truck doesn't have a heater."

"That's okay. We're almost there." When we arrived in Acorn, Ike didn't even slow down as he roared past the library.

"Hey, you passed the library."

"I know. Didn't I tell you? You're invited to my family's house for Easter Sunday dinner. It won't be much, but they all want you to come."

"You never mentioned it." I felt a wave of panic. My mother always prepared a big ham dinner for Easter, but what if Ike's mother fed me something disgusting like squirrel or possum or rabbit? It was too late to decline, now that she was expecting me. "Um . . . what's for dinner?" I tried to ask casually.

"My brother shot a wild turkey the other day. They live all through these woods, you know."

Turkey sounded safe enough. We pulled off the main road just past the post office and drove down the same dirt road that Ike and I had taken to the orchard. Ike's house sat perched on a little hill at the end of the road above the town. It was a clapboard house, not a cabin, and like the library, it was bigger than most of the other homes in Acorn. In fact, it was nearly the same size and age as the library, with an almost identical floor plan. The kitchen addition on the back of Ike's house was larger than Mack's tacked-on kitchen and it was connected to the dining room by a wide archway. They were the two nicest houses in Acorn, built by the two notorious great-grandfathers, the men reputed to have found a treasure and buried it somewhere. Could there be any truth at all to the legend?

Ike's living room was neat and cozy, with a fireplace just like the one in Mack's house. Framed photographs filled the mantel, and an embroidered sampler hung above it. The sampler looked familiar, and halfway through the afternoon I finally figured out why. It was just like the one that hung above Lillie's bed: *"There is a friend that sticketh closer than a brother." Proverbs 18:24.* I guessed that when the young girls in Acorn had been learning how to embroider, that verse had been more popular than the traditional *Home Sweet Home.*

We gathered around the dining room table, and after Ike's father said grace, we dug in to eat. The food was very good, the turkey small but tasty. I'd never had corn bread stuffing before, but it was wonderful. Mrs. Arnett's biscuits were so tender and flaky, they melted in my mouth, unlike the rock-hard cobblestone biscuits I baked. The table didn't overflow with food the way ours did at home on Easter or Thanksgiving, but the food was good and I ate my fill.

Ike was the youngest sibling from a large family of brothers and sisters, and the only one not married, yet. I couldn't even begin to figure out who was who with sisters and brothers and aunts and uncles and in-laws all milling around. No one in his family had ever learned the fine art of making proper introductions, so I was confused about who was who for most of the day. But they all knew exactly who I was—the new flatlander in town.

"So," his mother said when the meal ended, "I'm glad we finally got to see this young flatland gal that our Ike is so taken with." All of the other conversations around the table suddenly halted. Even the children grew quiet as everyone stared at me. I tried to smile.

"Um . . . the dinner was wonderful, Mrs. Arnett. Thank you so much for inviting me." They continued to stare at me the same way that Ike had stared when he had come into the library to watch me work. "Um . . . the library is open every day but Sunday," I said. "You're all welcome to come in anytime and check out a book."

Silence.

"Your son is very talented . . ." I paused when I saw Ike's uncles and brothers elbow each other. They began to snicker. "On the fiddle, I mean." They broke into loud guffaws. I decided to shut up. I looked over at Ike for help, but he seemed as amused as they were.

One of the younger women—a sister or sister-in-law—took pity on me and said, "You want to help me dish up the pie, Alice?"

"I would love to." I quickly stood and followed her to the kitchen. But she had something else on her mind besides dessert.

"I hope you ain't gonna toy with our Ike and break his heart." She held a very large knife in her hand—presumably to slice the pie, but I couldn't be sure.

"We're just friends. He knows I'll be going home soon."

"Because flatlanders have come down here causing trouble before, you know."

I started to point out the good example of Maggie and Hank Coots, then decided it would only make matters worse. "The pie looks delicious. What kind is it?"

"That's shoofly pie, made from sorghum."

I had never heard of it before, and I was a little leery about eating anything with a fly in its name. But I tried a small piece and found it deliciously sweet—and it didn't contain flies.

After lunch, Ike and his father and uncles and a brother or two gathered on the front porch for a jam session. The whole family joined in singing and clapping on some of the songs, and my earlier discomfort fled as the music swept me away. I could see that Ike's family was proud of him. They coaxed him to perform intricate fiddling tunes, then begged for more until his fingers must have been worn-out. "Ike's turned out to be the best fiddler of us all," his father told me.

Toward evening, Ike walked me home, taking the beeline path through the orchard, which really was halfway between the two houses, I discovered. He stopped beneath the trees, as I hoped he would, to take me into his arms and kiss me thoroughly. "I been waiting to do that all day," he murmured.

"I had a good time, Ike. Your family is very nice." I didn't mention his knife-wielding sister or her warnings. "And they're very proud of you, too."

"I sure wish I could get on *The Grand Ole Opry* program and make them even prouder."

"You know what? I have a feeling that you will someday."

"After we dig up the treasure?"

"I don't know about that," I laughed. "Besides, I think you're talented enough to get there on your own, without the treasure." He kissed me again, then we walked, hand in hand, the rest of the way to the library.

I enjoyed being with Ike. He made me feel cherished and pretty— and happy! But I didn't dare fall in love with him. I could never live in Acorn for the rest of my life the way that Maggie had. Besides, Ike had made it clear that he wasn't ready to get married, and I had no intention of getting my heart broken. One tragic breakup was enough for one lifetime. But I could enjoy the time that I spent with Ike, couldn't I?

On Monday I absolutely had to wash my clothing and bedsheets. It was a warm, sunny day so I knew they would dry quickly on the clothesline out back. I offered to wash Lillie's laundry, too, and she told me where to find two washtubs and a hand-crank wringer that would make the job a little easier. I built a fire in the stove, pumped water into two huge pots, and put them on the stove to heat up. Without modern conveniences and electricity, the housework around here was so tedious, and there was so much of it, that it overwhelmed me at times. I hadn't expected Lillie to help, but she limped into the kitchen just as I added more coal to the stove.

"You're up! I'm so glad you're feeling better, Miss Lillie." She was one of the most perplexing people I had ever met, but I'd come to realize how much I enjoyed her company.

"Guess I'm having one of my good days," she said. "So as long as you got the fire going, I think it's time you learnt to bake bread. You can mix the dough while you're waiting for the water to heat."

"Wait. I don't think I can learn something as complicated as bread, Lillie."

"You learnt to ride a horse, didn't you? Guess you can learn to do anything if you put your mind to it."

It had required a loaded rifle to get me on a horse the first time, and I didn't want to find out if Lillie would make me bake bread at gunpoint, too. "Okay," I sighed. "How do I make bread?"

She sat at the table and issued instructions while I mixed flour, yeast, and all of the other ingredients together. My arms and shoulders got a hefty workout when it came time to knead it. "Is it ready yet?" I asked repeatedly as my arms grew tired of kneading.

"Nope. Knead it some more." This went on for a very long time until Lillie finally decided I had kneaded it enough. "Now put it in the warming oven above the stovetop to rise, honey. I think the water is hot enough to wash clothes."

Lillie showed me how to set up the tubs outside with the hand-crank wringer on a stand between them. She also had a plunger-like device I could work up and down by hand like the agitator on my mother's electric washer to thoroughly clean the clothes. The sun finally reached the top of the hill, and Lillie sat on the bench outside the door, enjoying the spring sunshine.

After working the plunger up and down for a good fifteen minutes, I paused to rest. "I'm surprised that Mack didn't modernize this house," I said, puffing slightly. "He lived up north for a while, so he must have been used to having electricity. It sure would make this work a lot easier."

"No, it wouldn't. All them modern doodads put you in chains. Pretty soon you're a slave, just like I was."

"A slave? No, they make the work easier, Miss Lillie."

"Once you got electricity, then you got bills to pay. Then you got to work hard to pay them bills. Right now the mine is closed and there ain't no work, so you'd only get deeper and deeper in debt to them electricity people. Pretty soon the bank comes along and takes your house away. All because you want a washing machine and electric lights."

"I guess when you put it that way . . . But the mine won't be closed forever, will it?" I finished plunging and began feeding the clothes through the wringer, cranking by hand and watching them drop into the rinse water. I would have to plunge them again in the rinse tub to get out the soap, then crank them through the wringer again and hang them on the clothesline. By the time I finished, I would be as wrung out as the clothes.

"The least Mack could have done is put in indoor plumbing," I said.

"You want a toilet inside? That means you got to have a pump to get the water up from the well, and that pump needs electricity, too. More bills, same story. Where your treasure is, there's your heart, the Bible says. You can't serve both God and Mammon. Right now, you and me could get up and go anyplace God sends us and do whatever work He wants us to do because we don't have any bills to pay. But if you start serving Mammon, you ain't free to serve God."

I stopped cranking and leaned against the frame. Back home I was free from all obligations, with no job and no boyfriend. I had nothing to do all day but read novels. Yet Lillie made it sound as though God wanted to send me somewhere to work for Him. I could never be a missionary in some strange, foreign land. I couldn't even live in Acorn year-round the way Maggie had done. The reminder of Maggie made me sad—and eager to help her.

"Miss Lillie, how do you talk to someone about God when they've lost their faith? What do you say to them when they don't believe that God cares about them anymore?"

"Honey, you just saw the proof of God's love yesterday on Easter Sunday. Jesus bled and died for us. If that don't convince people that God loves them, then I don't know what will."

"Yes, but I don't think Maggie would ever go to church with me, on Easter or any other time. I think she's angry at God."

"You talking about Maggie Coots, honey?"

I nodded. "Her husband and little girl both died around the same time. I can't imagine how hard that must have been. I didn't know what to say to her when she told me about losing them."

"I knew Maggie when she first come here years ago. She was all on fire for Jesus back then. Came down with a whole bunch of people from some church up north."

"Cora called them do-gooders."

"That's right. They was gonna work for God and change everything for the good. And Maggie was very happy working for Jesus until things started getting hard for her."

"Maggie's husband and baby died, Lillie. That's not hard, that's devastating!"

"I know. Believe me, I know. But sometimes when people work for God, they get the idea that He should make their life all smooth and easy because they're doing His work."

"Well . . . He should, right?"

"It ain't so. Jesus said life is gonna be hard. Period. He said if you're gonna follow Him, then you're gonna carry a cross, just like He did. This world of ours is under a curse, honey. We need to expect things to be bad. But even if we lose everything, we still have Jesus."

"Don't you think that's a little . . . idealistic? How can you expect people to cling to Jesus after they've laid their loved ones in the grave, and after God didn't answer their prayers and keep them from dying?"

"I know Maggie's story. I know she lost her husband and child. And I know exactly how she feels because I lost my husband and my child, too."

"You mean Charley and Buster?"

"Not only them, honey. I lost my Sam and our little baby girl, too."

"Oh, Lillie!" I dried my hands on my apron and sat down on the bench beside her. "What happened?"

"Bunch of men in white hoods came and burnt a cross in our yard one night, and our house caught on fire. I was off delivering a baby, so I wasn't there. Sam and our little daughter were asleep and didn't get out in time."

"Oh, Lillie!" I hugged her as gently as I could. As she patted my back, I wondered who was comforting whom.

"Yes, I know all about hard times and wondering why God allows such a thing."

"I'm so sorry."

"That was a long time ago, honey. A long time ago."

"Were the men caught and punished for what they did?"

"Now, just who do you think was under them hoods? The reason they cover up their faces is because they don't want folks in town to know that they're the policemen and the judges and all them other officials. Those men will pay for what they done in the world to come, but not in this one."

I couldn't imagine the cruelty Lillie had endured, her first family snatched away and sold into slavery, her second family murdered. No wonder she had lied to the entire town and forced me to stage Mack's funeral. He was like a son to her, and she couldn't bear to lose him, too. "How did you ever get through such sorrow, Lillie?"

"Took a long time, honey. A long time. That's when I left and moved up here. I made up my mind to run far, far away and live all alone. I hated everyone—and white people especially. But little by little, the Good Lord healed my heart and coaxed me back into His arms again. Which is why I know He can heal Maggie's heart. And He will, I'm certain of it, in time."

"But how can you know for sure? Maggie told me herself that she's lost her faith."

"Jesus says if we belong to Him—and I know that Maggie Coots surely does—then no one can snatch us out of His hand. The Lord has a way of working things out so we'll find our way back to Him. He didn't let me stay lost, and He won't let Maggie stay lost, either. Believe me, I know."

"Is there anything I can do or say to help her?"

"Don't try to preach to her. She won't listen anyhow. Just be a friend to her."

I nodded, then thought of something else. "Lillie, why did you tell me to be careful around her?"

"Because bitterness and hatred can spread from one person to the next, just like a case of the measles. And I sure would hate to see you catch it, honey."

CHAPTER 24

Ike arrived at the library on Tuesday as I was getting ready to deliver books. "I'm here to take care of that bat for you," he said. He was armed with a burlap sack and a rake, and from the determined look on his face, he might have been here to slay a dragon for me. I longed to reward him with a hug for his bravery, but the other librarians were watching.

"Promise you won't kill it?"

"Not unless I have to. They get rabies sometimes."

I left him to his work and rode up to see June Ann. Her dog Rex ran out of the cabin when we arrived, barking ferociously, but both Belle and I were used to him by now. June Ann usually came to the door to greet me, but this time she didn't. Maybe she was busy nursing the baby. At least she wasn't working out in the field today.

I dismounted and tied Belle to the fence. "Good dog . . . nice dog," I soothed. "It's me, Rex. You know me." His tail started to wag and he finally quieted down. When he did, I could hear baby Feather crying inside the cabin.

"June Ann?" I called out. "It's me, Allie. I have your books."

No reply. The door was open so I went inside. The baby was in her cradle near the warm hearth, crying and red-faced, but June Ann was nowhere to be seen. Was she using the outhouse? I walked to the fireplace and lifted the baby into my arms.

"Hey, don't cry . . . it's all right." I propped her against my shoulder and rubbed her back. That was the full extent of my experience with babies. My soothing didn't help and I spent several long minutes walking around the room with her, humming, patting, and rocking. Feather continued to cry. I saw the two bottles of tonic on the mantel and they looked half empty, so June Ann and the baby must be taking their doses every day. Was it time to give Feather more? Where was June Ann?

I walked and patted some more until the sound of Feather's cries began to grate on my nerves. I couldn't make her stop. I could see how June Ann might become frustrated and depressed, dealing with this every day—and night. What if something really was wrong with Feather? I remembered Maggie's baby and the tiny tombstone that marked her grave. I hadn't wanted to ask how Rhoda Lee had died.

I felt Feather's forehead for a fever the way my mother used to feel mine. It wasn't hot. Maybe she was wet. I looked around for diapers and saw a pile of clean cloths on the bed. I laid Feather down and changed her, then walked with her some more. If she was hungry, there was nothing I could do about it.

By now, twenty minutes had passed. I decided to go look in the outhouse in case something was wrong with June Ann. She wasn't there. Nor was she sitting on the rock where she had waited the last time that I had rocked Feather for her. Next, I looked in the shed, still carrying the screaming baby. No sign of June Ann. I was getting worried. I had no idea what to do.

I longed to take the baby down to Miss Lillie so she could figure out what was wrong with her, but it would be impossible to get on the horse with a baby in my arms. I could barely get on empty-handed. Should I walk down to Mack's cabin? It was only a mile or two, but what could he do for a baby? It would take all morning to hike all the way into town, and the path was steep in places. What if I slipped and dropped Feather? Besides, Belle could slosh across the creek quite easily, but how would I manage the deep water? And what about the wildcat?

By the time I walked back to June Ann's cabin, the baby's cries were slowing down. At last, they quieted to whimpers and she finally fell asleep. I was afraid to lay her down, but my shoulders and arms still ached from cranking the wringer and kneading bread yesterday, so I finally laid her in the cradle. Then I went outside and sat on the doorstep to wait for June Ann. The cabin was much too dark and depressing inside to wait there.

"Hey, Allie." I heard June Ann's timid voice behind me and turned as she walked through the house and out onto the porch.

"June Ann! Where were you?"

"Sorry. I know I shouldn't have left Feather all alone like that, but I knew she was fed and her diaper was dry and . . . and she wouldn't stop screaming."

"The medicine didn't help?"

June Ann shook her head. I could see tears welling up in her eyes. "I had to leave her, Allie, I had to. I was so afraid!"

"Afraid of what?"

"That I might hurt her," she said in a tiny voice. "Sometimes I just feel like shaking her and shaking her, but I know that won't help. Then all kinds of crazy thoughts go through my head . . . like drowning her in the creek."

I didn't know what to say. The thought of June Ann shaking the baby or throwing her in the creek horrified me. I had felt a little of her frustration a few minutes ago, but what would it be like to deal with a screaming baby day and night? With no one to help me?

"I don't want to hurt her, Allie. I love her so much, but . . . I don't know what to do."

"There must be someone who would come and help you. Please, just tell me where to find your mother or a sister and I'll talk to them for you." June Ann started shaking her head before I finished speaking. "Why not?"

"I know what they'll say. They'll tell me that Feather is cursed because she's half Arnett and half Larkin. They'll say she cries all the time because the two families are fighting inside of her."

"That's ridiculous. You know it is. No one can possibly believe that."

"Sometimes I think it might be true, you know? The way she cries and cries?"

"Don't believe it, June Ann. She's a beautiful baby. Listen, please

271

come down and stay with Miss Lillie and me for a couple of days. We can help you take care of Feather. Lillie will find something that will help her, I know she will."

"I can't leave the garden and the animals. Wayne would shoot me after all the hard work he did to get us going."

"Not even for one day? Or maybe we can figure out a way to bring the animals, too." Although when I tried to imagine transporting a coop full of chickens, an ornery mule, and a couple of pigs across the creek and down the steep hill to town, I knew the idea was ridiculous.

"I can't leave. But please don't think I'm a terrible mother for leaving Feather alone in the house."

"I don't think that."

"I wasn't far away, honest I wasn't. I just didn't want to hurt her."

"I know. I know." I let June Ann lean on my shoulder and cry. "I'll figure something out, I promise." But what?

I stayed until she was calm and smiling again. The baby slept quietly the entire time. "I have to go," I finally said. "But please think about coming into town with me. Please?" She shook her head.

I felt drained by the time I arrived at the Sawyer farm. All nine children ran out to the edge of the woods to meet me. I never could understand how they could run in bare feet. I had been reading a short picture book to them each time I came, but now that Faye's boys had finished *Treasure Island*, I decided to ask the Sawyers if they wanted to hear a chapter from a longer book each week. The idea excited them, and even the very youngest kids listened so well to the first chapter that I rewarded them with a second.

Maggie had told me the reason Kentucky children were so attentive—unlike the students I had worked with back home—was because oral storytelling was popular among these families. By the time children started school, they would already know a dozen or more local tales by heart, told by their mamas and granddaddies. I loved reading stories to the children on my route, including the Howards farther up the mountain, now that their spring planting was finished.

But today I was anxious to get home and talk to Lillie about June Ann and Feather. I had planned to make a quick stop at

Gladys and Clint's cabin, staying only long enough to exchange books with them. Instead, they asked me to come inside and read aloud from the newspaper the way Cora used to do. I wondered if either one of them knew how to read or if they were simply lonely for company. Or maybe they were testing me. Maybe Clint believed in the old adage to keep your friends close and your enemies closer.

The newspaper he handed me was from February 1933, more than three years ago. The front page told the story of the assassination attempt on Franklin Roosevelt's life shortly before he had been sworn in as president. The bullet had missed Roosevelt but had killed the mayor of Chicago, Anton Cermak, instead.

"Ain't that where you're from—Chicago?" Clint asked when I finished reading the article. It required an enormous effort not to roll my eyes.

"I live *near* Chicago, not *in* Chicago. Blue Island is a perfectly safe little town, Clint. We don't have any gangsters or assassins." Although sometimes I did wonder about Uncle Cecil.

Gladys and Clint finally sent me on my way again, and I stopped to drop off more food supplies for Mack, including one of the loaves of bread Lillie had helped me bake yesterday. It had turned out pretty good.

"I'm impressed, Alice," Mack said when I pulled it out of the bag with a flourish. "I still have to chuckle when I remember your first day here, how you asked me for a hotel and a restaurant."

"You were so crabby that day. As if I had awakened you from hibernation."

"I had no idea what to do with you. And now look how well you're getting along."

He sounded condescending, as if he was patting me on the head. My temper flared. "Well, I might have a greater appreciation for your praise right now if you had *asked* me to stay instead of *forcing* me to stay." I hadn't climbed off Belle, so I was able to make a swift exit. Later, I was sorry I had snapped at Mack when he was trying to be complimentary, but he always brought out the worst in me.

By the time I arrived at the library, I felt so weary that I could barely lift the saddle off Belle and drag myself up to the house. I had forgotten all about Ike and the bat until he came bounding down the stairs from the second floor. Had he been here all day?

"Hey there, beautiful! I found the hole and plugged it for you, like you wanted. I checked the attic, too, and fixed a few holes up there. I don't think you'll be bothered by bats anymore."

"Thank you, Ike. I really appreciate it."

"How about showing me how grateful you are?" He pointed to his lips and puckered up. I stood on tiptoes and gave him a peck on the cheek.

"That will have to do until another time." I gestured with my head to where the other packhorse ladies were dismounting outside.

"Okay, but don't forget. And let me know if you see that bat again." Ike grinned and waved good-bye.

I could barely wait until everyone left and I could go upstairs and talk to Lillie about June Ann.

"I'm so worried about her and Feather," I told Lillie as I sat on the edge of her bed. "The tonics don't seem to be working."

"Give them time, honey."

"She shouldn't be all alone up there. I offered to talk to her family, but she wouldn't tell me where her parents live. Do you know who they are?"

"Of course I know them."

"Where do they live? I want to go talk to her mother and explain—"

"No, honey. Don't you go getting mixed up in this."

"But June Ann is afraid that she'll hurt the baby—and so am I. She says she feels like shaking her sometimes, or drowning her in the creek when she gets frustrated. I'll never forgive myself if something terrible happens."

"Why? This ain't your fault. That feud is more than sixty years in the making and there ain't nothing you can do about it. June Ann's mama ain't gonna go against her husband, and her husband ain't gonna go against his kin."

"Do those families really believe that Feather cries all the time because the two families are fighting inside her? That's what she told me."

"People believe all kinds of crazy things. But listen to me now.

I'm gonna tell you the same thing that June Ann and everyone else is telling you. Mind your own business."

That didn't sound like the charitable thing to do. Maybe Ike would tell me where to find June Ann's mother. I would ask him the next time I saw him.

As I was getting ready for bed that night, I had a brilliant idea. If I could find the treasure map, I could give it to Wayne and June Ann. They could dig up the treasure together and divide it between their families and end the feud. Both clans would finally accept baby Feather. She was the only person in town who could rightfully claim to be related to both great-granddaddies. Finding the treasure would solve everything.

I was in bed and about ready to blow out the lamp before I took a good look at my bedroom. Everything in the room looked just a bit . . . disheveled. I saw dust trails everywhere, as if furniture had been moved. It looked like Ike had even peered under the bed, and bats didn't hide under beds. The closet door stood open and I always kept it shut. One of Mack's bureau drawers was closed crookedly too, and it had been neatly closed when I left. I can't stand to see a drawer that isn't closed properly. I suppose Ike could have been looking for bats in the closet, but not in the dresser drawers.

Then I saw Freddy's letter on my nightstand, the one that I'd never mailed to her. I had described my date with Ike to her, and his kisses. I was quite sure I hadn't left it hanging halfway out of the envelope like that. Would Ike read my personal correspondence? Maybe, if he was truly smitten with me.

I asked Miss Lillie about Ike's activities the next morning. "It seemed like Ike was here for a very long time yesterday," I said when I brought her breakfast to her. "What was he doing all day?"

"I don't know. Rummaging around. He closed my bedroom door for me. Said he'd let me rest."

"Do you think he was up to something, Lillie?"

"What do you mean?"

"I don't know. Everyone in town seems to be up to something. Ike keeps offering to go through Mack's things, and he spent a lot of time up here once before, looking for that hunting jacket."

"I told him he could have it."

"You know what else Ike said? He said he didn't believe that Mack had shot himself. He said Mack had always been careful when he went hunting. Ike thinks someone from the mining company shot him."

"As long as he don't start guessing that Mack's alive, we'll be okay. If he starts blabbing that all over town, he'll ruin everything. You need to keep that boy's mind on other things, honey. Pretend you're sweet on him."

My face grew warm. I wouldn't have to pretend. "Ike has also been talking about the treasure map. He says that Mack was looking for it, too. Maybe he was searching through Mack's things because he was looking for the map."

"Or maybe he was just chasing the bat away like you asked him to. Tell me, did you see that bat flying around your room last night?"

I looked at her in surprise. "No. It was gone."

"Well, then?"

CHAPTER 25

All too soon, that fateful moonless Tuesday arrived. Tonight I would ride up into the woods, alone. Tonight Mack would break into the mine office to look for evidence that Hank Coots had been murdered. The moment I opened my eyes that Tuesday morning, my stomach began to writhe with dread.

"I don't think I should ride my route today," I told Miss Lillie at breakfast. "We should let Belle rest up for later." Lillie knew what Mack planned to do that night.

"What reason are you gonna give them others when they ask why you ain't working?"

"I don't know. Can't you tell them I'm sick or something?" I didn't like to lie, but Lillie had never seemed to have a problem with it. And I did feel sick.

"You gonna make everybody suspicious if you do that. First thing you know, they be up in your bedroom seeing what's wrong with you. Then that handsome Ike fella will be over here, worried about you. One lie's gonna lead to another until you're all tangled up in them. Best thing you can do is get on that horse today just like you always do."

She was right. I didn't need Ike coming up to my bedroom to bring me get-well flowers and hold my hand. Besides, if I went about the day as usual, maybe it would take my mind off my fears.

June Ann was sitting on her porch in the sunshine when I arrived at her cabin, holding Feather on her lap and talking baby talk to her. Maybe the tonics were finally working. Both she and Feather seemed happy and content. I sat beside them as we visited, watching June Ann kiss the baby's tiny hands and her bare kicking feet and stroke her soft red hair. I could have danced with relief.

At my next stop, the Sawyer children wouldn't let me leave until I read two chapters of *Treasure Island* to them. I agreed, willing to do anything to forget about what I had to do that night. When I finally stood to go, the oldest boy tugged on my hand.

"Want to see the pirate ship we built, Miss Alice? We make-believe we're pirates, sailing in it." I let them drag me over to have a look. It was just a pile of old wood and scraps of metal, but in their imagination it was a schooner that could sail all over the world searching for buried treasure. I marveled at the power of books to carry us far away to another time and place.

"There's buried treasure in Acorn, you know," one of the boys told me.

"You mean the treasure from Isaac Larkin and Wilbur Arnett?"

"Yeah. Whoever finds the map will be rich!"

"Tell me what you know about it." I listened as they all began talking at once, hoping I could unearth the treasure for Wayne and June Ann's sakes. But in spite of the children's enthusiasm for the subject, I didn't learn anything new. "I have to go," I finally told them.

"Can't you read just one more chapter?"

"You may read it yourself when I'm not here, you know."

"No, it's more fun when you read it to us."

I realized as I rode farther up into the hills that the children enjoyed the suspense of waiting nearly as much as they enjoyed the story. Mystery and suspense were what kept life from becoming boring. How exciting to have something to look forward to, a break from the daily routine of a hardscrabble life. My life back home had been an easy one but a boring one. I loved my job at the library, but aside from that, I had nothing else to look forward to day after day. Even my relationship with Gordon had become routine—not to mention my relationship with God.

Was that why I spent so much time reading books, because I had nothing else? I used to love the suspense of a stack of novels waiting to be read, the promise of something new in each story. I would live vicariously through the characters and share their adventures. Here in Acorn, people like Lillie and Mack and June Ann and Maggie were all very real, and so were the intrigues and heartaches in their lives. Maybe that was why I hadn't finished reading a single novel in the nearly six weeks I had been here. Why read a mystery when you're living one? Or two?

I visited Gladys and Clint, then rode straight back to the library. I would see Mack later and had no desire to talk with him before then. My stomach squeezed like clothes through the wringer as I passed his cabin.

I tried to work in the library for a while when I got home, carding books and putting them away. I couldn't seem to think straight. When I found myself forgetting the alphabet, I decided to give up. I was sitting at the desk, staring into space when Ike came in. He tossed his library book onto the desk and stood grinning like a boy with a secret.

"Hey, beautiful! I think I figured out a way we can see each other without anyone snooping."

"How?" My reply lacked his enthusiasm. The last thing on my mind was going off someplace and kissing Ike.

"I'll sneak back here after dark tonight and we can go for a walk."

"Tonight? But there's no moon tonight. It'll be pitch-dark!"

"I know. That's the point. And how'd you know about the moon?"

"Um . . . the *Almanac*."

"So what do you say?" He reached for my hands and held them in his, but I was too nervous about what lay ahead of me tonight to feel a thrill at his touch.

"I'm sorry, Ike, but I rode my book route today. I'm exhausted. I plan to go to bed early. How about some other time?"

His smile wavered and I could see his disappointment. "We don't have to walk far."

"I'm sorry, but I can't." I wished in vain for a movie theater or some other place of entertainment here in Acorn where a couple could go for a date. I liked being with Ike—maybe a little too much—but I didn't think it would be a good idea to be alone in the dark with him. "Do you want another book while you're here?" I asked, hoping I hadn't hurt his feelings.

"Sure," he said. "What do you recommend?"

He followed me into the non-fiction section, and I did let him steal a few kisses while we searched for a book. But I breathed a sigh of relief when he left, whistling a tune.

"Ain't you hungry?" Lillie asked as she watched me play with my dinner that evening. I finally pushed the plate away.

"I can't eat. I'm too scared."

"What are you scared of, honey?"

"Everything! Riding alone in the woods at night, meeting up with the wildcat, getting arrested by the sheriff, being shot at by whoever tried to kill Mack—all of it."

"Want me to pray for you, honey?"

I remembered her last bone-crushing prayer and didn't know if I could stand another one. But Lillie didn't give me a chance to refuse. She rose from her chair and clamped her hands on my shoulders and shouted out her prayer, loud enough for all of Acorn to hear, let alone the Good Lord way up in heaven.

"Jesus, you know who is on your side and who ain't. This little gal just wants to do what's right, Lord. Give her strength and courage. Make her as strong as Deborah was when she fought against your enemies. Give her the faith of Queen Esther to face all those people who would do her harm. Watch over her tonight, Lord, and bring her back here safely, I pray. Amen."

If I expected something magical to happen, and that I would instantly get a dose or two of courage, I was disappointed. My hands still trembled just as much after the prayer as before. My knees still threatened to buckle when I stood up and tried to walk. We waited for it to get dark outside, then we waited some more. Lillie had helped me find the miner's hat that Mack had asked for, and I watched as she filled it with fuel. It was time to go. She was about to load Mack's rifle when I stopped her.

"Wait. Don't put the bullets in it yet. I don't want to ride up there with a loaded gun on my lap."

"I thought you was worried about that wildcat?"

"I am. But I don't know how to use a rifle. I would probably end up shooting myself or Belle or some other innocent creature."

"If that's what you want." She shrugged and handed me the box of ammunition. I packed it in the saddlebags along with the miner's hat.

Belle was unhappy about getting saddled up and leaving her shed so late at night, and I didn't blame her. She kept moving away from me as I tried to get her ready, and she wouldn't stop stomping and snorting. I finally had to drag her out of the shed with both hands and tow her up to the back door so Lillie could have another talk with her to calm her down. Instead of talking, Lillie laid her hands on Belle's shoulder and prayed for her—although in a much softer voice since we were standing outside late at night.

"Oh, Lord! Keep that wildcat away from her tonight. Give her courage, I pray. Help her to see that justice needs to be done and that the right people should pay for what they done."

I thought it was asking a lot to expect a horse to be concerned about justice, but maybe Lillie had meant that part of her prayer for me. Belle did calm down after Lillie said, "Amen." I was glad that one of us had.

I climbed into the saddle, and Lillie handed me the rifle. I steered Belle toward the creek and up into the woods.

CHAPTER 26

T he night was horribly dark. Not only was there no moon, but a cover of low-hanging clouds hid any stars from view. I didn't know how Belle could see where she was going. I certainly couldn't. I hung on tightly, ducking tree limbs, remembering the first night that she and I had ridden up this trail with Mack. At least I was accustomed to riding a horse by now.

The woods were so black that I might have had my eyes closed. I knew this trail by heart in the daylight, but the familiar landmarks had disappeared in the darkness. Every sound, every hoot of an owl or whir of bat wings made me jump and flinch. The branches had leaves on them now and they made ominous noises when they rustled and swished and creaked in the wind.

When Belle finally turned away from the creek and climbed the steep slope, it took me by surprise. We had arrived at the cabin. Mack was sitting on the porch, waiting for us. He looked relieved to see us. "I was starting to get worried. I was afraid you wouldn't go through with it."

"Just hurry up," I said as I slid to the ground. "The sooner this night is over, the better."

"Are you staying here?"

I had been trying to decide what to do all day and still hadn't made up my mind. "It's so dark in these woods! Can't I light a lamp inside the cabin? Or even a candle?"

"No. On a dark night like this it could be seen for miles."

I listened to the eerie, unfamiliar noises of the forest as Mack removed Belle's bridle and replaced it with the halter. Even in daylight, Mack had been able to creep out of the bushes so stealthily that I'd never heard him, which meant anyone else could sneak up on me, too, including the wildcat. I knew if I sat alone in the cabin for hours and hours, every little noise would terrify me until my heart finally would give out. But did I want to ride up to the deserted mine with Mack? That was the more dangerous choice. The long night would seem endless while Mack searched the files. I suppose I could help him and make the work go faster. Or I could keep watch for him. Either way, it made me an accomplice. And what if the sheriff found me breaking in again? He wouldn't let me off so easily the second time.

"Well?" Mack asked. He had removed the saddlebags while waiting for my decision.

"I don't know what to do."

"Well, you'd better hurry up because I'm leaving in a minute." He unbuckled the saddle, but didn't slide it off her back. "Can you help me with the saddle? It's heavy and I don't want to drop it."

"Does your shoulder still bother you?"

"A little. It's going to take a while to heal right." I remembered how the bullet had gone all the way through him, and shuddered.

I helped him remove the saddle, and we carried it inside the cabin together. When we came out to the porch again, Mack stood looking at me with his hands on his hips, waiting for me to make up my mind. As I peered into the inky forest, a gust of wind lifted a pile of dried leaves and skittered them across the porch floor. The rattling, scraping sound startled me, and I let out a yelp, diving into Mack's arms for protection. He pulled me tight and murmured, "Shhh . . . It's okay."

I felt safe and protected in his embrace. I wanted to stay there. I also wanted to hold him back, beg him not to put himself in such danger. In spite of everything he'd put me through, I cared about him.

A moment later he released me. "You all right?" he asked. I nodded, but my heart had never pounded this hard in my life. "I think you'd better come to the mine with me."

He was right. I would go crazy here all alone. And if the wildcat did show up, I wanted to be with Mack and his rifle.

"You climb on first and sit in front of me this time," he said. "I'm afraid you'll slide off the back without the saddle. Can you climb on by yourself?" It was very hard to mount the horse without the stirrups, but Mack led Belle up to the porch and I balanced on top of the wobbling railing. It took several tries, but I finally made it onto her back. Mack handed me the gun, then climbed on behind me, following my lead by balancing on the railing. On this trip he would have to wrap his arms around me.

I exhaled. "Let's get this over with."

We followed the creek for a while, then plunged into the dark, featureless woods. At one point I thought that we might be close to Maggie's house and I remembered that she had seen paw prints around here. I was still holding Mack's gun, but that didn't mean I could aim and shoot it.

It seemed as though hours and hours passed as we plodded into the night. I had no idea where we were. Would we wander these woods until dawn?

At last, Mack drew Belle to a halt. I saw a clearing ahead and a large, hulking structure looming in the darkness.

"What is that thing?" I whispered.

"The coal tipple," he whispered back.

"You mean we're at the mine?"

"Yes."

"Wait . . . the mine is on the opposite side of the road from where we started. When did we cross the road?"

"A little ways back."

I hadn't even noticed. Mack could drop me off in this forest and I would be lost forever.

"What are we waiting for?"

"To see if there's a guard. Hand me the gun." I passed it to him, and we watched the clearing for what seemed like a very long time. My hips ached from straddling the horse. I had slid around a lot more without the saddle and I'd had to use my legs to stay seated. Now I longed to get off.

"Can't we get down and watch instead of sitting here?"

284

"We can make a faster getaway if we're on Belle. Besides, how will you climb back on again?"

"Oh." I hadn't thought of that. I should have stayed at the cabin. No, I should have stayed in Illinois.

More time passed. We changed vantage points a few times, watching the mine office from several different places while still remaining under the cover of the woods. I didn't see any movement. No one was guarding the mine.

"I think it's safe," Mack whispered. "Do you want me to leave you and Belle here while I walk to the office? She'll get you home if anything happens."

I was aching and sore and didn't want to stay on Belle a moment longer. But I was too proud to admit it. "No, I'll go with you." I would figure out how to mount her again when the time came.

"Okay, I'll slide off first," Mack said. "Hold the rifle." I held it while he climbed down, then handed it back to him. He laid it on the ground. Mack tried to catch me as I slid down, but I still landed awkwardly. "All set?" he asked when I had regained my balance. I nodded and Mack picked up the rifle.

"By the way, the gun isn't loaded," I told him.

"It isn't? Where are the bullets?"

My heart dropped to my stomach. "Um . . . in the saddlebags."

"But the saddlebags are back in the cabin." He opened the gun chamber to check, as if hoping I was mistaken, hoping he really had ammunition after all. "Great!" he said as he snapped it closed again. "Why didn't you tell me sooner?"

"Mack, I'm sorry. I didn't want to ride with a loaded gun on my lap, and . . . and then I forgot."

He turned away from me. He was upset. But at least I wouldn't have to worry about Mack shooting his gun at someone and landing us in even bigger trouble. He walked toward the mine office, leading Belle by her halter. I followed, looking down at my feet, trying not to trip or stumble or step in a hole. We crept through the trees, staying in the shadows and avoiding the open spaces. I couldn't see much. Everything about this journey seemed to be taking too long and I didn't know how we would have enough time to search through all those files, find what Mack needed, and then get all the way home again before dawn. Fear had turned my insides to water. I needed an outhouse. I didn't want to admit it to Mack, though. Maybe I could hold it a while longer.

At last we were as close to the office as we could get and still be under the cover of the woods. "I'm going to leave Belle here," he said. "Do you want to stay with her?"

I was tempted—until I remembered the wildcat. Besides, if the sheriff did catch Mack, how would I find my way home? The only route home I knew of was the road, where I was sure to be seen. "I'll come with you," I whispered.

Mack turned and gave Belle a good patting as he talked to her. "Now, you stay here, Belle. Don't go wandering off anywhere, okay? And don't follow us. We'll be back for you, I promise. That's a good girl."

He was being ridiculous. A horse couldn't possibly understand those instructions. But she lowered her head and began munching on a patch of weeds as if perfectly content to wait. Mack crept forward, crouching low.

"First, we'll run as far as the tipple and take cover behind it. Ready?" I nodded and we sprinted across the open space until we reached the towering structure. Mack waited a long moment, holding his breath, listening. "Okay, next, we'll run as far as that ditch along the railroad tracks." I nodded again and we ran across the open space toward the tracks, then dove into the ditch. I was shaking and winded. I expected to hear the crack and boom of gunfire at any moment. These people had murdered Hank and might have tried once before to kill Mack.

"Ready?" Mack asked when I caught my breath. We would have to traverse the widest open space yet, crossing the tracks and taking cover in the weeds beside the mine office. "I'll go first," he whispered. "If nothing happens, follow me a minute later."

I watched him stand and sprint across the tracks, staying low to the ground. Then I lost sight of him as he hid in the weeds beside the office. I thought about snakes—did they sleep at night or hunt at night? But I had bigger things to worry about than snakes. I drew a deep breath and followed Mack out of the ditch and across the tracks, watching my feet so I wouldn't trip. I didn't see where he was hiding until I was almost on top of him. He grabbed my hand and pulled me down next to him. I felt like a criminal for a very good reason—I was one.

Mack pointed to the back door, then crept toward it. I followed. My heart was about to thud right out of my chest. I was surprised to see that the window hadn't been repaired. Mack reached inside the same way I had and unlocked the door. He waited for a long moment after the door creaked open, listening. He held up his hand, cautioning me to wait. I was happy to comply. If gun-toting deputies were lying in ambush, I might be able to escape. Mack dropped to his hands and knees and crawled forward on all fours, disappearing into the darkness. A moment later he returned and motioned for me to crouch down and follow him. We both inched forward until we reached the file drawers.

"So far so good," he whispered as he sat down. He looked as relieved as I felt.

"Now what?"

"Now I start digging for evidence." Mack grabbed the handle on the first filing cabinet and yanked open the drawer. It was stuffed so full that it was going to take a week, not one night, to look through it. And there were two more drawers besides that one. He opened one drawer after the other, then groaned as he quickly rifled through the contents. "Look at all these files. There must be hundreds of them."

"What can I do to help?" I didn't want to be his accomplice, but I also didn't want to get caught. We needed to get out of here safely before daybreak.

"I'll start with this drawer. You take that one and just read the file names to me."

"I can't read anything. It's too dark."

"Where's my miner's hat?"

I didn't reply. We both knew where it was. In the saddlebags with the ammunition. In the cabin. "Well, you didn't remember to bring it along, either," I said when I saw his accusing look.

"Forget it." He sighed. "We'll just do the best we can."

I knelt on the floor and did what he said, squinting at the file tabs, my nose an inch away from the pages. Mack was doing the same. "Most of these are dated," he said a minute later. "Look for any files from 1934, the year that Hank died. It's a place to start."

I found receipts. Pay records. Invoices. The work was tiring and eye-straining. After a while I grew sleepy. Mack seemed discouraged.

Hours later, we had sifted through the first two drawers and were examining the third when Mack suddenly said, "Hey! This might be something. These are records of where they were digging right before Hank died. This one tells how many tons they mined . . . who was working. I think I found the year I'm looking for." He laid the file aside and pulled out the next one, leaning against the drawer to read through it. I was getting nervous. Was Belle still waiting out there? Mack hadn't tied her up.

"I think I'm getting close," Mack said, "but I'll need to read through all these files. Can you keep watch for me?"

"You never told me what will happen if the sheriff catches you here."

"He'll kill me."

"Don't be absurd. He might be crooked, but I don't think he would murder you in cold blood."

Mack looked up at me. "Alice, I'm already supposed to be dead, remember? If he kills me, who would ever know except you?"

"But . . . but what if I'm with you?"

"Look. If I tell you to run, just do it. Don't stop and ask me a million questions like you're doing right now."

I suddenly had a new incentive to stay awake and keep watch for him. Why hadn't he told me this before? Why hadn't I thought of it myself? I had read plenty of mystery stories. I should have figured out that they would kill Mack. Of course they would. He was already dead.

I wished I had waited for him back at the cabin.

My need for a bathroom was urgent now. Embarrassed or not, I couldn't wait. "Mack? Is it okay if I use the outhouse out back?"

"I guess so, if you have to. Just be careful. Stay low."

The outhouse wasn't far from the back door. I looked around carefully for any danger before dashing toward it and shutting the door. When I was done, I stood in the outhouse doorway for a moment, my senses alert, before dashing back to the office. I happened to gaze down through the trees toward the mine entrance when I saw car headlights approaching in the distance, traveling down the highway. Mack had been right: light really did travel a long way on a dark night, especially when there were no other lights for miles around. I wondered what business would take a traveler out on this lonely road in the middle of the night.

I waited in the doorway, expecting to see red taillights after the car passed the entrance to the mine and continued down the highway. Instead, the car seemed to vanish into thin air. I dashed back to the office as fast as I could.

"Mack! I think a car just pulled off the highway. I saw headlights on the road, but they disappeared when they reached the entrance."

"Is the car coming this way?"

"It's too dark to see." That darkness had been the reason for coming on a moonless night, and now it was working against us.

Mack stood and we went to the front window to peer out. "You're right! There it is!" he said, pointing. I saw it, too. The black hulk of a car, barely visible in the surrounding gloom, was moving slowly up the entrance road.

"We have to get out of here!" Mack turned back to the drawer and pulled out several more files, quickly checking their contents.

"Who's in the car, Mack? Is it the sheriff? H-how did he know we were here?"

"It's one of his deputies, more likely. He probably sends a man up here at least once a night to check for vandalism. People started stripping all the houses after the mine closed, taking anything they could find." Mack continued to sort through the files as he talked.

"And you just conveniently forgot to mention this nightly inspection to me?"

"They don't keep to a schedule, Alice. There was no way to know when or if they would come around, so why worry about it?" He stuffed a pile of files inside his jacket, tucking them into the waistband of his pants.

"Well, schedule or not, you should have told me!"

"I don't have time to argue with you. Let's go."

I followed Mack as we crawled toward the back door to the mine office. Sleepiness and fright made my legs heavy and clumsy.

I wasn't sure if I could run as fast or as far as I had earlier. "How are we going to get across the railroad tracks and make it through all of that open space without being seen?"

"Let's worry about one thing at a time," Mack said. He clutched the stolen files to his chest, trying to protect them. He handed the rifle to me when we reached the door. "Here. Carry this."

"Why me?"

"I don't want to lose these papers. The gun isn't loaded, remember?" When I still didn't reach to take it, he asked, "Would you rather be caught with an empty rifle or a pile of stolen documents?"

I took the gun from him. We crept through the door, then Mack reached through the broken windowpane to lock it again. I wouldn't have remembered. "Wait here," he whispered. I watched him go around to the front of the building. I held my breath, expecting to hear gunfire. A moment later he was back.

"We're in luck. The car went down to check on the houses and the store first. But we won't have much time to make a run for the woods. Are you ready?"

I nodded, even though I wasn't sure if my legs would cooperate. My heart was about to burst from fright. We had all of that open space to cross: over the railroad tracks, up to the coal tipple, all in plain sight if the guard happened to look our way. I drew a deep breath, and we retraced our steps, dashing across the tracks to the safety of the ditch, sprinting to the shelter of the coal tipple. I had to pause each time to catch my breath. Any minute now I might hear bullets whizzing past my head if we were spotted.

We made one more mad dash to the safety of the woods. Mack plunged into the bushes and hit the dirt, pulling me down to the ground beside him. I gasped for air. I didn't care about snakes or anything else except escaping without being seen. We lay still and watched for a moment as we caught our breath.

The dark shape of a car without its headlights on rolled up the road toward the office. The car stopped in front of the office. Someone got out and walked around the building, shining a flashlight. The night was so still that I heard his footsteps crunching through the weeds. No wonder Mack had decided to stay here instead of running deeper into the woods with branches snapping and leaves rustling beneath our feet. If one of us so much as sneezed, the man would hear that, too. I thought about Belle and the snorting and stomping she did when irritated.

The guard walked to the front of the building again and shone his flashlight into the window. Had we remembered to close all three drawers of the file cabinet? Had we put everything back the way it was?

Too late to worry about it now.

These were the longest minutes of the entire night, waiting, worrying, holding my breath as I watched the guard. I didn't exhale until he climbed back into his car. I started to tell Mack that I was ready to run again, but he put his fingers over my mouth and shook his head. We waited some more.

The car drove past the office and crossed the railroad tracks, heading in our direction. It continued up to the mine entrance and the man got out again, leaving the engine running. He walked up the narrow coal car tracks, shining his light in all directions, then stopped near the entrance to the shaft. It was boarded up, but he seemed to be inspecting it carefully. I prayed he would return to his car soon and drive away, but suddenly Mack gripped the back of my head and shoved my face down into the leaves. He pressed his own face against the ground, too. I soon understood why when the beam of the flashlight probed the edge of the woods. We remained flat as the light swung slowly past us. I could hear Mack breathing, my own heart hammering.

We waited. The light swept past us again from the other direction. We didn't dare move or look up. Would he spot Belle in the woods somewhere behind us? Time stood still. Finally, we heard the car door close and the sound of the vehicle moving away.

Mack lifted his head. "He's leaving," he whispered.

"Can we get out of here now?"

"Let's wait five more minutes." It felt like five hours. The ground was cold and hard beneath me.

At last, Mack rose to his feet. I stood, brushing dirt and leaves from my clothes, and followed him back into the woods. It was pitch-dark. Not even a pinprick of light was visible. If one of us stepped into a hole, we would break a leg. We reached the spot where I thought we had left Belle, but she wasn't there. Mack made a clicking sound to call her. We waited, listening.

"Belle wouldn't wander home, would she?" I asked.

"No, I told her to stay here and wait for us."

"Right. Like a horse can understand orders. Belle hates the dark, not to mention wildcats. She probably ran back to the safety of her shed and is sound asleep by now." I thought of the long, hard walk ahead of us through the dark forest and I wanted to cry. Mack clicked his tongue again, and a moment later I heard rustling in the bushes. Then Belle's familiar snort. I sagged with relief.

"There you are," Mack said. "Good girl. Good Belle." He patted her neck and rubbed her ears, then gripped her halter and led her deeper into the woods. My next worry was how I would climb onto her back.

We seemed to wander for a long time. I had no idea where we were. "Here's the trail," Mack said suddenly. "Want me to boost you up?"

"The trail? Where? I don't see a trail."

"You're the most argumentative, suspicious person I have ever met. Trust me, there's a trail here. Climb on . . ." He linked his fingers together to make a stirrup and motioned for me to put my foot into it. I did what he asked. Once again, I didn't make it all the way up, and Mack had to give my rear end a final boost. I would have complained, but he was grimacing and massaging his wounded shoulder so I knew the maneuver had hurt him more than me. He secured the files beneath his jacket, handed me the worthless rifle, then climbed onto a fallen tree trunk to boost himself up. He barely had enough strength to crawl on. Belle probably would have knelt down to help him if he had asked her to.

We rode in silence for a while before stopping at the edge of a narrow clearing. Mack waited, looking all around before venturing out of the woods. "What's wrong?" I whispered.

"Nothing. This is where we cross the road."

We continued on through the woods. I no longer cared about the wildcat. I just wanted to get home so my insides would stop wringing like a load of laundry. I knew we were close when I heard rushing water and the wonderful, familiar sound of Wonderland

Creek. We followed it downstream until Belle carried us up the steep rise to Mack's cabin. I was almost home.

We both climbed off, and I helped Mack put Belle's saddle and bridle on her. I performed my balancing act on the porch railing to climb on while Mack stroked Belle's shoulder, telling her what a good horse she was. Then he looked up at me.

"Thanks, Alice. I really appreciate your help."

His jacket hung open, and when he reached up to rub Belle's muzzle, I noticed a dark stain on the inside of his shirt, above his heart.

"Mack, your bullet wound is bleeding again."

He touched the spot and winced. "Maybe a little. It'll be fine. Let's hope this was our last trip to the mine."

The path seemed a little brighter as Belle and I followed the creek into town. Was I getting used to the dark or was dawn about to break?

At last I was home. Belle trotted into her shed like a thoroughbred racing to the finish line. I ducked just in time. I removed her saddle and gave her a little extra grain for her hard night's work. As I crossed the backyard to the house, I happened to look up. The clouds had disappeared, and I glimpsed the Milky Way like a river of sparkling lights shimmering across the sky. I couldn't recall ever seeing it so clearly, so magnificently before. The world looked glorious and beautiful to me as every cell in my body hummed with life.

"Wow!" I breathed. I was glad to be alive, to be safe.

To be home.

CHAPTER 27

I walked in through the back door, relieved my ordeal was finally over, and saw a dark figure huddled at the kitchen table. I let out a cry and retreated backward toward the door.

Lillie lifted her head. "You okay, honey?"

"You scared me half to death! What are you doing in the kitchen? It's nearly dawn!"

"I been sitting here praying for you and Mack and Belle. What'd you think I'd be doing all this time?"

"Sleeping."

"Well, someone's got to keep those angels watching over you. Did everything go all right?"

"Yes. Mack thinks he found what he was looking for."

"Good. Let's go to bed, honey." She started to pull herself to her feet.

"Wait. Before you do. You never told me why those men killed Sam and your daughter."

She stared at me as if she didn't understand my question. "You want to hear that story *now*? Can't it wait until morning?"

"No. I don't want to wait. You never finish any of your stories, Lillie. You'll forget by morning, and I'm wide awake now. I've been pondering death all day and worrying about it all night, so I want to hear the story right now." Lillie sighed and settled back into her chair. I was too wound up to sit. I understood how Belle must feel when she starts stomping and snorting.

Lillie took a moment to think, as if paging through a book to find the place where she had left off. Her voice sounded frail and sad as she told her story.

"Sam was trying to help the colored folk in our town," she began, "just like Mack was trying to help the miners. Them plantation owners didn't pay their sharecroppers a fair wage, and they charged too much for rent and all them other things folks need from the store. Sam stood up to them and asked them to be fair to us. The men in the white hoods didn't like that, so they come after Sam, hoping to scare him out of town."

I looked at her for a long moment. Fighting injustice seemed to carry a very high price tag. "Weren't you worried about Mack's safety when he came back to Acorn to do the same thing and fight for people's rights?"

"Sure I was. And even more worried after Hank died and someone stole that book Mack was working on. Mack had been to college, and he could have escaped from this place. I told him, 'Honey, you need to stay up there in Ohio with your good job. Stay where it's safe.'"

"Why didn't he listen to you?"

"I guess it was on account of the way he was raised." Lillie smiled slightly. "I taught him to care about other people, like the Good Book says. I taught him to always do what God asks you to do. The Lord made Mack real good at writing, and so he decided to write things to help other people, not to make a pile of money for himself. He don't run around saying Bible verses all day or toting the Good Book under his arm, but he's a good man, honey. Just like my Sam was. And God wants us to do good in this terrible bad world."

"But if Sam and Mack were doing what God asked them to do, why didn't He protect them?"

"Didn't we talk about this once before? We live in a fallen world. And we're the ones who made it that way, not God."

"I never understood why God doesn't get rid of all the evil people—like He did during Noah's flood."

"Because the Lord is merciful. He wants to give every last person a chance to hear about Jesus. He doesn't want anybody to die without knowing Him, whether they're wearing white hoods or cheating miners. That makes it harder for His children to live in this world, but Jesus said we're supposed to love our enemies and do good to the people who persecute you."

"This is more than persecution, Lillie. They killed your Sam, and they probably killed Hank and shot Mack, too."

"Yes, they might kill us. They killed Jesus, didn't they? But when He comes back someday, all of the evil in this world will be gone for good. Everything will be made new, and I'll see Sam and our baby girl again." Lillie struggled to stand and this time I helped her. We walked through the darkened library, then Lillie paused at the bottom of the stairs.

"Now, if only I didn't have to worry about my Buster," she said with a sigh. "It's been so long since I seen him, and I just wish I knew if he remembers what I taught him about Jesus, after all this time."

"But, Lillie, didn't you tell me that nobody can snatch God's children out of His hand?"

Even in the dark I saw her eyes glisten with tears. "That's true, honey. I did say that." She climbed up two steps, then stopped to look at me. "See? You learned something while you was here."

We climbed the rest of the way to the top and I helped her into bed. She was already wearing her white nightgown. "You still think about Buster a lot, don't you?"

"I do, honey. Especially now that I'm getting ready to cross over to the other side. That boy was so young when they took him from me . . . and I just wish I knew for sure if I'll see him again up in heaven."

"I'm sure you will." I bent to kiss her wrinkled forehead. "Good night, Lillie. And thank you for praying for us tonight."

I fell into bed. I was exhausted, but it took me a long time to fall asleep as my mind replayed everything I had experienced. I had never been through such a nerve-wracking ordeal in my life, and I hoped I never would again. And yet a tiny, stubborn part of me whispered that it had been an exciting night—now that it was over and I was safe, of course. I had lived through a real-life adventure instead of reading about one in a book. My life would seem boring when I got home. What in the world would I do with the rest of my life? I lay awake for a long time, but just before I fell asleep, I whispered a prayer—a real prayer—that God would help Lillie find her son.

I longed to sleep late the next day, still worn-out after only a few hours' sleep. But the packhorse ladies would arrive at the front door soon, and they would wonder why I wasn't up. I got dressed, let Belle out of her stall, and freed the chickens from their coop. Lillie remained in bed all day, so I spent the morning upstairs, working on her folk medicine book. She must be exhausted, too, and I wanted to be near her in case she needed me because I knew that in some strange, inexplicable way, I needed her. I couldn't bear it if she "crossed over to the other side" just yet.

Halfway through the morning I turned a page in Lillie's notebook and found a folded piece of paper stuffed between the pages. I unfolded it carefully and saw that the elegant handwriting, penned in ink, was not Lillie's:

May 2, 1855–

Charley Hammond sold to Edgewater Plantation, Midlothian, Virginia.

August 5, 1860–

Buster Hammond sold to Alfred Drucker, Thornburg, Virginia.

I stared at it in amazement. I thought I knew what this piece of paper was, but I was afraid to believe it. I carried it into Lillie's bedroom as if carrying a living thing, afraid the seventy-year-old note might disintegrate in my hand. She slept half-sitting up, propped by pillows and swaddled in the quilt to keep warm. She opened her eyes as I approached.

"Lillie, what is this? I found it in one of your notebooks."

"Let me see . . ." She reached for it with her spindly, wrinkled hand. "Oh, my. This is from my old missus on the plantation. This is the paper she gave me all them years ago, telling me where Charley and Buster was sold to. See here? August the fifth—that's the day they took my Buster away. I remember that awful day like it was yesterday."

My heart skipped with excitement. Could this clue help us find Buster? That's what I had prayed for before falling asleep!

"Is that your last name?" I asked. "Hammond?" I had never heard anyone call Lillie by her last name and realized that I had no idea what it was.

"No, honey. Hammond was Massa's name. All the slaves on them plantations had the same last name as their owners. But when we was set free, a lot of folks didn't want that name no more. They took new names for themselves. Some of them chose Lincoln—we thought the world of Mr. Abraham Lincoln. I took Sam's name when we got married."

"You never told me what happened when you and Sam went looking for Buster after the war."

"I didn't? Well, we found the plantation where he was sold, but Buster wasn't there no more. The Drucker family lived in a little town near Fredericksburg, Virginia, called Thornburg. Massa Drucker still owned the land, just like it says here. But the house was gone, burned to the ground when the army marched through. Massa Drucker mighta known where Buster was, but it didn't matter because he ain't talking to no colored people. Says he'll shoot us dead if we come on his property. Sam and me went to the colored town and asked around, but most of the Druckers' slaves was gone. A lot of them headed out West where they was supposed to get twenty acres and a mule."

"But Buster couldn't have gone out West by himself. He was just a boy, wasn't he? How old would he have been?"

"Twelve years old when the war ended. The colored folks told us that when the Yankees came through, everybody starved. Some tried to follow the army, and boys like Buster mighta worked for some of the soldiers, shining shoes or cooking for them—anything to try and stay alive."

"Did anyone remember Buster?"

"A couple of the old-timers remembered him from plantation days. Nobody knowed what happened to him, though. We searched and searched, but Buster was long gone."

I didn't let Lillie's news discourage me. I now knew some possible last names for Buster and I knew the name of the town where he had lived after he was sold. How far could a twelve-year-old boy travel on his own?

I was so excited about discovering this information that I couldn't wait to see Mack on Thursday and tell him the good news. I had to ride my usual route first, but when I finally arrived at his cabin, I dismounted and waited on the porch steps for him to appear.

I leaped up in excitement the moment Mack rustled out of the bushes. "Good news! I found out Buster's last name and the name of the town where he went after he was sold. He might have adopted his new master's name, Drucker. Or he might still go by his old name, Hammond. Lillie said he may have changed it to Lincoln after the war, too. But how many people could there possibly be named Buster Hammond or Buster Drucker? I figured it all out, and in the 1900 census he would have been about forty-seven years old. He'd be seventy-seven in the 1930 census, which means he'd be about eight-two or eighty-three today. Goodness, Mack. We'd better hurry!"

I was so excited as I babbled on and on about Lillie's son that I didn't notice how quiet Mack had been. "What's the matter? Is something wrong?" I finally asked.

"I have bad news, Alice."

"Does it have to do with Buster?"

"No. That's good news about him. But I have to go back to the mine."

"You're joking."

"I'm afraid not."

"Weren't the files any help to you?"

"They were an enormous help. I spent all day yesterday and today reading through them. But I've never been inside the mine, and I need a layout of the main shafts and where Hank's accident was in order to make sense of everything. I promised you that I would finish my work in a month's time and come out of hiding so you could go home, and I want to keep my promise."

"I know. But you can't go back there, Mack. It's too dangerous, especially if they've figured out the files are missing. Why not talk to some of the miners who worked there during that time? They should remember the layout, shouldn't they?"

"Yes . . . except that all of those miners think I'm dead."

"Oh. That's right." I sank down on the porch steps to think. "There must be some other way to get that information."

"Maybe you can talk to Ike Arnett. He worked in the mine before it closed. Is he still courting you? Are you close to him?"

My cheeks flushed, betraying me. My love life was none of Mack's business.

When I didn't reply, he added, "Didn't you say Ike suspected that Hank's death wasn't an accident?"

I had to respond. "He's hardly *courting* me. There's no place to go *courting* in Acorn, as you well know. Do you expect me to be another Mata Hari, pumping Ike for information between fervent embraces?"

"Who's Mata Hari?"

"Didn't you see that movie a few years ago with Greta Garbo and Lionel Barrymore?" Mack gave me a blank look. "Mata Hari spied for the Germans during the Great War. They made a movie about her life." He was shaking his head. "Never mind. What do you want me to ask Ike—assuming that I decide to do it?"

"I need to know the layout—where the active shafts were in relation to the site of Hank's accident. See if Ike can describe the two areas, how close together they are."

"I'll try. But in the meantime, what about finding Buster? Lillie isn't going to live forever, you know. We shouldn't put this off much longer."

"I'll send the information to my friend in Washington. Do you have time to wait while I write a quick letter?"

"Of course."

He disappeared into the cabin and came out a minute later with a small notepad. He sat down on the porch step, and when he reached inside his jacket to pull out a pencil, I saw him wince. I noticed the same dark stain on his shirt that I had seen the other night.

"Mack, is your wound bleeding again?"

"Just a little. I may have overdone it a little on Tuesday night."

He looked pale to me, and I reached out to feel his forehead. "You're running a fever!"

"I'll be fine." He pushed away my hand and continued to scribble his letter. "What were those names again?"

"Buster's first master was named Hammond. His new one was Drucker. And tell your friend to try looking for Buster Lincoln, just in case. He would have been born around 1853."

"And the town?"

"It's called Thornburg. Lillie said it was near Fredericksburg, Virginia."

I waited while he wrote some more. "I don't have an envelope," he said after signing his name. "If I give you the address, can you find an envelope and mail it for me?"

"Sure. And I'm going to ask Lillie to fix you something for your fever, too. In the meantime, you need to get some rest and take it easy."

He folded the letter and went back inside the cabin to rummage around for his friend's address. I didn't know where he was hiding all of these things, because every time I had peeked into the cabin, it had appeared to be abandoned.

"Here," he said when he emerged again. "And please try to get some information from Ike soon, okay?"

I looked at the address when I got back to the library and saw that it was a woman's name, Miss Catherine Anson. I felt a little prick of something that might have been jealousy. Who would have believed it? Mack had a sweetheart? The only affectionate female I'd seen him with was Belle.

CHAPTER 28

The next morning I went to the post office to mail Mack's letter. I didn't tell Lillie what the letter contained, afraid of disappointing her if we couldn't find her son. I used my return address in Illinois to alleviate any suspicion in the post office that Mack had written the letter. This time, the elderly gentlemen of Acorn were playing chess instead of cards. I bought a stamp, affixed it to the envelope and asked the postmaster to mail it, and once again my entire transaction took place without anyone speaking a word to me. How long did an outsider have to live in Acorn before people got over their suspicion?

Instead of walking back to the library, I continued up the road and took the turnoff to Ike's house. A few minutes later I reached the orchard. The blossoms were gone and the orchard looked perfectly ordinary, not at all like the possible burial ground for a hidden treasure.

Where was the treasure? Was it real? Like the pirates in *Treasure Island*, I had become obsessed with finding it. Everyone else in Acorn, Kentucky, wanted to find it and get rich, but I wanted to end the long-standing feud between the Arnetts and Larkins, for June Ann's sake.

I studied the grove from every angle, searching for a defining landmark. A huge, ancient tree? There were dozens of them in the woods beyond the clearing. An oddly shaped rock? There were plenty of rocks, too. At last I decided it was hopeless. If the Arnetts and Larkins hadn't been able to find this treasure after sixty years of searching, how could I?

I returned home, taking the path through the woods and along the creek, and came in through the library's back door. I had just stepped into the foyer when Ike walked in through the front door. I jumped, startled to see him—and felt a little guilty for searching for the treasure without him. Ike was the one who had figured out that the orchard was the halfway point between the two houses.

He gripped my arms to steady me. "You okay? I didn't mean to scare you."

"I'm fine. My mind was a million miles away, that's all. Are you here for a book?" I hoped he wasn't going to sit down and watch me work again or try to coax me into the kitchen to smooch.

"You promised to go for a walk with me, remember? And there's something I want to ask you."

"Okay. But it will have to be a short walk. I have work to do." We went out through the back door, and Ike paused as we passed the garden we had worked on together.

"It looks pretty dry," he said. "You been watering it?"

"No . . . Am I supposed to?"

"Well, yeah, if you want anything to grow."

My shoulders sagged. Here was another wearying job I would have to undertake. "Any chance it might rain?"

He laughed and patted my arm. "If it doesn't, I'll come over and help you haul water."

He reached for my hand and led me back to the orchard the way I had just come. We had forgotten to bring a blanket this time, but Ike cleared a spot beneath one of the trees and pulled me down beside him. He sat with his back against the trunk and I leaned against him, comfortable in his arms. A romance novel would describe Ike's arms as "brawny." The thought made me smile. All of the words that writers used to describe their heroes—broad-shouldered, manly, ruggedly handsome, brawny— had seemed like clichés to me when I had read them in books.

But Ike truly was all of those things. How much longer could we spend time together before we ended up falling in love? I remembered his sister's veiled threats about toying with him. Was I leading Ike on?

"I want to ask you something, Alice." He twirled a strand of my curly hair around his finger as he talked. "My band is playing at a dance over in the next county this weekend. Will you come with me?"

"Is it just for one day, like before?"

"No, it's far. We would have to stay there overnight."

"Ike, I can't. Even if we weren't . . . together, it wouldn't look right."

He turned my shoulders so I was facing him. "But I want to be with you all the time. I can't stand even one day apart. I . . . I think I'm falling in love with you."

My heart sped up. I had waited in vain for Gordon to confess his love for me, but he never had. Now I was glad he hadn't. Was I falling in love with Ike? Being with him felt exciting, and I missed him when he wasn't around, and his kisses made my brain whirl . . . but was that true love? He was waiting for me to return his declaration of love, but I stalled, afraid of getting hurt.

"I thought you had a girl in every town? You said you weren't ready to settle down with one girl."

"You're not like any girl I ever met."

He leaned forward and kissed me. How was I supposed to think straight with his lips on mine, his hands in my hair?

When he finally pulled away again, he looked into my eyes. "I know my future is hopeless right now. I don't have a steady job and no way to support you until the mine opens again, and who knows when that will be."

"You shouldn't go back into the mine, Ike—ever. You could make a living playing your fiddle if you could just catch the right break."

"What if that lucky break never comes? You already said you wouldn't stay here in Acorn unless I bought you all those modern things you want. I don't know what to do, except find the treasure. You gotta help me find it, Alice. It's the only way."

"I want to find it, too, but—" He started kissing me before I had a chance to explain that I wanted to find it so the feud would end. The feuding had gone on much too long and had torn the town of Acorn in two.

Ike was so sweet, so wonderful. I wanted to forget common sense and my home in Illinois and tell him that I loved him, too. I wanted to say that we could live happily-ever-after anywhere in the world as long as we were together. But happy endings only happened in books, not in real life.

Maybe Ike could come home with me to Illinois and we could live there. But where would an uneducated miner from Kentucky find work, especially during the Depression? Ike was talented and smart and he loved to read, but he would be as out of place in Blue Island as I was here in Acorn.

"I should get back to the library," I said when the kiss ended. "Lillie has no idea where I disappeared to."

"Will you come here with me some night and help me dig up the treasure if I figure out where it's buried?"

"But . . . it's against the law. This is someone else's property."

"Please, Alice?"

How could I refuse when Ike looked at me with those sad, dark eyes? I had helped Mack do illegal things in the middle of night. Why not help Ike?

"I'll help you, but first we have to find out where to dig. We can't just start making holes all over the place. Listen, Ike. Go play at the dance this Saturday. Have fun. We'll talk more about it when you return."

I was glad to stay home over the weekend and catch up on some of the sleep I had missed. I typed more of Lillie's folk remedies on Saturday, read a book on Sunday, and waited all day Monday for Ike to return, but he never did. Mamaw and the boys arrived on Monday afternoon, excited about starting a new story. I had chosen *Tom Sawyer*, which I had found on the nightstand in Mack's room. The boys were thrilled to read about a character who was as mischievous as they were.

I hoped Ike would return before I had to leave on my route Tuesday morning, but he didn't. As I passed Mack's cabin, I realized that a week had passed since the night we'd searched the mine office together. I decided to avoid Mack for a while. He had asked me to play Mata Hari with Ike and I hadn't done it.

When I reached June Ann's cabin, she was tearful again, and the baby was wailing. "Go take a little walk," I told her. "I'll rock Feather for a while." Thirty minutes later, the baby finally quieted and June Ann returned.

"Do you want Lillie to fix some more tonic?" I asked. "I see the bottles are nearly empty."

"It won't help."

Once again she rejected my suggestions to come into town or to ask her family for help, so I finally said good-bye and moved on. I rode up to see the Sawyers, then Gladys and Clint. And even though it wasn't my day to visit Maggie, I decided to pay her a visit. I needed to talk to her about my feelings for Ike and I knew she was the only person in Acorn who would understand.

Maggie was outside, hanging bedsheets on her clothesline. Maybe I shouldn't bother her. She'd told me that her mother-in-law was bedridden all the time now. But Maggie waved when she spotted me and looked happy to see me. I dismounted and tied Belle to the hitching post, then walked over to help Maggie hang the rest of her laundry.

"This isn't your day to visit me. What brings you here? Is everything all right?"

"I'm fine. Just confused," I said with a little laugh.

"Ah. It must be a matter of the heart. What else besides love can throw us into confusion?"

"You know my friend Ike, who I told you about?"

"The fiddle player?"

"Yes. He said he thinks he's falling in love with me."

"And are you in love with him?"

"I don't know. I've been holding back deliberately, telling myself not to fall in love with him because he said he had a girl in every town and he wasn't ready to settle down yet. Besides, I can't risk falling for him. I know I won't be staying here in Kentucky forever. I could never live without electricity and telephones and indoor plumbing for the rest of my life. How do you do it?"

"True love changes people, Allie. When you're in love, you want to do things to please the other person and make them happy. It wasn't hard at all to make sacrifices to marry Hank and live here, at first." We had hung the last sheet, and Maggie bent to pick up the laundry basket. "Do you have time to come inside and talk? I baked scones this morning."

"Sure. I'm not in a hurry." I watched her pump water and prepare tea in her rustic kitchen, completely at home with its limitations, as if she had never lived in a city with electricity and hot running water. Could true love really change people that much? Could I live this way for Ike Arnett?

"No matter how much you love someone, Allie, don't expect marriage to be easy. Hank and I loved each other, but it was still very hard. After all the changes I made for him, I wanted him to change, too. I kept pressuring him to leave Acorn and get an education. Hank was smart, no question about it. But the more I nagged him, the more convinced he was that I looked down on him for never finishing school. Maybe I did feel that way a little. After everything I had given up for him, it made me angry when he decided to stay here and work at the mine instead of going to college. I couldn't understand why he wouldn't do this one thing for me. Hank said, 'I am what I am. I was born a miner and I'll probably die a miner.'"

I winced at the prophetic words.

"We loved each other, Allie. But even true love doesn't always make things easy. When we got married, I never considered how little we had in common. The way we were raised, family expectations, goals and dreams. Those are all part of who we are."

"I know Ike and I don't have much in common. But we certainly are attracted to each other."

"How would your parents react if you told them you'd fallen in love with this man and have decided to marry him? And that you're going to stay here and live in a log cabin?"

"They'll think I've lost my mind. My mother will sign me up for a water cure. My father will give me a list a mile long of all the reasons not to do it."

"My family begged me not to marry Hank. They offered me everything from a new roadster to a trip to France if I came to my senses and returned home at once. And when I didn't listen to them, we became estranged."

"I would miss home. These woods and hills are beautiful, but they aren't home."

"The best advice I can offer is this: Don't go into any relationship thinking you can change the other person. Accept him the way he is right now, for the rest of his life. And he needs to accept you, too. If you can't live without hot running water, then he can't expect you to change your mind."

"Thanks, Maggie. I appreciate your honesty."

But I was still hopelessly confused when I got on my horse again and rode home.

Maggie's words rolled around in my mind like marbles that evening as I fixed dinner for Lillie and me—potatoes fried with onions and a little bacon, a recipe Lillie had taught me. I was so distracted that the fire in the stove died out and I didn't even notice.

"What's the matter with you tonight?" Lillie asked when she came out to the kitchen to see what was taking so long. She stood with her arms folded, a sure sign that she was annoyed.

"Lillie, how do you know if you're really in love?"

"You talking about that Ike fella?" Lillie didn't miss much. I might as well confide in her the way I had with Maggie.

"Ike said he was falling in love with me, and I didn't know what to say. I've never been in love before, even though I've read about it in books. I think it might be love because I feel all the same symptoms as in the books, so I guess it's the real thing, but—"

"It ain't love."

Her blunt certainty irritated me. "How can you be so sure?"

"Because I gave that boy some of my special love potion, that's why."

I dropped the wooden spoon into the pan of potatoes. "What? Love potion! I don't believe it. There's no such thing as love potion."

"Believe whatever you want, honey. But don't make the mistake of getting serious with him or you'll get your heart broken when that potion wears off."

"That's ridiculous!"

She gave me one of her knowing shrugs. "Don't say I didn't warn you. Now, you better put some wood on that fire or we won't be eating dinner until midnight." She started to walk away.

"Wait! Prove it to me, Lillie. Prove that you really know how to cook up some sort of magic potion."

She turned in the doorway to face me. "You see how Belle acts around Mack? I slipped her a little bit of that potion, too, so she would behave for him and do whatever he says. Mack's no good with horses. He got used to driving cars, up north."

I stared at her. Ike and Belle had been acting suspiciously alike, nuzzling necks, following Mack and me around like puppy dogs. But a love potion? My life had drifted into yet another genre of story—a fairy tale.

"Wait. Why would you give this so-called love potion to Ike in the first place—not that I believe it's true."

"That's my little secret, honey."

"Well, since it involves me, I think I have a right to know! And what will happen if you stop giving it to him? Or if it wears off?"

"Oh, it'll wear off one of these days. I'm just warning you ahead of time so you don't get your heart broke."

This was unbelievable. She had to be joking. Then I had another disturbing thought. "Did you give me any of this so-called potion?"

"Now, why would I do that?"

"I don't know! You won't even tell me why you gave it to Ike!" I was yelling. I wanted to shake her.

Lillie gave me her gap-toothed smile and said, "I never did see a person get as worked up as you do, honey. You worry too much about all sorts of silly things. See how upset it's making you? You need to sit back and enjoy your life."

"How can I possibly enjoy my life when you keep interfering with it?"

She turned away from me again, shaking her head. "You let me know when that food is cooked, honey," she said before hobbling away.

The stove may not have been red-hot, but I was.

After we finished eating, I went upstairs to Lillie's workroom. I sat down on the floor and leafed through her notebooks by lamp-light, page after page of blurred, wispy writing. I found recipes for curing everything from warts to whooping cough but not a single entry was labeled Love Potion. By the time I finished struggling through the third notebook, I couldn't read anymore. Love potion? Lillie had to be making that up.

Didn't she?

CHAPTER 29

Ike finally returned from his weekend travels on Wednesday morning. He burst into the library and picked me up by my waist and swung me around in circles. I'd seen couples do that in movies, but never in real life. I couldn't tell if I was dizzy from the spin or because I was happy to see him. "Where have you been?" I asked when he set me down again. "I was getting worried about you."

"I would have been here sooner, but my truck broke down on the way home. Hey, I got wonderful news!"

"Tell me."

"Someone heard me fiddling on Saturday night and asked me to play with his band on a road trip. They need a new fiddle player. It's a very popular group, and they travel a lot and play in more places than our little band does. They make good money, too."

"Oh, Ike! I'm so happy for you!" I couldn't help hugging him. "What a wonderful opportunity."

"It'll be sort of a trial run for me, to see how it works out. And one of the places we'll be playing is close to Nashville. Who knows? Maybe I'll get there yet."

"You can do it, Ike. I know you can." I remained in his arms, and he rested his cheek on top of my head. I closed my eyes, imagining us moving to Nashville. We would live in a real house, not a log cabin, and Ike would play his fiddle for the Grand Ole Opry every

311

week. He would be famous! We would both have to make a lot of changes, like Maggie said, but Tennessee would be middle ground for us, a compromise between Kentucky and Illinois. It could work.

"The tour starts this weekend and that means I'll be leaving again in a day or so. I'll be gone for at least two weeks, and boy, am I going to miss you, Alice."

"I'll miss you, too."

Would Lillie's love potion wear off while Ike was gone? Assuming that her ridiculous story was even true, of course. I was confused about being in love in the first place—why did Lillie have to confuse me even more by talking about a love potion?

Ike released me from his arms and sighed. "I guess we won't be able to look for the treasure until I get back. But I'll save every penny I make, and I'll come back. Promise you'll still be here?"

"I'll be here." I couldn't go anywhere until Mack finished his investigation at the mine and could be resurrected from the dead. Which reminded me, I was supposed to ask Ike about the mine.

"May I ask you a question, Ike? It has nothing to do with your good news; it has to do with Maggie Coots."

"What about her?"

"We've become friends, and we were talking the other day about Hank. I don't think she'll ever get over his death. You said you didn't think it was an accident. Why is that?"

"One of the reasons is because the company usually runs union organizers like Hank out of town. Instead, they put him in charge."

"What's it like inside the mine? Is it just one long tunnel going straight in? Or do you have to go down in an elevator or something?"

"The Acorn Mine is pretty new, so it's just a tunnel into the mountain. You can walk straight in. There are a couple of side tunnels off the main one."

"Did you ever worry about cave-ins or explosions, like the one that killed Hank?"

"You can't think about it. You just have to go in and do your job." Ike's habitual grin had changed to a frown. He looked down at his feet, not at me. I had never seen such a serious expression on his face before. He held my hand in his, squeezing it gently as he talked.

"Were you in the mine the day that Hank died?"

"Yeah, but the cave-in that killed him wasn't close to where we were working. They'd just found a new vein of coal in a side shaft, and Hank was supposed to set the charges. They went off too soon, before he was out."

"So you heard the explosion?"

Ike nodded. He still wouldn't look up. "Felt it, too. It was a horrible day for all of us. Makes you realize that it could happen to you, and no one wants to be reminded of that. It was hard to go back the next day. Everybody was jumpy. And you make mistakes when you're jumpy."

The conversation was upsetting him. I could tell he didn't like to talk about it. I no longer cared about Mack and his spying mission. I didn't want to make Ike remember any more.

"I hope you never have to return to the mines again." I gave him a hug, then looked up at him. "Will you come and see me when you get back from your tour?"

His smile returned. "Count on it."

I woke up on Thursday morning to rain pattering on the roof above my head. The rain would be good for my garden but not so good for riding a horse up the creek through the woods. I asked the other librarians about venturing out in the storm, and Cora seemed offended by my suggestion that we should stay home. "Of course we ride, rain or shine. It's our job."

"We've been out in the snow, too," Faye said. "Last winter we rode in a blizzard."

"A little rain never hurt anyone," Alma added.

I wasn't so sure. Didn't people in novels catch pneumonia and die from a chill? I was unable to convince the others, so I plopped a straw hat on my head, saddled Belle, and headed upstream in a miserable drizzle. I planned to stop and see Mack on the way home that afternoon and tell him what I'd learned from Ike about the mineshaft. I hoped the information would be helpful and that Mack wouldn't need to return to the mine. Ever since he'd told me that he would be killed if he were caught, I'd been afraid for him. There had to be a better way for Mack to solve Hank's death than by putting himself in danger.

I rode past his cabin and was nearly to the ford that led to June

313

Ann's cabin when I heard a grumble of thunder. The clouds had lowered like a thick gray sweater that seemed to be tangled in the treetops. The drizzle changed to raindrops the size of dimes. Any minute the gray sweater would tear and the rain would start to pour.

It thundered again, making Belle jittery. I nudged her to go faster, hoping we could get to June Ann's before the storm hit. I rode with my chin down to keep the rain off my face, but when I glanced up to see if we'd reached the ford, I saw a shadowy figure standing in our path. My heart leaped in fear. We were too far from Mack's cabin for it to be him. In all of my travels, I had never encountered anyone else out on the trail before. I was about to pull back on the reins when a flash of lightning lit up the woods and I recognized June Ann. I reined Belle to a halt beside her.

"June Ann! What are you doing way out here? There's a storm coming. I was on my way to your house to wait until it blows over."

"Here! Take this, Allie. Bring this to Miss Lillie for me." She was holding a plump bundle in her arms, wrapped in a feed sack and tied with twine. She thrust it up at me and I bent over in the saddle to take it.

"To Miss Lillie? What is it?" But the moment I had the bundle in my hands, I knew by its soft, warm weight that it was the baby. "June Ann, wait! I can't take her!"

She was already gone, disappearing into the woods. She wasn't following any path, and I quickly lost sight of her in the underbrush. How could she run like that? The baby moved in my arms and whimpered. Dread welled up inside me. I didn't know what to do.

"June Ann! Come back!" My voice echoed through the woods before being drowned out by a clap of thunder. Belle stomped her feet and flattened her ears as the rumble bounced off the surrounding hills like a dozen timpani drums. Before I could decide what to do, Belle decided for me, turning in a circle and heading downstream toward home. The rain was soaking me now, and I knew I needed help. Even if I went to June Ann's house, how could I dismount with a baby in my arms?

Thunder and lightning flashed and boomed as the storm intensified. Belle moved faster. She wanted to gallop, but I reined her in, knowing I couldn't stay in the saddle if she did. It was hard to control the reins and hang on tightly to the baby at the same time. I decided to head for Mack's cabin. It was only a mile or so down the mountain and much closer than going all the way back to Miss Lillie's house. I prayed he would be there so he could help me dismount. My hat was limp and dripping, the rain seeping through it. I was getting drenched. I unbuttoned my jacket and tucked the baby inside it. She was crying loudly now, and I didn't blame her.

Belle had the same idea that I did, and climbed the rise to Mack's cabin, coming to a halt near his porch. He came to the doorway before I had a chance to call out to him. "What are you doing here?" he asked.

"Can you help me down? I need you to take this baby."

"Baby? Did you say *baby*?"

"Yes. Please come here and get her." He walked out onto the porch, and I handed Feather down to him. He carried her inside while I dismounted. The storm was directly overhead now, and when thunder struck at the same moment that the lightning flashed, it startled both Belle and me. "Whoa. Steady, Belle," I soothed. I led her onto the porch where she would stay fairly dry, but she wasn't content with that. She pushed past me, pulling the slippery reins from my hands, and followed Mack into the house before I could stop her.

"Belle, wait! You can't go inside. Come back!"

"It's okay, Alice," Mack said. "I don't blame her for wanting to get in out of the rain, do you?"

The four of us—Mack, the baby, the horse, and I—all crowded into the tiny one-room cabin. Water plopped onto the floor from several leaks in the roof, and the wind blew more rain inside through the missing windowpanes.

"The driest spot is over here in this corner," Mack said. He slid to the floor and sat cross-legged, still holding the crying baby. I sat down beside him, expecting him to toss Feather back into my arms the first chance he got, but he surprised me. He had loosened the twine to unwrap her, and now he held her close to his heart, rocking and soothing her as though he knew exactly what to do. "Where in the world did this baby come from?" he asked above the sound of her cries.

"She's Wayne and June Ann Larkin's little girl. June Ann has been so depressed lately, and the baby is very colicky, crying all the time for no reason. June Ann waylaid me when I came up the trail today and she practically threw the baby into my arms, begging me to take her to Miss Lillie. I had no idea that she was handing me the baby, wrapped up like that."

"Where's her husband?"

"He finished planting all the crops weeks ago and went out looking for work. Mack, I didn't even have time to get down off the horse. June Ann just pushed the baby into my arms and ran off into the woods. I knew I could never dismount with a baby in my arms, so I came here."

"You don't think June Ann will hurt herself, do you?"

"I don't know what to think. Lillie's potion didn't seem to cure her baby blues. June Ann told me that she sometimes has terrible thoughts about drowning the baby in the creek whenever she won't stop crying. June Ann is up all night and she's exhausted. She told me to give her to Miss Lillie, but when the thunderstorm came up, Belle decided to come here."

"What's her name?"

"June Ann calls her Feather."

I realized that she had stopped crying. Mack had calmed her, somehow. He was surprisingly tender, gazing down at her, his dark eyes soft. Then he started singing. "Hush little baby don't you cry . . ." He had a fine baritone voice.

I couldn't help noticing the contrast between Mack's strong, muscular arms and the baby's tender, pink flesh; between his thick dark hair and Feather's wispy red hair. She seemed out of place in his sturdy arms, yet completely comfortable with him, and he with her. Mack seemed to have forgotten that I was there as he continued humming the melody after running out of words. The storm raged outside the wrecked cabin, but inside, the tiny infant slept peacefully in his arms. He unwrapped more layers, and we saw that June Ann had packed a few articles of clothing and extra diaper cloths inside the bundle, as if she wasn't planning to return for Feather anytime soon. But how could we feed a baby?

When Mack finally looked up at me, his faint smile turned to a frown. "You're soaked, Alice. Look at you, you're shivering. Here, you hold her while I make a fire."

He handed the baby to me, and as he laid her in my arms, I was aware that I held her more awkwardly than he had. "Wait. What if someone sees the smoke?"

"I'll climb out through the window if anyone comes, and you can pretend that you made the fire. But I don't think anyone will be out chasing smoke signals in this weather, do you?"

He ducked out through the rear door and returned a minute later with an armload of wood. Within minutes he had a fire blazing. I moved closer to the hearth, careful not to wake the baby.

Belle inched closer, too, to be near Mack. "You'd better hold the baby until my clothes dry," I told him, "or I'm going to get her all wet." I handed the sleeping baby back to him.

"Move closer to the fire, Alice." I sat on the hearthstone, running my fingers through my hair to dry it and control the curls. "How is Lillie?" he asked, watching me.

"She was fine when I left this morning. Speaking of Lillie, do you think there's such a thing as a love potion?"

Mack smiled. "Why? Has she been concocting one?"

I hesitated, then decided to tell him the truth—at least part of it. "Lillie said she fed a love potion to Belle so she would behave for you."

The words weren't even out of my mouth when Belle lowered her head and rubbed her muzzle against Mack's shoulder. He laughed out loud, and continued laughing for a good long time. His joy was contagious, and soon I was chuckling, too.

"That's fantastic!" he said, wiping his eye. "Now, if only I can figure out how to bottle her formula, I'll be a very rich man."

"So you don't believe it's true?"

"I didn't say that. I've learned never to underestimate Lillie."

"So you *do* believe in a love potion?"

"Don't you?" Belle nudged him again.

I was getting nowhere. "Mack, why did you come back to Acorn and try to make things better at the mine? Why not stay up north and forget the past?" I had heard Lillie's version of the story, but I was curious to hear his.

He began with a sigh. "When I left Acorn, I thought it was for good. I'd had a very long wrestling match with God that lasted for a couple of years. My father died in the mines and my mother died giving birth to me . . ."

"Someone told me you were born backwards."

"So I've heard. Anyway, Lillie raised me in the Christian faith and dragged me to church, but I didn't want much to do with God."

"Where did you and Lillie go to church? I've never seen any churches in Acorn."

"There used to be a nice one in town when I was a boy. But as the feud heated up and started tearing the town apart, we couldn't get any ministers to stay. The church building is abandoned now and practically falling down."

The baby sighed in her sleep, and Mack looked down at her again, stroking her soft hair. I loved listening to the slow, leisurely way he talked, pronouncing *I* like *ah*, and *my* like *mah*. He didn't have Ike's mountain twang or speak with poor grammar the way other folks in Acorn did.

"Anyway," Mack continued, "I studied at Berea, a Christian college, and that's where God started wooing me back. He said instead of being mad about the way things were, why not do something about them? I started investigating mine safety because of my father's death and decided to write my novel. I also decided to open the library so other kids could have a chance for a better life like I'd had. Or even if they stayed here, their life would be richer with books."

He was quiet for a long moment as he studied little Feather, then he looked up at me. "What about you, Alice?"

"What about me?"

"You never told me your story."

"There's nothing to tell. I grew up in Illinois, became a librarian, lost my job because of cutbacks, and then came down here."

"So your story is just beginning."

"I guess you could say that.

"Well, that's exciting. Think of all the possible directions you could go."

I nodded, but I couldn't think of any possibilities at all. How had Mack and Maggie and Ike figured out where they were supposed to go and what they should do once they got there? All my life other people had been making decisions for me. My parents had decided I should go to Cook County Normal School, and my instructors had decided I wasn't cut out to be a teacher. Even the decision to end our relationship had been Gordon's, not mine. One of the few decisions I had ever made on my own was to collect books for Kentucky and deliver them myself, and look how that had turned out! I would like to be more decisive in the future, but how? Especially when—as Mack had pointed out—there were so many possible directions in which to go.

"Penny for your thoughts," Mack said when I didn't reply. I needed to change the subject.

"What are your plans after you get justice for Hank and your book gets published?"

"I don't know. Maybe I'll write another book." He turned his attention back to the baby, lifting her tiny hand with one finger and smiling when she curled her fist around it. I wanted to ask where his experience with babies had come from, but I was afraid to. Every time I had asked an innocent question in Acorn, it seemed as though it led to another tragic story.

"Do you think you'll ever move up north again, Mack?"

"I don't know that answer, either. For now, my home is here with Lillie. I need to stay and take care of her and run the library."

"You know what I don't understand? Why don't the people in town ever come in to check out books? Faye's boys, Mamaw, and Ike are the only patrons we've ever had—besides the people we deliver to on our routes, of course."

"A lot of it has to do with the fact that the house belonged to the Larkins. But even the Larkins are reluctant to patronize it because they don't know what to do after they walk through the door. Most people are much more comfortable having books brought to their homes. That's why I want to expand the routes and get books out to more areas. And you'd be surprised how many people don't know how to read but won't admit it."

Eventually the storm blew over and the rain slowed to a trickle. Most of the water pattering on the roof and dripping through the leaks was falling from the trees. I had added a few more pieces of wood to the fire, but it would soon burn out.

"I talked to Ike about the mine," I said as I added the last few sticks of wood. "He says the mine is a straight tunnel that you can walk into, and there are a few shafts off to the sides. He was in the mine on the day Hank died and heard the explosion, but Hank was in a different place, where they supposedly found a new vein of coal. Does that help you at all?"

"Maybe. It would be better if I could send the mining bureau a sketch of the layout. I've been organizing the information to get it ready to send."

"Well, Ike is going out of town to play on a road tour with a new band. I don't know if I'll be able to ask him for a sketch until he returns, or even how I'd go about asking him to draw it."

The baby had begun to stir as we'd talked. Now her blue eyes blinked open and she gazed up at Mack curiously. "Hey there, little girl. Welcome to my cabin," he murmured. He looked so starry-eyed as he fussed over her that I began to wonder if he'd sipped some of Lillie's love potion, too.

"She's going to get hungry," I said. "How will we feed her?"

"We need to find June Ann and make sure she's all right. Maybe you should take the baby back home to her cabin."

"June Ann won't come out. Even if I did go back to her house, she'll hide. She's done it before. I think I'd better take her to Miss Lillie like she asked me to. But I'll have to walk home. Otherwise, I don't know how I'll ever dismount without help. Lillie is much too tiny to reach that far, and Feather probably weighs as much as Lillie does."

Mack shook his head. "Lillie doesn't have a cow, and this baby is too young to eat real food. I think you'd better take her up to Maggie's place. She has a cow and a few goats, too. At least the baby will get milk up there. Besides, Maggie will know how to take care of her."

"Won't it be hard for her—painful, I mean—after losing her own baby?"

"Yeah. She might refuse. But I think it's the best thing to do. Maggie knows more about babies than we do."

I looked at Feather, content in his arms, and smiled. "You're doing just fine, Mack."

"Thanks. But like you said, she's going to get hungry pretty soon. And when June Ann finally does show up, she can go up to Maggie's to get her baby back. She knows where Maggie lives."

I stood and stretched while Mack wrapped up the baby again. I was warm and dry and reluctant to venture outside. I enjoyed Mack's company and felt comfortable conversing with him. But Feather wouldn't be content much longer.

"What if Maggie refuses? Should I take the baby to Miss Lillie, then?"

"Don't give Maggie a choice. Just hand the baby to her the way June Ann handed her to you."

That sounded like a terrible idea. Maggie already took care of her ailing mother-in-law, and it didn't seem right to add to her burden without asking. But what other choice did I have? I reached for Belle's reins.

"Okay, Belle. Time to get going." I pulled her through the door and climbed onto the railing and into the saddle. Mack kissed the baby's forehead before handing her up to me. "Take care," he said. "Let me know how everything goes."

Belle tried to head home, but I took charge for once, making her do what I wanted. We rode to Maggie's house, and when we reached the clearing in front of her cabin, I called out to her. She came to her door.

"You're early today, Allie. I wasn't expecting you until this afternoon."

"I know. There's been a crisis and I've ended up with June Ann's baby. Can you take her so I can dismount?"

"Sure." She hurried over to Belle's side, and I handed the baby down to her. Maggie parted the feed sack cover and looked at Feather, then up at me again.

"You look chilled, Allie. Why don't you come in and warm up?"

I tied Belle to the hitching post and went inside where Maggie had a warm fire in the stove and fragrant bread baking in the oven. I quickly explained how June Ann had thrust Feather into my arms on my way up the creek. I left Mack out of the story.

"June Ann asked me to take her to Miss Lillie, but Lillie hasn't been feeling well, so I wondered if you would take her instead. Lillie's too old to take care of such a tiny baby, and I don't know anything about infants. You have a cow and some goats, so I know you could at least give her milk to drink. We don't have a cow, and I don't know where on earth to buy milk—"

I stopped, aware that I was babbling. But what if Maggie refused? What if I got stuck caring for an infant along with all the other endless tasks I already had? Even if someone loaned Miss Lillie a cow or a goat, I had no idea how to milk an animal, nor did I want to learn. Too late I realized I should have listened to Mack and not given Maggie a choice. "Please take care of her for me, Maggie. Please?"

"I'm the wrong person to ask. There must be someone else."

"Everyone I know is either a Larkin or an Arnett, and neither family will help. Please? I don't know what else to do with her or who else to ask."

"She's so pretty. How old is she?"

"She was born about a month ago."

"What's her name?"

"Feather . . . Maggie, I'm begging you."

"Well . . . I guess I could watch her until you find June Ann. Someone is out searching for her, right?"

"I don't know who to send or where to search. June Ann knows these woods a lot better than I do. She could hide for days."

"She'd better be careful, especially at night. I'm still seeing signs of that wildcat all over this area."

"June Ann knows about the wildcat. She loves her baby, Maggie. She'll come back for her soon, I know she will."

I watched Maggie and Feather as they gazed at each other. Maggie couldn't help smiling. I nearly sighed aloud with relief, then edged toward the door.

"I need to leave. Thanks so much, Maggie."

CHAPTER 30

The morning's ordeal wore me out. By the time I left Maggie and Feather and climbed onto Belle, I simply wanted to go home. Nobody on my route was going to get books today. I stopped at June Ann's cabin on the way home and called out to her, but she didn't reply. I wasn't surprised. I dismounted and sat on her porch to wait, but when it began to rain again, I finally gave up. I wrote her a note on a scrap of newspaper, telling her that Feather was with Maggie Coots, then I left the note on her table and rode back to Mack's cabin.

"Maggie agreed to take the baby," I told him when he came to the door. "I'm heading home now." I didn't even dismount. The rain had made Belle as eager to get home as I was. We were both cold and wet.

Belle went straight into her shed, where I removed her saddle and dried her off with an empty feed sack.

I trudged up the stairs to my bedroom to change my clothes. Lillie called to me as I passed her room. "You're home early today, honey. Did the thunder scare you off?"

"No, it wasn't the storm." I sagged onto the chair beside her bed and told her the entire story, beginning with June Ann waylaying me in the middle of the thunderstorm, and ending with Mack's suggestion that I take the baby to Maggie Coots. "Fortunately, Maggie agreed to take her for now, but I think we should contact

June Ann's family. If you'll tell me where to find her parents, I'll go talk to them and explain what happened. Maybe this crisis will finally bring the feuding families together."

"You don't need June Ann's folks. Maggie Coots will take good care of that little baby."

"But Maggie also has her mother-in-law to care for, and Opal Coots is bedridden."

"That don't matter. That baby's gonna save Maggie's life."

"Save her life? What do you mean? How?"

"The same way that Mack saved mine. That must be why the Good Lord sent that little baby here in the first place, and why He made her so fussy all the time, and why my tonic don't work. He wants to keep Maggie here until she settles accounts with Him, don't you see?"

I shook my head, bewildered. "No. I don't see anything."

"Maggie came down here to work for God, but that's not what He's wanting her to do."

"It isn't? I thought we're all supposed to work for God."

"He wants us to work *with* Him, honey. Not *for* Him."

I closed my eyes and rubbed them. "I'm so confused. What does working *with* God have to do with June Ann's baby and with saving Maggie's life and . . . and with Mack saving yours?"

She leaned against the pillow and sighed. "I had hundreds of children. All the babies I brought into this world are my children. I even watched some grow up and have babies of their own. But Mack is special to me. Raising him made up for the two children I lost, and for all them other hard things I went through. God gave Mack to me so I would keep on living. I got to see him grow up, take his first steps, learn to talk. I taught him how to read, and I made sure he had plenty of books. I kept my promise to his mama, and Mack went to college instead of working in the mine."

"He's a good man, Lillie. You raised him well."

"I know my time to leave this old world is coming real soon. If I can just see Mack settled, with his book all finished and a good wife by his side, then I can leave here in peace. I been hanging on just so he won't be all alone in the world."

"Has he found a wife?"

"Oh, yes. The Good Lord has found the perfect wife for Mack."

I thought of the letter he'd addressed to Miss Catherine Anson in Washington, and when I pictured Mack rocking baby Feather in his arms, I felt envious.

"Well, good. He'll make a good husband and father. But there's still a lot I don't understand, Lillie. Why would God go to all the trouble of arranging these complicated schemes—killing Mack's mother and making baby Feather have colic? It seems crazy. And why take Maggie's husband and child from her? Why did He make you suffer by taking Buster and Sam and your little daughter away from you?"

Lillie sighed. "I been around a long time, honey, and I seen a lot a things that don't make sense to us. Life is full of troubles, but this one with June Ann's baby will all work out for good. You'll see."

"I still think that if we talked to the Arnetts and the Larkins about Feather, maybe we could end the feud. Both sides need to see all the harm they've caused, and they need to start taking care of Feather and June Ann."

"Let it go, honey. That ain't gonna happen."

"How can you be so sure?"

"I quit trying to figure everything out a long time ago and learned to trust God to work it all out."

"But I want to *do* something!"

"Well, then, why don't you go fix us something to eat. It's past lunchtime, ain't it?"

"You know what I mean, Lillie. I want to do something important."

"It's the little things that make all the difference in the world. The kind words we speak and the simple things we do for people. Remember how that Ike fella helped you work in the garden? Now, he'd say it was just a little thing, but the Good Lord is gonna bless his labor with food for months and months to come."

"Is that what you meant by working with God, not for Him?"

"That's exactly right. See? You learnt something. Now," she said with a grin, "go work with God and fix us some lunch."

I went to my bedroom first, to change my clothes and dry off. I tried to make sense of what Lillie said as I stoked the kitchen stove and heated the leftover stew for us. After becoming so involved in the lives of people in Acorn, it was hard to let go and trust God. I wanted to fix everything. But when Mack had tried to do that, he'd only made things worse.

I had one more question to ask Lillie as I laid the lunch tray on her lap. "Where did Mack learn how to take care of a baby? You should have seen him today, holding little Feather on his lap, singing to her, rocking her to sleep." Her answer surprised me.

"Honey, as far as I know, Mack don't know a single thing about babies."

Early Friday morning, Ike came into the library to say good-bye to me. He could barely stand still from excitement.

"Well, I'm off! My brother's gonna drive me to the train station over in Hazard, and I'll meet up with the new band in Lexington. My fingers are itching to play, Alice. I can't wait to get going."

"I can see that."

"This is the best thing that's ever happened to me. If it works out, I'll be on my way to Nashville for sure!"

Ike was thrilled about what lay ahead, and although he swore he would miss me, I could see that he was eager to be on his way. I didn't want to delay him with a long farewell. "Write to me and let me know how you make out, okay?"

"I will." He hugged me tightly, but his kiss was quick and impatient. Then he was gone.

I knew I would miss him, yet as soon as the truck roared off, I felt as relieved as I had after the thunderstorm had blown over and the rain had stopped. Maybe now I could concentrate on my work in the library and type up more of Lillie's folk medicine book without any distractions. But as hard as I tried, I couldn't settle down and stop worrying about June Ann and Maggie and Feather. I needed to find out how they were doing. I decided to ride my route, even though today was Friday, and deliver books to the people I had neglected yesterday.

I stopped at June Ann's cabin on the way up the mountain. Her dog came out and barked at me, but June Ann didn't appear. The farm was obviously being tended. Her mule was out in the pasture, her chickens were scratching around the yard, and her garden looked weeded and hoed. I dismounted and went inside the cabin, calling her name. A fire burned in her fireplace, and the newspaper with my note was no longer on the table. In its place lay the book that I had brought her the last time I had come. I waited, hoping she would come out and talk to me, but she never did. I took the old book and left a new one for her. At least I knew she was safe.

I brought books to the Howard family, then stopped at the school, letting everyone think the storm had delayed me yesterday. Finally, I went to see Maggie.

"Come on in, Allie," she called from her doorway. I dismounted and went inside. The house was as peaceful and fragrant as always. Maggie stood by the stove, stirring something in a big soup pot.

"How are you?" I asked. "I've been thinking about you and the baby all night, so I decided to come and see how you're doing."

"We're fine. Have a seat." I removed my jacket and sat down at her kitchen table. Maggie poured me a cup of tea.

"Has Feather been eating okay?"

"Yes. She didn't like the goat's milk at first, but when she got hungry enough, she finally drank it. She cries a lot, Allie. I think she has colic. I've been feeding her several smaller meals instead of a bigger one and it seems to help. Have you found June Ann?"

"No. I stopped at her cabin on the way up here. I could tell she's been home, but she won't come out of hiding and talk to me. I wrote her a note yesterday, telling her that you were taking care of Feather, and today the note was gone. Where is Feather, by the way?"

Maggie gestured to the bedroom. "She's in with Miss Opal, sleeping."

"How is your mother-in-law?"

"Not good." Maggie sank onto a chair across from me with a sigh. "It's so strange to be taking care of the two of them at the same time. They're at the opposite ends of life; they both eat and sleep, but one is growing stronger, the other one weaker. My instinct is to nurture Opal and make her well again, just like I'm nurturing Feather. But there's nothing I can do for Opal. She's dying, Allie, and she knows it. She told me that she's ready to go. I don't know if I could be as brave as she is."

"I hope it's not too much work for you with the baby, too?"

"Not at all. I lay them side by side in the big bed, and they seem to draw comfort from each other. Miss Opal loves that baby. She talks to her when they're both awake and sings her to sleep when she cries. But she keeps calling her Rhoda Lee. I corrected her at first. But really, what difference does it make?"

Maggie didn't seem at all perturbed by her new responsibility. I realized it would be much harder for her to watch Miss Opal die if she didn't have Feather to care for, and I remembered Lillie's prophecy that the baby would save Maggie's life.

"Is there anything I can do to help you?" I asked as I stood to leave.

"Did you bring me another book?"

"I did. It's one of the new ones that I brought with me from Illinois. Wow, it seems like ages ago that I boxed up those books and climbed into my uncle's car."

"Today is the first day of May already. "

I looked at Maggie in surprise. I had lost track of the days and months. I was becoming like these mountain folks, who seemed perfectly content to ignore the passing of time. Mack had asked me to give him another month to finish his work, and surely the time must be up by now—wasn't it? It didn't matter. I couldn't leave now. I had grown much too fond of Maggie and June Ann and Feather. And I no longer took care of Miss Lillie and Mack out of duty, but because I cared about them. I would write another letter to my parents tonight, explaining that I would be further delayed.

The following week, riding my routes took longer than usual because I stopped at June Ann's cabin on both days, and took time to see Maggie and Feather on both days, as well. In between, I stayed busy with my library work and with typing Lillie's recipes and with all the hard work of running the household. I barely had time to think of Ike, let alone miss him. Was Lillie's love potion wearing off?

Being apart from Ike gave me time to think clearly about him without the distraction of his handsome face and cheerful personality. What had attracted me to him, besides his good nature and wonderful fiddle playing and heart-stopping kisses? Did we really have anything in common? And was it enough for us to spend a lifetime together? Maybe Ike would change his mind about me, too, while we were apart. He'd told me that women were drawn to him whenever they heard him play. If they started falling at his feet again, he might forget all about me. I watched for the promised letter from him, but it never came.

Belle and I were on our way back home to the library after delivering books on Thursday afternoon when Mack flagged us down in front of his cabin. "Do you have time for a visit?" he asked. "I want to tell you something. And I have a favor to ask." I would have been concerned except that he looked happier than I'd ever seen him. I knew it must be good news. I climbed down and we sat side by side on his front porch.

"It's finished," he said quietly. "My manuscript is finished. Done. The end."

"Mack, that's wonderful!" I gave him a quick, spontaneous hug. What must it feel like to accomplish such a task? I had read hundreds of novels in my lifetime, but I had never thought about how an author must feel when he wrote *The End*. If it was satisfying to finish reading a good book, how much more satisfying must it be to finish writing one? "Now what?" I asked him.

"Now I give it to my publisher."

"Do you want me to take it home with me and mail it for you? I assume that's the favor?"

"No. My manuscript was stolen from Lillie's house once before, remember? Besides, those nosy old geezers at the post office are going to wonder what you're mailing. They'll open up the package to look inside, I guarantee it."

"Isn't it against the law to tamper with the mail?"

"Of course it is. But making moonshine is against the law, too, and that doesn't stop anybody around here."

"How will you get your book to your publisher then?"

"I've given it a lot of thought and I've decided to deliver it in person. While I'm gone, I'll bring the information about Hank's accident to Washington. I have the evidence all compiled except for one crucial piece of information that's still missing. That's where the favor comes in. Moon or no moon, we need to go back to the mine."

"*We?* Oh no. Absolutely not."

"It'll be the same arrangement as last time, Alice. All I need is for you to ride up here with Belle. You can stay here at the cabin or come with me, it's your choice."

"Why do you have to go back there?"

"I need to go inside the mine and see where Hank's accident happened. Something doesn't add up. According to the documents we found and Ike Arnett's account, the accident didn't take place in the same shaft where they were mining coal."

"Ike said they had found a new vein."

"It doesn't make any sense to mine a new vein in another shaft if the old one hasn't played out. And according to those files we found, they could have kept digging in that original shaft for years. If they started a new one, they'd have to lay new tracks and hire more workers, yet production was slowing down after the stock market crash. I think Hank's accident was a setup. That's why I need to see the site."

"But the mine entrance is all boarded up. How will you get inside?"

"That shouldn't be hard. I'll just pry off some boards."

"Wait. The guard is going to come along and see that the boards are pried away. Remember how carefully he looked it over the last time?" I remembered lying in the bushes, terrified that we would get caught as we watched the guard search the mine entrance and shine his light all around.

"I don't have all the details figured out, Alice, but I know I need to go back there. Will you help me or not?"

My heart felt like a dead weight in my chest. "When?"

"Tomorrow night. I can't wait for the next new moon. If it rains like it has for the last few nights, it'll be dark enough."

"Oh, Mack. Isn't there any other way?"

"No." He rose to his feet and reached for my hand to pull me up. "Come on, I want to show you where I hide my manuscript, along with the papers for the mining officials—just in case. You'll need to mail them if anything happens to me."

"It sounds like you don't think you'll escape this time."

"Not at all. I'm simply taking precautions."

He led the way into the cabin and pushed aside a pile of dead leaves to reveal a trapdoor beneath the floorboards. Mack had lined the space with feed sacks and wrapped the two packages in oilcloth to make them waterproof.

"This packet of papers goes to Washington," he told me, "and this one is my book. The addresses for both of them are inside." Mack wore a satisfied smile, but I felt sick with fear for him—and for Lillie, if anything happened to him.

"Can't you just turn in the documents you already have? Why not let the government officials go inside to look at the shaft?"

"They may not want to come back to Acorn unless I can offer them some new compelling evidence. Please help me, Alice."

I closed my eyes. I knew he was waiting for my reply, but I didn't want him to go back to the mine. It was too big of a risk. I had a very bad feeling about his plan this time, knowing what would happen if he were caught. I needed to stall Mack, hoping he would change his mind. "Does it have to be tomorrow night? That wildcat is still roaming around, you know."

"We'll be fine. I swear that this will be the last favor I'll ever ask of you. Once I deliver this information to Washington, I won't have to worry about hiding out anymore. I can come home and take care of Lillie. And you can go home."

I could go home. It was what I wanted, wasn't it?

"But wait . . . you still don't know who tried to kill you, do you?"

"Well, no, not for certain. Why are you so reluctant to help me this time, Alice?"

"Because I care about you! I don't want anything to happen to you!" I blurted the truth without thinking.

Mack looked so stunned by my confession that I hurried to amend my words. "Everyone cares about you, Mack, but especially Lillie. She loves you like a son. She told me the other day that she's ready to leave this world, but she's just hanging on until you're settled down. She has lost so many loved ones already that it would be a catastrophe if something happened to you."

Mack reached for my hand. "Then help me, Alice. Please. I can't do it alone."

CHAPTER 31

The weather worked in Mack's favor on Friday night. Clouds padded the heavens like a layer of thick felt, obscuring the three-quarter moon and the stars, muffling the forest sounds. Rain drizzled on and off, as if unable to make up its mind. I hadn't been able to make up my mind, either. Should I stay at Mack's cabin where I'd be safe, or join him on his insane quest?

In the end, I decided to join him. Mack still hadn't fully recovered from his gunshot wound, and I'd been so wrapped up with Ike and Maggie and June Ann and the baby that I hadn't been paying attention to how thin and weak he looked. Worse, I kept forgetting to tell Lillie that he needed medicine. I knew how much he meant to Lillie, how she couldn't bear to lose him, yet I had been negligent. The least I could do was go to the mine with him and be his lookout.

Belle must have sensed my determination because she didn't throw one of her horse fits when I saddled her up late that night in the misty rain. Her attitude toward me had changed ever since I'd made her obey me on the day of the thunderstorm. It was as if I had earned her respect. Who would have ever thought that I'd learn to ride a horse—and a temperamental one at that?

We arrived at Mack's cabin without incident and left the saddle and bridle behind, like we had the last time. "Where's my rifle?" Mack asked, glancing all around.

"I didn't bring it. Lillie wouldn't let me."

"She wouldn't let you? Why not?"

"I don't know, but she got all funny about it when I asked her where the ammunition was, and she said you didn't need to bring your gun this time. She said the Good Lord would watch over us."

"That's just great! We need that rifle, Alice. Lillie didn't have a problem with us bringing it along the last time."

"Don't get mad at me," I said, holding up my hands. "I'm just the messenger. I would have brought the rifle, but I figured it would be useless without bullets—just like last time."

Mack huffed as if trying to control his temper. "Did you remember to bring the miner's hat?"

"Yes. And this time *we* won't leave it in the saddlebag, will *we*?" I wanted him to know that the responsibility for the mistake last time had been equally shared.

We rode Belle bareback up through the coal black woods. I felt untethered without a saddle and stirrups, as if I might slide off Belle's broad back. The eerie ride seemed to take even longer than it had the last time as we navigated the dark, featureless forest. Just as I spotted the coal tipple ahead of us, the rain began to fall in earnest. Mack drew Belle to a halt at the edge of the clearing and climbed off, then caught me as I slid off.

"I'm going to leave Belle here," he whispered. "Do you want to wait here with her?"

"No. I'll come with you. At least it will be dry inside the mine."

Mack didn't spend as much time surveying the area as he had before, quickly leading the way to the mine entrance, stopping every few yards to look around. There was no sign of a guard or any activity at the deserted mine. In the distance, the ghost town looked forlorn in the dismal rain.

"You be the lookout while I break in," Mack said. "Watch for the guard's car. You did a great job spotting it last time." Mack worked for fifteen minutes before finally managing to pry off a piece of one of the thick boards that sealed the entrance. But it had splintered in the process and would be noticeable to an alert guard.

"There's nothing I can do about it," he said when I pointed out the mess he'd made. "The hole has to be big enough to squeeze through. Is the coast still clear?"

"Yes, as far as I can tell . . ." I felt shaky with nerves. My mind had spun with fear ever since Mack and I had begun this journey. Mack put his hands on my shoulders as if to steady me and looked me in the eye, his expression serious.

"I need you to stay here and keep watch for me. If anyone comes, don't worry about me. You run into the woods, find Belle, and get out of here."

"How is that keeping watch? I'm not going to leave you trapped in the mine. You said they would kill you if you're caught."

"True. But that makes it dangerous for you, too."

"I don't think they'd dare kill me. My family would ask too many questions if anything happened to me." I didn't say it out loud, but I clung to the hope that no one would dare to harm Mack, either, if I was a witness.

"Are you sure?" he asked.

I exhaled, then nodded. Fear sat on my chest like a hundred-pound sack, making it hard to breathe.

We dropped to our stomachs on the wet ground and wiggled through the opening into the mineshaft. Mack went first. Once inside, I stood up and brushed mud and dirt from my clothes while he reached through the hole and tried to prop the splintered board in place so it wouldn't be as noticeable.

"Can we light the miner's lamp now?" I asked. "I can't see my hand in front of my face." Before Mack could reply, I head a rustling noise, like the wind rushing through the leaves, and I saw a dark mass moving and swirling just inches above my head. I recognized the sound from my experience with the bat in my bedroom, but this time it was multiplied a hundredfold. I crouched down beside Mack and covered my head, trying not to scream as the cloud of bats swarmed around us. At last, they poured out into the night, flying between the cracks in the boards that covered the entrance.

"They're gone," Mack said. I heard the relief in his voice.

"Can we please light the lamp now?"

"Not yet. We need to conserve fuel. I don't want to use it all up before I have a chance to inspect the accident site."

I felt shaky and out of breath. The shaft was as stuffy and airless as a closet and smelled like the coal cellar in the basement of my father's church. "I'm having an attack of claustrophobia. How can the miners stand it in here all day?"

"They get used to it. Let's start walking. We can follow the rail tracks for the coal carts. Here, hold my hand." He groped in the dark until he found my hand. I couldn't seem to breathe right. Mack's breaths were rapid and shallow, too, as we inched our way forward, deeper into the mine. We were going to get lost in this cave, like Tom Sawyer and Becky Thatcher. The town wouldn't hold another funeral for Mack, but maybe they would for me.

"I've read books that described 'stygian darkness,'" I said, "but this is the first time I've ever experienced it."

"How did they end—those books about stygian darkness? Happily-ever-after or not?"

"I don't remember. I just remember the word *stygian*. I thought it was a great word."

"Yeah, it is. I love words like that."

"Me too. But stygian isn't so great now that I'm experiencing it."

"Careful!" Mack said when I stumbled over one of the railroad ties. I was shuffling forward with one arm outstretched, like a game of blind man's bluff.

"The darkness feels so heavy!" I breathed.

"That's how it's described in the Bible, remember? During one of the ten plagues in Egypt, it was a darkness you could feel."

"I don't like it. And I can feel the weight of the mountain above us, too. Can't you, Mack? It feels like the rocks are closing in on us."

"That's what comes from reading too many books. They give you an overactive imagination."

"Well, you read a lot of books, too."

"I know, and I'm having the same problem you are." He gave a nervous laugh.

We edged forward in silence for a few minutes until I found it unbearable. The warmth of Mack's hand was comforting, but I needed to hear his voice. "Talk to me, Mack."

"Okay. What do you want to talk about?"

"For starters, I don't understand how you're going to find the place where Hank was killed when we can't even see each other."

"I have my right hand on the wall alongside us. The accident report said the cave-in that killed Hank was in a shaft on the north side, which is on our right. I should feel an opening when we come to it."

"Have you always been this courageous?"

"I'm not courageous at all. But I caused this mess, so I need to see it through. You're pretty brave yourself to come along, even though this has nothing to do with you."

"I'm not sure if it's bravery or stupidity. I've never done anything like this in my life. In fact, I've never done anything!" The truth gave me a lump in my throat. "You asked me about my story . . . well, the truth is, I've never really lived. Delivering books to Kentucky was the most adventurous thing I've ever done. But ever since I arrived in Acorn, I've been forced to do things I've only read about in books. My entire trip has all the elements of a badly written novel, with you getting shot, the corrupt sheriff, the buried treasure, the feud . . . and now this! My life is going to seem boring when I get home."

"But I'm guessing you'll be glad to get back to normal."

"You know, I don't think I want my life to be the same as before. Home will look different, I think. And I'm different. I want to get more involved in life from now on, instead of just reading about it in books. I want to spend more time with people." I was surprised by my own confession. "If I've learned anything while I've been here, it's how important it is to have family and friends and people around us to share our lives with. Miss Lillie is so . . . unique. I could never forget her. Or Maggie and June Ann, either. Then there's Ike and Cora and Faye and Marjorie and Alma. And the people on my route . . . they're all such characters."

"You must have friends and family back in Illinois."

"I do. I even had a boyfriend. But I was never involved in Gordon's life, not in a genuine heart-to-heart way. I'm ashamed to say that he was convenient and little else. No firecrackers ever went off. No romantic violins played music in the background when we were together. I'm thankful now that he broke up with me. What a tedious life we would have had."

"What about friends?"

"I have a best friend, Freddy. But I've come to see that I used her without giving very much in return. Most of the time, the characters I read about in books seemed more real to me than either Gordon or Freddy did. I spent all my time reading instead of living."

I didn't know why I was baring my soul to Mack. Perhaps it was the anonymity of darkness that made it easier. Or maybe fear and the threat of danger had prompted the need to confess and repent. Either way, I was finally seeing the truth—seeing the light, as they say—even though I was in absolute darkness.

Suddenly, Mack lurched sideways and nearly lost his balance. "Sorry . . . There's an opening here. Maybe it's the side shaft. Stay here, Alice. I'll go in a little ways and see where it goes." He released my hand.

"Don't get lost," I called. I longed to beg him not to leave me, but I made up my mind to be brave. I could hear his shuffling footsteps for a minute or two, then silence. What if he fell into a hole? What if something grabbed him? What if he got lost and never returned? I stood in the darkness, alone, trying very hard not to scream. It seemed like an eternity passed before Mack called out, "I'm coming back. Talk to me so I can find you."

"I'm here . . . keep following my voice . . . I'm right here." I could feel his presence moments before he bumped into me and reached for my hand. I couldn't even describe the enormous relief I felt from the comfort and warmth of another person, especially from Mack.

"That wasn't the place we're looking for," Mack said. "It came to a dead end after only a few yards, and there was some equipment or something stored in there."

We continued forward, hand in hand, following the rail tracks. I started babbling again, needing to hear my own voice. "I don't think I could ever get used to this darkness. This must be what books call 'absolute darkness.' And didn't Jesus say something in the Bible about sinners being thrown into outer darkness as a punishment?"

"Yeah, where there's weeping and gnashing of teeth."

"My father preached a sermon about hell one time, and he said we would not only be in total darkness in hell, but we'd be alone, isolated from other people and from God. You left me alone for only a few minutes back there, but I can see how spending an eternity like that would be the worst sort of hell."

"That was one of the reasons I came back to Acorn. I felt so alone when I was up in Ohio on my own."

Suddenly I ran smack into something hard and unyielding. I stumbled backward and fell, crying out in pain. Mack dropped to his knees beside me, feeling for me. "Alice! Alice, what happened? Are you okay?"

"I don't know. I . . . I bumped into something."

"Let me see." He moved away from me, and I could hear his boots scuffing on the loose stones as he felt around in the dark. "It's an ore cart. I'm sorry, I didn't realize they would leave one parked in the middle of the tracks. Are you hurt?"

"Nothing seems to be broken or bleeding. My shins feel bruised, but I'll be okay." He helped me up, then switched places with me.

"You feel along the wall for a while, and I'll follow the tracks in case there's another cart in the way." We started shuffling forward again.

"How far have we walked?" I asked. "And how far does this mineshaft go?"

"I'd say we've gone about half a mile. But the shaft might be miles long. And we've been going slowly downhill—have you felt it?"

"No. And I did not need to know that fact. I feel like I'm buried alive as it is."

I lost all track of time as we continued walking. Twenty minutes or two hours might have passed, I didn't know. My bruised shins throbbed. We moved slowly as if blindfolded, following the rail tracks. My left hand was in Mack's and my right hand trailed along the cold, rough wall, feeling for an opening. The thought of retracing our steps made me want to sit down and cry, but the alternative—being lost in here forever—was unthinkable.

Right then the wall vanished and my hand groped empty air. "Mack, wait! The wall just ended. There's an opening here." He let go of my hand to investigate, and I heard him moving around in the dark.

"There aren't any rail tracks going in," he said, "and the

338

opening is about six feet wide. Wait here for me, Alice. Keep facing the way we've been walking so we don't get turned around accidentally."

Great! That was another catastrophe I hadn't thought of—that we might get disoriented and confused and end up walking in the wrong direction without realizing it. There was no way to tell in the dark. I sat down on the cold stone floor beside the opening in the wall and waited for Mack to explore it. The mine entrance, I told myself repeatedly, was behind me.

Mack was gone even longer than the last time. I hated waiting all alone. I began to sing to keep loneliness and fear at bay, and I chose—appropriately enough—the hymn "Rock of Ages." It was comforting, even though I sang very softly.

"Alice . . . ?" Mack's voice sounded muffled and far away. "Alice, are you there?"

I scrambled to my feet. "I'm right here . . . Can you hear me?"

"Yes. Listen, I want you to turn around and walk back toward the mine entrance."

"What? Why?" He still sounded a long distance away and didn't seem to be coming toward me. "Is something wrong? Are you hurt?"

"I think this might be the right place, so I'm going to light the lamp. You need to get away from here in case there's an explosion."

"An explosion!"

"Sometimes the gas builds up and the spark might set it off when I light a match."

"Mack, wait—!"

"Just do it, Alice. Right now. Follow the tracks back a ways. If you don't hear an explosion, wait five minutes, and then come back."

I did what he said, my knees trembling as I backtracked. This time the unbroken silence was welcome—it meant no explosion had occurred. Time passed, and I kept glancing over my shoulder, hoping to see the glow of Mack's miner's hat, but the same inky blackness filled the shaft in both directions. When I thought five minutes had passed, I turned around and walked back, feeling along the wall for the opening.

"Mack?" I called when I finally came to the void. "Talk to me, Mack . . . I'm coming toward you, but I don't see your light."

"This way . . ." He sounded miles away. "I'll walk back to you. You should see my light in a minute."

I inched forward, my hand on the wall to guide me. "I still don't see it . . . Keep talking to me . . ." The floor was very rough, more uneven than the floor of the main shaft had been. When the beam of light finally burst through the darkness, it nearly blinded me. I squinted and held up my hand to shade my eyes. Even so, a shining light had never looked so wonderful to me before. Mack aimed the beam down toward the floor so I could see where I was walking, then he turned and led the way once I caught up to him.

"This way, Alice." We could barely walk side by side in the narrow shaft. The ceiling was a mere inch above Mack's head. The tunnel curved, continuing on for several yards before ending in a pile of rubble that had obviously fallen from a huge hole in the jagged, gaping ceiling.

"This is where Hank died," Mack said quietly. "You can see where they moved the rubble to dig out his body. And some of these rocks still have the drill holes in them."

I watched as Mack spent several minutes looking all around, shining his head lamp on the ceiling, on the wall at the end of the tunnel, on chunks of rubble. I had no idea what he was searching for. Mack probably didn't know, either. When he turned to face me, I had to shield my eyes from the glare again.

"There's no coal here."

"Is that good or bad?" I asked.

"It's good as far as our investigation is concerned. It means that Hank's death must have been staged. The investigators looked at how the charges had been set and if they were defective or not, but no one thought to look for a vein of coal. Why would the mining company tell Hank to set charges in this shaft if there wasn't any coal?"

"They wouldn't unless they were setting a trap."

"Exactly!" I couldn't see Mack's face because of the blinding light on his hat, but I heard the triumph in his voice.

"Are we all done? Can we get out of here now?" I had begun to shiver with cold and excitement and adrenaline.

"Yeah. We can go." But he took one last look around first, and

I saw him wipe his eyes. His friend had died here. My friend Maggie's husband. I rested my hand on his shoulder.

"I'm so sorry, Mack."

"Yeah. Me too."

He kept the light on as we made our way back down the narrow tunnel to the main shaft, then turned left to follow the tracks to the entrance. The shaft didn't feel quite so claustrophobic now that I could see. And now that I knew we were on our way out instead of walking into the unknown. Neither one of us was breathing hard anymore.

"I'd better turn out the lamp now," he said when we reached the ore cart parked on the tracks. He took my hand again to keep me from stumbling in the dark. Fifteen minutes later, I was amazed to see light shining through the cracks in the boarded-up entrance to the mine. Was it dawn already? Or was the night sky that much brighter than the inside of the mine? Before I could ask, Mack grabbed me in a tackle and shoved me to the side, against the wall. He pulled me to the floor and crouched with me in a tight ball.

Above the sound of our panicked breathing I heard a car engine running. The light came from headlights! I could hear rain pattering and the swish and squeak of windshield wipers. I held my breath, praying the guard wouldn't be able to shine his flashlight to the side and see us. My teeth chattered as I quivered with fear. I heard voices, more than one, and strained to hear what they were saying.

"Oh yeah? Well, how else would this board get broken off? I'm telling you, someone went into the mine."

"No one could fit through a hole that small. Must be an animal."

"You could fit. Try it."

"No, you try it."

Laughter. A brighter light poked through the opening we'd made and shone all around. I waited, enduring the longest minutes of my life.

The talking stopped. Had they seen us? Two car doors slammed. I heard the engine fade as the car backed away. The headlights vanished and everything went still. I was about to speak when Mack touched his fingers to my lips. He put his mouth against my ear and whispered, "One of them probably stayed here. He'll wait and see if we come out."

There was no way to know if Mack was right or not. We would have to stay hidden. I shivered uncontrollably. Mack held me tightly to keep me warm until my teeth finally stopped chattering.

We waited and waited. I was tired from the long hike and the stale air and the unrelieved tension. I finally drifted to sleep in his arms as fear and exhaustion made my body shut down. I don't know how much time passed before Mack nudged me awake. The shaft was growing lighter. The car had returned.

"See anything?" someone called.

"Nope. Haven't heard a peep. Let's go. I'm cold."

Mack had been right—someone had been watching the entrance.

"We have to fix the hole first. I brought a board to seal it up."

Hammering. It went on and on until no more light penetrated the opening we had crawled through. We were trapped.

"It's okay," Mack whispered in my ear. "We'll get out." At last the pounding ended. Soon the headlights and engine noise receded as the car pulled away. "We'll need to wait a little longer to make sure," Mack whispered. "Try to sleep some more."

Somehow I did manage to doze. I don't know how much time passed before Mack nudged me again. He stood and went to the opposite side of the entrance from where they had made repairs and peered out through the cracks. He started kicking and prying at the wood to make an opening. Little by little, the boards gave way. The hole was even smaller than the first one, but I was so desperate to get out of that gloomy dungeon, I would have crawled through any opening.

Freedom! Air! I inhaled deeply as the damp breeze tickled my skin. It was still raining, but it felt good to me. I was free!

"Come on," Mack said. He took my hand and led the way into the woods, stopping every few yards to call to Belle. She didn't come. We wasted fifteen minutes searching for her, without any luck.

"You forgot to tell her to wait for us this time," I said.

"I did? . . . Maybe all of that hammering scared her off. Or else the car engine spooked her. She isn't used to cars."

"I'm betting it was the rain. Belle hates rain. She probably made a beeline for home as soon as our backs were turned. I guess Lillie's love potion finally wore off and Belle no longer cares about winning your affections."

"Very funny."

Mack spent another few minutes tramping around in the brush and calling to her before giving up. The rain that had felt so good after leaving the mine, now felt cold and miserable. I was getting drenched. "Let's go, Mack. I need a warm fire and dry clothes. We can walk home, can't we?"

"It's a long way, you know."

"I don't care. Where's the trail? Lead the way."

The woods were a little lighter than the mine had been, but I still couldn't see much. We were both weary from hiking through the mineshaft all night, and Mack still hadn't recovered his full strength.

We fumbled our way through the thick woods for half an hour when I simply couldn't walk another step. "Can we stop and rest, Mack? I'm sorry, but I'm exhausted."

"That's okay. I'm getting tired, too."

We found a large, damp rock and sat down on it, side by side.

"There's a shortcut we could take that'll be faster—the road up to Maggie's house. We would risk being seen, though."

"Who's going to be driving up that road at this time of night?"

"Hopefully no one. We can cut through the woods along the highway to get to it."

We finished resting and set off again. Mack soon found the narrow dirt road that led up through the woods to Maggie's cabin. I had never been on it before. Mud puddles dotted the road in places, yet it still was much easier to hike on than the path through the thick trees and brush. We moved much faster. Before long, I saw the dim outline of the cabin and the hulking shape of the barn. Dawn was still a few hours away, but I heard squawking and flapping coming from the chicken coop directly in front of us. Had the hens heard us approaching? Mack pulled me to a stop.

"What's wrong?" I asked.

He held a finger to his lips. I saw him tense. I stared in the direction that he was gazing in but didn't see anything at all. When I looked up at Mack, his eyes were wide with fright. He wrapped one arm around my waist and began retreating slowly down the road, walking backward, pulling me with him. He was breathing hard again.

"What is it?" Then I heard the mountain lion's angry snarl. I smelled the animal, too—like the scent of a dozen feral cats. Its eyes flashed briefly, glowing in the dark, as it turned toward us. Mack didn't have a gun.

The cat began to move and came into sight. It was leaving the chicken coop and padding slowly up the road toward us. Mack pulled me tighter and whispered, "Don't scream and don't run. It'll attack."

The wildcat continued to creep toward us, sniffing the air, stalking us. The books all say that your life flashes before your eyes when you're staring at death, but my life didn't flash—maybe because I hadn't really lived it yet. Instead, I found myself staring into the future, desperately wanting to live, wanting to experience joy and sorrow, love and friendship. My life couldn't end this way. I wanted to begin living it.

The cat crept closer. It was only a few yards from us now, moving faster than we were able to back away. I was going to die, and I didn't want to.

Suddenly a gunshot cracked through the silence of the night. The cat leaped in the air as if trying to turn and run, then fell to the ground after only a few steps, its limbs twitching. I leaned against Mack in relief and began to sob.

"Who's there?" someone called. I recognized Maggie's voice. She walked toward us wearing her nightgown and Hank's hunting jacket, her rifle still raised, ready to fire again. I was so relieved, it never occurred to me that Mack should hide from her—that he was supposed to be dead.

"Maggie! It's us, Allie and Mack. Thank God you came when you did! You saved our lives!" I would have run to her, but Mack hung on to me, holding me back.

Maggie halted in the middle of the road, some thirty feet from where we were, the dead wildcat lying in the road between us. Maggie was close enough that we could recognize each other in the faint light. But she didn't lower her rifle.

"Step aside, Allie. I don't want to hit you, but I don't plan on missing a second time."

"But you didn't miss, Maggie, you shot it. See? The wildcat is dead." Why was she still holding her gun to her shoulder, looking down the sight, pointing it at us?

"I know the cat is dead. And now you need to step aside," she said, "so I can finish him off."

"But—"

"She's not talking about the wildcat," Mack said softly. "She means me. Maggie is the one who shot me."

"No. That's not funny, Mack. Both of you, stop fooling around."

"Tell her, Maggie," he said, loud enough for Maggie to hear.

"He's right. I'm the one who shot him. I thought I'd killed him, but I see I was wrong. I won't miss this time."

I instinctively moved in front of Mack, shielding him. I didn't think my heart could possibly beat any faster, but it did. "But . . . but why, Maggie? You're such a kind, loving person. I've seen the way you take care of Hank's mother and little Feather, and I know Mack well enough by now to know he isn't the villain." I felt dizzy and feared I might faint. I didn't want to believe that Maggie would shoot Mack—now or the first time. "Why would you do this? What did Mack ever do to you?"

"He came back here, that's what he did. It's his fault that Hank died."

"Listen, if I could do it all over again, Maggie, believe me, I would do things differently." Mack sounded breathless, as though he had just run up a steep hill. "I know I was wrong to get Hank involved. But listen, Alice and I just came from the mine. We found proof that his death wasn't an accident. If you let me take the evidence to Washington, they'll send an inspector up here and put the real culprits in jail."

"And then what? Is that going to bring Hank back to me?"

"No," Mack breathed. "No, it won't bring him back. I'm so sorry, Maggie."

She was still pointing the gun at us. I knew what a crack shot Maggie was. She could wound me in the arm or leg and then finish off Mack after I fell to the ground.

"Y-you don't want to do this, Maggie," I stammered. "They'll put you in jail for murder."

"I don't care. Miss Opal won't live much longer. She might rest easier if she knows that the man responsible for Hank's death is dead, for real this time."

"But Mack didn't kill him. The mining company did!"

"No, Maggie's right," Mack said. "Hank would still be alive if it hadn't been for me. I blame myself every single day for what happened to him, so why shouldn't she blame me, too?"

"Shut up, Mack," I hissed, poking him with my elbow. "Please, Maggie . . . You have your whole life to live. Don't throw it away on revenge."

Maggie gave a short laugh. "What do I have? Nothing! I'm going to join Hank and Rhoda Lee in the graveyard right after I send Mack to hell. Now step out of the way, Allie. You're my friend, and I would hate to shoot you, but I will if I have to."

"No . . . please don't!" I wanted to live, and I wanted Mack and Maggie to live, too.

Suddenly I saw a flicker of movement alongside the cabin. A dark figure burst out of the shadows behind Maggie and raced straight toward her. Before I could react, the figure plowed into Maggie and tackled her to the ground. The gun fired with a loud crack. Mack's arms went limp and he dropped to the ground behind me.

"No! Mack, no!" I sank down beside him, weeping, shaking him. "Mack? Please be okay . . . please!"

"I'm okay," he breathed. "She missed me. I'm just . . . I'm just . . ." He covered his face. His shoulders shook with tears of relief.

Maggie's gun!

I scrambled to my feet and ran over to scoop up the rifle. I was stunned to see that the person who had tackled Maggie was June Ann Larkin. She lay on the ground beside Maggie, panting. "Are you okay?" I asked them.

"Why did you stop me?" Maggie moaned. "Why? You shouldn't have stopped me!"

June Ann slowly sat up, pulling her dress down over her bare legs. She wasn't wearing any shoes. "Listen, Miss Maggie. You took good care of my baby and I'm grateful. But Alice is the only friend I have in the whole world. I couldn't stand by and let you shoot her."

"What are you doing out here in the woods in the middle of the night?" I asked June Ann.

"I come over here all the time to be close to Feather. Some nights I sleep out here so I can hear her. I ain't very good at taking care of Feather myself, but I love her just the same."

I crouched down to give June Ann a hug, holding the rifle well away from us. "I'm so glad you were here tonight. You saved Mack's life."

Maggie rolled to one side and struggled to stand. I handed the rifle to June Ann and reached to help Maggie, but she pushed me away. "No! Let me go! Leave me alone!"

"I won't, Maggie. I care about you." I fended off her blows as I tried to pull her into my arms. "I won't let you go."

She finally stopped resisting and sagged into my embrace, weeping on my shoulder.

CHAPTER 32

I stayed with Maggie, trying to comfort her as she mourned Hank's death all over again. June Ann disappeared into the night as silently as she had appeared, taking Maggie's rifle with her. Mack vanished, as well.

Nothing I said to Maggie could console her, so eventually we went inside the cabin where I simply held her and let her cry. The sky was growing light when the baby woke up and began to fuss. Maggie dried her eyes and went to her. I stoked the stove so she could heat a bottle of milk, then watched Maggie feed Feather, rocking in the chair beside the stove. Neither of us said much; there simply weren't any words that could express Maggie's sorrow or my sympathy.

I cooked oatmeal for breakfast for us and helped Maggie feed some to Miss Opal. Maggie gathered the eggs and took care of her animals, and the normal morning routine seemed to help her compose herself. Before long, she appeared as calm and gracious as she usually did whenever I visited her. I found it impossible to believe that this gentle, loving woman had tried to kill Mack—twice. Neither of us mentioned him.

I realized that two other people besides Lillie and me now knew that Mack was alive. But Maggie wasn't likely to tell anyone since she was the person who'd shot him. And poor, lonely June Ann had no one to tell.

"You probably should go," Maggie said when I'd finished my tea. "You have a very long walk back to the library, don't you?"

She was right, but I was reluctant to leave her. "Are you going to be all right?"

"Yes, Alice. I'll be fine. I have Opal and Feather to take care of, and you have Miss Lillie."

I hugged her good-bye and walked down the trail that had become so familiar to me, stopping at Mack's cabin. He wasn't there. The compartment beneath the cabin floor was open and the documents he'd hidden there were gone.

I reached the library around noon, and when I emerged from the woods alongside the creek, there was Belle grazing peacefully in her pasture by the shed, safe and sound. I would have to lead her up to Mack's old cabin to fetch her saddle and bridle, but not today. I was much too tired today. I simply wanted to sleep.

"Mack told me the whole story," Lillie said when I walked into the kitchen.

"He made it back home?"

"Yep, he got here just after dawn." Lillie had a fire going and had made potato soup. The house felt warm and cozy. I slumped onto a kitchen chair. "You okay, honey?"

"Yes, but I'm exhausted." Lillie ladled soup into two bowls for us and sat down to eat it with me. I had worked up an appetite on the long walk home. "Well, Lillie, you said that baby Feather would save Maggie's life, and you were right. But it didn't happen the way we thought it would. The baby saved Mack's life, too—indirectly."

"He told me how brave you was, stepping in front a him so Maggie couldn't shoot him."

"Where is Mack? Upstairs sleeping?"

"No, honey. He's gone."

"Gone? Where?"

"He left to take his book to the publisher and to deliver them other papers to the mining people in Washington. He'll be back just as soon as he can. He said he hoped you'd stay a little longer."

"But . . . How did he get into town to a train station? I saw Belle out back."

"Mack knows a trail over the mountain and through the woods. Shouldn't take him long."

I breathed a weary sigh. "I don't know how he'll manage it. I don't think I could walk another step."

We finished our lunch, and I went upstairs and climbed into bed. I slept like a dead woman. When I finally woke again, I spent the remainder of the day staring into space like a mannequin in Marshall Field's store window. I had used up a year's worth of emotions in a single night—fear, sorrow, love, grief—and my heart needed time to replenish the supply. Lillie took care of me for a change, hovering over me, patting my shoulder or my hand. It took all weekend for my mind to stop replaying the image of the wildcat padding toward me, head lowered, ready to spring. Or the sight of Maggie's gun barrel aimed at me. And Mack.

On Monday morning I decided to calm my nerves by typing more of Miss Lillie's recipes. It was one of the few tasks I could do that didn't require any thinking on my part. I was on the very last notebook and making good progress when I found an envelope tucked between two pages. Someone had printed *Miss Lillie* on the front, but the envelope had never been opened. I brought it into her bedroom to show her.

"What is this, Lillie? The seal has never been broken."

She took it from me and studied it for a moment before handing it back. "It's a letter that tells where the treasure is hidden."

"What? Are you joking? Is it the same treasure that the Larkins and Arnetts have been fighting over all these years?"

"Mmm hmm. Old Granddaddy Larkin gave me that letter when he was dying."

"Mack's grandfather?"

"No, his great-grandfather. That was years and years ago now. Way back when I first come to Kentucky, long before Mack was born. Old Isaac Larkin asked me to come take care a him when he was sick and dying. That's when he gave me that letter."

"But why didn't you ever open it up and see what it says?"

"He said to keep it safe for him. He said I would know when to open it."

"You've had it all this time? Why didn't you use it to dig up the treasure?"

"That money ain't mine to dig up."

"So the treasure is real? And it's still buried?"

"Far as I know. Ain't none of my business, honey. But I can tell by the way both families have been fighting over it that neither one of them has that treasure."

"Do you know the whole story, Lillie? Where the treasure originally came from?"

"Sure I know it. Isaac told me all about it."

"Please tell me. I've heard romanticized versions of it, but never the real story." I sat down on the chair beside her, listening in breathless suspense, just as Faye's boys and Mamaw had listened to *Treasure Island*.

"Wilbur Arnett, Isaac Larkin, and Abe Coots were like brothers," Lillie began.

"Wait. Who's Abe Coots? Is he any relation to Maggie?"

"Yes, he was Hank Coots's great-granddaddy. All three men growed up together and all three went off to fight the War Between the States. Wilbur and Isaac lived through all that marching and shooting and fighting and came home again, but their friend Abe Coots was killed in some battle down around Lookout Mountain. His two friends put all their money together and had Abe's body shipped back home so he could be buried in the cemetery here in Acorn. That's where Isaac and Wilbur are buried, too."

"Is that the same graveyard where Mack . . . where he's supposed to be buried?"

"No. There's an older cemetery over behind the churchyard. When those graves filled up, they started that new cemetery."

"Wait. Where is this churchyard? Mack said you used to take him to church, but you told me there wasn't one here in Acorn."

"That's because nobody uses it no more. Everybody stopped going on account of the feud. That church used to be filled with Arnetts and Larkins every Sunday morning, singing and praying and praising the Lord. Then this feud started up and the families decided they ain't gonna worship together no more. Pretty soon there ain't enough people left to keep the church going, so

351

the minister gave up and left town. That poor old building is all falling down now."

Lillie and I had wandered down a side trail, talking about the church. I wanted to get back to the treasure hunt. I rose from the chair and sat on the edge of her bed, restless with anticipation. "So where did the treasure originally come from?"

"A few years after the war, Isaac Larkin and Wilbur Arnett was out hunting turkeys along Wonderland Creek when they seen a plume of smoke back in the trees. They figured it was from a still, and they decided to see who was cooking moonshine. Turned out they was two robbers, sitting by a campfire and talking about how they stole money from a bank in Lexington and made off with the loot. Seems they killed a man while making their getaway, and they needed to hide out for a while. Wilbur and Isaac knew them men was dangerous, so they decided to keep an eye on them and make sure they stayed out of Acorn.

"Well, the robbers kept on drinking moonshine all afternoon, and by the time night fell, they'd passed out cold. Isaac and Wilbur crept into their camp and stole the loot right out from under them crooks."

"They robbed the robbers? Were they crazy?"

"That's what greed does to you, honey. It makes you go a little crazy. Isaac and Wilbur had all sorts of plans for what they was gonna do with that money. But come morning, the real robbers was out roaming the hills looking for their loot, and they was madder than a mess a hornets. The two friends was scared to death they'd be shot dead if they spent a cent of it. Weeks went by and the bad men was still out looking for it. In the end, Isaac and Wilbur kept just enough to build two houses, and they give a little to their friend Abe Coots's wife, then they buried the rest of it until they was sure it was safe."

"Is it still there? Did they ever dig it up?"

"Far as I know, they never did. I told Isaac he should give the money back to the folks at the bank, but he said he was too scared. He thought the sheriff would accuse him and Wilbur of stealing it because the robbers wore masks over their faces. Besides, the whole town wanted revenge on account of the dead bank teller, and Isaac figured there'd be a lynch mob before there'd ever be a fair trial."

"What a mess."

"Them two friends couldn't decide what to do, so they left the money buried. They decided it was cursed. Wilbur Arnett died first, and just a short time later, Isaac Larkin lay dying. He told me the whole story and gave me that letter just in case his kin might need the money someday. He said God would show me when it was time to dig it up. And since God never said a word about it to me, I kept the letter sealed up, just like I promised."

"That's incredible . . . unbelievable!" In fact, the story sounded like a work of fiction. Yet why had the two families been feuding all these years if there wasn't some truth to the tale? "Did you ever show this letter to Mack?" I asked her.

"What for?"

"Maybe he would know what to do with the money."

"I know exactly what to do with it—leave it in the ground where it belongs."

"But the Larkins and Arnetts have been fighting over it for sixty years. This could end the feud."

"Honey, if you believe money could end the feud, then you don't know people very well. You think they gonna share it? Uh uh. Each side's gonna want all of it. There'll be shooting and killing around here for sure."

I looked down at the yellowing envelope. I was dying to know what the letter said, where the treasure map was, and where the money was buried. I looked up at Lillie. "May I open it?"

"You ever read the story of Pandora's box?"

"Yes, I've read it . . . but I'm dying of curiosity, Lillie. Can't I just see what it says and then seal it up again? I promise I won't tell anybody. I'm going back to Illinois as soon as Mack comes back, and if I don't open this it'll be like reading a good book and discovering the last chapter is missing. I have to find out how it ends."

"It'll end with more fighting if you open that up, I'll tell you that much."

"I really don't see the harm. Please?"

"I can warn you not to, but I can't stop you if your mind is made up. You'll just do it when my back is turned."

"Then I'll do it in front of you. I'm going to open it."

I turned the envelope over and ran my finger around the flap. The glue was so old and brittle that the seal opened easily. I expected to find an elaborate treasure map inside, like something out of a pirate story, with a big red X marking the spot. Instead, I pulled out a single sheet of plain paper, folded in half. I read it out loud to Lillie:

"To my family,

Never let money come between family and friends. Keep following the Good Book and always do what it says: 'Thou shalt not steal.' And that means stealing money from bank robbers, too. The Bible is right when it says, 'The love of money is the root of all evil: which while some coveted after, they have erred from the faith, and pierced themselves through with many sorrows.' And always remember, 'There is a friend that sticketh closer than a brother.'

Signed,

Isaac Larkin"

Lillie laughed out loud when I finished reading. I dropped the letter to my lap in disappointment. "It doesn't say where the treasure is buried."

"It says exactly what I just told you—don't dig it up! Believe me, the Bible is right and the love of money does lead to all kinds of evil. I seen it happen again and again in this long life of mine. Why do you think my old massa and his friends fought that awful war? They wanted to keep owning slaves because they can't make money without us. Money starts all kinds of wars, honey, like this war between the Larkins and Arnetts. Finding that treasure will only start an even bigger war."

I didn't want a sermon. I wanted a map. I read the letter through again, trying to find a message hidden between the lines. I even held it up to the light to see if there was a hidden map. When nothing magical appeared, I read it through a third time. Nothing. Lillie watched me, shaking her head in amusement.

"What does this verse about a friend mean, Lillie? Is he talking about the friendship between the three men? Were they closer than brothers?"

"That verse comes from the Bible, and it's talking about the Lord Jesus. He'll stick by us when nobody else will. Ever hear that hymn 'What a Friend We Have in Jesus'?"

"That's the same verse that's on your sampler." I pointed to the picture frame hanging on the wall above her bed. "Did you embroider that?"

"Nope. It come with the house."

My heart began to pound. "Lillie! I saw another sampler just like it in Ike's house—which used to belong to Wilbur Arnett. Maybe that's where the map is hidden!"

"I'm telling you, honey. Leave it alone."

I didn't listen. I stood and reached for the sampler above her head, blowing off the dust. "May I take this down and look at it, please?"

"There's a story in the Bible about a great big basket, and inside is a woman named 'Wickedness.' God put a big heavy lid on top of her, made out of lead, to keep the wickedness from jumping out. Ever read that story?"

"No." I wasn't interested. I had the frame in my hand and I looked it over carefully. I didn't see anything on the back that looked like a map. I studied the embroidery to see if the instructions were concealed in the design. Nothing. I would have to take the frame apart. I sat down and turned it over on my lap.

"May I take this frame apart?"

"It don't belong to me, honey. It belongs to Mack."

"He won't mind. He was searching for the treasure map, too."

I began to pry off the nails that held down the backing, being very careful not to damage anything. The date on the sampler was 1875, for goodness' sakes. I expected to find a map concealed behind the backing, but there was nothing there. I looked between the yellowing fabric and the wood—in vain. I had torn the entire sampler apart for nothing.

"I'm sorry, Lillie . . . I'll put it back together."

"Leave it, honey. I'll fix it."

"I'm really sorry. I should have listened to you."

She waved me away, still shaking her head.

I went back to my typewriter in Lillie's workroom, but I couldn't concentrate. I couldn't stop thinking about Isaac Larkin's mysterious letter. Maybe I needed the other sampler from Ike's house. Maybe if I put the two samplers side by side, I'd see the solution. But who knew when Ike would return home. Besides, if I told him what I had discovered, he'd want to keep all the money for himself, not divide it between the two families. Should I wait for Mack? He was a Larkin, but he didn't care about the money. He wanted to end the feud, too. In my opinion, Wayne and June Ann should be the ones to dig up the money. The treasure rightfully belonged to Feather.

The next time I went into Lillie's room, she had put the sampler back together and hung it on the wall again. But it didn't look the same. I had damaged it for nothing, and now I was sorry.

CHAPTER 33

As I waited for Mack to return, time felt suspended. Day after day, nothing happened. It was as if someone had waved a magic wand and the town of Acorn froze in time. My garden continued to grow. The packhorse librarians checked out piles of books and returned piles more. I finished reading *Tom Saywer* to Faye's boys and began reading *Huckleberry Finn*.

Meanwhile, I could sense my parents' growing concern in their letters as they asked about the delay and wondered how much longer until I came home. I couldn't give them a clear answer. I worried that my father would show up at the library door one day and insist that I return home with him, but I couldn't leave now! I had grown to love Miss Lillie and I felt responsible for her—and for June Ann and Feather and Maggie, too. And I needed to find out how the story of Acorn, Kentucky, would end when Mack did return and all of the loose ends could be tied up.

I rode my usual book route twice a week, after retrieving Belle's saddle from Mack's abandoned cabin. Each time I stopped at Maggie's house, I found June Ann there. Maggie had become a second mother to her. June Ann was little more than a teenager, after all. Together, the two women took care of Miss Opal and Feather.

As time passed, I became more and more annoyed with Mack. I hated waiting. The least he could do was write to us with news about his book, and the investigation into Hank's death, and the search for Lillie's son. I hadn't received a letter from Ike, either—or even a postcard from his travels.

Then one day, someone waved the magic wand again and broke the spell. Time became unfrozen, and after waiting and waiting for something to happen, everything happened at once. First, Ike Arnett strode into library on a Thursday morning just as I was packing my saddlebags for my trip up the creek.

"Ike! Welcome home! It's so good to see you." I remembered how he had once picked me up and whirled me around in a circle, but he didn't do it that day. He looked dead tired, and maybe a little hungover as he slumped into Lillie's chair in the non-fiction room. "When did you get back in town, Ike?"

"Late last night. I know it's early in the morning, Alice, but I came to tell you I'm sorry for not writing like I promised. We've been doing so much traveling and playing that I've barely had time to eat or sleep."

"I understand." It wasn't quite true. I was irritated with him. How much time does it take to mail a postcard? But I held my tongue. "Everything is going well with your new band, I assume?"

Ike grinned and his face beamed brighter than the miner's hat in the gloomy tunnel. "It's like I died and went to heaven, Alice. When me and the other fellas in the band play together, it's like we can read each other's thoughts. We might be six separate people playing six different instruments, but we make one beautiful sound, and it's music! Heavenly music! I never felt anything like it before. It's like we were born to play together."

"I'm really happy for you." And I was. Ike Arnett did not belong in Acorn, working in the coal mines.

"The pay's been real good, but I gotta tell you, Alice, I'd do this for nothing. I love playing my fiddle and making people happy. Everyone seems so beaten down here in Acorn, especially these past few years. I don't think I ever want to come back. But when our band plays, we make everyone happy. You should see them dancing and singing and tapping their toes." Ike couldn't stop grinning.

One of the things I had missed the most about him was his cheerful spontaneity with romantic picnics in the orchard and stolen kisses. The town had been much too quiet without him. "How long will you be home?" I asked.

"I'm leaving again in a few minutes. I just came home to give my folks some money and to pick up a few things. Then I'll be gone for another month, maybe more. We have so many offers to play that we're turning jobs down. It's like I rubbed a magic lamp and a genie popped out and granted my greatest wish."

"That's wonderful." I would be sad to see him go. But I was even sadder to realize that I had no idea what I would wish for if a genie offered to grant my greatest wish.

"I know we said we'd find that treasure, but to tell you the truth, I don't care about it anymore."

When Ike mentioned the treasure, I was tempted to ask him if I could borrow the sampler hanging above his fireplace. I resisted the urge. Not only had I promised to keep Isaac Larkin's letter a secret, but I still felt guilty for ruining the sampler in Lillie's room. I wouldn't ruin another one.

Ike stood up and took my hands in his. This was it. I would probably never see him again. But instead of kissing me good-bye and walking away, he began to *hem and haw*, as my grandmother would say, acting very much like a boy who has been caught being naughty.

"What's wrong, Ike?"

"I have a confession to make—something that's been bothering me. I hope you'll forgive me when I tell you."

"I could never stay mad at you for very long."

"Okay . . . Well, remember when I went upstairs looking for Mack's hunting jacket? The truth is, I was snooping around to see if Mack had found out anything about the treasure. Before he died, he'd said he was looking for it, so I wanted to see what he'd found. The same is true about the day I got rid of that bat for you. I did take care of the bat like I said, but I was also searching through Mack's things for a map. I made friends with you at first because I thought he might have told you something about it."

I pulled my hands away from his. "So our time together was just a lie?"

"No! Not at all! It might have started out that way, but I fell for you, Alice. I fell hard! That's why I'm coming clean about the treasure and about snooping in Mack's room. And that's why I'm trying to say I'm sorry. I never should have lied to you."

I felt a little hurt, a little angry, but mostly sad. "Why are you telling me the truth now?"

"It's been eating my conscience, and I don't want to be punished for my wrongdoings. I want the Good Lord to keep on blessing my music. This band is important to me. It's what I always wanted my whole life. And it's my ticket out of the coal mines. I won't need the treasure now."

"You were born to play the fiddle, Ike. Of course I forgive you."

He moved closer and rested his hands on my shoulders. "I'd love to ask you to wait right here for me, but that ain't fair to you. I'd like it even more if you came with me, but that's no kind of life for you, either—traveling with a road band. I'm guessing you'll be heading home soon?"

"Yes. Soon." I didn't really know when it would be, and I couldn't tell him that I was waiting for Mack to return.

"I hate saying good-bye, Alice. But if the Good Lord wants our paths to cross again .... well, then, I guess He'll take care of it."

"I guess He will." God had seemed to manipulate a lot of other events lately, such as giving Feather the colic and having June Ann appear just in time to save Mack and me. What Ike said was probably true. The Good Lord could arrange anything.

Ike looked down at me with his big, sad, brown eyes and said, "May I kiss you good-bye, for now?"

I nodded. His kiss was tender and loving—and final. Another good-bye. Ike had treated me kinder than Gordon had when he'd broken up with me, but this parting was sad, just the same. Ike's love potion had worn off. And so had mine.

I closed the door behind him and stood in the foyer, trying to figure out exactly how I felt. When I turned around again, there was Lillie, standing at the bottom of the stairs.

"Is he going away?" she asked.

"Yes. Which means you were right, Lillie. It's wearing off, isn't it?"

"What is, honey?"

"The love potion you gave Ike. It's starting to wear off."

Lillie smiled. "Ain't no such thing as a love potion, except in storybooks."

"But you told me that you made some and gave it to Ike."

"Why would I give a love potion to Ike?"

"I don't know! You wouldn't tell me why!" I was shouting. Was Lillie becoming senile? Or was this one of her tricks? "You said you gave some to Belle, too, remember?"

Lillie eyed me as if I were the one who was senile. "Honey, if I knew how to make a love potion, I'd be selling it up in New York City." She chuckled as she limped away.

Good thing I had grown to love her, because she infuriated me.

I saddled up Belle and left on my route, still sad over Ike's departure and my bruised feelings—even though, if I were honest with myself, I would have to admit that a relationship with Ike never would have worked, any more than a relationship with Gordon would have worked.

I rode past Mack's vacant cabin as usual, and I found myself missing him, too. And not just because I had to clean Belle's hooves and groom her all by myself now that he was gone. Mack and I had become good friends during the weeks I had visited him up here, bringing him food. And our friendship had deepened the night we'd explored the deserted mine tunnel together. I missed talking to him. I missed his quiet strength.

My first stop of the day was June Ann's cabin. I was in the habit of stopping to see if she was there, although I usually found her at Maggie's house, my final stop. Today I was in for a surprise. Not only was June Ann at home, but so was her husband, Wayne. June Ann came running out of the house to tell me the good news before I even had a chance to dismount. She was carrying baby Feather in her arms.

"Guess who came home last night, Allie—Wayne! And he's got a pocketful of money that he made working for that Conversation Corpse."

I smiled at her mispronunciation of the *Conservation Corps*. "That's wonderful, June Ann. Is he going to stay home for a while?" I remembered how brief Ike's visit had been.

"He's staying home with us for good. And he says maybe now we can buy a couple of windows for the cabin."

"I'm so happy for you." And I was. I had rarely seen June Ann so joyful and excited. She was even smiling. Then I thought of my friend Maggie and the effect this might have on her. "Was it hard for Maggie to say good-bye to you and Feather?"

"Oh, we're gonna keep on visiting her. Feather and I love it up there."

My sad mood over Ike's departure began to lift, and I couldn't stop smiling as I made my rounds, delivering books and reading stories to the children. But as I approached Maggie's house, I grew apprehensive. How would she cope without June Ann and the baby? For as long as I'd known her, Maggie had seemed perfectly fine to me until the night she'd tried to shoot Mack again. Now that I knew how fragile she really was, I worried about her.

She was standing on her front porch when I arrived, leaning against the post, her face serene. "I've been waiting for you, Allie," she said as I dismounted. "I need to ask a favor."

"Sure. Anything."

"Miss Opal died this morning."

"Oh, Maggie! No . . ." I moved into her arms, not sure who was comforting whom. Why did this have to happen now, just when Wayne Larkin had returned home? "I'm so sorry, Maggie."

"It wasn't unexpected. Miss Opal was ready to go. And she went peacefully, in her sleep."

I pulled away to wipe my tears. Maggie's face was dry. "Are you okay?"

"Yes. But would you please let everyone in town know? I'll need help burying her. I would like to hold her funeral tomorrow. She wanted to be buried in the family plot in town, behind the church."

"Yes, of course. But I'm worried about you, up here all alone."

"You don't need to be. Let's go inside, so we can talk. I'll make tea."

Maggie seemed so calm, but I couldn't help wondering if it was a façade. I remembered her telling me that she had lost her faith, and also that she'd planned to turn the gun on herself and join Hank and Rhoda Lee in the graveyard after killing Mack. With Miss Opal gone, I feared for her life, but I had no idea what to say.

"I'll be happy to stay here with you, now that June Ann and Feather have gone home," I said as Maggie poured the tea.

"Thank you, but Hank's brothers will be coming as soon as they hear the news."

That didn't ease my fears. I took a deep breath, praying for the right words. "You told me once how you didn't think God loved you—and I'd probably question His love, too, if I'd been through everything that you have. But I just want to say . . . you gave up your rich life in Boston because of your love for Hank, and you said it was what people did when they were in love. They made sacrifices for each other. Well, that's how you can know that Jesus loves you, Maggie. He came a lot farther than from Boston to Kentucky when He came down from heaven to earth. And He gave up so much more—for us. Including His life."

Maggie nodded faintly. Her eyes were still dry as she stared into her teacup.

"You used to love God, Maggie. Please give Him another chance."

She nodded again and breathed a sigh. "I'm going home, Allie. To Massachusetts."

"For good?"

"For now, anyway. Maybe I'll be back, maybe not. I'm going to ask Hank's brothers to take over the farm." She looked up at me and her tears finally came. "I need time to heal. I've been messed up ever since Hank died. Taking care of Feather made me realize how much I want a family of my own again. Hank would have wanted me to keep on living. He'd be horrified by what I tried to do to Mack, and by how bitter I've become. I need some time away from here so I can get over everything." I reached for her hand and silently took it in my own. "Anyway . . . I suppose you'll be going home, too, Allie? Now that Mack can take care of Lillie again?"

She was right. There would be no reason to stay once Mack came home. But I was surprised to discover that I was no longer as desperate to return home as I once had been. "I think I'll be very sad to leave here," I told Maggie. "I've enjoyed being a packhorse librarian. But you're right, I will be leaving as soon as Mack returns. He went to Washington to talk to the mining officials about reopening the investigation into Hank's death. I expect him back any day."

"Be sure to let me know when you're ready to go. I'll give you a ride to the train station, if I'm still here."

"A ride?" I pictured us swaying up the road on the back of Maggie's mule with my suitcase tied on the animal's rear end.

"Yes. A ride in my car."

"You have a *car*? Where is it?"

"In my barn. Didn't you know that?" I leaned back in my chair, shaking my head in amazement. Maggie smiled. "How did you think I got into Pottstown to buy supplies and things?"

I put my hand over my mouth to try to hold back my laughter. It didn't work. My giggles sputtered out, and I laughed until the tears came. I felt terrible for losing control when Miss Opal lay dead in the next room, but I couldn't help it.

"What's so funny?" Maggie asked.

"If you had a car all this time, I could have left Acorn months ago!"

"That's true, but just think of all that you would have missed."

Yes. Just think.

CHAPTER 34

I was reluctant to leave Maggie, even though she assured me that she would be fine. But I finally hugged her good-bye and rode back to town to tell everyone about Miss Opal. The packhorse ladies returned at the same time that I did, and I told them the sad news. They promised to spread the word to all the other folks in town.

"What a day!" I said to Miss Lillie as I sank into my chair behind the library desk. "People have been coming and going—Ike Arnett and Wayne Larkin and Miss Opal—and now Maggie will be leaving soon, too. How much more can happen in one day?"

"When it rains it pours, they say."

"How quickly everything can change."

No sooner had I spoken the words than I heard the kitchen door open and close. I didn't even have time to rise from my chair before Mack strode into the room, smiling and out of breath. He dropped his carpetbag on the floor and wrapped Miss Lillie in a tender hug. She was so tiny and he was so tall that Mack seemed to swallow her up. Tears filled my eyes to see them together.

"Praise the Good Lord! You're home!" she said, her voice muffled against Mack's shirt. He lifted her into his arms and carried her to the chair in the non-fiction room.

"Welcome home, Mack," I said, following them.

"Thanks. It's wonderful to be home. The big city is exciting, but I missed the hills and hollows. And I missed you, Lillie."

"Tell us about your trip, honey. Did those city people like your book?"

"Oh yes, ma'am. My editor sure did. Now we just have to wait and see what the publisher thinks."

I couldn't contain my excitement. "Mack, that's wonderful! I can't wait to read it. I've never met a real live author before."

"Have you met any dead ones?" he asked with a grin. "Because technically I'm still dead, you know."

"We're gonna have to fix that real soon, honey," Lillie said. "Now, what about those mining folks in Washington. Did you talk to them?"

"Yes, I had a very good meeting with them. I showed them the documents I found and explained what Alice and I discovered at the mine. They promised to send a team out here to inspect the mine as soon as they can arrange it. They're going to reopen the investigation into Hank's death."

"Let's hope there's justice finally for Hank Coots," I said.

"Sounds like you got a lot done, honey. We're so glad you're back."

"There's one more thing I did while I was away." Mack left us for a moment to retrieve his carpetbag, then knelt in front of Lillie to rummage through it. "I have a surprise for you, Lillie. There's a letter in here somewhere I want to show you."

"A letter? Who's it from?"

"It's from your blood kin. A descendant of your son, Buster."

"My Buster?"

"One and the same. I asked a friend of mine in Washington to do some research for me, and she was able to find out what happened to him after he was sold away from your plantation before the war. Buster has gone on to heaven now, I'm sorry to say. But this letter is from his grandson. He remembers Buster quite well and wrote this letter to tell you all about him."

"Oh my . . . oh my, I don't know what to say . . ." It was a good thing Lillie was sitting down because she looked as though she might faint.

Mack located the letter and pulled it from his satchel with a flourish. "It took a lot of work, but my friend not only found Buster, she found his family. It helped a lot when Alice found that piece of paper telling us that Buster had been sold to a Mr. Drucker in Thornburg, Virginia. My friend in Washington discovered his name on the U.S. Census register and learned that Buster grew up and got married and had five children. This letter is from one of his grandsons."

Lillie looked from Mack to me and back again. Tears rolled down her lined face, but I could tell from her expression that they were tears of joy. She couldn't speak. I knelt beside her chair, too, and put my arm around her tiny shoulder as Mack pulled the letter from the envelope. "You can read the whole thing later, but I especially wanted you to hear this part:

> " 'My grandpappy used to tell stories about how he grew up as a slave, and how his Mama Lillie taught him all about Jesus. He was trusting Jesus when the Union soldiers came through and set all the slaves free on his plantation. An army chaplain took a liking to him, so Grandpappy Buster traveled all around with those army folks until the war ended. That's when he decided he wanted to be a preacher, too, and he kept right on preaching the Gospel until the day he died. Folks would come from miles around just to hear him.' "

Lillie wiped her eyes on her apron. "Well, the Good Lord can take me on home now. I know I'll see my boy up in heaven. I guess it just wasn't meant to be that we found each other this side of heaven. Our lives mighta been much different if we'd had our way instead of God having His way."

We talked until suppertime, and it would have been wonderful to kill a fattened calf and celebrate this glorious reunion with a banquet. But our food supplies were sparse, as usual, and there wasn't time to prepare a big meal.

Mack told us more stories about his travels as we ate leftover corn bread and eggs scrambled with bacon. Lillie listened to the rest of the letter, spellbound, as it told about Buster and his family. The way she gazed at Mack reminded me of my dried-up garden soaking in the rain. She barely ate, barely breathed, as if afraid this was a dream and she didn't want to wake up.

"How did you find Buster's family so quickly?" I asked at the end of the meal. I had gotten up from the table to heat water to wash the dishes.

"My friend Catherine Anson in Washington did the research before I got there. She really worked hard at it and turned out to be quite a detective." I felt an emotion I couldn't quite place as he talked about Miss Anson, and I was surprised to realize it was jealousy.

"What's been happening here while I was gone?" Mack asked after a while.

"Opal Coots passed away," I told him. "The funeral is tomorrow. Do you think you might attend? You can let the town know you're alive now, right? And come out of hiding?"

"No, not yet. I will soon, I promise. But not tomorrow. I don't want to disturb Maggie and her family by showing up and reminding them of Hank. Is the funeral up at Maggie's cabin?"

"No, Miss Opal wanted to be buried in the churchyard. Which reminds me—where is Acorn's old church? I've never seen it, you know."

"It's across the road from the post office and back in a hollow. It isn't very far."

I couldn't help smiling. "Nothing around here is very far. I'll never forget my first glimpse of Acorn. Uncle Cecil drove straight through town and out the other side before we even knew it."

"I'll never forget the look on your face," Mack said, "when I told you Acorn didn't have a hotel or a restaurant." We both laughed, but at the same time I felt a sense of loss. I would be going home now, and I would probably never see Mack or Miss Lillie again. I had grown to love them both, and I would miss them. It was impossible not to grow fond of the man whose life I had helped save, a man who had stood alongside me facing danger and death. I turned away to hide my tears.

"Maybe I'll walk over to the church after I finish washing these dishes," I said. "It's a nice warm evening." I needed time alone to sort through my feelings. I had waited so long to go home to Blue Island, and now the time of my departure had come too soon. I realized that in the beginning I had wanted to leave Acorn because of all the hard work I'd been forced to do, the inconveniences of rural mountain life. But ties of friendship and love now exerted a much stronger pull than my own selfishness.

I finished the dishes and followed Mack's directions, walking up the road toward the post office, then turning down a dirt road I'd never explored before, across the main road. I passed several houses wedged into the side of the hill before finally arriving at the church, nestled in a hollow. It looked as though it had once been a nice little building, but it had fallen into extreme disrepair over the years, the white paint peeling, the roof sagging, the exposed wood weathering. Most of the window glass was missing. I wondered if people had "borrowed" little pieces of the church whenever they'd needed a spare board or a new window to patch up their own homes, just as they had "borrowed" from the mining camp. But the main reason the church had deteriorated was because of the feud. "What a shame," I murmured.

The front door was boarded up, yet I didn't care to go inside, knowing that snakes and bats and other creeping things liked to inhabit deserted buildings. Instead, I walked around to the back to explore the graveyard. The cemetery wasn't very large, with graves crammed into every available space. Some of the plots had been tended over the years while others were unkempt. I walked up and down the rows, pushing vines and weeds aside and idly reading the names on the tombstones.

The gravediggers had been at work, and I found the large, gaping hole where Miss Opal would be buried tomorrow. A dozen other Cootses were buried in this section of the cemetery, including one whose name I recognized: Abraham Coots. He was the man who had died in the Civil War, the close friend of Isaac Larkin and Wilbur Arnett, the two men who had stolen from the bank robbers and inadvertently started Acorn's long, bitter feud. I bent to read the epitaph on the weather-beaten stone:

Abraham C. Coots
October 2, 1838—November 24, 1863
"There is a friend that sticketh closer than a brother."

I stared at it in amazement, suddenly breathless. Could this be where the treasure was buried? The clues in the two embroidered samplers and in Isaac Larkin's letter finally made sense. Of course! Isaac and Wilbur had buried the treasure in their friend's grave!

I walked home in a daze, wondering if I should come back with a shovel and dig up Abe Coots's grave to see if I was right. But night had fallen by the time I reached the library, and I lacked the courage to skulk around the cemetery at night, much less disturb the dead with my digging.

"What's wrong, Alice?" Mack asked when I walked through the door. "You look like you've seen a ghost."

I couldn't tell him. The treasure should be unearthed by an outsider, not a Larkin or an Arnett. And Mack was a Larkin. "It's nothing," I mumbled.

Mack and Lillie sat in the non-fiction room talking, but I barely heard their conversation as my mind spun with plans. Lillie had once told me that the feuding families would lay aside their differences and get together when someone died—and Opal's funeral was tomorrow. All of Acorn's families would be there, and June Ann might attend the funeral, too, because of her friendship with Maggie. I could ask June Ann and Wayne to help me do the digging, and the entire town could witness it. I imagined it all as if watching the climax of a dramatic, epic film. The feud would end and Acorn, Kentucky, would experience healing at last.

I hardly slept that night and did my chores in record time the next morning before dressing for the funeral. Hank Coots's brothers brought the casket down into town on the back of their wagon, but Maggie was kind enough to stop by the library and give Miss Lillie and me a ride in her car. Mack stayed hidden, unwilling to upset Maggie or the rest of the townspeople, who still thought he was dead.

It was a lovely funeral, very similar to the one we'd held for Mack, with harmonicas and fiddles and banjos. The entire town had already gathered behind the church when I arrived, including people who lived way up in the hills, like Clint and Gladys, and the Howard family. Miss Lillie gave a short sermon, and one of Hank's brothers gave a eulogy for Opal. I hated to spoil the solemnity as

Hank's brothers lowered the coffin into the grave and shoveled clods of dirt on top of it, but the time had come for my stunning announcement. I pushed my way to the front of the crowd.

"Wait, everyone. Don't go home yet. I have something to tell you." Everyone stared at me, some unkindly. "I know I'm an outsider and a flatlander and I have no right to interfere in your business. But I'll be going home in a few days. Maggie has offered to give me a ride to the train station, and I'm going to accept it. As you may know, she's leaving, too." My eyes met Maggie's, and she nodded slightly.

"Anyway," I continued, "I've been as curious as all of you folks are about the legend of Acorn's buried treasure, so I've been playing detective and following some clues. It turns out that Isaac Larkin gave Miss Lillie a letter before he died, offering a hint about where the treasure is buried, but she has kept the letter sealed all these years. Well, I opened the letter, and it helped me figure out where Isaac and his friend Wilbur Arnett buried their treasure—"

Everyone began talking at once, drowning out my words. The excitement reached such a pitch that no one seemed to remember that we were at a funeral. The crowd eyed me with curiosity and more than a little suspicion as if wondering what this crazy flatlander was up to. Faye's boys wove through the crowd and planted themselves directly in front of me, staring up at me in anticipation the way they had when I'd read stories to them.

"You gonna tell us where?" someone finally shouted above the noise. I held up my hands, waiting until the rumble of excited voices died down before speaking again.

"Now, I'm not entirely certain the treasure is there because I didn't dig it up. I wanted all of you to be witnesses so that if it is there, you can see for yourselves that neither family stole it. And I think that Wayne and June Ann should do the digging since they represent both families."

The crowd murmured some more as Wayne and June Ann walked forward with their baby. Then it grew so quiet that I could hear the rushing waters of Wonderland Creek a few blocks away. I was suddenly petrified.

What if I was wrong about the treasure and I ended up looking like a fool? What if someone had dug it up already—or if it had never been buried there at all?

"What are we waiting for?" someone shouted. I was pretty sure it was Clint.

"I'm waiting because I want all of you to swear to me first that if we find the treasure, the feud between the Larkins and Arnetts will end. You've been arguing about this money for years, each family accusing the other of stealing it. Shame on you! Wilbur Arnett and Isaac Larkin were friends. They survived the war together and looked out for each other. They'd be horrified to see how their families have been treating one another all these years."

I looked out at their expectant faces, hoping my speech had thawed a few hearts. Instead, I saw the Larkins and Arnetts still trading hostile looks. Had Lillie been right? Would finding the treasure lead to more fighting and shooting and killing? Then I saw Miss Lillie smiling at me, encouraging me, and remembered her joy when Mack had come home.

"Families belong together," I said. "Life is too short for arguing and feuding. And now that America has fallen on hard times, you need each other more than ever. See that church behind us? Your bitterness and neglect are what destroyed it. But if you end the feud and divide the treasure among those in need, think how rich you *all* will be. Maybe you can use some of the money to rebuild the church, too. The Bible says we're supposed to help each other, and that if one of us has a need, everybody should pitch in."

I surveyed the crowd again, then walked over to June Ann and Wayne. I lifted Feather from June Ann's arms and held her up. "Look at this beautiful baby. She's worth more than any treasure. And she belongs to all of you—Larkins and Arnetts alike. You have *so* much wealth here in Acorn—the mountains and creeks, your families and your children. Don't squander another day on this ridiculous feud."

I saw Cora and a few other women wiping their eyes. "Are we in agreement?" I asked. "Should we dig up the treasure and use it for everyone's good?" The two clans took a moment to talk amongst themselves, then one man stepped forward from each family and met in the middle to shake hands. A cheer went up from the crowd.

"Let's start digging!" someone shouted.

I turned and led the way, still carrying Feather in my arms, and stopped to point to Abraham Coots's grave. I prayed I hadn't made a mistake. "I think it's right here," I said, sounding more confident than I felt. "I think Isaac and Wilbur buried the money in their friend's grave."

I stood back to watch as Wayne and a few other men grabbed the gravediggers' shovels and began to dig. As they did, I looked around at the faces of all the people here in Acorn whom I had grown to know and love. For the first time I realized how much I had missed in life by reading books day and night about imaginary people. From now on, I wanted to live with real people and become part of their real stories. And as I saw Miss Lillie gazing at me, smiling her gap-toothed grin, I wanted more than anything else to have a faith that was as real and vibrant as hers.

I was still lost in my thoughts when I heard the dull *thunk* of a shovel striking wood. The men had only dug down a few feet, not six, so I knew it couldn't be a casket. My heart raced with excitement as the men brushed off the dirt with their hands, unearthing a small wooden box. Wayne Larkin pried off the lid, and cheers erupted from the crowd as he held up two fistfuls of strange-looking money. I felt shaky with relief and had to sit down on a nearby tombstone to avoid dropping the baby.

"What kind of money is that?" Clint asked, pushing his way forward to see. "Them don't look like real dollars."

The crowd parted to let one of the older men from the post office examine them. "They're greenbacks," he said. "The government printed these during the War Between the States and for a few years afterward."

"Are they any good?" Clint asked.

The old man shrugged. "Guess we'll have to take them to a bank and find out."

But the odd-looking greenbacks didn't dim the joyful mood as the townspeople continued to laugh and cheer. I searched for June Ann and saw a woman rush toward her and pull her into her arms. I guessed by the woman's red hair that she was June Ann's mother.

The long, bitter feud was finally over. And although I knew that fairy-tale endings only happened in books, I wasn't at all surprised that my story-like visit to Wonderland Creek would end with "happily-ever-after."

CHAPTER 35

It seemed very strange to be home in Illinois again. I wandered around Blue Island in a daze, as if I had been shipwrecked like Robinson Crusoe and finally had returned to civilization. Simple things that I'd once taken for granted amazed me. The array of fruit and vegetables on display in the market brought tears to my eyes. The contented *swish-swish* of the agitator on laundry day sounded like music. Electric lights seemed nothing short of miraculous. It took me weeks to get used to reaching for a light switch when I walked into a darkened room instead of searching for a box of matches. And when I sat on the edge of our porcelain bathtub and turned the knob, I laughed out loud as I watched the hot water pouring in, and the steam rising, and the bubbles frothing. But I didn't enjoy soaking in our tub half as much as I had enjoyed my first long-awaited bath in Lillie's copper tub in Kentucky.

The world back home seemed loud and angry and aggressive. I couldn't get used to the constant blare of the radio. Halfway through a film at the movie theater, I got up and walked out, finding the show too noisy and fast-moving after the slow pace of life in Acorn. To be honest, the plot of the film seemed too contrived and coincidental to be believable. But then again, if they made a movie about my adventures in Acorn, it might seem unbelievable, too, with murders and feuds, stolen loot and buried treasure, and a happily-ever-after ending. And who would believe there could be a one-hundred-year-old former slave who could cook up a love potion?

I missed the trees and the hills. It was too flat in Illinois, and the trees looked scrawny and lonely. I couldn't get used to the rush of traffic in the streets or the rumbling freight trains blasting their whistles. Everything moved too fast. I wanted to tell everyone to slow down and take time to enjoy life and each other.

I missed waking up to the sound of the creek every morning. And the birds singing. And fresh eggs, still warm from the hen house. I missed Belle and our leisurely journeys up Wonderland Creek. Freddy didn't believe me when I described how I had learned to scrape out Belle's hooves.

I went next door to see Freddy before I'd even unpacked my suitcase. She gave me a huge hug and invited me inside. "I want to hear all about your trip, Allie. Come on out in the kitchen." But I knelt in front of her mother's chair and greeted her first. "Hello, Mrs. Fiore. How are you? I've thought about you so often while I was away."

She looked at me in surprise. "I'm fine, Alice. Well, as good as can be expected under the circumstances. Welcome home. Freddy missed you."

I stood and turned to Freddy. "Before I talk about my trip, I want to hear all about what you've been doing while I was away. Don't leave out a single thing." She looked stunned. I was the one who usually dominated the conversation. She led me out to her kitchen, and we sat down at the table.

"Well, there's not much to tell," she began. "I've been teaching school, taking care of Mom . . . you know, the usual."

"She's seeing Gordon Walters," her mother called from the next room. "The young man from the funeral home."

"Really, Freddy? I'm so happy for you!" I wanted to jump up and hug her, but she held up her hands, holding me back.

"Gordon and I are just friends."

"Friends? But why, Freddy? Why not be more than friends?"

"You tell her, Alice," Mrs. Fiore called from the living room again. "Tell her to stop giving that nice young man such a hard time and marry him already."

"Why are you giving Gordon a hard time, Freddy?"

She shrugged and started picking at the hem of the tablecloth. "I didn't want to go out with him at all, at first. It felt as though I had won second place . . . as though you gave him to me and I was getting leftovers, a consolation prize."

"But Gordon broke up with me, not the other way around."

"He's in love with her," Mrs. Fiore shouted.

Freddy smiled. "Gordon has won Mother's heart, as you can see. And he insists that he won't give up until he wins mine. He's been very persistent. Some nights he comes over just to listen to the radio with my mother and me, and he sits there and watches me grade papers. Can you imagine?"

I could imagine. I remembered how Ike had stood in the library doorway watching me work. "It must be love," I told her. "Gordon *never* came over to sit and watch me."

"That's because you always had your nose in a book," she said, laughing. "Who wants to watch that?"

I recognized the truth in what she said. And though books would always hold an important place in my life, I silently vowed not to let them dominate it. "Give Gordon a chance, Freddy."

"We'll see. I'm making him take things slowly."

I grabbed her arm and gave her a shake. "No! Don't do that, Freddy. If I've learned anything at all from my time away, it's that you've got to take chances in life. Jump in with both feet and do things you never dreamed of doing. We only get one life, and we've got to live it to the full. Most of all, we've got to love others to the full."

Freddy stared at me for a long moment. "What happened to you down in Kentucky? You've changed, Allie. You were always the cautious one."

"I'm all finished being cautious. You would never believe all of the shocking things I've done these past few months."

"Like what?" She looked bemused, as if she didn't believe me.

"I broke into a mining office and got caught in the act by the sheriff. I explored a deserted coal mine in the pitch-dark because we couldn't light a lamp or the coal gas might explode. I helped stage a man's funeral when he wasn't really dead and then stood in front of him to shield him when the shooter tried to kill him a second time."

"You're making this up."

"No. I'm not. I learned how to make tonics and elixirs to heal people. I learned how to ride a horse named Belle, and I rode her up into the woods, all alone, to deliver books to people who lived way back in the hills."

"Is this the plot of a book you read?"

"No, Freddy, it's not! It all really happened—and more. I figured out where a lost treasure was buried, and the whole town came together to help me dig it up. And I fell in love with a handsome musician for a while, and even though it couldn't last, it was fun. Fun! Don't hold back with Gordon for one more day. Let yourself fall in love with him, and even if it doesn't work out, it isn't the end of the world—it's only the beginning."

"If all of this is really true, you should write a book about your adventures."

"No one would believe it," I laughed.

The front doorbell rang. Freddy glanced up at the clock on the kitchen wall. "That's probably Gordon now."

I scrambled to my feet. "Then I'm going out the back door, not because I don't want to see him but because you need to be alone with him."

"You've lost your mind, Allie."

"On the contrary—I've finally found it."

The Depression hadn't eased much while I was away, and hoboes still came to our back door begging for an odd job to do in return for a meal. I viewed them differently now. I surprised my mother by offering to make soup and homemade bread to serve them. I shocked my father by going to Floptown with him to help the poor. And one afternoon as Mother was leaving to visit Aunt Lydia, I asked to go with her.

The maid answered the door and led us into Aunt Lydia's morning room. "You look so different, Alice," Aunt Lydia said the moment she saw me. "Why, you're positively radiant! You must have had an adventure."

"I did, Aunt Lydia. In fact, I had several."

"Sit down, my dear, and tell me all about them." She reached for my hand and made me sit on the antique settee beside her. I was happy to see that the water cure hadn't changed my exotic aunt into a replica of my mother. She still carried her crystal tumbler of amber liquid. And the stuffed moose head on the wall still wore a babushka on its head.

"You know, dear, when Cecil and I came back for you, he wasn't convinced that we should leave you there with that wizened old woman. But I told him, 'Oh, why not! Let the poor girl live a little!' I just knew you must be having an adventure."

"I'm so glad you did." I leaned back on the sofa beside my aunt and told her stories that I hadn't even shared with my parents yet. When I got to the part about the wildcat, Mother's face turned pale.

"Alice Grace Ripley! You should have come home immediately if you were in danger!"

"Nonsense," Aunt Lydia said. "A little danger makes life fun. Tell me, Alice, did you fall in love?"

"I did, for a little while. With a handsome fiddle player who made music like an angel." I leaned close and added in a whisper that my mother couldn't hear, "He kissed like an angel, too."

"Oh, how delicious! Love is the spice of life!" Aunt Lydia picked up her glass and took a long drink before setting it down again. "Did it end in heartache, dear?"

"Well, yes . . . but it was the good kind of heartache, Aunt Lydia. The kind where you'll always think fondly of each other, even though you know your love could never be."

My aunt squealed with delight. "Ooh, I just love stories that end that way! Those happy, sappy endings in romance novels aren't realistic at all. But if you can gaze up at the stars at night and think fondly of your lost love, then it's worth falling in love and losing him."

"You're absolutely right."

Mother looked from one of us to the other, bewildered, as if she was watching a tennis match and had lost track of the score.

"Each time you fall in love, dear, it will be even more exquisite than the last time."

"In that case, I'm looking forward to it."

I thought of the people I'd met in Acorn every single day. Summer had arrived, and the one-room school on Wonderland Creek would be closed until fall, but I wanted to make good on my promise to send textbooks to them. I made an appointment with the school superintendent, and when I explained the situation in Kentucky, he agreed to donate his used books. Father let me speak to some of the groups at church about donating books, too. "I wish you could see how much these people appreciate books," I told them. "How happy a simple story makes a child who has nothing."

Speaking of church, it seemed like a very different place to me now. I no longer thought of my attendance as an obligation or of the Sunday service as just a nice, stately ritual. Church was a place to be with other people who also wanted to do God's work. It was a place to hear from God about what He wanted from me. I'm still waiting to find out all the details, but at least I'm listening now.

When I went to the library to ask Mrs. Beasley about starting another book drive, everyone seemed happy to see me. "We've missed you, Miss Ripley. We all wondered what happened to you until someone from your father's church explained how you've been helping out down in Kentucky."

"I've missed you, too. In fact, I'd like to come in and volunteer, if I may. I would like to start a story hour and read to the children once a week the way I read to the children in Kentucky. I'm sure they'll need something to keep them occupied this summer."

Mrs. Beasley agreed, and before I left that day, she pulled me aside to whisper confidentially. "The part-time clerk is leaving to get married this fall. Would you like to come back to work? It's only part time—"

"Yes!" I shouted, before remembering to use my library voice. "I would love to," I whispered.

Several months after I returned home, a package arrived in the mail from New York City. I ripped it open and found a preview copy of Mack's novel. The dedication read, *"To Miss Lillie—my mentor, mother, and friend."*

I sat down on our living room sofa and started reading immediately. I continued reading, too, barely stopping to eat, and sleeping only when my eyes would no longer focus. Mack was a fine writer and had penned a compelling, edge-of-your-seat story. One of the characters—a naïve young woman with a tendency toward melodrama—sounded a lot like me. I didn't mind. Mack treated her with fondness in the novel.

He had not only composed a great plot, but the language he used was a feast of words. His lyrical descriptions of the hills and hollows made me homesick for Kentucky. His sentences and paragraphs sang just like Ike's fiddle. I no sooner read *The End* than I went back to the beginning and read the novel through a second time just to enjoy Mack's delicious writing. He used such wonderful words in his novel. I had to smile when one of them was *eschew*.

I wrote Mack a letter to congratulate him and to let him know how very much I had enjoyed his book. I also mentioned that I had collected several boxes of donated books for his library and promised to ship them along with the used textbooks as soon as the school board gave their approval. I watched the mail every day, hoping for a letter from Mack in return. Instead, the doorbell rang one morning while I was helping my mother in the kitchen.

I went to answer it with flour in my hair and wearing a smudged apron—and there was Mack. He wore a suit and tie, his hair neatly cut and combed. I had forgotten how tall he was.

"Mack! Wait . . . how . . . why didn't you write and tell me you were coming?"

"I thought I'd surprise you the way you surprised me, remember? Showing up on my doorstep with your suitcase?"

I was thrilled to see him, yet all I could do was stand and stare at him. And Mack stared back. Mother finally broke the spell when she called from the kitchen, "Who's at the door, Alice?"

"Um . . . You won't believe it, Mother. Mack is here. My friend from Kentucky? The librarian I told you about?"

She came into the living room, drying her hands on a towel so she could shake his hand. "Well, don't leave him standing there, Alice. Invite him in. Offer him something to drink."

I eventually recovered from my shock and led Mack inside to make proper introductions. Mother offered him a chair in our front room and brought him a cold drink. I sat down on the sofa across from him, marveling at how Mack could look so completely at home in my living room in Blue Island. My mind began to spin with a hundred questions for him.

"How is everything in Acorn? Are the two families still living peacefully?"

"Yes, remarkably so. They've even begun rebuilding the church together."

"Have you heard from Maggie? Has she come back to Acorn?"

"No, not yet."

"How's Belle? Does she miss me?"

Mack smiled. "You know, Belle doesn't say very much, but I'm certain she does miss you. She isn't getting nearly enough exercise now that you're gone, and she's looking a little pudgy. I asked Alma to please ride her once in a while."

"Are you keeping up with your work at the library? I seem to recall that it was quite a mess when I first arrived, with books piled everywhere and cards that needed to be filed."

"Oh, it's a mess again," he said, laughing. "And now that the feud has ended, we have a lot more patrons. By the way, you might be interested to know that I used some of my advance money from the novel to put in electricity and a pump for the well. We finally have indoor plumbing and lights."

"Really? I can't imagine that . . . What happened to my garden?"

"We had a great harvest, Alice. Faye and Marjorie helped Lillie and me with the canning."

Thinking about Acorn made me teary-eyed. I missed that place. "And how is Miss Lillie?" I asked.

Mack's smile faded. "That's another reason I came to see you. I wanted to tell you the news in person, not in a letter . . . She's gone, Alice. She had a long life, a hard life. But at least she went peacefully. I brought breakfast to her in bed one morning, and she was gone . . ." Mack's voice choked with grief.

I couldn't stop my tears, either. I could barely talk. "I'm so sorry."

"Yeah. Me too."

"I'm glad you found Buster for her, and that she got to learn something about her son."

"You helped me find him, Alice. I'll always be grateful to you. And for typing Lillie's book, too. The university is going to publish it."

I pulled a handkerchief from my pocket, but it was damp in a matter of minutes as my tears continued to fall. "Lillie once told me that she was hanging on to life because she wanted to see you settled down, with your book published and a good wife by your side."

Mack smiled. "Did she now?"

"Yes. And before I left, she told me you'd found the perfect wife. I'm assuming things worked out for you and your girlfriend in Washington?"

"What do you mean?"

"The woman who helped you find Buster. I figured you and her—"

"You mean Miss Anson?"

"I think that was her name."

Mack laughed out loud. "Alice, I met Catherine Anson at Berea College. She was one of my history teachers. She retired from there a few years ago. She's in her seventies."

"Well, who did Lillie mean, then?"

He moved forward to the edge of his chair. His voice got very quiet. "It's funny you should ask. I know it sounds ridiculous, but . . ." He looked embarrassed. "Not long before Lillie died, she told me that I should marry you."

"What?"

Mack did a perfect imitation of Lillie's scratchy voice and thick accent: "'Honey, why do you think the Good Lord sent that gal down here to us in Kentucky—and why I kept her here? God wants you to marry her!'"

"Oh boy."

"I know. I thought she was crazy, too." Mack waited until I looked at him, and our eyes met. "But I trust Lillie's judgment, Alice . . . don't you?"

I was speechless.

"I couldn't stop thinking about you," he continued. "And the more I did, the more I began to see that maybe the idea wasn't so crazy, after all. So I decided to come here in person to pick up the books . . . and the closer I got, the more I couldn't wait to see you. And so I've been wondering . . ." For a man who wrote words for a living, Mack was becoming very tongue-tied. "If I were to stick around Illinois for a while, and if we had a chance to get to know each other better . . . I mean, we'd have a lot of things to talk about first, and I know you were once sweet on Ike Arnett . . ."

"It never would have worked out for Ike and me," I said. "We're too different."

"Well . . . what do you think about you and me?"

I smiled when I remembered the first day I'd met Mack and how he'd sat cross-legged on the floor in the library foyer caressing the cover of one of the books I'd brought him. He had even lifted it to his nose to inhale the scent. I remembered my surprise when he'd used the word *eschew*. I pictured him holding baby Feather in his arms, singing to her, as thunder rumbled and rain dripped from the cabin ceiling. I remembered how panicked I had been at the thought of losing him when we faced the wildcat and the barrel of Maggie's rifle.

I took so long remembering all of these things that Mack finally said, "Don't leave me hanging here, Alice. Please . . . tell me what you think."

What did I think? Hadn't I lectured Freddy about taking a chance on love and jumping in with both feet? My logical side said that a mutual love of books was an excellent starting point for any relationship, and that I had much more in common with Mack than I'd ever had with Gordon or Ike. What better match could there be than between a man who loved to write books and a woman who loved to read them? And even if I threw logic out the window, a life with Mack was certain to be an adventure. Our time together had been an adventure already.

"What do I think?" I repeated. My smile must have given me away. Before I could finish, Mack leaped to his feet and grabbed my hands, pulling me up to face him. Then he planted a kiss on me that made me forget all about Ike Arnett's kisses.

When he pulled away and I could breathe again, I looked him in the eye and said, "I think Miss Lillie is the wisest woman I've ever met."

Author's Note

President Franklin Roosevelt founded his relief program, the New Deal, in 1933 to help alleviate the effects of the Great Depression. One of the most innovative programs of Roosevelt's Work Projects Administration was the Packhorse Library Project. Considered a rousing success, the program employed mainly women who served their neighbors and community by bringing reading materials to isolated one-room schoolhouses and homes located in the very rural and remote areas of eastern Kentucky.

The packhorse librarians provided not only entertainment in the form of books and magazines, but also practical help on home health care, cooking, agriculture, parenting, canning hygiene, and machinery. They also opened the world to these isolated people, allowing them to learn not only about their own government and country, but of lands and people across the globe.

The inspiration for this novel came from a children's nonfiction book titled *Down Cut Shin Creek: The Packhorse Librarians of Kentucky* by Kathi Appelt and Jeanne Cannella Schmitzer. It tells the true story of the packhorse librarians, complete with photographs. Many thanks to my editor, Sarah Long, for bringing this book to my attention as a great premise for a story.

I'm also grateful to Wayne Collier and his wife, Jean, for sharing Kentucky history with me, and for taking me on a journey into the mountains of eastern Kentucky where I saw the real Cut Shin Creek. The mines and villages and creeks in the beautiful mountains of Kentucky inspired the fictional town of Acorn and Wonderland Creek.

Discussion Questions

1) What were some of the lessons Alice learned as she stepped out of the imaginary world of books and into real life? What did she discover about life that was different from reading about it in fiction?

2) Which specific books and genres of stories "sprang to life" for Alice, a lover of novels, while she was in Kentucky?

3) In what ways was Alice different after her visit to Wonderland Creek? Which events or persons had the biggest influence on her?

4) Compare the three men in Alice's life: Gordon Walters, Ike Arnett, and Mack. How did each of them view Alice? How did they influence how she viewed herself?

5) What events in Miss Lillie's past shaped her life and her faith? Were any of her actions in the novel contrary to her role as a spiritual leader in Acorn and a woman of faith? If so, do you think her actions were justified?

6) Jesus said, "For where your treasure is, there will your heart be also" (Matthew 6:21). How was the truth of this verse demonstrated in Acorn, Kentucky?

7) How did Alice's shallow faith as a "preacher's kid" grow or change? Compare her faith journey with Miss Lillie's, Maggie's, and Mack's.

8) What did Alice learn about relationships from these people in Acorn: the packhorse librarians, June Ann and Feather, Maggie and Opal Coots, Mamaw and Faye's boys, Ike Arnett and his family, Clint and Gladys, the other patrons on her route, the sheriff, and even Belle the horse?

9) If you could write the next chapter in Alice's life, what would it be?

About the Author

LYNN AUSTIN has sold more than one million copies of her books worldwide. She is an eight-time Christy Award winner and an inaugural inductee into the Christy Award Hall of Fame, as well as a popular speaker at retreats, conventions, women's groups, and book clubs. She lives with her husband in Michigan.

Don't miss any of these novels from Lynn Austin!

To find out more about Lynn and her books, visit *lynnaustin.org*.

A world at war again. A horrific accident. And three lives forever intertwined. In the midst of God's silence, can faith and hope survive?

While We're Far Apart

As three sisters flee unexpected sorrow and a tainted past, they find they have nothing to rely on except each other—and hope for a second chance.

Until We Reach Home

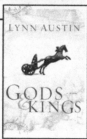

Experience the history, drama and promises of the Old Testament in this dramatic series of truth and loyalty. When invading armies, idol worship, and infidelity plague the life and legacy of King Hezekiah, can his faith survive the ultimate test?

Chronicles of the Kings *Gods and Kings, Song of Redemption, The Strength of His Hand, Faith of My Fathers, Among the Gods*